I owe him nothing.
He owes me everything.

WE BECOME RAVENS

MARIA DEAN

WE BECOME RAVENS

HOT TREE PUBLISHING

MARIA DEAN

For information, contact the publisher, Hot Tree Publishing.

WWW.HOTTREEPUBLISHING.COM

EDITING: HOT TREE EDITING

COVER DESIGNER: BOOKSSMITH DESIGN

E-BOOK ISBN: 978-1-923252-21-9

PAPERBACK ISBN: 978-1-923252-22-6

Dedicated to the memory of Edgar Allan Poe
Let his work live on, forever more.

"All that we see or seem is but a dream within a dream."
Edgar Allan Poe

Once upon a midnight hour,
Whilst my mind did creep and cower
From the sleep that begged to take me
To a place that would forsake me
There came a presence all-consuming
To which my soul did want to lose me
And I thought my grief forgotten
Washed aside by dreams so wanton
Wrapped in wings of feathered darkness
Where he devoured me in my starkness
I danced amidst his roaming touch
Until his hold became too much
And I questioned my own sanity
Was my need for him pure vanity?
Or was this dream a brand-new entity,
This world and him my new reality?

I'm alone.
Nothing ever changes.

CHAPTER ONE

"What do you wear to meet a murderer?" I ask my mother as I scan my closet.

My mother doesn't answer.

She never does.

She sits on the window seat, mauve curtains framing her like a portrait with high cheekbones, glassy eyes, pearlescent skin, and thick lashes. I rifle through shirts, jumpers, tops, and dresses, all of which are either steel grey, navy blue, or black, an ombre of bleakness devoid of colour or pattern reflecting the past ten years of my life.

A dress? Too formal. Jeans? Too casual. I look to my workwear, but my job as a journalist has no dress code other than comfort and practicality.

After pulling on black trousers and a skintight grey jumper, I select a waist-length jacket to complement the look.

The letter remains in the kitchen, stuffed behind a bottle of olive oil and the large peppermill a work colleague bought me years ago as a Secret Santa gift. I know its contents word for word, as I've read it a thousand times, wondering whether my day would be an entirely different one if the vowels and consonants were to rearrange themselves.

> *Dear Miss Evangeline Bransby,*
>
> *I've been approached by many journalists over the years, as my story is one that is much sought after. I have refused all of them.*
> *But it is time, and I don't think it would be right to tell anyone my story other than you.*
> *A visit has been arranged for Tuesday 5th January at ten o'clock in the morning, if you would do me the honour.*
> *I realise this must be difficult, but I think you and I have both been waiting long enough.*
> *Yours sincerely,*
> *Valdemar Montresor*

The paper is creased from when I'd screwed it up and thrown it away, a higher force stopping me from tearing it up and burning it. But shortly after, I'd found it back on the kitchen table, the paper smoothed out, the words staring at me along with my mother, who'd been sat at the table with compelling eyes and thin lips.

"Are you seriously telling me I should do this?" I'd asked her.

Silence had been her reply, a quiet I had to interpret, like all the other empty answers she's given me over the years.

"Will this outfit do, or do I look like I'm heading up a meeting?" Turning towards my mother, I'm faced with a bare window seat, the oversized scatter cushions plumped as if no one had just been sitting there.

I'm alone.

Nothing ever changes.

"You choose now to disappear," I accuse the air. "This was your idea, remember?"

I press my hand against my churning stomach and glance down at my clothes. It doesn't matter what I wear, as my anger always manages to radiate through my layers.

It's been ten years.

It feels like more, but at the same time, it feels like it was only yesterday.

A lot can happen in ten years.

People can change, heal, and forgive.

But what about murder?

Can that be forgiven?

The letter doesn't mention forgiveness; that isn't what he's asking for. So, what does Valdemar Montresor seek to gain from this meeting? What can the man who murdered my twin brother possibly have to say to me other than he is sorry?

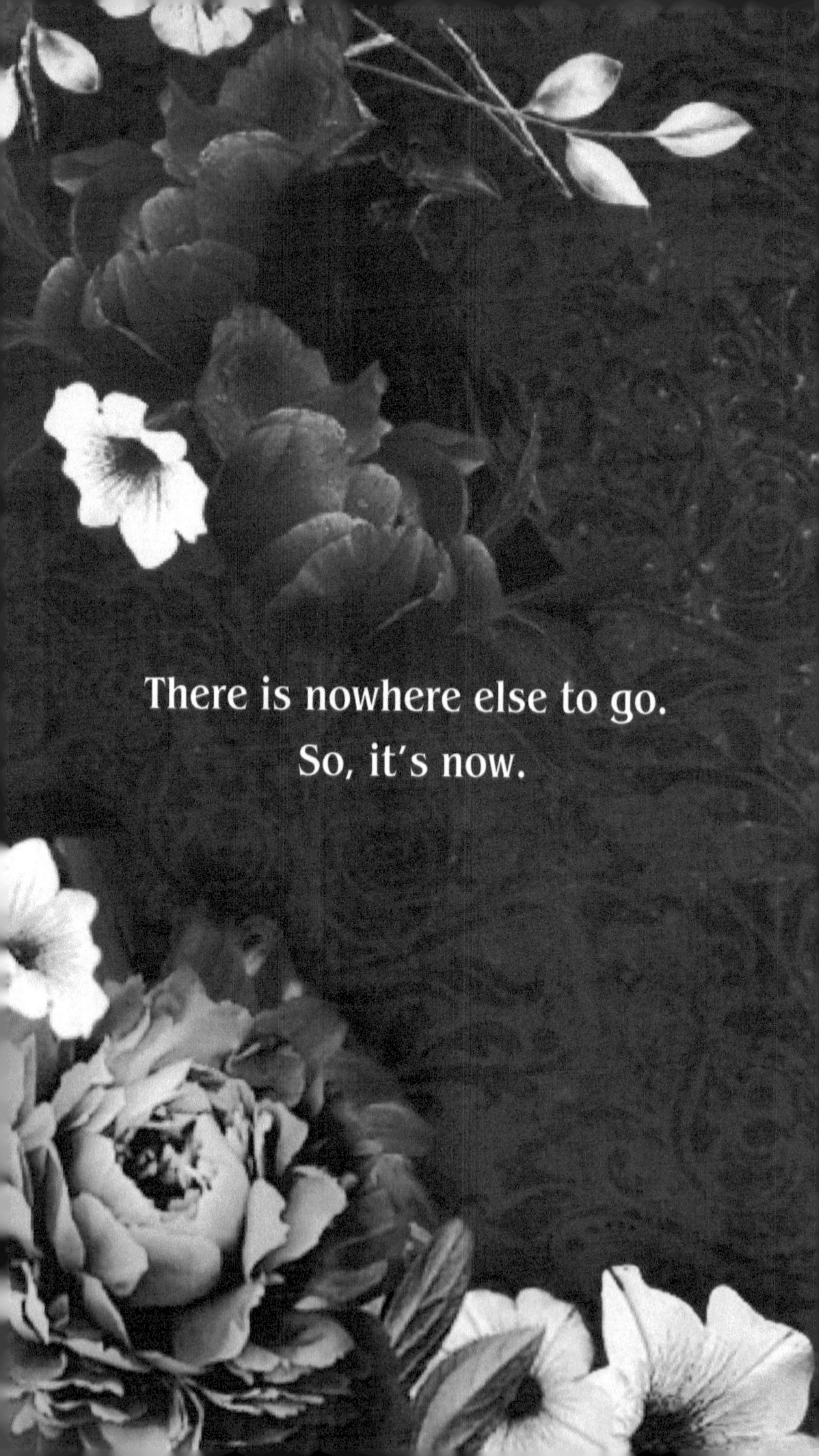

There is nowhere else to go.
So, it's now.

CHAPTER TWO

January brings a raw greyness to the small city of Amontillado, the sorry place I call home, a mere smudge on the map famous for its sherry wine, casks of which are exported daily when it isn't being consumed on street corners—the only way the citizens can ignore the debauchery and corruption that pollutes the cobbled streets.

The ferry chugs across the murky waters of the Maelstrom, the giant lake that forms the epicentre of Amontillado. Monroe Penitentiary—or The Pit, as it's known locally—threatens from a distance, cresting the small island of dense rock.

The concrete building was originally an old military base that was converted into a prison fifty years ago when the crime rate in Amontillado was climbing higher than the walls behind which criminals could be contained. The desolate structure was the perfect location to banish the condemned, doused in chaotic history and lampooned on an island. What better place to dump the scum of the city? Not that the justice system here is anything to shout about. With the right name, the right tattoo, and the right amount of money, the law can be bought, bent, and bribed.

The sky, an impenetrable film of ashen clouds that smothers any chance of winter sunlight, mirrors my mood. The air feels charged as if a storm is brewing—and not only inside me.

I grip the handrail of the upper deck. The ferry bobs as the waves try to tell me to leave this place, turn around, and go back. Nothing good will come of this.

A man in a dark blue raincoat eyes the prison like it's the last place he wants to be travelling towards. Noticing he's armed with paperwork and a laptop bag, I guess that he's a lawyer or solicitor making the dreadful journey to converse with the damned.

Despite my good sea legs, my stomach vaults.

A bell sounds as the ferry nears the dock, and the engines cut out.

There's no backing out now.

I let go of the rail and edge towards the stairs.

The man in the blue raincoat registers me for the first time since we boarded ten minutes ago. "After you." He motions with his free hand as we approach the narrow stairs, his polite gesture feeling more like he's daring me to be the first one to step foot on this austere island.

Maybe he knows what awaits us once our feet hit the dry soil. His stark eyes and trembling hand suggest he's been here many times and that it never gets any easier.

Taking a deep breath, I reach the bottom of the stairs, where a man in a dirty cap and stained hoodie winds a ridiculously thick rope around an iron post, securing the boat to the dock and us to this place.

"Watch your step," he tells me as I tread onto the metal dock, my legs feeling strange as they acclimatise to the solid surface.

As I inch forwards, my gaze follows the stone steps that lead up to the cold building that appears as if it's glaring down at me.

"Going my way?" The voice startles me as Blue Raincoat Guy arrives at my left, his bald head and wire-rimmed glasses looking too normal for this bleak venue.

"There's only one place to go, isn't there?"

"You're not wrong." He shakes his head, averting his gaze from the prison. "Your first time?"

"Is it that obvious?" I clutch my coat, wondering how the cold is penetrating my thick layers.

"I've never seen you before, and I think I would have noticed you."

I glare at him, but he doesn't seem to notice my disdain as he continues.

"I can show you the way. Shall we?" He nods at the steps.

It's now or never.

Clouds collect, light rain spotting my face, the solitary jail with eyelike windows looming, the gated entrance like an open mouth ready to consume us.

There is nowhere else to go.

So, it's now.

You can do this.
Just breathe.

CHAPTER THREE

After being searched by hand, machine, monitor, and scanner, I wonder if they'll perform a cavity search, but, to my relief, the iron-fisted prison guard seems content with knowing the contents of my bag, my bra, and my coat. I'm just relieved they can't search my brain, because there's no way they would let me in if they could glimpse my thoughts.

It's no special treatment that I've received, as Blue Raincoat Guy has had the same reception, albeit by a male prison guard who wouldn't look out of place in a Roman amphitheatre, his hands splattered with blood to the roar of a feisty crowd.

"She's good to go," my less-than-friendly prison guard says as she steers me towards a man whom I've already named The Gatekeeper. He's small yet lean, his beige uniform looking stiff. Attached to his belt is a large keyring that must have at least thirty keys jangling from it, the weight of so many condemned men being a hefty one to bear.

The inner door—one of many, I expect—is metal, like that of a bank vault.

Blue Raincoat Guy is beside me, pulling his coat back

onto his shoulders while trying to balance his now disrupted pile of papers.

"I guess this is goodbye," he begins, pushing his glasses up his nose. "Unless we're here to see the same inmate. Who *are* you here to see?"

The Gatekeeper reaches for his keys, not even looking as he selects the correct one. It's already in the lock, his fingers on the handle and ready to pull the door open as I glance at Blue Raincoat Guy and reply, "Valdemar Montresor."

His eyes widen, the colour draining from his face as the name leaves my lips. "Are you… serious?" His glasses start to steam up, but he appears oblivious as the door is pulled open, the squeal of metal hinges grating down my spine.

"I wish I were joking."

"But how? Why? Are you family?" He glances at my silver hair, possibly wondering what blood relation I could be with such colouring.

"No. I'm a journalist."

"But he hasn't spoken to anyone since his arrest. No one. How did you…?"

"He asked for me."

His shock turns to scepticism. "We are talking about *the* Valdemar Montresor—head of the Raven Hands, murderer, madman?"

I find it ironic that "madman" is the one label that stands out in my mind, the newspaper headlines still fresh as I recall the front-page spread: *Madman Montresor Murders Man*. An eyewitness statement claimed that the notoriously calm Valdemar Montresor had lost his head that night and rained gunfire on an entire casino.

"I swear his eyes were red," the croupier had told the *Amontillado Gazette*. "He had two guns, one in each hand, and he just kept firing and firing and firing up in the air until the chandelier collapsed and everyone was screaming."

"Yes, that Valdemar Montresor," I tell Blue Raincoat Guy.

The door is now open, and two large men wearing brown uniforms and armed with batons, stun guns, and Tasers await us against the backdrop of an artificially lit corridor.

"I'll see you on the return ferry," Blue Raincoat Guy says, eyeing the men.

"This way, please." The larger of the men beckons me while Blue Raincoat Guy remains.

"Good luck!" he shouts as I'm taken down the corridor.

I glance at all the doors, trying to guess which one contains my criminal. Feeling like Clarice Starling, I wonder when I'm going to get the lecture about not making eye contact, not asking certain questions, and what to do if I need to leave the room, but the guard remains silent, as if there's nothing he can say to prepare me for this.

When we reach the end of the corridor, we go through a fob-activated door and into a smaller waiting area that isn't dissimilar to one found in a hospital, although it's lacking the posters on what to do if you find a lump in your breast or advice on how to quit smoking.

We approach a blue door, which is metal again but painted this time and has a reinforced glass window.

"I'll remain in the room with you. Just let me know if you want to leave. You have an hour with him."

The guard opens the door with the same fob, and my stomach drops to my toes.

You can do this.

Just breathe.

Suppressing the urge to turn and run, I follow the guard into the room.

It's so much worse
than I imagined.

CHAPTER FOUR

I would be lying if I said I haven't thought about meeting Valdemar Montresor these past ten years, but it's always been a vision of bloodshed, of me stabbing him over and over, thrusting a knife into his chest until the blade comes out of his back. After my brother's death, my dad encouraged me to see a therapist. I attended for a few years, and in the later stages of my sessions, Dr Tarr suggested meeting Valdemar as part of my recovery to come to terms with my loss. However, it was an avenue I was never willing to venture down, my grief too volatile, too unpredictable.

I've only ever seen photos of Valdemar in newspapers, and even then, it was ten years ago. Incarceration has meant he's ceased to be in the limelight.

But none of my wonderings have prepared me for the man sitting behind the metal table, his wrists clad in cuffs secured to the floor, his white T-shirt tight against his well-sculpted upper body, tattoos clawing their way from underneath each sleeve and around his collar. And if the canvas of his body isn't enough to grab my attention, then the startling blue of his eyes against his sleek dark hair is enough to command my gaze.

All my well-rehearsed composure has taken flight along with the flock of ravens tattooed down his left arm and hand.

A tremor runs through my body, and I hear a whooshing sound in my ears as I recall the day Valdemar Montresor shattered my life.

Had it been hours, minutes, or seconds before the news reached the media? I can't remember, but I can still taste the bile that burned the back of my throat, the dread that threaded its way up my spine and wrapped its tendrils around my trachea. And then there was the pain—the blinding hot pain between my eyes that I blamed on a migraine as I stumbled around the newsroom of the Amontillado Gazette.

"This just in. The notorious Valdemar Montresor, head of the organisation the Raven Hands, has been arrested this evening on a suspected murder charge," the well-groomed reporter announced on the flat-screen TV as behind her, the flashing lights of police cars and paparazzi cameras went off like a disco.

I was the gofer, covering the garbage they called news, like local man Johan Hermann trying to marry his dog or when The Gold Bug Coffee Shop started offering oat milk, and I was still trying to earn my wings as a serious reporter.

"Hold the fucking headline!" Captain hollered as he flew out of his office, a plume of cigar smoke following him despite the smoking restrictions in the building.

As he was our highly-strung editor-in-chief, who never appeared to leave the building, no one ever dared to challenge him on any accounts, such as the way he barked orders at us or the fact that he expected us to understand everything he said the first time he said it.

"What are we standing around for, people? Dupin, get your arse down there!" Captain glared at Dupin, his best reporter, who'd been halfway out the door, about to head home for the evening.

Dupin stared at the screen. "Where? Where the hell is this going down?"

We all glared at the lovely news reporter, urging her to tell us where she was reporting from.

My voice was faint at first, the stabbing pain between my eyes almost blinding me.

"It's at the casino," I said, my throat dry, my eyes burning.

"What did you say?" Dupin asked.

"Fortunato Casino. That's where she is, where it's happening."

"How do you know?" Captain asked, his cigar wobbling between his lips.

If I said, "Because I felt the bullet, heard the shot, and sensed the terror," they would look at me as if I were a madwoman, so instead, I replied, "Because my brother works there."

Like all twins, we had a connection, an unwavering bond. And I'd known the exact minute he'd stopped breathing because I had stopped breathing as well.

Tearing my thoughts from the past, I challenge myself to look directly at the man who murdered my brother.

It's so much worse than I imagined.

Searing, jarring pain rips through my heart, leaving me unable to move.

And if he, Valdemar Montresor, isn't enough to stop the flow of oxygen around my body, I notice that he isn't alone.

I owe him nothing.
He owes me everything.

CHAPTER FIVE

When I was younger, I didn't think of it as anything more than my imagination or the norm; surely everyone sees them, right? But then I got older and quickly realised it *wasn't* the norm, that talking to your dead mother isn't considered part of daily life. And there was a time when I wished I couldn't see her. I just wanted to be like everyone else.

But then my brother died, and I lost someone who had never missed a single beat of a single day with me; after that, seeing the dead became all I desired.

It's difficult to pinpoint when I began to see my mother. She died in childbirth; my brother and I took the very last air she breathed. Knowing that my first feat on this earth was to murder my own mother is something that haunts me still. I've always felt that it tarnished us and set us up on the path of things to come.

We didn't miss her; it's hard to miss someone you never knew.

I don't remember the specific day I started seeing her. She

was always appearing in her glimmering halo of light—but I do recall the first time I mentioned it to my father.

"You look beautiful, sweetheart," my dad cooed from the corner of the sitting room as I twirled around in my new satin dress bought especially for Christmas Day.

"Thanks, Daddy." I giggled before looking over at my mother standing next to him, her smile as radiant as her skin. "Mummy likes it too."

My father's face wilted and his cheeks hollowed. It was like letting the air out of a balloon. "What did you say?"

"I said Mummy likes it too. I can tell because she's smiling." Flapping the skirt, I danced around the room, unaware of what I'd conjured.

"But Mummy isn't here, sweetheart. She's in heaven, remember?" His tone was soft but laced with conviction, and I'm still not sure who he was trying to convince that my mother wasn't standing in the room with us.

I stopped dancing and smiled at my mother before telling my father that heaven must be here in our house, then.

We never talked about it again. I never mentioned her clasping her hands to her heart every year as I blew out the candles on my birthday cake or how brightly she appeared to shine the day I opened my exam results in the kitchen. And after I left home and bought a place of my own, she came with me, culling the idea of there being a heaven at all.

And I've often wondered, after Ed's passing, why I haven't seen him. Why he hasn't visited me like my mother does. Ed had been the other half of me. Until the age of around seventeen, we'd been inseparable, like twins are supposed to be.

And when he died, I wanted to see him, if only to soothe the wound his death had opened.

Ten years of searching for a ghost amongst the living.

And now, he's here, standing behind Valdemar, his face hollow, his eyes watery, the bullet hole encrusted with dried blood imbedded like a third eye in his forehead tarnishing the silver-blond of his fringe. His hand rests on Valdemar's shoulder, his raven tattoo stark against the paleness of his skin. There's no halo of light like there is around my mother, no shimmering translucent skin, just ghostly limbs and the smell of sulphur.

And I want to cry.

My mother, although dead, looks beautiful and at peace, whereas Ed looks lost and broken.

Why here?

Why now?

What is he doing standing behind the man who shot him?

As if this interview isn't going to be difficult enough.

Gulping hard, I drop my gaze, not wanting to look like I'm staring at thin air. My mind is racing, my heart hammering against my ribcage as if it's trying to break a bone. I want to talk to Ed, to reach out, but Valdemar is watching me.

Grabbing the back of the chair, I drag it out and then sit down. My hands shake as I pull out my tiny Dictaphone and notebook.

There's an abrasive silence as I sit here, nerves swamping me, anger fermenting.

Once I'm ready, I inhale deeply before looking up to find my brother has gone. The only eyes now staring at me are those of Valdemar Montresor.

I take in his slick black hair swept back into a man bun, his murderous eyes a biting blue, his jaw covered with a close-cropped beard. The calm exterior he exudes is a sharp contrast to the concoction of emotions mixing inside me.

"Angel." The gruffness of his voice counters with the beauty of the word, and I'm annoyed that something so innocent can come out of his mouth.

"I beg your pardon?"

"Your name… Evangeline. It's a Latin name meaning gospel, the bringer of good news, and you remind me of an angel with your silver hair and pale eyes. Thank you for coming."

He sits back in his chair, and I'm lost, his accent a melting pot of so many continents. There's a hint of Spanish, a dash of Italian, and a smattering of New Yorker all mixed together, making it impossible to tell where he comes from. It's like he's brewed it himself and branded it his own.

As my insides harden, I remind myself of some of the rules I read online about interviewing notorious criminals.

Rule number one: Don't let them take control of the interview. You are in charge, not them. They will try flattery, insults, outrageous remarks, and even promises of secrets they've never shared. Don't be fooled. Stay in control.

But he's already in control. He asked me to come here, and I agreed. I'm here at his behest.

"I nearly didn't."

"I understand, and thank you again for agreeing to be here. I know this must be very difficult for you." I want to sense insincerity in his tone, to complete the picture of the bad guy sitting before me, but I don't. Instead, his words are carefully placed as though he's contemplated them for a long time.

"You have no idea."

His jaw twitches. "I know more than you think."

The fluorescent light flickers as a sting of cold air splinters into my lungs and almost takes my breath away. What does he mean? What does he know about me?

I tap my pencil on the first page of my notebook, trying to keep this professional and concentrate on the job I'm here to do rather than my personal reasons for being here.

Valdemar's eyes roam the empty page. "You know why I asked you here."

Unsure as to whether this is a question, I answer it anyway. "Your letter said you have a story to tell."

"I do, but it's not one that can be printed."

Annoyance bristles my shoulders. "You asked me here as a journalist."

"I asked you here as *you*. Some of the things I need to tell you can't be printed."

My shoulders drop. "So, you lied to get me here." I shouldn't be surprised. Thou shall not murder. Thou shall not bear false witness against your neighbour. The commandments seem to be a to-do list for this guy.

"Not at all. I said I have a story to tell and that I want you to hear it. I didn't specify that you should publish it."

I let out an audible sigh. "Then why am I here if not to write a story?"

"Because you *need* to be here."

I wait for him to elaborate, but instead, he moves on.

"Before I begin, do you have any questions?" He nods to the blank page of my notebook.

"I have questions. Lots. But they're all in here." I tap the side of my head with my pencil.

He leans forwards, his T-shirt pulling against his chest, images of the tattoos underneath the thin material bleeding through. "I wonder what else is in there."

Rule number two blares in my ears: Don't let them get inside your head. They will play mind games with you and try anything to learn personal details, your strengths, and especially your weaknesses. Keep your guard up and your personal life to yourself.

But he's already in my head. He's been there for the past ten years.

Clearing my throat, I straighten in the flimsy chair. "I already know enough of what happened that night from the police and the press."

Valdemar crosses his thick arms. "And working for the press, you know first-hand how much bullshit they print. And here I was thinking you were here for a real story."

He's playing games again, luring me in with promises of something exclusive, something sensational. But I can't staunch the reporter in me.

"Why now?" I ask. "You've been locked away for the past ten years. You could have told me these things anytime."

He clenches his jaw, and something flickers behind his eyes as if he's contemplating his words carefully. "Because in six weeks, I'm being released."

"What the fuck?" Anger railroads the journalist, my blood a tempest.

"My case has been reviewed and my sentence reduced." There he goes again, being careful with his words. All I want to do is bulldoze them from the room.

"That can't be right." I shake my head, my hands twisting under the table.

"I'm afraid it is."

"This cannot be happening. Who did you have to bribe for this?" Heat crawls up my neck.

"No one," he says.

"Liar. You killed my fucking brother, and you get to walk free after ten years? Where is the justice in that?" I'd promised myself I wouldn't get cross, that I would keep my emotions in check and not lose my shit, but I'm already a bubbling volcano of fury.

"This is why I wanted to talk to you."

"To assuage your guilt?"

"No, to put the record straight." He's so calm, so cool, which makes me even madder.

"And why should I believe you?"

"Because you're here. That alone tells me you want

answers. And I can give them to you, but it'll take more than one hour."

I regard him with caution. What is this about? What game is he playing?

"I have a visitor slot every Thursday at four o'clock. I would like for you to attend for the next six weeks." He sounds businesslike, formal and professional, not the hot-headed thug I've pictured for the last ten years.

My skin crawls at the thought of having to repeat this visit. It's been hard enough; I'm not sure I can go through it all again. But then I remember Ed, and even though his ghost appeared ghastly—the pallid skin, the rawness of his wound—I would give anything to see my brother again, even if it means having to sit across from the monster who made him what he is now.

"What about your other visitors?" Does he *have* any visitors? Friends, family?

"They can wait."

Uncertainty mixes with my curiosity. "What can you possibly have to tell me that will take us six weeks?"

"Everything you want to know."

This thought rattles about in my skull.

He's a murderer. What else is there to know?

"I know you're the head of one of the most prolific organisations in Amontillado. I know you're a ruthless monster with no soul, no empathy, and certainly no morals. And I know you killed my brother."

Valdemar places his elbows on the table, his restraints jangling as they slide down his forearms. "Wouldn't you like to know why?"

"The papers reported—"

"What they wanted to report."

I try a different angle. "At the hearing, the witnesses said—"

Again, he interrupts me. "What they were told to say. No one was interested in my past or my reasons behind what happened. But you, angel—you are. You deserve to know the truth and to hear it from me rather than anyone else."

I tut. "And I'm sure it'll be a pack of lies."

"What would be the point? And, like you said, I have no morals, so why would I feel the need to lie to you?"

Valdemar is giving me six weeks of access to him and an exclusive story that most journalists would give their right arm for. He said I can't publish it, but what right does he have to ask that of me?

I owe him nothing.

He owes me everything.

After Ed's death, I was a mess, incomplete, half of me having died with my brother. I was on sick leave from the paper for over twelve months, and when I did return on a part-time basis, I functioned on a cocktail of drugs and grief. I felt like a ghost. Dead on the inside, dead on the outside, sharing my days with my deceased mother, wishing I could join her.

And then one day, I caught sight of myself in the mirror and didn't recognise the person staring back at me, saw nothing of my brother, only a shell with vacant eyes. So I decided enough was enough. I couldn't languish with the dead any longer.

I've spent the last few years trying to retrieve the dream of being a successful journalist, but my past won't seem to let me, and other reporters are being assigned the best leads while Captain views me with wary eyes, as if I might break down at the slightest sign of stress.

This could be my big break. This could be the story that puts me up there with the greats. But do I want that? Could I live with myself knowing that the death of my brother put me in the limelight? But Valdemar is right—I don't want anyone else reporting on this. I don't want to read about it in some other paper, some bull-headed journalist putting their slant on things. If this story is to be told, it has to be by me.

"All right," I reply slowly, unsure of what exactly I'm agreeing to.

"Thank you." He shifts in his seat like the handcuffs aren't the only thing restraining him. "Being locked away makes you realise you won't be around forever, and I don't want my story to die with me."

The sound of me swallowing is louder than I would like.

"You don't sound like a man who is being given a second chance and being released in six weeks," I say.

"Maybe not. But I've been safe in here. Well, as safe as a man can be, locked away with a thousand other criminals. But I'm well aware of the price on my head, angel."

It's as if he's sliced through my cranium and examined my brain, and for the first time since this all began, I wonder just what and who I'm tangling with.

"I'm sure your flock will keep you safe," I say before I have time to think.

"What is it they say—keep your friends close and your enemies closer?" I wait for him to smile at this little joke, but his mouth remains firmly set, which suggests he isn't joking at all.

"Five minutes," the guard says.

I'd forgotten all about the prison guard standing behind me, and his announcement makes me jump as I automatically look to the clock for confirmation.

"I have one question before I leave." I close the empty notebook and tidy away my scant belongings.

"Go ahead."

My hand hovers over the Dictaphone. And I'm not sure where the question comes from, but it's out before I can stop it.

"Do you regret killing him?"

Valdemar's face hardens as if he isn't going to dignify my query with an answer.

"Time's up." The prison guard appears to my left, and I rise, wondering whether if Valdemar were to answer, it would change anything.

The guard ushers me to the door, and I turn to get one last look at Valdemar, but he's not alone. My brother has returned, blood spattered on his white shirt, his empty eyes staring right at me as his waxen hand rests on Valdemar's shoulder.

Blinking to clear my vision, I try to erase the blood, the bullet hole, and the look of sorrow on his face, but Ed isn't some hallucination to be tampered with. My brother remains as Valdemar answers me.

"There's a famous saying by a man named Sydney J. Harris," he begins, his eyes narrowing. "'Regret for the things we did can be tempered by time; it is regret for the things we did not do that is inconsolable.'"

Maybe this wasn't such
a good idea after all.

CHAPTER SIX

IT'S BEEN TWO DAYS SINCE I WAS LAST AT THE PRISON, YET IT feels like longer. Valdemar's parting words have stewed in my brain, bubbled with possibilities, and boiled over into an unhealthy obsession with what he could have meant by them.

"Regret for the things we did can be tempered by time; it is regret for the things we did not do that is inconsolable."

Seeing Ed standing behind Valdemar, his pale hand with its raven tattoo resting on Valdemar's shoulder, how he looked so haunted even though he's the one who is dead, has kept me awake every single night.

After the visit, I'd stormed out of the room and marched back to the ferry, my anger at Valdemar coiled into a spitting viper that I would have loved to have unleashed on him.

Blue Raincoat Guy hadn't been on the return ferry, and I was glad I didn't have to make idle chitchat about my first meeting with the notorious madman Montresor, because I would have only spat poison. But I've found it hard not having anyone to talk to. My one-way conversations with my mother are a sounding board only.

"I'm not going back there," I'd told her on Wednesday

morning as I'd made coffee. But as I'd gone back into my bedroom, a frame had been placed on my bed, the first school photo taken of Ed and me together, our uniforms crisp and stiff, my hair braided tightly in pigtails, Ed's silver hair slicked to the side with glossy gel, our smiles as fake as the skylike background behind us. I've never seen my mother move things, never seen her touch objects, but somehow, she manages to make them appear as if by magic, her way of silently telling me what I need to do.

When I got up this morning, my mother had been waiting for me in the kitchen, a knowing look on her face over the fact that today I was due to visit Valdemar.

So, I'm back at the prison, and after a long wait, I'm now being patted down by a different prison guard to the one who searched me on Tuesday, her hands just as ruthless as the last one's had been. Blue Raincoat Guy isn't here. Instead, I'm surrounded by a handful of haunted-looking friends and family who've made the dismal ferry ride over to see their criminals without the bars—like petting time at a human zoo.

It's an eclectic mix of people. A young man with a fresh crop of acne is accompanied by an older man with a receding hairline and a beer belly that doesn't want to be restrained under his zipped-up jacket. Then there's a middle-aged lady who looks like she used to be tall but has shrunk, possibly worn down by these visits. And then there's a young woman with jet-black hair, unnaturally long acrylic nails, and glossy lips. She was chewing gum when we arrived, and the guards immediately asked her to get rid of it. She seemed to take great pleasure in spitting it out into the plastic bin they held up for her. Unlike the rest of us, she doesn't look afraid. She looks like she wants to be here, like it's part of her weekly routine along with sunbeds and a pedicure.

And then there's me. I've dressed in skinny jeans and

black Converse, not wanting to stand out as a reporter. I wonder what the rest of the people must be thinking when they look at me, wondering which criminal I've been coerced into visiting.

To add to the rest of the thoughts that have been gnawing away at me these past two days is Valdemar's warning about not printing his story. I'm unsure whether to honour this request or to print it anyway just to spite him. Either way, I told Captain I wouldn't be available on Thursday afternoons for the next few weeks. He began to enquire as to why, but the mention of my gynaecologist stopped him in his tracks.

Once scanned and searched, we're ushered by The Gatekeeper towards the main door, two large prison guards flanking each side of it, one male and one female in appearance who holds a clipboard in her meaty hand.

"As you're probably aware, we're running late due to unforeseen circumstances," the female officer says, and I wonder what "unforeseen circumstances" could mean in a prison such as this. An attempted escape? A mass brawl? A security breach? The possibilities are endless. "So, I regret to inform you that visiting time will be cut short today." She glares at us, the sarcasm rolling off her face like the mist off the lake.

No one protests. No one argues. No one demands their time back with their precious loved ones. In fact, most of the visitors look relieved.

The guard smirks before scanning the list she holds in her hand. She stops, looks up, eyes the black-haired woman, then returns to her list before stepping forwards.

"Jacinta, you're not down for a visit today." The prison guard's voice is deep, her tone matching her stern look and the severity of her brown hair, which is pulled into an eye-wateringly tight bun sitting obediently on top of her head like a doughnut glazed in dark chocolate ganache.

"What?" The black-haired lady who I now know is Jacinta still appears to be chewing invisible gum as she eyes the prison guard whom I've aptly named Trunchbull, as she reminds me of the headmistress from *Matilda*, one of my favourite childhood books. After reading the book, I'd practised for weeks, trying to move a pencil with my eyes and contemplating the things I could do with magic like that instead of being able to see the dead.

"You're not on the list," Trunchbull repeats, tapping the paper with a chunky finger.

"There must be some mistake." Jacinta bristles. "He's expecting me."

"Not today, he isn't." There's a hint of satisfaction in Trunchbull's voice.

"Well, I'm here, so just add me to the list. It's not like I haven't visited him before."

Trunchbull shakes her head. "No can do."

"Of course you can," Jacinta argues. "Just get a pen and write my name down."

"I can't do that, as he has another visitor booked in." Trunchbull glares at Jacinta as this revelation settles on her, wrinkling Jacinta's perfectly drawn brow before she eyes the rest of us.

"Who?" Jacinta murmurs. Then she points an elongated finger at me. "It's her."

It isn't a question, and it strikes me as odd that she knows I'm the one who's visiting Valdemar. Has there been a mix-up? No, Jacinta isn't on the list, but obviously, she thought she was; otherwise, she wouldn't be here.

I stare at Trunchbull as I realise what's happened. Jacinta is a regular visitor of Valdemar. God, she could be his girlfriend, and he's replaced her with me.

Heat prickles up my back. My worries have always been about how safe it is to visit Valdemar Montresor, a notoriously dangerous criminal, and how damaging these interactions could be for my already precarious mental health, yet I'm more afraid now of what might go down in the reception area. Jacinta's nails look sharp; maybe they aren't just for vanity's sake.

Trunchbull seems to pick up on my pleading look, as she says to Jacinta, "I'm not at liberty to say."

"Like fuck you aren't," Jacinta spits as she eyes me up and down like I'm a vagrant who's just asked her for some money. "Who the hell are you, and why are you visiting Valdemar?"

"I'm not here to see him." It's weak, but the last thing I need right now is to be tangling with a disgruntled girlfriend.

"Liar." Jacinta steps forwards as the two guards flank her. "I've been here before and seen the same bunch of people, but I ain't never seen you here. Who the fuck are you?"

"That's enough." One of the guards positions himself between me and Jacinta as Trunchbull tells them to get her out of here. Wasting no time, they flank her and march her back through the main doors.

There's no time to consider who Jacinta is, or what this could mean for me when I leave the prison, as Trunchbull swings back into action.

"Okay, show's over, folks," she barks as The Gatekeeper unlocks the door, and we're ushered through it.

"I don't need to remind you of the rules, but I will anyway for those of you who are new to this." Trunchbull leads us down the same corridor I walked down on Monday. "Take the seat facing the rear wall as you enter the room. No leaning over the table. No shouting. Do not leave your seat for anything or anyone. If an alarm sounds, remain seated until I or another guard tells you to move, and absolutely no touching. Is that clear?" She turns quickly to face us, the murmurs from the others telling me they've heard this speech a thousand times. Checking her watch, she tells us, "You have forty-two minutes."

After flashing her fob against the scanner of a different door to the one I went through three days ago, she opens it and tells us all to find a seat and sit down. The room is sterile, with grey walls and a matching floor that seem to bleed into each other, making it feel like an enclosure. There are no posters, no smell of brewing coffee, no sound of laughter, just emptiness.

The rest of the group shuffle in and take their seats, like commuters who sit in the same seat on the bus every day.

I take the only seat remaining at a table at the back of the room.

It's a little surreal when the door opens and the inmates are led in. They're all cuffed, but as they spot the person who's waiting for them, the cuffs are removed.

My heart leaps into my throat.

Their cuffs are removed.

Shit. I hadn't realised they wouldn't be cuffed during visits. I'd felt safe during our last meeting, knowing Valdemar was shackled to the table, but this feels different.

Nervousness ripples through me.

Is this the reason he asked me to return, so he could have his hands free? Does he know I've pictured him dead a thousand times over, and now with his release imminent, he thinks I'm going to be seeking my revenge? Does he want to get to me before I get to him?

Maybe this wasn't such a good idea after all.

Fate has a lot to do with it.
Being in the right place
at the right time.

CHAPTER SEVEN

Panic floods my bloodstream.

There are three prison guards in the room, and I suspect another on the other side of the door. Valdemar won't have a weapon. What could he do to me in the confines of this small space?

Well, for starters, he'll have the full use of his hands, which would be enough.

Breathe. Calm. Stop this nonsense.

He has six weeks before he's released. Surely he wouldn't jeopardise that for a pre-emptive strike at a scrawny journalist?

The inmates rub their wrists, a crew of motley men all weathering the telltale signs of incarceration: pale skin, dull hair, and hopeless eyes.

Valdemar is the last to enter the room. I'm disappointed that the ghost of my brother doesn't follow him. Instead, alarm taps at my subconscious, and I'm convinced there's a hint of a smile as his cuffs are removed and he's brought over to the table.

He'd been sitting when I last visited, so now I see him at

his full height, all six feet of him. His tattoos appear animated as he walks, the ravens looking ready to take flight, the white T-shirt he's wearing rubbing against his skin, his sweatpants hugging his hips.

The air feels thick, danger surrounding him like lethal smog.

"You came." His voice is deep, rich, and flavoursome, as if he's been saving it for me.

"You asked me to," I reply, my words feeling like they're caught in the back of my throat.

I've spent the past ten years researching this man. I've read all manner of things about him, like how, fifteen years ago at the age of twenty-five, he became the youngest man ever to lead the Raven Hands, which on the outside appears to be a men's club, their signature raven tattoos on their left hands a marker of their allegiance, yet underneath, it operates as a suspected prolific criminal gang, dishing out violence, threats, and God knows what else to those who they deem deserve it. The Raven Hands once ruled Amontillado with iron fists and brutal force, and it's no secret that during their reign, the crime rate in the city was at its lowest.

Most reports speak of how calm Valdemar Montresor is, how controlled, and how all of it's a façade concealing the ruthless killer underneath it all. But here and now, as he towers over me in the flesh with no restraints, I realise just how dangerous this man is. The charisma, the piercing eyes, the lull of his intoxicating words. He doesn't need to hold a gun to your head to make you do his bidding; he simply needs to look at you.

As he lowers himself into the chair opposite, I exhale slowly through my nose.

"You look tense, angel." Valdemar settles his elbows on the table and steeples his fingers as he stares at me until I'm forced to look away. "Is something the matter?"

Caught out by his perception, I scramble for an answer other than the fact that I'm shit scared of him, and then I remember Jacinta.

"Just a little confusion on the way in." Irritation pricks my skin as I recall her harsh words and the way she'd looked me up and down.

"Confusion?" His eyes haven't left my face, and I almost feel as if he's reading me like a book, searching for something that isn't written in words.

"Jacinta was here," I say, trying not to squirm under his gaze.

"I've had a lucky escape, then." His top lip curls.

"She wasn't very pleased to see me," I tell him.

"I bet she wasn't." This feels like it should be accompanied by a smirk or a smile, something to show he's joking or finds this funny, but his face remains stoic, the serious air that surrounds him never seeming to lift.

"Who is she?" I ask, but do I want to know? If she's going to jump me on the way out, I do. "Your girlfriend?"

His laugh takes me by surprise, his cool, sober expression gone for a fleeting second. "No, she isn't my girlfriend." He delivers each word slowly and purposefully, so there can be no doubt about his answer. "She's Jupiter Prospero's."

I wouldn't be able to call myself a journalist if I didn't know who Jupiter Prospero is—Valdemar's right-hand man and the guy who's been babysitting the Raven Hands for the last ten years.

"Why does she come and visit you? Is she a Raven Hand?"

I seem to have lost my head, my journalist training forgotten. I know to only ask one question at a time; otherwise, the previous questions remain unanswered. But Jacinta has annoyed me, and I need to know who I'm up against. Valdemar is caged—for the time being at least—but Jacinta is out there on the other side. She knows what I look like and that Valdemar has replaced her visits with mine, and she was pretty pissed off about it.

"There's no such thing as a female Raven Hand." He's serious now, the previous bout of laughter having dissolved.

I furrow my brow. "Really?"

"Why are you so shocked by this? It's common knowledge that all Raven Hands are men." This is true, yet still, I can't quite grasp this "no women allowed" rule.

"I know that. It just seems a little archaic."

"The Raven Hands were established centuries ago."

I wait a beat, wondering if I'm in for a history lesson, but he doesn't elaborate, so I push on.

"Times change, people change, things move on. You're telling me the Raven Hands haven't moved into the twenty-first century?"

"I've tried, over the years, to make changes. I allow women into our meetings and to attend all social events, something that would never have happened fifteen years ago, but it's not as simple as you think."

"Why not?" I try not to scoff at this. It feels like it *should* be simple.

"It just isn't." He emphasises the *s*, almost making it sound like a *z* between his teeth, and once again I sense his reluctance to elaborate.

"Then explain it to me."

Lowering his arms, he glances to his right before answering. "The Raven Hands were established hundreds of years ago by a man named General Vankirk who was fed up with the lawlessness ravaging Amontillado, so he took it upon himself to clean the city up by whatever means he felt necessary. But it was no easy feat, and he soon realised he couldn't do the job alone, so he enlisted the help of like-minded men. Vankirk was well-known for the large raven tattooed on the back of his left hand, and his recruits became known as Raven Hands."

"I thought it was a men's club," I say.

"On the surface." Valdemar squints as if he's testing me.

"You're telling me the Raven Hands aren't a men's club and are, in fact, a vigilante group?"

"Something like that." There's a wryness to Valdemar's voice that I pick up on but ignore for now.

"So, this Vankirk guy gets a bunch of his mates together and decides to fight the bad guys? Not the most original of origin stories." I can't hide my smirk. This is kid stuff. Men playing at being boys.

"Not just anyone." He's so severe, his face lacking any emotion other than complete concentration on what he's saying, and I wonder if this is because he's been locked away for ten years and has only had the scum of the earth to converse with.

"Who, then? Are people chosen?" I hate that he's got me squirming on the hook in his fathomless waters, wondering when the beast will bite.

"You don't choose to be a Raven Hand. You become one."

An eerie silence settles on my shoulders, making me shiver.

"You've lost me." I'm floating now in open water, nothing to grab onto.

"Raven Hands are different from other people. We possess things others do not." His eyes sharpen as if he's trying to tell me something without saying the words.

"You're saying you're special?" I hate this guessing game, but I'm used to it, being a journalist.

"Gifted is the term I prefer to use." His voice has a silky quality now, as if he's spinning this tale for me with the finest yarn.

The room swirls, the other visitors and inmates merging into a morbid mass of body parts.

I press on, trying to settle the voice niggling inside my brain. "What kind of gifts are we talking about? Ambidexterity? The ability to roll your tongue? Holding your breath for longer than three minutes?"

"Those things are not gifts. This is not a talent show, angel. Gifts are something extraordinary that are bestowed upon someone for a purpose." His eyes narrow, and I know I've hit a nerve.

"Well, now you do sound like a bunch of tattooed anti-heroes who have special powers." I sit back in my chair and try not to roll my eyes. "Next you'll be telling me you wear masks and capes and find the nearest phone box when there's a crisis."

Ignoring my joke, Valdemar says, "You surprise me, angel. I thought you of all people would understand what I'm talking about." He clasps his hands together, interlocking his fingers.

A draft of cold air rushes over the back of my neck.

Trying to rein the conversation back in, I sit up.

"You're a Raven Hand. You must have a gift. So, what is it?"

"That, my angel, would be telling."

This time, there's no holding back the roll of my eyes. But I'm rattled now. As if this guy isn't dangerous enough. What can he do? What power does he possess?

I try a different approach. "So, how did you know you were a Raven Hand?"

"Deep down, I've always known. It's not like a revelation, a Before and After. You grow up knowing you're different, that you don't fit in."

His words are like a cold shower, the water running over my skin and giving me goose bumps.

"And then what? You get a calling?" There's a mocking to my voice, but I can't help it. This is like something from a movie.

"Fate has a lot to do with it. Being in the right place at the right time."

"And what about my brother? You can't tell me he was in the right place at the right time." Tears choke me, anger stifling my nerves. How can he sit there and be so calm?

"No one can predict the actions of others; we are at their mercy." His voice is as cold as his stare, and it does nothing to abate the goose bumps that are still erupting on my arms.

"What about *your* actions? How do you sleep at night?" I ask.

Valdemar stares at me, and I wrap my arms around myself, the bite of his glare enough to stoke the chill I'm feeling.

"Who said I do?"

"You deserve to rot in hell for what you've done," I spit.

"I don't dispute that."

"So, what's your purpose here? You think you're going to tell me what happened to my brother, and I might see a different side to things, that maybe you're not the monster everyone thinks you are and you deserve forgiveness? Are you trying to redeem yourself in my eyes? Because I can tell you now, that will never happen. I will never see you as anything other than a murderer, and if your story were to ever be written, it would portray you as what you are—a monster." The chill in my body has gone now, thawed out by the mounting rage that heats my skin.

"I'm not here to change your opinion of me."

"Then why *am* I here?" I clench my fists under the table, feel the nip of my nails as they dig into my palms.

"You tell me," he asks, leaning in slightly.

He's in my head again. How does he do it? Is this his gift?

Why *am* I here? Ed. That's why I'm here. Because my brother is here, and even though I can't see him now, I can feel him as if he's lurking in the shadows. I haven't felt his presence these past ten years, yet here, I can.

"I'm here for my brother," I tell him.

"You and me both." He delivers this with such authenticity that I can't help but believe him, yet hisanswer puzzles me. But I don't have time to ponder it, as the prison guard shouts unnecessarily loudly that our time is up.

The visitors look blearily around the room as if they're relieved it's over, yet I find myself annoyed at the time having gone so quickly.

"You look tired, angel," Valdemar says, examining my face. "Are you sleeping?"

"I haven't slept in ten years," I snap.

My answer pins him to his chair.

"Do I need to worry about Jacinta?" I ask, breaking the awkwardness as a prison guard moves to the rear door and starts to usher the inmates out one at a time. "Am I going to get my eyes scratched out as soon as I leave this building?"

"You don't need to worry; I will deal with her." He's so sincere that I have no doubt he *will* deal with her, even though I can't see how when he's locked up in here.

A prison guard arrives behind Valdemar, though he doesn't touch him like he did the other inmates, merely waiting for Valdemar to rise.

"Until next week, angel."

"Next week," I reply, wondering what will happen between now and then as I watch him being led from the room.

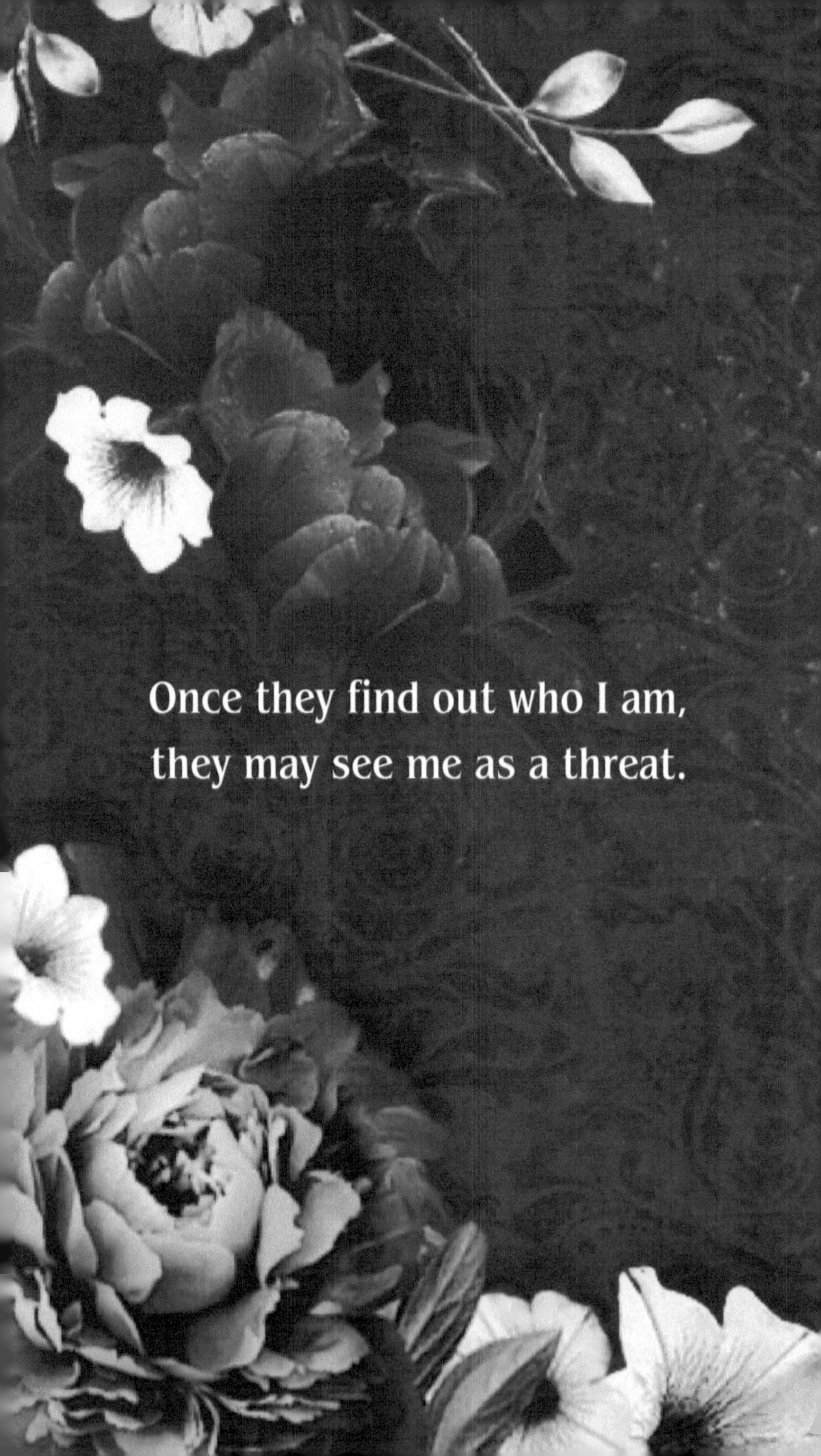

Once they find out who I am,
they may see me as a threat.

CHAPTER EIGHT

 came about when my colleagues, Una and Pierre, decided that Mondays were so dismal, we needed something to douse the start-of-the-week blues, and although I have no intention of telling them about my meetings with Valdemar, I crave some normality.

I've worked with Una at the *Gazette* for five years. She joined the team wanting to be a reporter, had the drive and the nose for it, but her wildly opinionated nature kept her from producing a story we could print. The first piece she submitted for the *Gazette* was about a local man who had gone missing, but instead of writing an objective piece on the matter, she turned in a full-page article implicating his girlfriend of foul play. Needless to say, her journalist career never took off, but her photography is out of this world, which led to her being hired as a photographer.

Pierre has been with us for a year and is the baby of the team, being both the youngest at twenty-two and also the newest recruit. He's still finding his feet, a position I remember only too well. He's nice, a little quiet, but seems to be immune to Una's pit-bull nature.

The three of us gravitated to one another, though I'm not sure why, as Una can be feisty, so you have to know how to handle her, and Pierre is quite reserved. And me? Well, let's just say that I've never had a queue of friends all lining up to spend time with me. When I was younger, I had Ed, and he had me. We never needed anyone else. And by the time I got older, no one wanted to be friends with the pale twin who carried an air of death around with her. Which is probably the only reason Una warmed to me when she started working at the *Gazette*, as she's a total goth chick.

Tonight's venue is Una's choice, a newly opened wine bar on Pym Street named Bon Bon. Because of its name, I'd imagined pastel walls and a sweet scent in the air along with a casual atmosphere—not the type of place Una likes to hang out—but I couldn't have been more wrong. The bar is cloaked in darkness, low-hanging lights casting the tables in a red glow, mauve velvet seat covers, and melancholy-looking staff all giving vibes of dark chocolate truffles rather than pink sugary sweets, which is definitely her preferred environment.

"How did you get lumbered with the college story?" Una asks as she arrives at our table, laden with a pitcher of something looking more like a potion than a drink. Her black hair appears almost blue tonight, the half-up, half-down style bunched into two pigtails on either side of her head conjuring an image of a goth poodle.

Pierre takes the tray from her and hands out the glasses as I play mother and pour the drinks. Music is playing, but it doesn't seem to have a tune, just a beat and a rhythm. This is not a bar I would have come to if Una hadn't suggested it. The black walls and crimson lampshades are stifling.

"There was nothing better on offer," I reply, eyeing the contents of the pitcher with curiosity.

"I would have gladly swapped with you, Evangeline,"

Pierre says, his wavy brown hair flopping into his watery eyes. Pierre's sun-kissed skin and umber hair boast exotic roots, yet his origins change daily depending on what mood he's in. I've heard him tell people he's of Mexican descent, yet on the same day tell someone else he's Italian. When I quizzed him about this, he told me that his mother never disclosed the race of his father, so he likes to cover all bases.

He takes a long swig of his drink. "God, what is this?" He glares at Una, his mouth morphing widely like that of a frog as he winces at the glass.

"Just a little pick-me-up cocktail. Sounds like you both need it." Una grins, her black lipstick looking even darker against her pearly white teeth. Her goth subtype changes regularly and can be anything from nerd goth to faerie goth depending upon her mood. Tonight, I think she's gone for traditional goth with heavy eyeliner, pale foundation, and a corset top that's pulling her in and making her appear taller than her five feet two inches.

"I can't argue with that." Pierre grips his glass like he's debating with himself whether he hates the drink or loves it. "I got stuck covering the rat infestation on Arnheim Street."

"I think I would rather have covered the rats than the college story," I tell him, and he raises a thick eyebrow at me.

"Really?" he says.

"The college story was a dead end. A parent called in and told us the headteacher had been suspended for the suspected embezzlement of school funds. After a little digging, I found out he hadn't been suspended at all but had handed his notice in on grounds of ill health. Not really the story of the century," I explain.

"Still had to be better than rats." Pierre's eyes narrow as he sips his drink, the jury still out.

"You two sound like you struck gold, as I've spent the day

tagging along with Dupin on a sighting of the infamous singer Morella," Una tells us.

Dupin remains our top reporter, and Captain thinks the sun shines out of his arse. Continually given the best leads, Dupin keeps on shining, whereas the rest of us are left withering in his shadow. Una is our top photographer and would be up there with Dupin in Captain's estimations if her look didn't scare the life out of him. Despite her scary appearance and her sharp bite, she can be a softie, but you have to get to know her to see this side of her. It took me a while to see the real Una under the all-black façade.

"Rumour had it Morella was spotted at an elite gym down near the lakeside," she continues.

"I take it she was a no-show?" I enquire, sampling my drink and grimacing at the burn as the liquid snakes down my throat.

"Oh, she showed up all right, but she was more mozzarella than Morella," Una laughs.

I snigger and shake my head.

"I don't get it," Pierre says, his open mouth suspended as he glances from Una to me.

"She was a cheesy lookalike, and not even a good one. Blonde hair, blue eyes, big tits, but that's where the similarity ended," Una explains.

Pierre laughs, sticking a straw into his glass before offering me one.

"Thanks." Leaning over the table, I pluck the straw from his hand. As I do, the cuff of my jacket skims the edge of my glass, sending it toppling over the table.

"Fuck." Catching the glass, I avert a major spillage, but my sleeve is soaking.

"I have tissues." Una stands, fumbling about in her skull-shaped bag before telling me she doesn't have any after all.

"Don't worry. I'll go to the ladies." I slip off my chair and head towards the washrooms.

I hadn't thought the lighting could be any worse in this place, but as I near the rear of the bar, the lampshades give off a cardinal hue that makes the room feel like it's draped in blood. Tables are replaced with booths, their occupants devoured by the depths of black leather upholstery and muted conversations.

The washroom is as opulent as the rest of the bar, with large gilded mirrors and red-and-black cubicles. I don't waste any time rinsing my sleeve under tepid water and then drying it the best I can under the noisy hand dryer.

Heading back to our table, I pass the booths, and a female voice startles me.

"It's you."

I'm stopped in my tracks as Jacinta emerges from a booth, blocking my path.

Fuck.

If our last meeting is anything to go by, this is not a friendly hello.

"Jacinta." It comes out as a whisper.

"You don't need to worry; I will deal with her."

Valdemar's words rattle through my head. But whatever he's done or said—if anything—can't help me here and now.

"This is the woman who was visiting Valdemar." She jabs a finger at me as she speaks to the darkened booth. I can't see who she's talking to until a long leg emerges from the gloom, pulling a body into the swathe of red.

"Sit down, Jacinta," a male voice says.

Jacinta suddenly seems like a pussy cat as I'm met with the coldest stare I've ever seen. He's tall and thin, his grey shirt and dark jeans hugging his slender frame. His black hair is closely cropped, making his head appear as if it's too large for his body, and his full lips do nothing to soften the brutality of his glare. Even against his dark skin, there's no mistaking the raven tattooed on the back of his left hand.

"And you are?" His face doesn't flinch as the words leave his mouth with an undertone that's used to getting answers whether people want to give them or not.

"No one you know."

My dad always said my cockiness would get me into trouble one day, and I'm wondering if today is that day as the Raven Hand narrows his eyes, sizing me up before laughing in my face.

Following his instructions, Jacinta has disappeared back into the depths of the booth, so now it's just me and the Raven Hand.

"There's more than one way for me to find out your name, lady," he says.

"How about you tell me yours first?" I goad.

He licks his lips, a glint in his eye, and for a moment, I wonder if I have a death wish.

He quirks his eyebrow. "You don't know who I am?"

From all the research I've done, I know he's Jupiter Prospero, but I don't want to give him the satisfaction of thinking he's infamous enough to be a household name.

"I've no idea who you are," I lie.

"I find that hard to believe, seeing as you're visiting Valdemar Montresor. Unless you don't talk to him during your visits. Is that it, lady? Do you have your mouth full when you go see him?"

His eyebrow arches, and my stomach coils. I've heard rumours of corrupt prison guards who, for a price, can arrange for special visits in private rooms, but I hadn't considered that maybe it's what Jacinta's visits were for. Do the Raven Hands share such things?

"What do you want?" I finally ask.

"I want to know why you're seeing Valdemar."

"If he hasn't told you, then it isn't my place to do so."

"Fuck, lady, you're trying my patience." His words feel like they hit my cheek, and I fight the urge to wipe them off. "I don't see what the problem is. Any friend of Valdemar's is a friend of mine." He opens his arms wide as if wanting a hug.

"Then I'm sure if you ask him, he'll tell you who I am and why I'm visiting him." I'm not sure why my allegiance is to Valdemar, but it's clear he's not shared our arrangement with the rest of his flock, including his number two—and once they find out who I am, they may see me as a threat. "You'll have to ask him. Now, if you please." Easing past him, I catch an earthy scent with a hint of spice.

I march back to my table, my heart racing and my fists clenched.

Why *hasn't* Valdemar shared our arrangement with his closest adviser? And if having Jacinta on my case isn't bad enough, I now have Jupiter Prospero to contend with.

All that remains is the
stone-cold stare of a killer.

CHAPTER NINE

THERE AREN'T AS MANY VISITORS THIS WEEK, AND I WONDER IF the torrential downpour that's lasted several hours has put some of them off the treacherous ferry crossing. With only a few of us, it doesn't take as long to be searched and processed before we're herded off to the visitors' room.

Taking the same seat I did last week, I wait for Valdemar to be brought in.

I can't deny the fear that's settled in my bones after my encounter with Jupiter Prospero. The risks have always been there. You can't walk into the lion's den and not expect a fight, but I hadn't anticipated tackling the pride as well as the alpha. My anxiety has always been aimed at Valdemar—he's the one in here on a murder charge.

But he's caged. For now.

Jupiter Prospero isn't.

When I'd arrived home from the bar on Monday, I'd recounted meeting Jupiter Prospero to my mother, who was perched on the window seat of my bedroom. She'd listened as she does, her eyes wistful, her skin pale, and even though she'd offered no words of maternal wisdom, she'd smiled, which settled me slightly.

But I've been unable to sleep for the entire week, my nights spent scouring the internet for information about the Raven Hands, taking copious notes, and drinking camomile tea. During the past few days, I've only managed a few hours of sleep, and even that has been laden with dreams of large ravens with their wings outstretched, their sleek black feathers oil-like in the moonlight, their beaks sharp and shining like razor blades.

My breath is stolen from me as Valdemar is brought into the room by a small but sturdy-looking prison guard. Unsure as to whether I'm reading too much into things, I notice that the guard barely touches him, as if he daren't lay a finger on him. But I don't get a sense of fear from the guard. They seem at ease with each other, as if they're old friends.

I straighten in my chair as Valdemar's cuffs are removed and he stalks over to our table.

Our table.

He's alone. No sign of my brother. But I feel Ed's presence, as if he's in the walls.

"Angel." A sharp scent like fresh night-time air accompanies him as he lowers himself into the chair.

"Valdemar."

Sweat beads between my shoulder blades as he stares at me, the intensity of it too much to look away from.

"You're still not sleeping," he says at last.

"I'm fine." I glance away, hoping he won't pick up on the lie.

"No, you're not," he argues.

"We aren't here to talk about me."

"You might not be, but I am. Humour me." He cocks his head to the side, and a small smile graces his lips.

Swallowing the number one rule of interviewing criminals, I tell him about my encounter with Jacinta and Jupiter. His body stiffens with every word.

"Did he touch you?" Valdemar leans forwards, and I note the guard checking us out.

I shake my head. "No." This is the first time I've seen Valdemar less than relaxed, and it not only accentuates the blue of his eyes but also the snarl to his lips.

"Are you sure?" he asks.

"I think I would have remembered if he had." I replay our meeting in my mind, focussing on Jupiter's hands, where they were, whether they came anywhere near me, but I'm certain they didn't.

"Even the slightest of touches, like he caught your hand or brushed up against your shoulder," Valdemar pushes.

I hesitate.

Sensing my confusion over his overreaction, he says, "It's important."

"No, I'm sure he didn't. But why does it matter?" I'm confused by this insistence about whether Jupiter touched me. What does it mean? Why is Valdemar so bothered by this?

He eases himself back into the chair. "If you're sure he didn't touch you, then there's nothing to worry about."

"Don't give me that. Something is going on. What is it?" I ask.

Valdemar grins. "There she is."

"Who?" I glance behind me.

"My reporter."

My reporter. Annoyance licks at my insides.

"You're not being fair," I tell him. "Am I in danger? What's going on with Jupiter?"

"I'll deal with Jupiter." That phrase again, like he still has command of his flock from inside these walls.

"That doesn't answer my question," I snap.

Valdemar pauses as if he's considering his words carefully before he speaks. "Jupiter is looking after the Raven Hands."

I wait, but he remains silent. "I'm sensing a 'but.'"

Valdemar regards me. "But there's been some unrest. The flock doesn't respond to Jupiter as they do to me."

This I can understand. When I'd met Jupiter, his stare had been hard, cold, nothing behind it but brutality. But with Valdemar, there's a hypnotic quality, a lull to his voice, a strength to his stare that makes you want to sit on your hind legs and beg for him. I've seen the way the guards are with him, the way I continue to visit even though I want to kill him. He's a charmer, a seducer, and no one is immune.

"Ten years is a long time. Is Jupiter trying to take over?" I guess.

"I'm the sworn leader, and while I breathe, there will be no other. You can't just take over. Jupiter is well aware of that." He says this as if Jupiter is in the room with us and Valdemar is reminding him of the fact.

"How do you become a leader?" I ask.

"There are two ways. One is to have the title bestowed by the previous leader. A ritual is performed and the reign handed over," he explains.

"And the other?"

There's a glint in his eyes, reminding me of what he is and why I'm here.

"The other is to kill the head Raven Hand and take the title for yourself."

I swallow, knowing what path this line of questioning is going to take me down.

"Who was head Raven Hand before you?" The reporter in me is lapping this up, but then I remember that there is no story here other than Ed's.

"Victor Rue. He was head Raven for many years. He was

ruthless, devoted—everything you would expect from a leader."

He knows what I'm about to ask, even though I'm not sure I want to know the answer.

"So, how did you become the new leader?"

In a blink, the charm, the charisma that has you wanting to eat out of the palm of his hand, is gone, and all that remains is the stone-cold stare of a killer.

"I killed him."

And just like Pandora,
I feel I've opened the lid on the
curses of mankind.

CHAPTER TEN

He has flesh, yes, breathes oxygen, and talks and thinks just like a human, but looking into his icy eyes, knowing he murdered his way to power, reminds me of the man he truly is.

The enchanter is gone.

The devil remains.

"You think I'm a monster," Valdemar says, placing his elbows on the table and interlocking his fingers.

"I know you're a monster," I reply.

"The world needs monsters." His voice is so cold, I can almost feel it in the air.

"How do you work that one out?"

"Because sometimes things need to be done. Horrible things that most people don't have the guts for. They won't get their hands dirty, so someone else has to." He unclasps his hands at this, as if showing me just how sullied they are.

"That's how you justify killing someone to gain power?" I lean forwards, my hackles raised.

"I don't kill to gain power." His words slice through the air as if he's brandishing a knife.

"You just said you killed Victor Rue to become head Raven Hand."

"Ever the journalist." He smirks. "You're putting words in my mouth. I never said I killed him for that reason."

"It was just a bonus, then?"

Valdemar places a hand flat on the table. "Consider this. You have a dog who's been loyal and faithful to you his whole life. He stayed by your side and listened to all your problems without judging you, without betraying you, until one day your dog doesn't remember who you are anymore and starts shitting in his bed and pissing on the floor. And your dog looks at everyone who visits with large begging eyes and a low whimper to be put out of his misery, but they don't listen, don't act; they don't want to get blood on their hands, murder on their conscience. So, your dog turns to you, his loyal friend, his faithful servant. And he asks you to do this one last thing for him. Is it easier to say yes or to say no?"

"You're saying Victor Rue was ill?" I probe.

"His body was strong and able. His mind was not."

"You think that justifies killing him?" I can't keep my voice neutral, something else I know as a journalist. Keep your own views under wraps; don't let them know what you think about what they're telling you, even if you think it's the most heinous thing you've ever heard.

"These decisions don't come easily. To kill someone you don't care about is easy, but to kill someone you admire and respect is impossible."

"And barbaric," I add.

"You're telling me you wouldn't put your dog out of his misery? Wouldn't save him from sitting in his own shit and wandering out into the road in the middle of the night because he has no idea where he is?" Valdemar asks.

"There are places that will care for people," I argue, but he sneers at this.

"All they do is mop up the shit and lock them up for their own safety. Is that really how you would want to spend the last of your days?"

"It doesn't matter how you justify it, it's still murder. You still have blood on your hands." I motion with my eyes towards his hands.

He's telling me that Victor Rue was a mercy killing, but it's not as if Victor is his only victim.

He's a murderer. A murderer.

"What about you, angel?" He cocks his chin at me as if batting this question over to my side of the table.

"What *about* me?" My voice wobbles despite the strength I'm trying to uphold.

"Do you think you would be able to get your hands dirty?"

The room spins, and I'm about to topple from my chair when the guard announces that there are only a few minutes left.

"Should I be worried about Jupiter?" I ask, changing the subject.

"I will speak to him," Valdemar replies.

"How?"

"I'm allowed phone calls."

"What do I say if he comes looking for me?" I'm not sure why I'm looking to this man for advice, but the question is out before I can stop it.

"He won't." There's a sharpness to his words, like they're his only weapon in here.

"But if he does?"

"Then he's a bigger fool than I took him for." The corners of his mouth twitch as if he's almost smiling.

Chairs scrape on the floor as the other inmates rise and are shackled, then led to the rear door. Just like on my previous visit, Valdemar is last. The guard hovers as Valdemar offers him his wrists.

"But if, for some reason, you find yourself in his company again, don't let him touch you," Valdemar warns.

"Why?"

He stands, and I want to stand with him, but I have to remain seated until all inmates have been removed.

"Because no one is allowed to touch you." He delivers this with such sincerity, such passion, that I shiver.

It's not what he said but the way he said it, what he's insinuated about the type of touch he's referring to. No one has touched me, in that way or any other, in a very long time. I've been grieving for so long that there hasn't been room for anyone else in my life. Last year I decided to go on a date with a guy I'd met in the deli. He was nice, but after our second date, when he'd learned that my twin brother had been shot by Valdemar Montresor, his interest in me waned. It was as if he didn't want to get involved in what my world might look like or didn't want to be tainted by my grief, let alone by any involvement with the Raven Hands. And I knew from then on that if I was going to date, I would have to hide the death of my brother, which is something I simply can't do. He was part of me. Still is.

"What will happen if Jupiter touches me?" I ask.

Valdemar glares at me, anger flirting around the corners of his eyes.

"If I'm in some sort of danger, then I think I need to know. I know you don't care, but—"

"Whatever gave you that idea?" he cuts in.

Before I can respond, the prison guard urges Valdemar to move. "Come on, Montresor. Visiting is over."

Just before they exit, Valdemar turns and shouts over his shoulder, "I hope you sleep better tonight." He smirks and then vanishes through the door.

THE MAELSTROM IS CHOPPY ON THE RETURN JOURNEY TO THE mainland, but I know it's not the rhythmic churning of the water that's stirring the contents of my stomach. It was supposed to be one visit for closure. But now I'm a regular visitor of Valdemar's, and Jupiter Prospero—who, for some unknown reason, I can't allow to touch me—has started sniffing around.

This state of affairs couldn't be further from what I hoped facing Valdemar Montresor would achieve. I could back out, tell him I'm not coming to visit him anymore, and hopefully put a stop to Jupiter poking around, but I can't deny the curiosity box Valdemar has presented me with.

And just like Pandora, I feel I've opened the lid on the curses of mankind.

At what point do you recognise
your dreams as just that—
dreams?

CHAPTER ELEVEN

Maybe Jupiter can read minds or control people through physical contact, or is his touch lethal? The possibilities of his "gift" spiral through my mind, Valdemar's warning of not letting him touch me fresh in my thoughts as the ferry docks, returning me to Amontillado.

Keeping a vigilant eye open for Jupiter or any other possible Raven Hands, I pull my coat tight against the biting chill of the wintery air and scurry to the car park where I left my car earlier today.

Though it's not quite six o'clock, the sky resembles charcoal, and despite Christmas lights that still adorn the nearby lampposts, the car park feels polluted with a darkness that isn't just to do with the sun having disappeared.

Convincing myself I'm just a bit wary after visiting the prison, I spot my little black Ford and thrust my hand into my bag to retrieve my keys.

Under the flickering glow of the broken streetlight, I fumble with my fob, my hands seeming to have lost all dexterity.

As soon as the door is open, I slip into the driver's seat

and lock myself in. I hadn't realised how tense I'd been until my shoulders drop.

Not wanting to remain here any longer than necessary, I go to put my bag on the passenger seat when I notice a white envelope.

Holding my bag like a shield, I stare at the letter.

How the hell did it get in my car?

I definitely unlocked the car just now, so there's no chance I left it open.

So, what is it doing on my passenger seat, and who the fuck put it there?

All the horror films I've ever watched come crashing into my brain—the helpless heroine in the front seat, the murderous madman emerging from the back seat where he's been lying in wait.

I almost cry out as I swing my head around to examine the back of the car, a blast of obscenities at the ready to attack the crazed intruder.

But there's no one.

The back seat of my car is empty.

I return to the envelope, the starkness of the paper making it appear as if it's glowing against the grey upholstery. I could ignore it until I get home and then just throw it in the bin, but the reporter in me is already composing headlines.

Ed's death only served to elongate the career ladder I started climbing ten years ago, and last year, finding myself still writing up the dregs of what some people considered "news," I contemplated a career change. Maybe I wasn't cut out to be a hotshot reporter. Maybe my calling lay elsewhere in the world, and I'd yet to hear it because I was being deafened by the world of journalism. At what point do you recognise your dreams as just that—dreams?

But the thought of starting a new job with new people

and a new role to learn filled me with such dread that I knocked the career change idea on the head and have still been waiting for my big break.

What if my big break is in this envelope? What if it's a lead from a friend? What if it's the story of the century, something Captain will love me for and that could set me on the path towards journalist stardom?

Carefully, I pick the envelope up and turn it over. There's nothing written on it. The flap has been tucked inside, and it takes no effort to open it.

Holding the thick white paper, I scan the typewritten words.

YOU KNOW WHAT HE IS

YOU KNOW WHAT HE'S DONE

CAN YOU LET HIM LIVE ANY LONGER?

KILL HIM

With shaking hands, I drop the note onto my knee and swivel to look in the back seat again, making sure the bad guy hasn't been there all along and I missed him the first time I checked.

Holding my breath, I scan the back of the car.

But there's no one here except me.

My mind starts racing with questions. Who left this note for me? How do they know I'm visiting Valdemar Montresor? How do they know this is my car, and how did they leave this note in my passenger seat without breaking in?

Shit. This is such a mess.

KILL HIM.

What the hell?

The idea of killing Valdemar Montresor isn't new to me. I've had many a daydream of sticking a knife into him, glorying in the justice I would serve. But it's always been fanciful thinking, as I never thought I would even meet the man, let alone be given an opportunity to push a blade into his stomach and gut him like he deserves.

But here I am with a free pass, albeit one that would require getting a weapon past security, which seems doubtful. But it appears as if I'm not the only one who wants him dead.

What would become of me if I did deal out the retribution my brother so deserves? What would that make me? A monster? A murderer? Where does the line end where murder would be justified? And if I do kill him, won't that make me just like him?

Valdemar's words whisper through my head.

"Do you think you would be able to get your hands dirty?"

Valdemar Montresor
is a murderer.

CHAPTER TWELVE

up as something it isn't.

Valdemar Montresor is a murderer.

And I'd like to say that he appears like any other man when he walks into the visitors' wing in his plain white tee and grey sweatpants.

But he is far from average.

There's an aura to him, an atmosphere that shrouds him in

The cursor blinks at me. I'm unable to finish this sentence. I'm not lying when I write these words—I would never lie when writing a report. Dress up the truth—absolutely. Embellish things to satisfy the reader—of course. But lying is not on my agenda. The last thing I want to do is humanise Valdemar Montresor. There are crazy people in this world—vulnerable, impressionable people—who look up to guys like him, and worse, there are others who are happy to turn a blind eye to the bad things he's done. They see his antihero image as something to be revered and admired.

I just see a killer.

Powering down my laptop, I glance at the clock. It's one in the morning, and there's no rush to write my piece on Valdemar, as I'm still not sure whether I'm going to publish it. He said I couldn't report our interviews, but there's no harm in having a backup plan. So, I'm documenting our conversations before I forget everything he's told me.

I've made notes and scribbled down some of the more important things he's disclosed, but I feel we've only scratched the surface. There's more to Valdemar Montresor than meets the eye, but I have no doubt that whatever he tells me, my opinion of him will never change. How can it?

The note I received is tucked in my bag, reminding me I'm not the only one who wants him dead.

After brushing my teeth and replacing my loungewear with an old T-shirt, I climb into my double bed knowing that the next few hours are going to tick by with me staring at the ceiling. But as I lie down, a strange heaviness pulls at the back of my head, as if my pillow has hands that are ready to embrace me.

My body feels as though it's been moulded into the mattress, my limbs relaxing, weightlessness surrounding me.

Maybe it's the exhaustion of the past few weeks finally catching up with me. Maybe it's the heaviness of the thoughts lodged in my brain—Valdemar, Jupiter, Jacinta, seeing Ed's ghost, the note—all of it having burrowed so deep, I feel like I'm being pulled under.

There's no time to panic over this surreal sensation as my eyelids give in and slumber takes hold.

Clutching the iron railing of the balcony, I take in the night sky, which is a wash of inky blue dotted with diamanté stars, the air fresh and ripe with the flavours of the night. Dense trees surround the grounds, which are beautifully manicured with a gigantic maze in the middle, its pathways swallowed up in thick foliage guarding the centre. It's as if I'm standing on a cliff edge, looking down upon the shrunken ground below.

I feel intoxicated, my body swaying slightly, my head floating. The fitted silver dress I'm wearing isn't one I recognise, and neither are the heeled sandals, but I feel good in them—powerful, even.

The balcony is abuzz with people, none of whom I know, and they don't appear to be paying me any attention, lost in their own world of espresso martinis and hummed conversation. The dress code is formal, men in sharp suits and women in glitzy dresses, all of them black.

Glancing up, I see that the balcony is attached to an old building with wrought-iron railings, trailing ivy weaving its way up the side of the ancient stone, and gargoyles scowling above the glass doors that open into a grand room.

I return to the view, recognising the Ragged Mountains off in the distance, holding me in their clasp like two cupped hands.

Someone arrives behind me, the smell of cedarwood and bergamot adding to the night-time bouquet.

He's male, I'm sure, as the heat from his body and the powerful fragrance sing masculinity.

It's been a long time since I've been this close to a man.

Too long.

As I lean against him, his warmth seeps through the thin material of my dress, relaxing my thoughts and stripping me of my inhibitions.

A hunger to be touched, to be wanted, coils within me.

Please, touch me.

No words are spoken as his hands travel over my skirt, the sensation sending a shiver of pleasure up my spine.

It's not enough.

I want to feel him.

As if my thoughts have reached him, he tugs at the hem, sliding his hands over my skin. Goose bumps erupt at the feel of his fingertips.

I rest my head on his chest as my dress is pulled up, the hem now sitting on my waist. It doesn't occur to me who the man is or whether the people on the balcony are watching us. My only concern is that he doesn't stop touching me.

I tighten my grip on the railing as his hands smooth over my backside, brushing my soft skin rhythmically and purposefully as heat grows between my legs.

Wordlessly, I encourage him.

More.

I want more.

Give me more.

One hand moves over my thigh, inches from the fabric of my underwear. Shifting my right foot, I widen my stance in the hope that his touch won't stop there, the craving growing.

Closing my eyes, I block the night out, the people and their voices, and focus solely on his hands.

One of them snakes up my stomach and traces my nipple through my dress as the other glides over the sheer fabric of my underwear. Biting my lip, I stifle a cry as he strokes me through the gossamer of my knickers.

I lean into his caress, and he slides my underwear to the side, his fingers slipping inside me with ease as his thumb explores my clit.

Butterfly kisses land on my neck, the softest lips buttering my skin.

He plays my body like a musician with a rhythm all his own, hitting all the right notes.

It's bliss.

It's beautiful.

It's beautiful bliss.

The night air claims my groans as the buzz builds, the fire inside me raging until my body starts to shake and my mind explodes.

Shuddering, my breathing becomes tight as I roll through the longest orgasm I've ever had.

When I open my eyes, my vision blurs, the stars shimmering against the indigo sky as my body comes back down to earth. As my eyes recalibrate, I glance down just in time to see his hand retreat from around my waist, adorned with the unmistakable tattoo of a raven.

The room spins as I bolt upright, my body hot and damp, bitter bile rising in the back of my throat. Throwing the covers off, I examine my skin for evidence of his contact, but there's nothing other than a throbbing between my legs.

I don't need to touch myself to know how wet I am, how turned on I was by him.

"It was just a dream," I say aloud, as if verbalising it will verify the fact. *Just a dream.* There's no way on this fucking planet I am attracted, sexually or otherwise, to Valdemar fucking Montresor—although, right now, my body would argue otherwise.

Checking the time, I note it's nearly morning, and for the first time in forever, I've slept for more than a couple of hours. I've never been touched like that before. In the real world, my sexual encounters were limited even before my brother's murder, and I'd always wondered if men kept their distance because I was tainted by death, the aura of the dead following me around.

I clamber out of bed and head to the bathroom to take a very cold shower.

I can feel it all.

CHAPTER THIRTEEN

 brought in. It's been a week since I've seen him and seven nights of the same goddamn dream.

It's consumed me during the waking hours as well as during sleep. I've tried sleeping on the sofa, drinking herbal teas, and exercising before bed in the hope that I'll banish the dream. But no matter what I do, every night I'm on the balcony, the silver dress clinging to my body, craving him like a junkie needing a hit. And what sickens me the most is the fact that when I wake, I'm hot and panting with a growing throb between my legs and a thirst for more.

I woke this morning still feeling the vibrations of Valdemar's touch on my skin as if his hands had only been there seconds before. The ache within me has been unbearable, but I've not given in and relieved myself, as I will not yield to this demonic dream.

He murdered my brother.

He took Ed's life from him with the simple pull of the trigger.

He killed the other half of me.

Yet, when I move, I can feel the memory of his hand, his fingers, the tremor of the orgasm.

I can feel it all.

He enters the room with a swagger, his head low and a glint in his eye, his broad shoulders swaying, his hair scraped back into a smooth bun. Trying to block out the recollection of his fingers inside me, I stare at him, stony-faced and tight-lipped, until he sits down.

"Are you sleeping any better?" Valdemar enquires.

"Why do you ask?" I snap. Why would this be his first question? Then I remember that last week, he told me I looked tired, and his parting words had been something to do with getting a better night's sleep.

"There's colour in your cheeks," he observes.

Fuck.

"Yes. No. I mean, I have been getting some sleep." There's no way he can know about the dream. Unless he's a goddamn mind-reader. The thought prickles my skin. "Your gift. Can you read minds?" I ask, though I almost don't want to know.

He smirks and gazes at me from underneath his thick lashes. "Fortunately not."

Hiding my relief, I ask, "Why fortunately? I thought that would be a great gift."

"Being plagued with the thoughts of everyone in the room is more like going mad than a gift. Not something I would like to endure. Living with my own thoughts is bad enough," he says.

Jupiter springs to mind, and I ask, "Are there Raven Hands with this gift?"

"Not for many years. Our gifts aren't something we talk openly about." He glances at the table, something I know people do when they don't want to talk about the subject you've raised, but I won't be deterred.

"Why?"

"Because they're personal to us." Valdemar sits back in his chair, as if he's keeping his secrets at bay.

I've never told anyone I can see the dead. It's not something I feel comfortable talking about, and Valdemar is right —it's personal. But mine isn't a gift. A curse, yes, but a gift, no.

"How did you become a Raven Hand?" Folding my arms, I try not to look at his hands.

"I've always known, deep down, that I didn't belong with the rest of society, but I didn't officially become a Raven Hand until I was seventeen."

"That young?" It shouldn't come as a surprise. The corruption in this city doesn't discriminate against age.

"My mother was a single parent. My dad walked out on her the minute he found out she was pregnant. She worked three different jobs to keep food on our table and a roof over our heads. She was always working, whether it be cleaning the offices in Charmion Square or waiting tables at The Haunted Palace restaurant."

"So, you were left to your own devices."

"To fend for myself in every way possible. But only because she didn't have a choice." His eyes soften. "I was walking the streets one night, trying to avoid being alone in the apartment. I'd been texting my mother, telling her I was okay and that I was on my way home, when a man came up behind me and grabbed my phone from my hand.

"It took my mother months to save up the money to buy me that phone, and it was my only way of contacting her when she was at work. And he took it, just like that. I hadn't got a good look at him. He could have been seven feet tall with a machine gun in his hand—I didn't care. The anger was blazing, the rage taking over the controls."

The room stills as if everyone else has faded into the

background and only Valdemar and I remain with his memories.

"So, I ran after him. Down Locke Lane, onto Hunter Grove, and then right through the Blackwood estate until I caught up with him on Fay Road. I was seventeen, lean, and in shape. He was a thirtysomething slob who couldn't keep the pace, but even so, I only caught up with him because someone had got to him before me." Valdemar's eyes have lost their focus, as if he's looking into his past rather than at me.

"By the time I rounded onto Fay Road, the guy was being held aloft by a tall man all dressed in black with light hair and large hungry eyes. He held the thief like he was a sack of rubbish. 'Does this belong to you?' he asked, eyeing me as the guy dangled in midair, his high tops scraping the ground and his hands grappling with the chokehold the other guy had on him. I told him that he'd stolen my phone, and I just wanted it back. The man eyed the thief and then dropped him. And before the thief could run, the man stepped on his forearm, pinning him to the pavement.

"He searched the thief, pulling my phone from an inside pocket and asking me whether it was mine. I nodded. He told me to come and get it. I should have been terrified, but I wasn't. I stepped closer, reached out to take the phone, and the man said to me, 'You gonna let him get away with this?' I wasn't sure how to answer, and he carried on. 'He took what was yours. He had no right. He'll do it again unless you teach him a lesson.' I thought he meant for me to beat the guy up and send him away with a black eye and a fat lip, but when he pulled the knife out of his pocket, I knew he meant more of a permanent lesson."

Valdemar presses his lips together before he continues.

"I'd been in fights at school, so I was no stranger to a bit of violence, but I'd never handled a weapon before. He handed me the knife, telling me it was my lesson to deliver and to make sure it was one the guy would heed. The thief was now squealing, tears swelling in his eyes, pleading with me not to hurt him. But as he did, all I could think about was how easily he snatched my phone from my hand, how hard my mother had worked to buy it, and how he'd taken it from me without a second's hesitation."

Valdemar pauses as if savouring the memory. "I don't think I drew a breath as I cut off two fingers from his right hand."

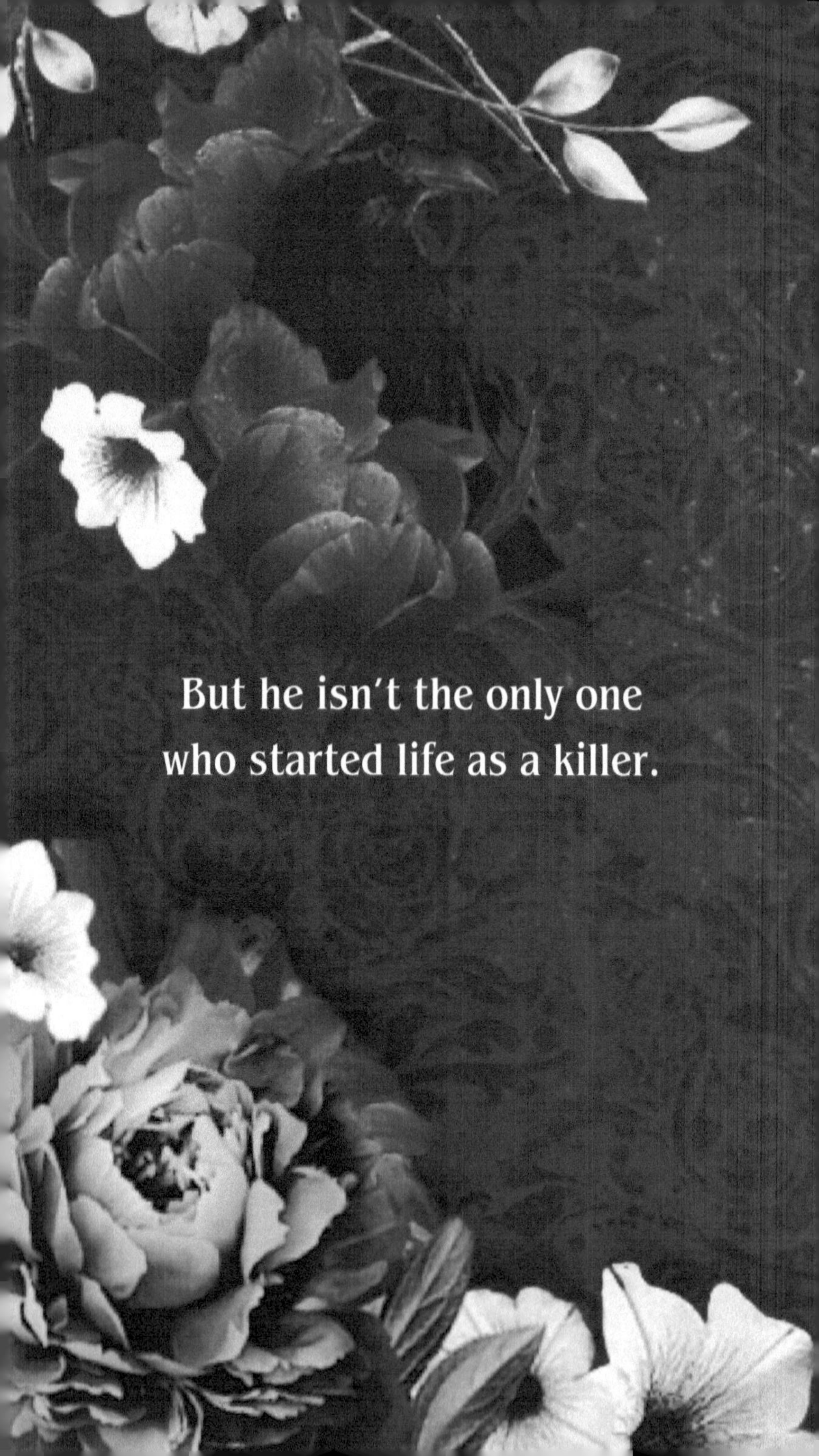

But he isn't the only one
who started life as a killer.

CHAPTER FOURTEEN

I so shocked by the revelation that he cut two fingers from some guy who tried to steal his phone from him?

"You were seventeen?" I ask.

"Yes."

"And you just met this strange guy on a street, and he told you to cut off a thief's fingers, so you did?" I clarify.

"He told me to teach him a lesson he wouldn't forget. I had to interpret the punishment myself." Valdemar's voice is husky now, as if the story he's just told has scratched at his throat.

"And this led to you being a Raven Hand?" I'm mentally writing a piece on this, constructing the sentences, delivering the lines.

"I'd heard of the Raven Hands, but I had no idea who Victor Rue was. After I'd cut the thief's fingers off, he looked at me and laughed, then told me I was fucking nuts and that he could use a guy like me."

"A boy. You were a boy." I lean forwards, emphasising my point.

"Have you lived in Amontillado all your life?" Valdemar arches an eyebrow.

"Yes."

"Then you know as well as I do that you become an adult a lot younger living here than anywhere else."

I sit back as Ed comes to life in my head, the nights he would come home in the early hours smelling of strange scents, a haunted look in his eye like he'd seen things he shouldn't have. And he was just a boy. Just like Valdemar had been.

Ed wasn't the only one who'd been corrupted by this city.

"So, Victor Rue takes you under his wing"—I smirk at my unintended pun—"and you became a Raven Hand."

Valdemar doesn't answer me, and the journalist in me senses there's more to this.

He swallows hard before glancing down at his hands. "It was a couple of months after I met Victor that I became a full-fledged Raven Hand."

He's gearing himself up for something, and I'm poised, waiting until he opens his mouth.

"My mother was attacked one night on her way home from work. It was late, she was alone, and someone jumped her, stole her purse, her phone, the cheap gold ring that belonged to my grandma." He pauses, readying himself, his eyes lost. "They hit her on the side of the head and again on her cheek—not enough to kill her, but enough to knock her out." He looks up at me before continuing. "She was left unconscious. When she didn't come home on time, I took to the streets looking for her. Anyone else would have survived —they would have been traumatised, needed a few stitches and some rest, but they would have lived. Unfortunately, my mother was a haemophiliac. When she was left unconscious, her blood didn't clot, and she bled to death. By the time I found her, it was too late."

Something unravels inside me, and I don't want it to be sympathy. I don't want to feel sorry for this man—he doesn't deserve it. But I am only human, and somewhere, under those tattoos, so is he. I'm also aware that this all could be a ruse, a lie, laying the foundation of the sob story so that I feel sorry for him and his poor start in life that led to him being a killer.

But he isn't the only one who started life as a killer.

"I'm sorry for your loss" is the best I can come up with, but Valdemar bats this away as if it's inconsequential.

I want to know what happened to the man who killed his mother. But if the thief who tried to take his phone is anything to go by, then I presume he came to a rather unfortunate end at the hands of Valdemar and Victor. Aware that time is pressing on, I change direction.

"What I don't understand is your gift. You said you can't be a Raven Hand without a gift. Did Victor Rue get lucky and just happen to stumble upon you by accident?"

Valdemar sits up, seemingly happy with the change of topic. "When you become the head of the Raven Hands, you're delivered an extra gift—a foresight, if you will. He'd been looking for me."

"He knew your gift?" If Valdemar picks up on the scoff in my voice, he doesn't show it. I don't mean to sound so dismissive, not after what he's just told me, but I can't help thinking this all sounds like something from a comic book.

"He didn't know exactly what it was, just sensed that I had one."

"I take it you now have this same foresight?" I guess.

"Yes." He's reluctant to discuss the gifts, this much is clear, but I push on.

"And you recruit—or recruit*ed* when you weren't in here."

"Yes."

There's a bitter taste on my tongue, metallic and tangy,

and it isn't until Valdemar glances at my mouth that I realise I've bitten my lip.

"Is that why you took it upon yourself to recruit Ed?" Any earlier sympathy I had for him is gone.

"Your brother had a gift."

The room tilts, memories washing over my skin: Ed and me in the park, him pulling on my hand as I set off running for the swings.

"No!" Ed shouted, grabbing my wrist so tight, it left a red mark on my skin.

"Hey, let go." I tugged my arm back, but he held firm.

"You're going to get hurt," he insisted.

"I'm not a baby. I'll be fine." Then I pulled my arm harder and ran straight to the swings.

I mastered them easily as Ed watched from the side, a paleness to his already colourless skin. I laughed, flailing my legs wildly as the rush of air enveloped me, the feeling of freedom swallowing me before my left sandal flew from my foot. The momentary distraction caused me to lose my grip on the chains, and I was flung forwards, flying weightlessly through the stagnant sky before hitting the ground with an undignified thud.

Ed rushed to my side, his utter panic delivering his breath in raspy gusts.

"I told you not to go on them."

My tears fell, and I wiped them away with the back of my sweaty hand as I surveyed the two grazed knees I'd suffered despite the rubber tarmac that was supposed to soften my landing.

"Hey, are you okay?" Another parent had arrived, a mother in a thin jacket and worn sliders armed with tissues and a bottle of water.

Ed pulled me to standing, the pain in my ankle making me dizzy.

"I'm fine. We're fine." I gestured to Ed for him to steer us away from the woman. The only thing worse than not having a

mother of your own was having to endure the pity of someone else's.

I hobbled over to a large sycamore on the edge of the park that doused the grass in shadow and would shelter us from prying eyes.

"Are you okay?" Ed said at last, but all I could think of was what he'd said to me before I'd run for the swing.

"You're going to get hurt."

"How did you know?" I asked him.

He did what he always did and ignored my question, fussing over the graze.

"Ed, how did you know?"

Startled at my insistence, Ed stared at the ground, scuffing the dry dirt with his muddy Nikes. "I just knew."

"Was it like a feeling, or did you know exactly what was going to happen?"

He took his time, probably considering whether it was worth lying to me.

"I saw it," he said at last. "I saw your shoe fall off, and then you fell with it."

It should have come as a surprise, but this wasn't the first time Ed had said he'd seen things before they happened, I'd just never paid enough attention to warrant it with any credibility. He'd always had a wandering imagination, coupled with a sense of dread that comes with growing up knowing you killed your mother. But this was different.

"You knew about his gift," he says.

Valdemar's smoky voice pulls me back into the room, and I feel as if he'd seen the memory for himself. There's no point in lying to him, so I say nothing.

"There are things I wish I could change, things I wish I'd done differently, but there are some things I didn't have a choice in. Your brother was born with his gift. That was out of my control."

"What a bullshit excuse." Squeezing my hands into fists, I

try to keep my voice down, as the guard at the back is eyeing me across the room.

"Did he talk to you about his gift?" Valdemar asks.

"His gift is irrelevant. You groomed him, lured him in with promises of a gang-style life, the glamour, the money, the violence, and then you shot him in cold fucking blood, so don't give me your pathetic excuse about a gift and him being chosen," I spit.

The hand creeps over Valdemar's shoulder, its fingers the colour of old chewing gum. I track the bitten-down nails, the blood-spattered sleeve, the elongated neck, and the protruding Adam's apple, and finally my gaze lands on the face—his haunting porcelain face.

Ed stares through bloodshot eyes as my breath catches in my throat, and I want to clasp my hand over my mouth to stop the shrill cry that's about to erupt, but I can't let Valdemar know something is wrong, that my brother is here.

"I wish that were the case. Truly, I do. And I'm not arguing with you about me being the bad guy because I am. I know I am. I have so much blood on my hands, I'm not sure what colour my skin is anymore. But when I tell you that your brother was a Raven Hand, born a Raven Hand, bled like a Raven Hand, and that his gift had everything to do with his death, then you have to trust what I say."

I don't have to trust anything this man says, and I have to stop myself from saying so out loud.

My eyes glaze over, the room blurring beneath the stagnant tears I refuse to cry. I feel trapped. I want to look at Ed, but I don't want to arouse Valdemar's attention. It'll look strange if I'm staring over his shoulder. And my brother's face is not the smooth portrait I remember.

"*You* pulled the trigger. *You* shot him. *You* spilled his blood. No one else," I remind him.

Valdemar's shoulders rise and fall, the sheer force of his stare keeping my tears at bay.

"And I'm truly sorry, but…."

I'm about to interrupt, but he continues, bulldozing my argument right out of the room.

"He asked me to shoot him."

It's like an avalanche, the cold rushing into my bloodstream, the world as I know it buried under his words.

"He asked me to shoot him."

My brother doesn't move, doesn't even flinch. I want him to nod, to confirm what Valdemar has just said, but just like my mother, he remains silent, his face conveying nothing but pain.

The guards move away from the walls in unison, and I almost scream at them to stay put, just for one more minute.

"Time, everyone," one of the guards shouts, and my eyes remain rooted on Valdemar. I can't look at my brother—the torment is too much.

"He asked me to shoot him."

Leaning over the table, my voice breaks as I hiss, "What do you mean?"

When a guard appears behind Valdemar, my brother vanishes as if someone has turned the TV off.

Valdemar rises, and I'm swallowed by his shadow.

"Sleep well, and I'll see you next week, angel," he says, that hypnotic quality to his voice back.

One whole week. He can't tell me something like that and expect me to wait an entire week before finding out what the hell he's talking about. But the moment to argue is gone, as Valdemar is led away, the coldness of his shadow remaining.

What am I missing?

CHAPTER FIFTEEN

THE RETURN FERRY CROSSING TAKES LONGER THAN NORMAL, the lake eager to hold on to me, giving me ample time to ponder Valdemar's words.

"He asked me to shoot him."

Valdemar was seen shooting my brother by a police officer at the casino, and in the court hearing, he pleaded guilty; it was an open-and-shut case. Per the terms of his plea deal, he was sentenced to twenty years in prison—nothing compared to the taking of someone's life.

I didn't attend the court hearing. My grief was too fresh, my wounds too raw. I would never have been able to sit in the courtroom mere feet from Valdemar Montresor and watch him breathing when my brother wasn't.

But years later, when my grief had soured and only bitterness remained, I read the newspaper reports, applied for the transcripts of the hearing, and asked Dupin to pull in a favour with one of his sources in the police department who got me the case files on the investigation. And I learned everything there was to know about what happened at the casino that night. Once I started reading, I couldn't stop, hungry for something to explain the inexplicable, to shed some light on the darkness that had consumed me.

"He asked me to shoot him."

I can't recall reading anything that suggested my brother had begged to be killed or that he wanted to die, a detail I would have remembered. What had I missed? And why did Valdemar not mention this during his case? Was it because it was something that might compromise the Raven Hands? Or because it's a lie to keep me where he wants me.

Ed started at Fortunato Casino when he turned eighteen and worked there for five years. He never professed any delight in his job, but he never complained about it either. It was just after he started working at the casino that Ed had changed. I always thought it was his job, the people he saw, and the fact that he lived in the hours of obscurity. Preferring the night shifts, he slept during the day, only waking when the sun had set and the world hid under the cover of darkness.

We'd always come as a pair. Same womb, same home, same school. When he got the job at the casino, it was the first time he'd done something without me, and that was when I started to lose him.

When he wasn't working, I had no idea where he went or who he was mixing with—until he went to work one evening and didn't come back.

Once home, I switch the kettle on even though I have no intention of making a cup of tea, and after throwing my coat on the back of a chair, I grab the box file that has taken up permanent residence on my kitchen table.

I pull back the lid and delve inside, shuffling the creased papers and photos filed in a system only I understand.

I fish out the *Amontillado Gazette* that ran the day after the shooting, skimming over the article on the front page until I find the interview with eyewitness Alberto Montani.

Ignoring the part about him and his wife being there for their fifteenth wedding anniversary and it being a trip they'd planned on doing after they'd first met in the casino, I find the quote I'm looking for.

"We'd played the tables, but you gotta know when to quit, so we'd moved on to the slots when someone screamed," Alberto Montani told the *Amontillado Gazette*. "It came from over near the roulette tables. There'd been a buzz around those tables all night because Adolphe Fortunato, the owner, had made a rare appearance. I remember saying to Marie that we might get a chance to see the man himself, but we never did. I thought the scream was someone fooling around after having just lost a load of money, but then there was a loud crack and the smashing of glass, followed by more screaming. We couldn't see the tables from where we were, but others must have, and that's when people started lying on the floor with their hands over their heads and hiding behind the machines. It's a classy place, not the sort of venue where you expect trouble, and I thought it must be a hold-up, so I grabbed Marie's hand and pulled her down onto the floor."

I stuff the article back into the box, then carry on digging until I find what I'm looking for. I pull out a chair and sit, scanning the already familiar words of Sergeant Psyche in his statement that was taken as the first officer on the scene.

We were called by dispatch to a disturbance at the Fortunato Casino after the report of a gun having been fired.

We entered the casino at 21:24 and made our way to the back of the casino where the roulette tables are.

A smashed chandelier lay broken on the centre of the table, and there was glass underfoot. A female croupier (later identified as Miss Louise Olivia) told us that

the men with the guns had gone to the
private suites at the rear of the building.

On arriving at the suite, we found the
doors locked.

I said: "Police. Open the door now."

When the doors didn't open, Officer Massa
Will and I broke them down.

Valdemar Montresor was standing on the
far right of the table with Jupiter Prospero and Jacinta Alessandra. Adolphe Fortunato, Dr Ollapod Tem-Pest, Julius Rodman,
and Edgar Bransby were on the other side,
facing the other two men.

Valdemar Montresor had a gun pointed at
Adolphe Fortunato.

I unholstered my weapon and said to
Valdemar Montresor: "Put the gun down and
put your hands behind your back."

Adolphe Fortunato said: "There's no need
to cause a fuss. Valdemar Montresor is
going to put his gun away."

Valdemar Montresor kept his gun trained
on Adolphe Fortunato.

Valdemar Montresor glanced around the
room and then lowered his weapon, but then
he raised it again and pointed it at Edgar
Bransby before shooting him between the
eyes.

Dropping the statement onto the table, I wonder how
doctored this account is. I can't imagine Valdemar was the
only one with a gun in his hand; he made no bones about
how corrupt the police are and how Adolphe Fortunato had
them in his pocket and still does. Fortunato's grip on this city

is one we all feel the pressure of, but it doesn't explain why Valdemar shot my brother.

There is nothing in this statement, whether true or not, that gives me any motivation for why Valdemar shot Ed or any indication that Ed asked him to. What am I missing? Valdemar wants me to hear his side of the story, but how truthful is he being? And why is the ghost of my brother standing over Valdemar?

I haven't forgotten about the note either. Who wants Valdemar dead? Why are they expecting me to do the honours?

And all the while, I'm having raucous dreams about the man who has now turned my life upside down for the second time in ten years.

Let it go, angel. I've got you.
Come for me.

CHAPTER SIXTEEN

My Sunday is spent unblocking the sink in my bathroom and then trying to write up some more from my talks with Valdemar. By eight, I throw in the towel and pack my laptop away, knowing I'm never going to be able to write an objective piece on Valdemar Montresor.

After a long bath and rereading the same page of a trashy thriller I've been attempting to finish for well over two weeks, I give in and climb into bed.

The sheets are cold, and the smell of lavender and ylang-ylang oil is already attacking my nose, my latest effort at trying to send myself off into a dreamless sleep and rid myself of the rising stress the last few weeks have evoked. Despite my bedroom smelling like an apothecary, the dreams have still come, Valdemar's hands upon my skin, his breath on the back of my neck. Although I've never seen his face in my dreams, I know it's him.

After slipping the knife under my pillow, I turn the light off and close my eyes. It's not much of a plan, but I'm hoping the prick of the blade against my palm will be enough to wake me and release me from his touch.

It's crazy, I know, but after enduring night after night of the same dream, I'm ready to try anything to make it stop.

Settling on my front, I slide my hand under the pillow and curl my fingers around the handle of the blade. My eyes close, the familiar pull of the night gripping me with both hands as reality ceases.

Swathes of silver silk wrap themselves around my calves as I run down the long corridor of the old mansion. Paintings adorn the walls, the light of the moon slipping in through the large windows and kissing the gilded frames.

My bare feet are silent upon the hardwood floor, my hair whipping my shoulders as I race against the night. Something squawks outside, and I see the black wings of a bird beating against the glass.

Running harder, I notice a large oak-panelled door ahead of me, yet no matter how fast I run, no matter how much distance I cover, I don't seem to get any closer to it.

Then I hear it, just over my shoulder—the whisper of his husky voice.

"Who are you running from, angel?"

Feet pounding the boards, I sprint for the door, fear and adrenaline coursing through my veins, pushing my body to its limit.

"There's no point in running, angel."

His words bounce off the high ceiling, making it impossible to tell where they're coming from.

"Because eventually, angel, you will stop."

As soon as I hear the word stop, *my body freezes as if I'm on a leash and he's pulled at the slack.*

The corridor lengthens, the oak door shrinking, seeming the furthest away it's ever been.

There's a large window to my left, the moonlight casting a spotlight upon the floor where I stand.

Something niggles at my brain—something I should be looking for. There are no pockets in my dress, the thin material barely covering me.

What is it I'm looking for?

I flex my fingers, wondering what I should be holding in my hand.

"Looking for this?"

I feel it first, the cold metal pressed against the side of my arm.

Sucking air in through my teeth, I glance down and see the glint of the blade as it runs over my skin and up to my shoulder.

"Hold still, angel." His breath is hot against the back of my neck as the knife travels over my collarbone and then down onto my chest.

Holding my breath, I try not to move.

The urge to flee has gone, the need to stay overwhelming.

His fingers trail over my shoulder and pull at the thin strap of my dress. A shiver runs down my spine even though I'm hot. He slides the knife underneath the strap and cuts it with ease. He then repeats the process on the other side, the flimsy dress falling, leaving me naked, the moonlight, his hand, and the knife the only things upon my skin.

"That's better," he says as he smooths the weapon over my abdomen, goose bumps rising as I shudder against the chill of the metal. It travels up my side, the tip of the blade kissing the underside of my arm as he brings it up to my breast.

He teases the knifepoint over my nipple, his other hand flat on my hip.

"I told you there was no point in running," he says as he moves the blade up to my throat.

The beat of my pulse pounds my ears, my heart drumming against my ribcage that I'm sure is going to crack.

Holding the knife steady, he slips his hand between my legs.

"Keep perfectly still, angel. Perfectly still."

I find myself leaning against him, his solid frame holding me up, my head resting on his chest, his breath caressing my hair.

His fingers brush tentatively over my sensitive spot, the electricity surging through my body making the command to stay still nearly impossible. Biting my lip, I close my eyes as I try not to grind my crotch against his hand.

"That's it, angel." As he dips his fingers inside me, I feel the nip of the knife against my throat, the thrill surpassing the fear of the blade. "You're so wet, angel, so pliant."

I twist my hands behind me, and they find him, gripping his shirt, steadying the mounting pleasure threatening to topple me.

"I've got you." His fingers pulse as his thumb massages me, and the moan escapes the confines of my head. "I want to hear you. I want to hear what I do to you."

"Oh God." Pressure mounts, the buzz building, gaining momentum until I can't keep it at bay. "Yes," I cry as Valdemar's fingers fuck me, my throat exposed to the knife's edge.

"Let it go, angel. I've got you. Come for me."

Hard and ferociously, my orgasm rips through my body, shattering the moonlight, my cry piercing the night.

My breath catches in the back of my throat as my eyes spring open, the tail end of the orgasm still rolling through my body.

But it isn't the pleasure that shocks me, or that the dream has changed, but the fact that in my right hand, I'm holding the knife.

How can you control
your dreams?

CHAPTER SEVENTEEN

"How can you control your dreams?" I ask Pierre and Una as the large vegan pizza is placed on the table by a skinny teenager who looks like he would rather be anywhere but serving pizza on a Monday evening.

We all finished work late due to Captain changing his mind at the last minute on a story we had planned to run midweek, so it was a unanimous decision to grab a bite to eat to accompany our usual Monday night drinks. Being a strict vegan, Una has brought us to The Hop-Frog Vegan Veg-Out on Hicks High Street.

Tucking her dark hair behind her ear, Una reaches for a slice. "Depends what you mean by controlling your dreams," she says as she curls her pizza slice into a cone and takes a bite without smudging the dark red lipstick she's worn all day as part of her romantic goth look.

"Do you mean you don't want to dream?" Pierre asks, wrinkling his nose up and poking the soy-based cheese topping.

"I've tried all the stuff to stop myself from dreaming, and

none of it works. What I really want is to be able to control my actions during the dream."

"Why would you need to do that? The best part about dreaming is letting yourself do things you would never do in real life." Pierre sucks leftover flour from the pizza-making process from his fingers before continuing, "Unless you're chopping up kittens or something?"

"I'm not chopping up kittens," I reassure him. "I'm just doing things in my dream that I would rather not do in real life."

"Evangeline Bransby, what are you doing that's so bad?" Una asks, wiping the corner of her mouth on the back of her fingerless-gloved hand and trying to adopt a mischievous tone.

"Let's just say I'm in a compromising position with someone I would never touch in real life."

"Holy shit, who?" Una's eyes widen, her heavily winged eyeliner appearing to expand.

"No one you would know," I lie. Although Una and Pierre weren't working at the *Gazette* when my brother died, they would have to have been dropped off here from another planet to not know who Valdemar Montresor is.

"Damn. Male, female, trans, neutral, or neither?" Pierre asks.

"What difference does it make?" I squint at Pierre, whose pizza is suspended in the air, inches from his mouth.

"I can't paint a mental picture if I don't know who I'm imagining." He grins.

I shake my head.

"Seriously, though, I'm not sure you can control yourself during a dream," Pierre adds.

"That's where you're wrong," Una corrects him. "There are techniques that revolve around lucid dreaming where you recite a mantra while you're awake and then try to recite the mantra in your dreams. It's possible, but it can take years to master. And then there's hypnosis."

"I'm not getting hypnotised," I say.

"I think you're tackling this from the wrong angle." Pierre swallows and then picks up another slice. "I think you need to address why you're having this dream and whether, on some subconscious level, your brain is telling you that you really want to engage with this individual."

"Absolutely not." I snort. "Subconscious, unconscious, semiconscious, or even comatose, I do not want anything to do with this guy." As I say the words, I feel the pull of something within me, like there's a little voice in my head asking me if this is true.

"So, he's a man." Pierre's eyebrows rise.

I throw him a stern look.

"Hey, I'm not saying that you want to bone him. All I'm suggesting is that there might be something unresolved between the two of you, and maybe you just need to confront it," he points out.

"I hate to admit it, but he does have a point," Una says.

"I do come in useful sometimes." Pierre takes a small bow, and Una pats him on the back. "But what I really want to know—" He leans forwards, eyes darting between the pair of us. "—is why you, Una, choose to eat this stuff that claims to be cheese?" His eyes drop to the pizza in his hand.

"It does not *claim* to be cheese, merely an alternative to the processed rubbish the rest of you Neanderthals stuff in your mouth on a daily basis. Besides." Una smacks her lips together. "You don't seem to have had a problem with it, having polished off half the pizza."

"Everyone knows you have to try something thirty times before you decide you don't like it," Pierre says.

"Is that so?"

"And I'm hungry." He rips a bite off like a caveman, and Una laughs.

Plucking a mushroom off my pizza, I wonder what my dream could possibly be trying to convey. Is it that I hate Valdemar Montresor? Is the dream some kind of metaphor that I have no idea how to interpret? Is it about me confronting him over the death of my brother? Or is it to do with the note suggesting I should kill him? The dream doesn't feel connected to any of this, but I'm not a dream expert. No matter which way I look at it, I can't convince myself that having erotic dreams about a man I loathe could be some sort of hidden message about how to move on from the loss of my brother.

I haven't told Pierre and Una about my visits to Valdemar Montresor, mainly because I know Una wouldn't understand my motivation. Pierre would probably get it, the fact that I need closure or to understand what happened, but Una's moral compass is firmly set on wrong and right, no in-between, and she wouldn't want me to be manipulated by him or to give him the airtime. Despite her mean-girl vibes, she's protective when it comes to those she cares about. And I can't tell Pierre without telling Una. And I certainly can't disclose that my dead mother convinced me to go visit him, so it's no surprise that they don't even consider him a possibility. I should confide in them, but I need more time to gauge what Valdemar's motivation is and what he really wants from these visits first.

Why him?
Why me?

CHAPTER EIGHTEEN

Why I was under the illusion that my conversation with Una and Pierre might put a stop to the dreams, I have no idea, but by Thursday, I've had the same one every night— the long corridor stretching before me, the moonlight drenching my naked body, and the brutal blade against my skin.

The only thing that differs is what Valdemar says to me, his filthy mouth working me into a frenzy even more than his touch.

My insides are in turmoil, my body at war with my head.

Why him?

Why me?

I'm beginning to wonder if this is a new form of torture, one there appears to be no end to.

These night-time escapades have stretched my days out somehow. The week has felt longer than normal, and I feel strange sitting here waiting for Valdemar to be brought into the visitors' room when I've felt the touch of his hands and heard the purr of his voice every night.

"I can't wait for my tongue to replace my fingers, angel, so I can taste you properly."

Picking at my chipped nail varnish, I try to banish the words he whispered last night, their seductive tone still stroking my skin when I woke this morning amidst the aftermath of another orgasm.

Maybe I'm going insane.

Valdemar struts into the room, his guard looking like he's the one being escorted in and not the other way around.

"Angel," he says as he sits.

A tiny tapping sensation dances down my spine at the sound of the endearment falling from the same lips that have said it every night this week and asked me why I'm so wet and if I can take one more finger. The mouth that calls me angel, his and only his.

These dreams are fucking me over in more ways than one.

"Are you all right?" His husky voice stirs the memory of the dream, and I have to bite the inside of my cheek to stamp it out.

"Yes," I lie.

"You don't seem it. Are you still sleeping okay?" he asks.

I glare at him. "I think the state of my emotional wellbeing has more to do with the fact that I've spent an entire week wondering what you meant when you told me my brother asked you to shoot him."

"Of course. I apologise. I shouldn't have left you wondering, and I understand if you don't trust me, but all I can say is that you will, in time."

I want to flip him off and tell him I will never trust him, but instead I press on, ignoring his cryptic words. "We have fifty-four minutes, so please, don't waste any of them."

His eyes narrow as if he's assessing me before deciding to speak. "You weren't at the hearing."

"No."

"And I'm sure you've done your homework on what happened that night." Valdemar presses his lips together, and I try not to focus on them, or the words that slipped out of his mouth in my dreams.

"That goes without saying," I reply.

"Then I can tell you that what you've read is a pack of lies."

I raise a brow. "Surely not everything."

"All the statements from the authorities were doctored, falsified in favour of Adolphe Fortunato. You know as well as I do how much of the local police force he has on his payroll or you wouldn't be the hotshot journalist I took you for." The corner of his mouth quirks upwards.

"I'm aware of his sway," I confirm.

Everyone knows that Adolphe Fortunato rules this city, his ruthless grip having only tightened over the past ten years. He has eyes and ears everywhere. There's a rumour that he's been sniffing around the *Gazette*. Captain has remained tight-lipped, but you can't keep the gossip mill from turning around a group of scoop-sniffing journalists who make their living from airing the dirty laundry. The thought of Fortunato buying the *Gazette* is one that truly gives me sleepless nights. If he were to own the largest newspaper in Amontillado, God knows what he would have us publishing, how he would use the paper for his gain.

"More than sway, angel. The guy is a serpent that has slithered its way into every mind in this city. He has the whole police force in his fucking pocket along with other high-ranking officials, and even the general public have their price—a cheap one when you consider how frightened everyone is of him. The witnesses who swore I pulled two guns out and shot down the chandeliers—fucking priceless, as that didn't happen." He laughs at this, shaking his head.

"Why would Fortunato pay them to lie about something like that? And if that didn't happen, then how did they explain the lack of broken chandeliers at the scene? Surely not everyone involved with the investigation was on his payroll." It's my turn to shake my head.

"Fortunato can be very resourceful when he wants to be, and there are more ways than cash to get people to lie for him."

I turn this over in my mind. There have been rumours of what Fortunato does to people who don't do as he says. Terrible things. But I've always thought they were just that—rumours set about to frighten people into doing his bidding.

We're veering further from the path I want to be on, and I don't want to run out of time like last week and be left on a cliff edge again. "Okay, so what's your version of events?"

"Before I tell you about that night, I need you to know how I found Ed."

My silence is enough to get him to proceed.

"Ed joined us shortly after he started working at Fortunato Casino. I was at the casino the night he was shadowing one of the croupiers, learning on the job. At the time, I didn't know who I was looking for or what exactly Ed's gift was. I just knew someone would be there and I'd know when I saw them." His voice takes on a slightly mystic tone, adding to the seductiveness I've got so used to hearing in my dreams.

"The first I noticed something was amiss was when a scrawny guy started pushing Ed at the roulette table. Afterwards, when we'd got Ed out of the casino and into one of our cars, he told me he'd seen what was about to happen through a vision, saw the scrawny guy lose his winnings and pull the knife out to slash the croupier's forearm. He saw it all, just like he'd been seeing things his entire life, and it frightened him—the knife, the violence, the blood. So, he'd tried to stop his vision from happening and asked the scrawny guy to leave, but Ed was eighteen, a trainee member of staff. The scrawny guy lost it, got all up in his face, asked him who the hell he thought he was, and then started shoving him. I stepped in when the scrawny guy pulled the knife."

He's the storyteller again, the man with so many words, words that hold me captive whether it be in the waking hours or in the dream realm.

"The scrawny guy was wasted, so it didn't take much for security to disarm him, but in the scuffle, one of the security guards was caught with the knife, a deep slash to his forearm —not exactly as Ed had foreseen, but close enough. Ed was visibly shaken, more frightened at the repercussions where Fortunato was concerned than he was over the confrontation, so it was at that point that I steered him out of the casino and into one of my cars."

"You stepped in, just like Victor Rue did with you," I confirm.

Valdemar dips his head in agreement.

"I asked him about his gift, learned quickly that it was getting out of control. The images would come like flashes in his mind, and he didn't know what to do with them or how to control them. He told me that no matter what he did, he didn't seem to be able to change the future, to stop whatever he saw happening, that even when he tried to intervene, the event would happen anyway, if slightly altered. And the whole time he spoke to me, he was clawing at the sides of his head as if trying to remove it from his shoulders."

Hot sweat gathers at the base of my neck.

"Can you imagine what it must have been like to see things before they happened?" Valdemar asks. "To have visions of things yet to come, to know the future before it's played out, and know that you have no way of stopping it?"

My voice cracks, my throat dry. "He hardly ever talked

about it. I'm not sure whether that was because he didn't want me to worry or he just didn't know what the hell was going on." Truthfully, I always thought he had it under control. As much as I was living with seeing the dead, he was living with seeing the future, but I can begin to see now just how impossible his life had been and how distressing it must have become.

"As a Raven Hand, I'd never come across such a gift, but I assured him we would work things out. He was relieved to have found someone to talk to, to share his burden. And it was then that he joined us to become a Raven Hand like he was always meant to."

The timeline plays out in my memories. I can recall Ed being withdrawn in his late teens, pulling away from society and locking himself in his room for days on end. Then he got a job at the casino, and I barely saw him at all due to the night shifts.

"As much as Adolphe Fortunato is a slimy serpent, he's also an influential figure in this city. The Raven Hands have always tried to stay clear of him, but a few years after Ed joined us, he discovered, quite by accident, just some of the things Adolphe Fortunato was up to."

I leap in. "You used my brother as a spy."

"No. I would never have put Ed or any Raven Hand in that position. And this was nothing to do with Ed's gift. This was something he witnessed while at work."

"What did he see?" I ask.

Valdemar's tongue pushes over his front teeth as if he's recalling the taste of this tale.

He lowers his voice. "Ed believed Adolphe Fortunato was trialling the use of a new drug—something that would lower inhibitions."

"I'm not sure dealing drugs from inside the casino would be much of a story. People would be more shocked if it *wasn't* going on. You said yourself that everyone knows what kind of businessman Adolphe Fortunato is," I point out.

Fortunato's exterior exudes the air of a confident businessman, the man who's made sound investments and amassed an empire due to hard work and a head for business, but underneath the façade, everyone knows the unspoken reality of the lawlessness, the drugs, the weapons, and God only knows what else he deals in.

"You misunderstand me, angel. This wasn't to do with drugs being dealt in his casino. This was to do with him slipping a drug into the drinks of gamblers," Valdemar explains.

I sit up, the reporter in me jolted awake. "Wait—you're saying he was spiking people's drinks?"

"Think about it. People go to the Fortunato to drink and gamble, but what are the things that hold them back and stop them from making stupid bets and ill-considered judgments?"

I inhale deeply, considering his question before answering. "Their emotional stability. Time to think and take in all the relevant information before making an informed choice. Fatigue. The list goes on." I shake my head. "But all those inhibitions can be lowered with alcohol, so why not just pour everyone double measures at the bar and get them all wasted?"

"You ever been to a casino?" he asks.

I roll my eyes, so he continues.

"They're classy establishments. They don't let you in when you're rip-roaring drunk, and they certainly don't let you stay when you lose the ability to stand around a table. No, alcohol wasn't the way. But this new drug was different. It made people drop their defences and abandon their analytical thinking, just like alcohol, but without affecting their cognitive functioning. From the outside, people would look sober, calm, and totally in control, yet inside, the brain would be thinking, 'Fuck it, let's gamble ten grand on black thirty-one.'" He wafts his hand over the table as if laying down the cash.

"How would they even begin to do something like that?" But even as I ask the question, I see Adolphe Fortunato's right-hand man and confidant, Dr Tem-Pest. No one knows what he's a doctor of, exactly, but he's been working with Fortunato for years, pulling strings and whispering in ears. He would have the know-how, and a man like Fortunato would jump at the chance of turning over his revenue, of expanding his empire even further, and just the sheer possibility of manipulating people at his whim.

My palms are sweating. This is a reporter's wet dream—the big scoop—but I'm beginning to see why Valdemar has said I can't publish this story, as there's no way on earth Fortunato would stand for this. I would be dead before it even hit Captain's desk.

Valdemar sits back, picking up where he left off. "One night, Ed overheard a conversation between Fortunato and a barman named Angelo. Fortunato put Angelo on one of the quieter bars and told him, 'G and T only.' Ed guessed Angelo was to spike gin and tonics. So, he kept watch during his shift, taking note of the people who bought a G and T and how their behaviour changed during the evening.

"Ed told me it was like watching the transformation from Jekyll to Hyde. They would start the night cautious, only placing small bets, keeping close track of their money, and keeping their wits about them, but within the hour of that one drink, they would be gambling large sums, throwing their money around like it was water, and not batting an eyelid when they lost thousands of pounds."

"Jeez." The implications of this are starting to slot into place. "How long did the drug last? What about when these people left the casino?" I ask.

Valdemar holds my gaze. "You see where this is going. This is the part where Fortunato didn't give two shits about what he was doing."

My mind races at the thought of people leaving the casino with their inhibitions lowered, what stupid decisions they might make, the reckless things they might do all because Adolphe Fortunato wanted to line his already bulging pockets. How vulnerable would they be when they couldn't decide if a situation was dangerous or not? How many would accept lifts from strangers, would take someone home who they didn't trust? How many would have their money stolen from them if they couldn't recognise a bad situation? How many would be attacked or violated because the alarm bell in their heads wasn't blaring at the first sign of danger?

As I contemplate the various implications, dust particles swarm within a shard of light that splits through the air from the barred window.

"How does this fit in with the night you shot Ed?" Although I'm intrigued and alarmed by all this, I haven't forgotten why I'm here.

His eyes glaze over, and his face drops as if the memory is pulling on his skin.

"We couldn't sit back while Fortunato was drugging people, but we were smart enough to know we couldn't just walk through the front door of his casino and tell him to stop being a bad boy. We knew it would take time and planning.

"The night of the shooting was only phase one. We were to go in and get a location on Adolphe Fortunato." Valdemar straightens in his seat.

"The Raven Hands have always stayed clear of Adolphe Fortunato and him of us—a mutual agreement that has gone back years—so when Jupiter and I entered the casino that night, we were met with the assumption that we were there to kick back and enjoy ourselves. Thanks to Ed, we knew when Fortunato would be at the casino, so once we had the go-ahead, Jupiter and I arrived with Jacinta and her friend Ada. Ada knew nothing of the plan, as we needed her reactions to be genuine, but Jacinta knew and played her part.

"Ed told us that the drinks were being spiked at the bar near the roulette tables by a tall, lanky bartender named Bobby, and that the beverage of choice that night was whisky.

"I ordered the drinks: a Manhattan for Ada, a craft beer each for Jupiter and myself, and a whisky for Jacinta."

"You made Jacinta take the spiked drink?" I jump in, shocked by this.

"She didn't drink it. We knew where all the cameras were and which staff on the floor were watching the people who'd taken the spiked drinks, so as soon as we were in position, Jupiter pressed himself up to Jacinta, blocking the view of the cameras and prying eyes, the whisky held low in her hand, and he kissed her. As he did, he slipped a wad of tissue into the glass and soaked up the liquid. They'd practised it a thousand times, so when it came to the real thing, it was seamless.

"We gave it ten minutes before Jacinta started to perform. She'd trained as an actress when she left school but never pursued the career—why, I don't know, because she was so fucking believable."

As much as I try, I can't help but get lost in the art of his words, the way he paints the picture. I feel like I'm in the casino, amongst the gamblers, watching the events unfold.

"We were by the roulette table when she started to shake, just her hand at first, then up her arm. She kept licking her lips as if her mouth was drying out, and she started to twitch."

"You pretended she'd had an allergic reaction to the drug?" I ask.

Valdemar nods. "Jupiter was the first to notice and asked her what was wrong. Ada dashed over to Jacinta, her reaction completely genuine. Jacinta's eyes rolled in her head as someone shouted to get her a chair.

"The game had stopped at the table, and one of the croupiers came over to see what was going on. Jupiter played the panicked boyfriend while I took charge, getting Jacinta to lie on the floor as I told Jupiter to call an ambulance. His hands shook as he dialled and faked the call.

"Ed had told us what happens when there's a medical emergency on the floor. The staff carry the casualty off to a private function room as quickly as possible, as no one wants to see someone potentially die in the middle of the casino—it's bad for business. Management is also notified. And, of course, Adolphe Fortunato when he's on the premises."

Valdemar pauses for a second, as if getting his bearings, before continuing. "Ed arrived, announcing that he was a first aider, and a middle-aged man joined him, one of Fortunato's more senior employees, who we guessed had been tailing Jacinta since she ordered her drink. His name badge read Julius.

"Ed shouted for us to move back and give him some room. Jacinta was on the floor, a gurgling sound coming from her throat coupled with erratic breathing. There was a second when I thought she wasn't acting at all.

"Julius pushed his way through and knelt next to Ed, who was trying to put Jacinta in the recovery position. Julius told him they needed to get Jacinta to the medical room, this being the private function room.

"Ed scooped Jacinta up, not wanting Julius to touch her and possibly become suspicious. Julius argued that the rest of us needed to stay on the floor, but Jupiter was like a man possessed and said she wasn't being taken anywhere without him. I followed, telling Ada to wait for the ambulance she believed was en route.

"We reached the function room. Ed went in first, carrying Jacinta, and Julius was behind him, then Jupiter and me."

Valdemar's head drops, his eyes searching for something on the empty table before he returns his gaze to me.

"And that's when the whole fucking thing went wrong."

And that's when the whole
fucking thing went wrong.

CHAPTER NINETEEN

The visitors' room shrinks, and I feel it as if I'm there in the casino, the dread that comes when the tables have turned, when you think you're in control, and then suddenly, you're not.

"And that's when the whole fucking thing went wrong."

Valdemar takes a minute before he continues, the thread of the tale momentarily dropped.

"I walked my people into that casino knowing the calibre of humans we were dealing with. I never suspected, never had a plan B, and never considered what came next—and that's where I failed Ed, failed you and your family." Valdemar holds his hand up, pre-empting my interruption. "I know I'm beyond retribution, but I need you to know what happened, why your brother asked me to shoot him. But to do this, I must divulge something that I would never normally tell anyone, and this is the reason why I've asked you not to report any of this, coupled with the fact that Fortunato would have you killed before you'd even finished typing his name."

He places his hands flat on the table. "You must swear to me that what I'm about to tell you goes no further than here."

His words slip into my core, and I don't even hesitate. "I swear." My voice is light, and I wonder how I've come to be swearing allegiance to a murderer.

He shifts in his seat. "The gifts of the Raven Hands aren't something we want known to the world. We're sworn to secrecy. Some Raven Hands don't even know what other Ravens' gifts are, they're that closely guarded. Other than Ed, no one has known what my gift is, and I need to keep it that way."

"Then why are you telling me this? What's to stop me telling the world what you all are?" I ask.

"Because of Ed," he replies.

As my brother's name simmers in the air, the grey hand lands on Valdemar's shoulder, and I fight the pull to look up to find Ed's eyes boring into me, his lips dried and cracked, the gunshot a perfect hole between his eyes.

"Ed would not have wanted the world to know what he could do, and you can't tell this story without revealing who he was," Valdemar points out.

"How the fuck do you know what my brother would have wanted?" I snap.

Valdemar takes his time, as if adjusting to the guest standing behind him. "Because Ed was my Blood Brother."

Have I misheard him? Did he say *Blood Brother*?

"Your what now?" I ask.

"There's a ritual, a pledge that some Raven Hands take when they feel a connection to another within the fold." He flips his hand over, and I spot the scar running diagonally from his wrist to his finger. "I felt it with Ed, like we were bonded in some way, like he was important to me, so, after a year of him being a Raven Hand, we took the Blood Oath, cutting the palms of our hands and sealing our fates, making us Blood Brothers." Valdemar clasps his hand together as if reenacting the ritual.

"This is like something out of a fantasy film." I shake my head. "As if it wasn't bad enough that you inducted him into your little boys' club, then you had to spit on each other's hands and swear loyalty for the rest of your lives," I scoff.

"It's hard to understand, I know. But this is ancient power, a ritual that's been performed over centuries, and until you experience it, you can never understand. Some Raven Hands never take the Blood Oath. They don't want to be bound to another for the rest of their lives."

Glancing up at Ed, I realise why he's never visited me. It's because even in death he's still tethered to Valdemar Montresor.

I search Ed's eyes, trying to find a spark of life, a glimmer of the brother I once knew, but all I get in return is the stony stare that's accompanied him every time I've seen him—until Valdemar's words snap me out of my trance.

"He's here, isn't he?"

Like with all rumours,
there always has to be an
element of truth.

CHAPTER TWENTY

"WHAT?" A COLDNESS CREEPS OVER MY SKIN AS I FEEL LIKE I've been stripped bare for the world to see.

"Ed is here with us now," Valdemar says, his voice low, quiet, as if keeping this between the two of us—*three* of us.

"How?" Tearing my eyes from Ed, I try to hold my gaze on Valdemar. "Can you see him? Is that your gift?"

"No. But you can."

"I don't know what you mean." The speed of my response betrays me.

"Yes, you do," he says.

Ed was the only person who knew I could see the dead. I've never spoken to anyone about my ability, yet Valdemar is regarding me as if I've just told him I can hopscotch. Like it's the most natural thing in the world.

"It's not a gift, if that's what you're thinking," I blurt out, forgetting myself for a split second.

"I never said it was."

"No one would want this. It's of no use to anyone other than to drive them insane," I say.

"Yet here you are, and so is Ed." He sounds pleased about this.

"Is he always with you?" I ask.

"Not all the time. There are times when I can't seem to reach him, but I always know when he's here. I can feel him."

"This is so messed up." Placing my hands over my face, I rest my elbows on the table. "It's your fault he's here, your fault I only get to see him like this. Because you killed him."

"He asked me to," Valdemar stresses.

"Why? Why would he want that? He had his whole life ahead of him. Nothing is as bad as taking a bullet to the head," I argue.

Valdemar's eyes widen as he leans over the table, closing the gap between us. "Believe me when I tell you, angel, that the bullet to the head was the better option."

There's a coldness running through me which I ignore, too rattled by this conversation to pick up on the chill.

"How can that be?" I feel like I'm on a roller-coaster—the ups and downs, the speed at which this tale is racing, and the wind harsh against my face. I just want it to stop, to get off and catch my breath.

"Because we'd been set up." Valdemar sits back, his body slackening as if he has no energy to retell this part of the story.

"Set up?"

Licking his lips, he straightens as if bracing himself to relive something he has no desire to. "We thought that once Jacinta had faked her reaction to the drug, the staff would carry her off into the private function room and Fortunato would be called to deal with the situation, seeing as she happened to be the girlfriend of a Raven Hand. He wouldn't want any bad blood between us or suspicion raised about why Jacinta had reacted the way she did to a harmless glass of whisky."

"Then why use yourselves? Why not use some lesser-known Raven Hands?" I ask.

"Because I would never send another Raven Hand to do my dirty work." There's anger behind his words, as if I've insulted him by even insinuating this.

"You did with Ed," I point out.

"Ed and I were equals. He was my Blood Brother. And he was integral to the plan, as was Jupiter." Glancing around the room, he tenses his jaw. "What I'm about to tell you has to stay here. I wouldn't tell you at all if I thought I could withhold it, but again, I owe you this—the truth, all of it. I just have to hope you honour these secrets, not out of consideration for me but for what you'll do to these people if you tell the world what they can do."

Swallowing hard, I nod. I would never want the world to know I see the dead, that my brother could see the future. We would be ridiculed, disbelieved, taunted at the very least —or at worst, hunted down, rounded up, deemed a menace to society, or experimented on until there was nothing left of us.

"We had much bigger things in mind than trying to catch Fortunato out at drugging his customers. We figured if we could track him at all times, we could assassinate him."

"How were you going to get a tracker on him?" I ask.

A smile creeps into the corners of Valdemar's mouth. "Jupiter can track people—anywhere, anytime. That is his gift."

"How?" But then it hits me when I recall my first meeting with Jupiter and Valdemar's subsequent reaction.

"Once he's touched a person, he knows exactly where they are at any given time. One touch," Valdemar confirms.

Shit. I see now why Valdemar doesn't want me to publish this. I can't imagine the outcry if the general public knew that someone was walking the city who could track anyone just by touching them. No wonder Valdemar had been so insistent that I didn't let Jupiter touch me. But why would he care about my privacy? Surely it would be to his advantage to have his second-in-command know my whereabouts?

"So, you guys faked the reaction to the drug to lure Fortunato into the room so Jupiter could touch him. But it didn't work out?"

"No. Fortunato was already there along with Dr Tem-Pest, but they weren't interested in Jacinta. They had their sights set on Ed."

A freezing fog fills my lungs.

"They knew he was a Raven Hand," I guess. The tattoo on his left hand would have been a giveaway. "They knew you were there to foil their little experiment." I'm surprised there isn't a mist curling from my lips as I speak, the coldness having wrapped itself around my chest cavity.

"And to this day, I don't know how. Maybe they'd been watching Ed. Maybe they'd known all along what we were planning. Who knows, but either way, they were waiting for us in a good old-fashioned ambush."

Stalling, Valdemar blinks and pushes back in his chair as if he's trying to get away from what happened next.

"Do you know what Adolphe Fortunato does to people who cross him?" he asks.

"Not specifically. But I've never looked into him. Like you pointed out, he's not a man to tangle with."

"I never saw for myself what he did to traitors, but there were rumours, whisperings on the grapevine of what would become of someone who'd crossed him. And like with all rumours, there always has to be an element of truth."

My stomach drops to my toes. I can't look at Ed or I'll crumple in the chair.

"What did you hear?" I swallow hard.

"Angel, you don't have to—" Valdemar leans forwards as he speaks, but I don't let him finish.

"Don't patronise me. I'm not some delicate wallflower. I'm here for the truth. You said that yourself. So give it to me. All of it."

His eyes pool, a sadness seeping into the depths of his pupils like those of a consultant before he tells his patients they only have hours to live. "The rumours were that he would skin people, then cattle-prod the open wounds or pour acid onto the skin and watch it bubble. He would infect people with a disease Dr Tem-Pest had cooked up in his lab, aptly named The Red Death, that would make his victims dizzy and experience sharp pains before bleeding profusely from their pores." Valdemar's voice goes quiet, like he had more things to add to the list but can tell that I don't want to hear anymore.

There is no air in this room. My head spins, the room sways, and Ed's outline shimmers.

"Fuck." My throat closes because I know exactly how the next part of this plays out. "He saw his death, didn't he? Ed saw what that fucker was going to do to him," I guess.

"He wasn't the only one."

Confused, I stare at Valdemar.

"In times of great stress, the brain works in strange ways. As I walked into the room, I saw Ed being manhandled, realised this whole thing was a set-up, and then, through our bond, I saw exactly what Ed saw," he explains. "As soon as I saw his vision, the look in his eyes, and the nod he gave me, it ripped me in two and broke me in ways no one should ever have to endure."

My tongue swells, and I feel like I can't swallow. I may not be able to see the vision as my brother or Valdemar did, but I know that whatever he's about to tell me is going to haunt me for the rest of my days.

But I have to know.

"What did you see?" I dare to ask.

Valdemar pauses as if gearing himself up or waiting for me to change my mind. Eventually, he speaks, his voice low and smooth, as if he's trying to soften the blow of each word. "I saw Ed being bricked up behind a wall, alive, and screaming for someone to kill him."

Gripping the edge of the table, I almost fold in on myself.

"That's why he asked me to shoot him. He knew what awaited him, what agony he would have to endure, knew the arduous death that would claim him slowly with pallid breath and invisible hands."

A cry claws its way up my windpipe. I manage to swallow it.

"Wait a minute." Pressing my hand to my forehead, I point at Valdemar. "You said he was never able to stop his visions from happening, that no matter what he did, they happened anyway. Are you telling me this was the only time my brother managed to cheat fate? Please tell me it was, or I swear to God…." I glance at Ed, wishing he would open his mouth and tell me something, anything.

But just like my mother, he is silent.

I look back at Valdemar, knowing I'm not going to want to hear what comes next.

"Ed always said his vision would happen regardless of his interventions. Fate is like that. But we learned, over the years, that he could influence minor parts of the scene—blur the details, so to speak." Valdemar pauses and eyes me carefully before continuing. "The only way we cheated was that Ed was dead before they bricked his body up."

"No." Sucking back tears, I wrap my arms around my waist. "We cremated him. My dad had to identify his body. I put my hand on his coffin. I kissed it before they took him away. It's not possible."

Loss swells inside me, anger, fear at what Valdemar is about to say.

"It's with the greatest sadness that I tell you the box you burned was empty, as your brother's dead body had already been taken from the morgue by Fortunato's men and placed within the walls of his mansion along with all the other unfortunate souls who crossed him. Ed was to be made an example for the rest of Fortunato's followers that even in death, you didn't escape his wrath. The only comfort we can take from this is that he wasn't alive when it happened like Fortunato intended him to be. Ed succeeded in that part."

I will not let him take me.

CHAPTER TWENTY-ONE

"No." A single tear rolls down my cheek, and I brush it away quickly as my eyes lift to the ghostly figure of my brother.

My brother who saw his death.

My brother who begged to be shot rather than bricked up alive behind a wall.

My brother who, after his death, was placed there anyway to rot in an empty cavity, his body slowly devoured by the rodents.

"I'm sorry," I tell his ghost. My words are barely a whisper, my breath caught in my grief at how I failed him, how I didn't see what was happening, what he was being drawn into, and that I did nothing to get him away from it.

"You have nothing to be sorry for, angel," Valdemar says.

Glaring at him, heat rising up my neck, I'm about to tell him to go fuck himself when he continues.

"Ed's words, not mine."

Mouth parted, I stare at Valdemar. "What do you mean, Ed's words?"

"I may not be able to see him, but I can hear him," he says, his expression sincere, as if he's almost sorry about this.

Searching my brother's face, I squint to see if his cracked lips are moving, but they remain tightly closed, seemingly unable to open.

I look back at Valdemar. "He can talk to you?" I ask.

He nods.

"Why can't he talk to me?" Bypassing Valdemar, I look at my brother. "Why can't you talk to *me*?"

"It's through the Blood Oath that I'm able to hear him," Valdemar explains.

Shaking my head, I sit back in my chair, unable to believe what Valdemar is saying, yet annoyed that it all makes sense. I have never been able to converse with my mother. She's never spoken to me in all the years she's visited me. There were countless times when I would have given anything to hear her voice, to know what it sounded like, to hear her words of advice or just simply that she loves me.

And Ed.

What I would give to talk to him one last time.

Turning back to Valdemar, I say, "I want to speak to him." I place my hands flat on the table as if we're about to conduct a séance.

"Go ahead," Valdemar says.

"How can I trust your answers? You could tell me anything."

His eyes narrow. "What would I have to gain by lying to you?"

"I don't know. To hide the truth," I suggest.

"I've told you what happened." Each word is said slowly, clearly, almost robotic.

"So you say." I hold his gaze, trying to see what he's holding back, because my journalist instinct is telling me that I'm missing something—I'm just not sure what.

"Why don't you ask him something only he would know," Valdemar says.

I stare at Ed as I sift through my memories, conscious of the ticking clock on the wall and the hour that's almost up.

"Okay. That day in the park when we were kids. You saw something, and then it happened. What did you see?" I ask Ed.

Valdemar's mouth creases into a faint smile as if he's seeing the memory for himself.

"He said he saw you fall off the swing. You were going crazy high, and then your shoe flew off and you along with it. You sprained your ankle and couldn't play dodgeball for at least a week. You got him to wait on you, bringing you drinks and snacks, and even tried to get him to do your homework for you, but he drew the line at that," Valdemar says.

My lip wobbles, so I bite it. Holding Ed's lifeless gaze, I imagine these words coming out of his mouth, the soft hush to his voice that wasn't unlike the whispering of the wind through your hair.

"He said he loves you, and he's sorry for what happened. But it was inevitable. He'd already seen it and knew there was no other way. He said he misses you, and he's sorry he was so distant in those last few years. He hopes you've learned how to make pancakes and aren't relying on shop-bought ones," he continues.

Stifling a half cry, half laugh, I press my hand to my mouth. "He used to make the most amazing pancakes. He would make a whole stack and then drizzle them with maple syrup and chopped bananas. We survived on those pancakes when our dad was working long hours and we couldn't be bothered heating the microwave dinners he'd left for us." My eyes meet Ed's. "I haven't eaten a pancake since the day you died."

Valdemar shakes his head. "I'm not telling her that."

"Tell me what? Just say it. What does he want to say to me?" My eyes dart between them.

"He's asking you to trust me." Valdemar holds my gaze as time is called, and I want to punch the guard. Just like before, I'm not ready to leave. I want to talk to my brother. I want to stay with him.

"I'm sorry, angel." Valdemar stands as the guard arrives behind him.

Is he sorry I can't talk to my brother like he can? Is he sorry that the only time I can see my brother is when I see him? Or is he sorry my brother is dead in the first place?

He's led to the door at the back of the room, and I stare, dumbfounded by what I've learned today. In the span of fifty-four minutes, my world has been ambushed and ransacked. Everything I thought I knew, I didn't. My world feels different, and I don't know whether this is a good thing or a bad thing. It's a known fact that sometimes the truth hurts, but what about when it numbs you? What about when the truth turns you inside out so you don't recognise yourself anymore?

Ten years is a long time to wait for the truth, and I was ready—more than ready.

But now that it's out, I'm not sure what to do with it.

I will not let him take me.

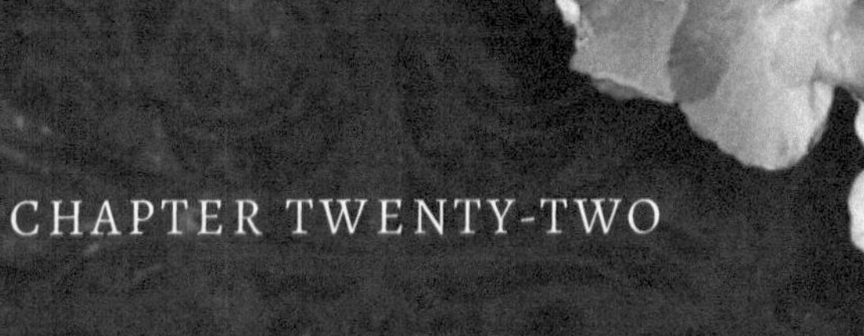

CHAPTER TWENTY-TWO

After leaving the prison, I head straight home, where my mother is waiting for me at the kitchen table. Sitting opposite her, I tell her everything, and her placid face never changes, her eyes almost looking through me. Pain spears my chest at her reticence, jealousy overwhelming me that Valdemar can hear my brother, yet all I'm surrounded by is quietude. The world of the dead is a silent one that leaves me with only my thoughts for company.

By evening, I'm drained, yet my brain refuses to shut down. Although I've been sleeping better, my dreams pulling me into a deep and immersive slumber, I wonder if sleep will come as easily tonight given that today's visit yielded so many revelations, my head can barely hold on to them.

Yet the numbness remains, my body feeling nothing, my heart pumping purely out of necessity to keep me alive.

Ed spoke to me.

It doesn't feel real. I want to hear his voice. I want to see his lips move, to hear the soft hiss of air through the small gap in his front teeth. I want his words the way he would have delivered them, with a smile or the curl of his top lip or the dimple in his right cheek. I don't want Ed's words coming out of Valdemar Montresor's mouth; they aren't his to utter.

Nonetheless, it's Valdemar's voice I hear every night.

In my waking state, I feel shame and embarrassment at my actions in the dreams. Why do I give myself to him so freely when in the cold light of day, I can't stand to be around the man?

Yet I'm not sure how true that is anymore. When my last few visits have ended, I've been annoyed, wanting to stay, to talk to him further, but surely this is only because he's telling me things I have a right to know, things I should have known a long time ago. I've never been able to talk about my brother with anyone, or about my ability to see the dead, and I'm ashamed to say it's been a relief to share some of my troubles. But that's all it is. It has nothing to do with Valdemar as a person and everything to do with the fact that he's the only one with whom I can talk freely.

After placing the book I've been trying to read on my bedside table, I switch off the lamp, thrusting my bedroom into an unnatural darkness.

Willing myself to fight him, I drop my head onto the pillow.

I will not let him take me.

I will tell him no.

I will stop this.

It isn't right, and although it's just a dream, it feels so real, too real for it not to eat away at my conscience.

My eyes close and sleep calls, and I can almost feel him waiting for me.

Barefoot, I run through the maze, my hands full of my gossamer skirt, my silver hair loose around my shoulders. Glancing back, all I see is the neatly trimmed shrubbery surrounding me, looking no different from the foliage I was looking at not five minutes ago. The night air is still. An owl hoots in the distance, and the towering mansion watches with cold amusement as I try to find my way out of the labyrinth.

Like a jungle explorer, I push past the overgrown branches, wondering if I've taken a wrong turn or if the hedges are growing taller around me. My feet sink into the undergrowth, my arms exposed to the night air as the halter-neck dress swishes around my legs, the smell of dense earth connecting me with nature.

Tuning into the night, I hear the rhythmic flow of water. Following the sound, I run faster, push harder, and race against non-existent time.

A few seconds, minutes, hours, eternity. Time passes in its dreamlike way as I finally reach an opening, the leaves parting to reveal a square courtyard, an imposing fountain taking centre stage. The fountain is shaped like a chess piece within a large bowl of water with gargoyle heads dotted around its lower half. Water spurts from their gaping mouths, the sound menacing.

I shuffle towards the edge of the fountain, then bend down and place my cupped hands in the cool water to scoop some up before letting the liquid drain through my splayed fingers. The gargoyles appear to grimace, their mouths cavernous, eyes set in stone.

"Angel."

His voice startles me even though I've been waiting for it, readying myself for his arrival. I don't see him, only hear him.

"I've been looking for you." His hand snakes around my waist, pulling me up to stand.

"I want to be cleansed. I want to forget," I tell him.

He runs his hand up the side of my body, his fingers gliding along the underside of my arm as he pulls it outwards and then holds on to my hand.

"Step into the water," he commands.

The hypnotic quality of his voice renders me docile as I dutifully do as he says, a shiver trickling through my insides. The *bottom of my dress floats around my feet, the material hungrily soaking up the water as if it's been starved.*

There's no sound of him entering the pool behind me, yet I know he's there, his hand still holding mine. The water is cold, but all I feel is heat working its way up my legs as I wade into the middle.

"This pool is made up of tears, angel," he tells me, the water circling my ankles. "It's all the tears you've cried—every single one."

The moonlight glistens off the tears, my movements sending slow ripples across the surface, the patter of the fountain getting louder as we move nearer.

Without a word, he beckons me to stop, and when I do, droplets spray against my shins. Releasing a clasp at the base of my neck, he pushes the dress from my shoulders, and it falls into the water, gathering like a billowing cloud before I step out of it and watch it float away.

He slides his fingers up my arms, and the heat from his hands joins the warmth swirling inside me. There's a moment when I think I should be telling him to stop, but I don't have the will to do it. Something is at work here, and I don't know what trickery it is, what magic lies at the heart of these midnight escapades or within this wonderous mansion with its haunting songs, but I'm lost to it all, giving myself freely to whatever this man has in store—because I want it.

I want this.

I crave this.

So, when he tells me to sit, I obey, lowering my naked body slowly into my fallen tears.

His body acts like a chair as I lean my back against his chest, using his thighs like armrests. His hand curls around my throat, pulling my head back so all I can see is the blackness of the night sky with a thousand twinkling stars winking from above.

The rhythmic rushing of the fountain floods my ears as the water hits my inner thighs, the pressure of it massaging my muscles. He inches me closer, my legs spread and my eyes straining on the nightscape.

It's when the water hits between my legs that I cry out. He tightens his hold around my throat, and his other hand holds me under the gushing fountain, the water assaulting my most intimate area.

"This is beautiful." His words sink into me, pleasure building at the onslaught of the water. "Watching you spread out like this, holding you, tasting your tears." His tongue licks at the droplets that have landed on my face.

It's unrelenting, the power of the stream, the pummelling against my clit, the overwhelming pleasure it produces, and all because this man decides it will be so.

And I revel in it, pushing my hips into the torrent, letting it drum against my skin and stoke the heat that is raging within me.

"Let yourself go, angel," he whispers, his fingers squeezing my throat until I'm not sure which stars I'm seeing, the ones above or the ones inside my head. "Come for me."

And it hits, like a tornado that's been building, a tsunami that's been escalating. I break against the sheer pressure that's intensified between my legs.

"Valdemar!"

Breathing hard, my eyes strain against the darkness of my room, my body shivering, the fire wild between my legs. Rubbing my hand against my throat, I swallow hard, trying to get my breath back.

A dream.

Just a dream. Like all the others.

But it had felt so real.

Like all the others.

My emotions are playing tricks on me. Ten years of snowballed grief has resulted in night-time hallucinations, reminding me of the trauma I've lived through. Growing up with no mother, knowing that mine and Ed's birth was the cause of her death, is not something you live lightly with.

Spending your days talking to your dead mother is also not the norm. Then losing my brother the way I did—no wonder I'm having nightmares.

But they don't feel like nightmares. Not while I'm having them. Not now that I'm awake.

They're a guilty pleasure—pure, unadulterated indulgence. They feel like a sanctuary, a time and place that is just for me and Valdemar.

They feel like heaven.

What is wrong with me?

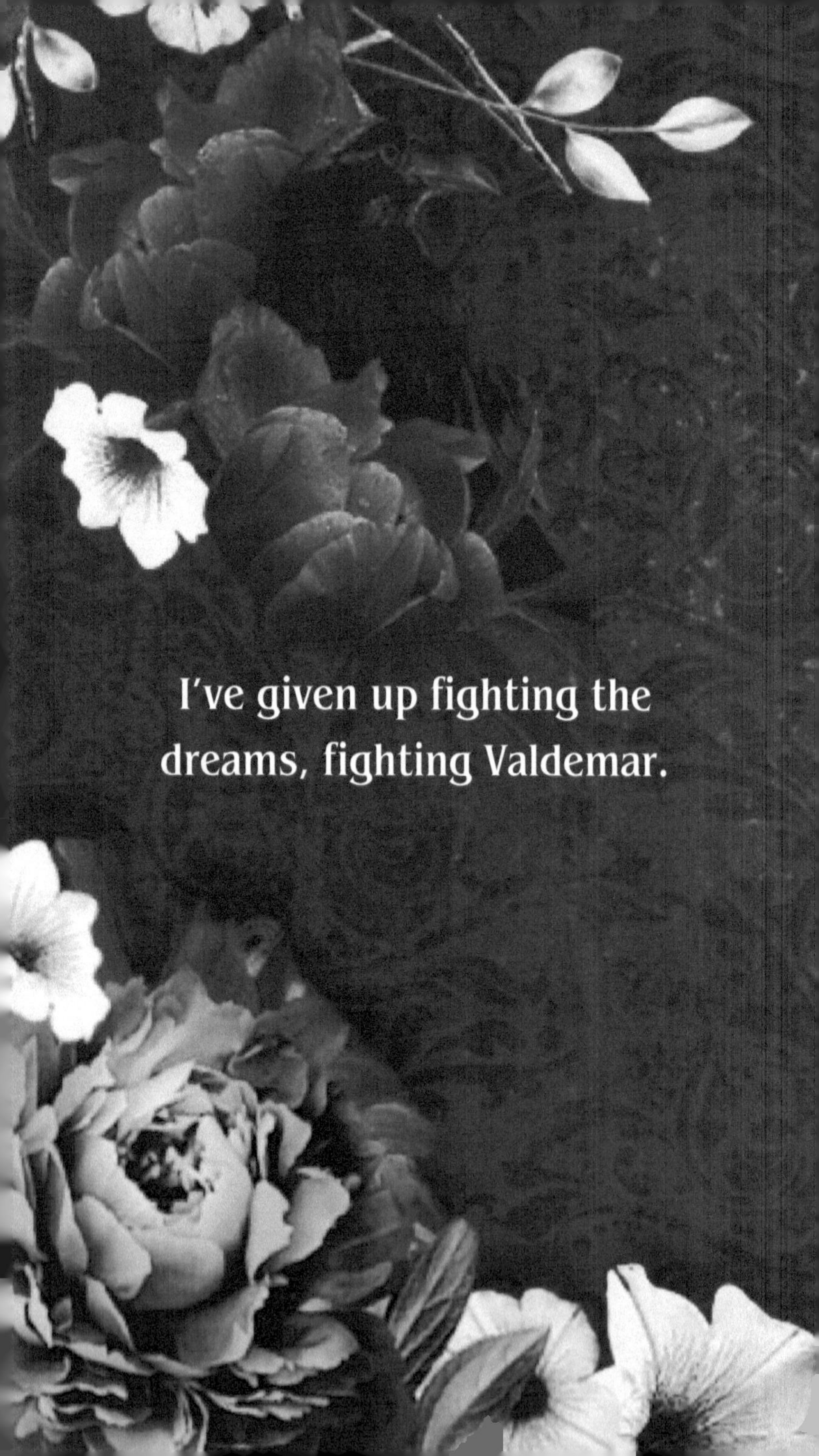

I've given up fighting the
dreams, fighting Valdemar.

CHAPTER TWENTY-THREE

It's Monday evening, and Una and I are sitting in Baldazzar, a Turkish bar on the outskirts of the city. The tables are full, the chatter rowdy as lavish lamps drench the room in a cosy warmth I could happily bask in all night.

Pierre sent his apologies earlier today. It's his mother's birthday, and the family have gone out for a celebratory meal, so Una and I have the conversation to ourselves. Taking the opportunity of our time alone, I tell her a little bit more about my dreams, leaving out the intimate details.

"I'm still having these crazy dreams about this guy. It's literally every night. And they feel so real. When I wake up, I feel like I've done the things in my dreams. It's like it's an actual memory."

Una toys with the paper straw protruding from her tall glass. "Are you ready to tell me who you're dreaming about yet?"

"No." My reaction is sharp, my cheeks heating.

Una side-eyes me, and I know she's picked up on the guilt on my face. I focus on the long cuffs of her emerald top where they dangle onto the table, then slide back to reveal the gold bracelets adorning her wrists. Her dark hair is crimped and flowing over her shoulders as part of her medieval goth look.

"It could be several things. Stress making you overtired. Maybe you're working too hard," she suggests.

I heave an internal sigh that she isn't going to push me to reveal who my mystery dream-man is. There have been whisperings in the newsroom about Valdemar's release. I knew it wouldn't be long before Dupin got hold of that story, but as expected, no one is talking about it around me with obvious reason. Even Una hasn't broached the subject, which suggests they're all handling me with kid gloves.

"I don't think the lame stories Captain has me covering can be referred to as 'hard work,'" I tut. "I just wish I had a bit more control in the dreams. I seem to lose myself in them."

Chewing on the straw, Una regards me like I'm a fraction that needs converting to a decimal. "Maybe it's more than a dream."

I look up from my drink. "What do you mean?"

"Have you heard of astral projection?" she asks.

"Yeah, but I've no idea what it is." I shrug.

"It's an out-of-body experience where your astral self, or your soul, leaves your earthly body and goes on rampages throughout the city," Una explains.

"That doesn't sound possible," I tell her as I consider the likelihood of seeing your dead relatives, foreseeing the future, or being able to track people through touch alone.

"Some cultures think so. They believe your consciousness can function separately from your physical body. It's an ancient belief, but one I'm here for, although I've never been able to accomplish it."

"I don't think this is a case of astral projection. Surely I would remember seeing myself asleep on the bed or hovering above myself."

Una shrugs, the straw losing its appeal. "If it isn't astral projection, then I'm out of ideas." She looks sad for me. This is the Una people don't see, the one who doesn't rear her head very often, the one who cares, who empathises, who takes on everyone else's problems and tries to solve them.

"I'm sorry," I say.

"For what?" she asks.

"Dragging down the mood of our Monday night pick-me-up drinks."

"Hey, don't apologise." Una pats my hand. "I love a good mystery. Besides, it beats talking about how my cat woke me at three in the morning, coughing up a furball."

"Just one of the reasons I don't have pets." I laugh.

"I wouldn't be without him, though. Pluto is my only companion at home."

This reminds me how lonely Una is and how much we've come to rely on each other over the years. In the five years I've known her, she's never spoken about her family, other than telling me she was brought up by a strange aunt who passed away when Una was nineteen. She's had a string of boyfriends, but none of them have stayed for the duration, probably because they found the sting in her tail too sharp to handle.

My thoughts stray to my dead mother, who, at one time, was my only evening companion. But now there's Valdemar, and as much as I hate him, he doesn't cough up furballs.

"Say, do you want me to sleep over? I could do a night-time stakeout and see if I can see your astral self leaving your body. I don't mind."

I balk in my seat. There's no way I can have Una watch me orgasm in my sleep.

"Thanks for the offer, but it's fine," I say quickly.

She doesn't look convinced.

"I can't put you out like that," I demur, hoping to mollify

her, "but you have given me an idea. I have a security camera I can set up. It's an old one from when I shared a flat with some fellow students and was convinced one of them was stealing my food. I don't know if it'll pick anything up, but it's worth a try. I might see a hazy mist coming in from under my door or the sandman in my room." I laugh, trying to lighten the atmosphere.

"Just as long as you share your findings. I want to know what's going on," Una says.

You and me both, I want to say.

EVERY NIGHT THIS WEEK, THE DREAM HAS FOLLOWED ITS USUAL course.

It begins in the maze and ends in the pool.

I dug out the security camera and set it up on the tall drawers opposite my bed, but all it's shown is me sleeping, nothing more, until I wake once I've cried out Valdemar's name in the dream.

There's no sandman, no shimmering mirage of astral projection.

And I've given up fighting the dreams, fighting Valdemar. There's no point, as no matter how much my waking self despises the man, my nocturnal self can't get enough of him.

On Wednesday night, the dream unfolds like it has every night this week.

I run through the maze until I reach the fountain, where Valdemar guides me into the water and his embrace. I spread my legs, and he holds me under the thrashing of my tears as I gaze at the stars and lose myself in the abyss of bliss.

"There's nothing more beautiful than the sight of you laid bare for me, angel." His words cut through the drumming of the water, working their way to my centre and the mounting orgasm about to

rip through me. "I love to watch you come undone, to feel you writhe under me." His hand tightens around my throat, and my head falls to the side as pleasure devours me, clawing away at my insides and crying to be let out.

I whimper and moan as Valdemar holds me until my climax snowballs and hits me in my core, my orgasm ravaging me.

"Say my name, angel. I want my name on your lips as you come."

And as his name is carried on my breath, his feather-soft kisses along my collar transform into a hot burst of pain.

His teeth sink into my neck, the bite hard and bloodthirsty.

Waking with a start, I sit up, the throbbing down my shoulder burning through my T-shirt. I leap out of bed and make my way to the bathroom, where I pull the neck of my T-shirt to the side—and there they are.

Teeth marks.

Perfectly formed, red teeth marks embedded into the crook of my neck.

"What the fuck?"

No one answers me as I stare into the mirror. But even as I ask the question, an answer is forming, one that makes me want to vomit, one I can't believe I didn't think of before. And now that it's here, I can't believe how stupid I've been.

Returning to my bedroom, I check the time, working out how many hours there are before I'll be sitting in front of Valdemar Montresor, asking him what the fuck is going on.

He knows what he's done.
I can see it in his eyes.

CHAPTER TWENTY-FOUR

IT'S A STORMY CROSSING TO THE PRISON, WHICH HAS NOTHING to do with the weather and everything to do with the bite mark now decorating my skin.

After a brisk search by a new guard, I take my usual seat and wait for Valdemar to be brought in.

I've toyed with ideas of how I'm going to confront him, whether to draw the truth from him slowly or try to catch him out, but as soon as he arrives in the room with a smirk on his face, I know I'm going to blow.

He knows what he's done. I can see it in his eyes.

Lowering himself into his chair, he doesn't take his eyes off me.

Chewing on the side of my cheek, I watch as his gaze falls from my face to the side of my neck, the bite mark peeping out of the open-necked shirt I've purposely worn.

"I owe you an apology, angel," he says.

"You owe me more than that, goddammit," I hiss like a kettle that's reached boiling point.

"I lost control." His stare is hard, like he's trying to hold me down under it.

Fighting the urge to shout, I whisper through my teeth, "What the fuck?" The guards are poised by the back wall, and the other visitors are settling down to talk to their criminals. It won't do to cause a scene. I can't risk getting kicked out when I need confirmation of what I suspect is going on here. "Your gift."

Now it's me holding him under my glare.

"You can infiltrate people's dreams, can't you? And that's what you've been doing with me, isn't it?" I try to deliver this with venom, but by the time I reach the last question, my anger has turned to shame. I'm embarrassed to learn that he's seen me naked, touched my body in the most intimate of ways, that he's made me come over and over again, and that I've cried out his name as I've done so.

His silence is all the proof I need.

"The bite marks," I begin, pulling my shirt up over my shoulder. "How did you…?" I don't know how to finish the question, but Valdemar is ready with his answer.

"My gift allows me to visit people's dreams. I see what you see, feel what you feel. And sometimes, when the dreams become intense, I can leave physical marks upon people, just like I did with you."

"You can hurt people in their dreams?" I ask.

"It's possible, yes."

I don't want to ask how often he's hurt people in their dreams, how often he's used his gift as a weapon against others, as it's not them I'm thinking of right now but me.

"You've violated me in my sleep." I stretch each word out, making sure he hears them loud and clear because I can't raise my voice in here.

"I've done nothing of the sort."

"How can you **say** that? I am asleep. It's as good as coming into my room and assaulting me in the night."

Valdemar's cheeks flare, his face flush with anger. "No. I would never."

"But you have. Repeatedly." Crossing my arms, I sit back in the chair, trying to put some distance between us.

"I've never abused my gift with you. You don't do anything your subconscious won't allow you to," he says.

"Bullshit," I spit.

"It's true."

"So, when a person dreams of leaping off a building, you're telling me that's really what they want to do?" I have to fight to keep my voice down.

"For some people, yes. Dreams allow them to do the things they want to do in real life but can't or won't or aren't brave enough to do. When you dream, your imagination is untamed and free from judgment, even your own," he explains.

My laugh earns me a glare from the old guy sitting next to us.

"Is that what you tell yourself to keep your conscience clean?" I throw at Valdemar.

"I'd like to think you know me well enough to understand that my conscience is anything but clean and I have no desire to cleanse myself of all the terrible things I've done. And to add to that, I'd like to think that you know I would never do anything you weren't comfortable with."

"This is bullshit," I repeat, shaking my head.

"Angel—" he begins, but I cut him off.

"Don't *angel* me."

He waits as I compose myself.

"Do you know how violated I feel?" I say.

As he presses his lips together, I note the glint of satisfaction in his eyes, the delight he's taken from this.

"I've only done what you asked. In that very first dream, you took the lead, angel. You told me what you wanted, and I gave it to you. I've touched you like no one else has, worshipped you in the way you deserve. You can't sit there and tell me you haven't enjoyed it."

"You fucking...." I close my eyes, reining in my anger. I can't lose my temper here. I'll get kicked out. Taking a deep breath, I open my eyes. "I don't want you to touch me again. You don't have my permission. Do you understand?" He doesn't respond, isn't even looking at me, and my blood boils. "Are you even listening to me?"

His eyes have wandered, focussing somewhere over my shoulder, and for a second, I wonder if Ed is here. I pray to God he isn't. This is embarrassing enough without having my dead brother present.

Following his gaze, I glance over my shoulder to see two men sitting opposite each other. I've seen the inmate—a bald guy, lean cut and clean-shaven—before, but his visitor—a man with dark features, broad shoulders, and a scar running down the side of his face—is new.

They look hostile, and I wonder how different their argument must be to mine and Valdemar's.

I turn my attention back to Valdemar, whose gaze is still on the men behind us.

He speaks, but his voice has changed; it's cold, efficient. Not the usual tone he takes with me. "Put your hand on the table."

"What?"

"Just do it," he insists.

His eyes never leave the men, and I feel a drop in the atmosphere, the churn of something that Valdemar senses like the darkening of the sky and the eerie silence before a storm.

Sliding my hand over the table, I lay it flat in the middle as my stomach rolls.

Over the past few weeks, I've grown complacent, forgetting that this is a prison containing some of the most ruthless men to have walked this earth—one of whom is sitting opposite me.

"Valdemar." His name barely leaves my mouth as he grabs my hand and pulls me up from my seat at the same time as what I can only describe as a bloodthirsty cry erupts behind me.

I'm pulled across the room and pressed into a corner, Valdemar's body against mine, shielding me from whatever is going down behind him.

I've never been in a warzone, never reported from a rally gone wrong or about angry protestors, but that's what it feels like as I hear the shouts from the guards, swearing from inmates, raucous war cries, the sound of fists pounding flesh, the thud of kicks hitting stomachs, and the guards ordering people to get back, to get down, to stop.

From my vantage point, I can only see the large form of Valdemar as he huddles around me in the corner. Taking my head in his hands, he moves my gaze to his.

"You're okay," he tells me. "You're safe. I'm here."

I find myself nodding. He doesn't look away from me, never even glances over his shoulder to see what's happening.

"I need you to get on the floor," he instructs.

"Why?"

"Please, just do it," he insists.

I hold on to his forearms as we slide to the floor, Valdemar still keeping me protected from the riot behind him, and even amongst the carnage, I can't help but notice how natural it feels to touch him, how familiar.

"That's it. Now take this." Letting go of me, he pulls his T-shirt over his head and presses it into my hands. Reading my puzzled expression, he says, "They're going to let off tear gas. It's what they do when a fight breaks out. I need you to put my shirt over your face. If we stay low, we should be okay, but I need you to do as I say."

I grab his T-shirt and hold the soft material over my mouth and nose.

The smell of warm spice and damp oak fills my nose as the shirt swallows me.

"Put your head against my chest," he tells me. "We need to block out as much of the gas as we can."

His chest, now bare, looms over me, and I want nothing more than to gaze at the perfection of his skin, to take in the artwork of his tattoos, the intricacy of the designs, to examine the large raven whose wings are spread across his pecs.

"What about you?" I ask, wondering when I started to worry about Valdemar Montresor.

"I'm not the concern here. You are. Now do as I say."

I push my forehead into his chest as he cups the back of my head with his hand, holding me in place as the riot wages out.

My sense of sight gone, fear should be overwhelming me. I should be shaking, nausea eating away at me from being in a locked room with angry criminals at large, the threat of impending tear gas looming in the air. But I feel none of these things as I'm held by Valdemar, the smell of him thick and heavy, the security of his arms around me, the pressure of his body against mine. It's exactly like it is in my dreams, yet this is real.

Someone wants
Valdemar Montresor dead.

CHAPTER TWENTY-FIVE

I'M NOT SURE HOW LONG I'VE BEEN LOCKED IN VALDEMAR'S embrace, but like an injection of poison, fear floods me as he's pulled away.

"Evangeline," he says amidst raspy breaths. It sounds odd, him using my real name, but I don't have time to decide whether I like it or not.

"Take my hand, miss," a new voice says.

Letting Valdemar's T-shirt drop from my eyes, I try to get a look at the guard who spoke, but my vision is diluted.

"You can remove the shirt. We're going to place a visor over your head." There's a hand on my shoulder, bony and sharp with fingers like hooks, and I almost shrug it off.

Disorientation is setting in now that I'm bereft of Valdemar's safety net. I need my senses back if I'm to stay calm. Taking his T-shirt from my face, I blink against the smog.

It isn't like a foggy day. Amontillado has its fair share of mist that rolls in off the lake and hangs around all day like an uninvited guest, but this hazy drape is different. Even on those misty days, you can always see what's directly in front of you, the fog always a few metres in the distance. This cloud of vapor is right in front of my face, tangling itself in my hair and caressing my skin with its artificial movement. In the seconds my eyes have been exposed, they burn, water springing from the corners as if to douse the fire they believe is raging.

Rough hands arrive, strapping an elasticated band over the top of my head and securing it as a clear plastic visor is pulled down over my face.

I'm plunged into an unnerving enclosure that protects my face from the tear gas.

Blinking furiously, my eyes begin to adjust, the burn subsiding to a sting, my watery tears washing away the last of the toxin.

Although the scene isn't clear, the room having been wrapped in a thick blanket of grey, I can make out the shapes of people, including the guard beside me who's wearing a matching visor and newly acquired body armour.

"Okay, miss, I'm going to lead you to the exit, and then we'll get one of our medics to check you over before you leave."

There's no sympathy in the guard's voice—he's used to dealing with criminals, not the public—but I take his hand.

As he pulls me up, he moves to my right, and from behind the clarity of the visor, I can just make out the shape of Valdemar being manhandled by two guards.

"Make sure she's okay." His words travel through the obscurity, his usual smooth, deep voice replaced by a wheezing gasp.

"We will," the guard says briskly, "but I'm not doing anything until you get moving, Montresor. You need to see the doctor."

"I don't need to see anyone," Valdemar fires back.

"You can barely see and breathe. Now do as you're told and get moving," the guard barks.

Their shapes begin to move to the rear of the room as I'm led to the door on the other side.

A new feeling taps at my insides, one I never thought I would feel for the likes of Valdemar Montresor, but the guard's words have lodged in my chest, and no matter how hard I try to push them down, they won't budge.

"You can barely see and breathe."

Being a reporter, I know what tear gas is designed to do. While I'd been sheltered from the gas by Valdemar's T-shirt and his body, he'd left himself open to it, letting it attack his eyes, burn his throat, and invade his nasal passages.

"Will he be okay?" I ask.

The guard doesn't even turn, let alone answer as he leads me through the exit and out into the corridor, the gas lifting like magic. Following the other visitors who have all had visors placed over their heads, I pull mine off, needing to return to the elements and not hide behind a piece of Perspex.

"There might be a wait for the medic. We only have two on site, so one will deal with the inmates while the other sees to you guys," the guard says.

Trailing the line of people, we reach a door that leads into a small room containing a few plastic chairs and a rectangular coffee table.

Running my hand through my hair, I take stock of the other visitors and suddenly wish I hadn't.

Most of them have removed their visors and are swiping at red-rimmed eyes, tears streaming down their faces. There's a woman rocking in the chair in the corner, pressing her hands so hard against her eyes that I fear she'll push them into her brain. A middle-aged guy is standing there, squeezing his eyes tightly closed and clawing at his throat. It's like the aftermath of an apocalypse.

I tug on the sleeve of the nearest guard, who eyes me suspiciously. "Hey, I don't need to see a medic. I'm fine."

He just continues to stare at me.

"Look at me," I demand. "I don't look like any of these people. I'm fine, honestly. I just want to leave and get some fresh air."

Glancing at the rest of the people, he turns and, with a nod, ushers me out of the room. Taking me back through the maze of corridors, he leads me to the entrance.

"What happened in there?" I ask, almost running to keep up with his large strides.

"Not sure yet," he answers without slowing his pace.

"Was it a disagreement between family members?" The journalist in me hasn't been quelled by the tear gas.

"God, no." The guard tuts. "That, we would have been able to deal with. No, this was an organised job."

"What do you mean?" I ask.

"I mean that someone from the outside wanted a message sent and used a visitor to send it."

"I don't understand." I shake my head.

"The inmate who was attacked will have a list of enemies as long as your arm. These guys usually do, or they wouldn't be in here. And it doesn't take much to get someone to send them a message from the outside, just like you saw today," the guard explains.

"How do you know that?"

"Because the guy who attacked the prisoner wasn't your average Joe Bloggs throwing a punch in a bar. This guy knew where to strike." Pausing to open a door using a fob, the guard glances at me, eyes wide. "He broke Luchesi's fucking neck," he tells me, and for a second, he isn't a prison guard anymore. He's just a guy who came to work today to earn his living to pay his bills and put food on his table and ended up witnessing a vicious attack.

"Is Luchesi alive?" I ask, assuming he must be the prisoner who was attacked.

Rubbing day-old stubble, the guard blinks. "Not sure, but if he is, he might never fucking walk again."

"Why did Luchesi agree to see that man if he knew he was going to attack him?"

"He didn't know, and the guy will have been sent by someone and probably registered by a different name. There are ways of getting in. Trust me. If someone wants to send a message to someone in here, no amount of policies, rules, and procedures will stop that message from being sent."

A sinking feeling glugs in my stomach, the note I received weeks ago coming into my mind's eye.

Someone wants Valdemar Montresor dead.

Someone knows I've been visiting him.

Someone has asked me to kill him.

But who?

It's strange, unfamiliar,
to feel this safe and comforted.

CHAPTER TWENTY-SIX

On my return from the prison, I head straight home, not trusting the streets of Amontillado not to have their eyes on me. The fight has left me shaken and angry, and I hate to admit how vulnerable I feel without Valdemar's protective wings around me.

My mother is waiting at the table in the kitchen as I drop into the chair, and I tell her everything that happened, pulling the note out of the drawer I'd stashed it in and slamming it down.

I fire question after question at her. Who knows I'm visiting Valdemar? Why do they want him dead? Are they hoping I'll do their dirty work for them? How do they even know who I am? Am I being watched? Do they want me to kill him while I'm visiting him like what nearly happened to Luchesi today? I'm no fighter and certainly no trained killer, so what the hell do they want me to do? How do they expect me to smuggle a weapon into a prison when I'm searched before every visit? Valdemar said he has enemies, and the guard confirmed that all those men in there do, but how do they know I've been visiting him, and more importantly, what will they do if he continues to live?

A chill trickles down the back of my neck.

The under-cabinet lights highlight small grease stains on the splashbacks above the hob. Ignoring them, I return my gaze to my mother. Her hands rest on the table as she watches me intently.

The note is between us, its contents belying how innocent it looks—just paper and words and not the death sentence it is.

"What am I going to do, Mother? What have I got myself involved in?"

She stares at me, her eyes so wide, so full of love, and I wish more than anything that she could answer me, tell me what I need to do, what the next step is. Instead, she reaches for my hand, which I give her. As I do, she disappears, and I'm left alone in the kitchen, the tap dripping and the clock ticking.

THE THOUGHT OF SLEEPING TONIGHT FILLS ME WITH A mixture of anxiety and curiosity. After the drama of the fight, I haven't had time to consider what Valdemar confessed about his gift, the confirmation of his ability to visit me in my dreams and to leave puncture wounds on my neck.

Knowing he's seen me laid bare, legs spread, and screaming his name only heightens the embarrassment of something that already felt illicit and dangerous. Irritation bores into my skin at the fact that I can't seem to control myself in the dreams, that I'm under his influence even though he professed the opposite. He told me my body was only doing what my subconscious willed, but I don't buy it. I don't want him touching me. I don't want him to see me the way he does.

At least, I thought I didn't. Today, when he held me, I let him. I felt safe. It felt so right, like I belonged, just like in my dreams, and the thought makes me want to cry.

Having never felt the safety of my mother's arms, I grew up with a hardened shell, no touch to gently thaw it. My dad wasn't the hugging type even when he was around, and the rest of the family kept their distance, always a little unnerved by the pale twins who had managed to kill their mother.

Ed had never hugged me. We'd never needed physical contact. Our wordless bond was enough.

In the bathroom, I pull off my clothes and toss them in the laundry bin, shivering against the chill that permeates my apartment. Reaching for my nightshirt that hangs on the radiator, I stop for a second as a thought blooms boldly in my mind. Deciding against the nightshirt, I then grab a towel and wrap it around myself as I pad back into the kitchen.

Holding on to the towel, I stare at Valdemar's T-shirt that I threw on the table when I got in. The guard never questioned it when I left the prison, too preoccupied to notice an old prison-issue T-shirt.

Cautiously, I hold it to my nose and inhale, afraid of what memories it might conjure. As soon as his smell hits me, I'm back in his arms, warmth seeping through my body, a calm enveloping me like a drug.

It's strange, unfamiliar, to feel this safe and comforted. It's what I've been missing all my life, and I almost laugh at the prospect of a convicted murderer being the person to provide me with the one thing I've never had.

Unsure as to why I'm doing this, I let the towel drop and pull the T-shirt over my head before making my way into my bedroom and slipping under the covers.

Apprehension fizzes in my stomach. What if he doesn't

visit? What if he's too ill to use his gift, his vision blurred, eyes still burning even in his sleep?

This feeling gnaws at my gut until I realise that the thought of him not visiting fills me with dread. For three weeks now, his nightly visits have invaded my slumber, the narcotic I've needed to finally get a full night's sleep, and now I'm hooked, addicted to his presence in a way I never thought possible.

Avoiding the question of how my feelings towards Valdemar Montresor have so quickly morphed into something I don't care to assess, I lay my head on the pillow and close my eyes, wondering where the night will take me.

They are dead.
Both of them.

CHAPTER TWENTY-SEVEN

Blinking quickly, I let my eyes adjust to the gloom of the large room. Vaulted ceilings and corniced archways are evidence of its splendour, and the rows of orderly chairs with ornate legs and cushioned backrests tell me I'm standing on a stage.

There's a clicking noise, and the stage is flooded with light. Placing my hand over my eyes, I squint at my new view, the blood red of the velvet backrests coming into view along with the dark wood of the floor, the gold legs of the chairs—and him.

He's in the middle of the first row, wearing a white shirt and black dress trousers. His arms rest over the backs of the chairs on either side of him, and his right leg is balanced by its ankle on the other knee.

My mouth hangs open. Although I've heard him, felt him, touched him, I have never seen him in the dream before.

The dream.

This is a dream.

A dream he's engineered.

For the first time, I feel a sense of place, of ownership over my thoughts.

"Nice choice of attire," he says.

Glancing down, I smooth his T-shirt over my body, pulling on the hem to ensure it covers me.

"What are you doing here?" I ask.

"I'm here to make sure you're okay and to help you sleep." The lull to his voice sends shivers down my spine.

"How very selfless of you."

"I would be lying if I said I wasn't also here for my pleasure. Ten years is a long time to be locked away. The night is my only freedom."

"Then why waste it here with me?" I cast my eyes over the room.

"There's nowhere else I'd rather be." He says this with such sincerity, no hint of sarcasm.

"If the previous dreams are anything to go by, this is the part where you tear my clothes off."

He smirks. "But several hours ago, you told me I don't have your permission. So that won't be happening this evening."

An ugly silence fills the small theatre, a sinking feeling settling in my stomach.

"Then what are you here for?" I ask.

A ghost of a smile brushes his lips. "To watch the show."

Glancing behind me, I falter. "What show?"

His grin elongates as a shiver whips down my spine.

To my left, a woman appears from nowhere, her skin translucent, her eyes glassy, her hair smoothed down in a centre parting with blonde ringlets adorning each side of her face. Her bodice is laced tightly, her full skirt and the cut of her sleeves indicating an outfit from the 1800s.

She smiles at me as she runs her hands over my arm. I see her, but I can't feel her. Her touch is nothing more than the flow of air around the stage.

To my right, another woman joins us, similarly dressed but with long dark curls and flowers in her hair.

Their movements are fluid. Their appearance is crystalline.

They are dead.

Both of them.

Not mere actresses in this unscheduled play but tethered to this place, wherever it may be.

To be visited by the dead during the night is new even for me.

"Do you see them?" I ask, shooting my gaze back to Valdemar.

"No. I only see you."

"Then why—" I begin but am cut off as they raise my arms.

I can't work out what trickery this is, as they make no impact on my limbs, their touch like feathers, yet my arms move at their bidding, rising above my head.

The dark-haired woman lowers herself, smiling at her friend as she bends down in front of me and places her fingers under the hem of my T-shirt.

"What are you doing?" I ask, but her only reply is another soft smile as she pushes the material up over my thighs, revealing my nakedness beneath.

Her partner gathers my hair at my nape as the other continues to work my T-shirt up until it reaches my neck, and then together, they remove it and toss it to the floor.

"That's better."

Valdemar's gruff voice reminds me of his presence. I can't see him, as my view is now blocked by the dark-haired woman in front of me, but all he can see is me, now naked on the stage.

The blonde woman runs her hands through my hair, pulling my head back and baring my throat like I'm a puppet on invisible strings. Gliding her hand over my chest, she touches my breasts, the barest of tickles igniting my senses.

The dark-haired woman lowers herself again and runs her hands up the inside of my legs, stopping only to lick her lips as she nears my inner thighs.

"What is this?" I plead, trying to stay focussed and not let the growing need between my legs take over.

"You forbade me from touching you, and I will never let

another man or woman alive touch you, so this is the best I could come up with."

"I can't feel them."

"No? Then maybe you just need to fantasise. Though I doubt you can imagine their touch as mine."

"Valdemar—" I begin, but I don't get to finish as the dark-haired woman's hand disappears between my legs and the blonde woman continues to touch my breasts. Although the image of them is there, all I can feel is a shadow of their touch, a suggestion of what I could be feeling, and I want to scream.

"This is torture," I say.

"For you or me?"

"Why would you do this to me?" I almost cry.

"I'm only doing what you asked. I want to indulge you to help you forget, but you told me no touching, so I'm adhering to your wishes." Valdemar stands, pushes his hands deep into his pockets, and walks towards the stage.

The dark-haired woman's fingers work me just before her head dips to replace her hand. I grab for her hair, but my hands grapple at thin air.

"Valdemar, please," I whimper as he climbs the steps to the right of the stage and stalks across the boards, his hands still hidden in his pockets.

"Please what?" he says.

Pleasure kisses me all over but only lightly, too lightly. It's not enough to satisfy the arousal these women have ignited, and I want more—need more. It's like the smell of your favourite dessert as the waiter flounces it before your eyes on a shiny silver platter.

"I don't care what I said. Just touch me. Please," I beg.

He's close now, his eyes boring into my naked skin. The women move behind my back as he stands before me.

"Believe me, I wish I could." His eyes drop to my breasts, then below my waist before rising back to meet my own. "But I can't."

"Why not?" I loathe the desperation in my voice, but my need is growing with every second his hands aren't upon me.

"I need your consent," he says.

"I give it. Now. I consent. Just touch me," I plead.

The corner of his mouth twitches. "I need you to give consent in the real world, not in this one."

"You never had my consent before, yet you touched me anyway, so why is this different?" I argue.

"I was relying on your subconscious before, letting you lead the dream, but today you explicitly told me I wasn't allowed to touch you, so I have to honour that."

"Like fuck you do. When did you grow a conscience?" I snap.

By the flicker in his eye, I can tell my remark has stung him.

"I didn't mean that. I'm sorry."

"Don't be."

"But I am, so please, just make me feel the way you do every night. Please," I whimper.

"Not until I have your consent, angel."

And with his last word, the whole room dissolves, taking Valdemar with it.

Laying my palms flat against the mattress, my breathing comes thick and fast as a yearning growls in the pit of my stomach. Running my hands across my chest and down my arms, I confirm I'm alone and that the ghostly hands of the women have gone. But Valdemar remains—not in person, but his voice, his words, and his stare are all imprinted in my brain so I will never forget them, never sleep another night without his presence.

Five weeks ago, I wanted nothing more than to kill him, to watch his blood spill at what he did to my brother, to me, to my future. But now….

What's changed in the last few weeks?

Is it because I know his background, where and how he grew up, and what he went through to get to where he is now? Is it because I know my brother asked him to shoot him, a mercy killing to avoid being bricked up alive? Is it the dreams, his invasion of my nights, the knowledge of what his touch is like, what his words sound like, or is it because of yesterday when he protected me like I was the most precious thing he'd ever held?

Or am I just being a complete fool and letting sexual desire rule my head? Have I been coerced by these dreams into thinking he can give me what I want, what I've failed to find?

Fighting the urge to relieve the throbbing between my legs, I swing myself out of bed and pad into the bathroom, not knowing the answer to any of these questions but aware I will have to endure this dream for the rest of the week until my next visit with Valdemar and that the dream will change again if the pattern is to continue.

Next week is my last visit before he's released, and then what? I've been naïve in thinking that our contact will end after his release when really it will only just begin.

Don't touch me.

CHAPTER TWENTY-EIGHT

In my youth, I imagined life as a hotshot journalist would be action-packed, fraught with danger and intrigue to the point where I would almost feel like a spy. I wanted to change the world, to make it a better place, to make people feel like they had a voice and that their story mattered. But today marks an all-time low in my career as I stand in the frozen-food section of The Eldorado Food Emporium, surrounded by row upon row of fish fingers and faced with a terrified old lady who had her purse stolen from her two days ago.

"Can you tell me what happened, Mrs Wyatt?"

Marian Wyatt tugs at the sleeves of her grey coat as if she's trying to disappear inside it.

"We can do this interview somewhere else if you'd prefer," I say.

Interviewing Mrs Wyatt in the very aisle where she had her purse stolen was not one of Captain's better ideas. She's clearly traumatised by what happened to her, and she'd be far more happier talking to me in the safety of her own home.

But Captain had argued that revisiting the scene of the crime might bring back some memories and would make for a better story.

"The readers will feel her fear," he'd said. "Nothing is frightening about an old lady sitting in the comfort of her own home while drinking tea and telling you all about the thief who snatched her purse."

"I'm fine, honestly," Mrs Wyatt tells me, her wide eyes saying otherwise. "I've been shopping here for twenty years, ever since my husband, Ronald, died. I don't want these thugs to win. They've already stolen my purse and my money. Why should they get to steal my life as well?"

There's a glimmer behind her rheumy eyes, and for a second, I almost believe her. But I think we both know the thugs *have* won, and it breaks my heart.

"So, you were in this very aisle when the theft happened?"

"Yes. I was buying Napoleon his favourite fish fingers." Mrs Wyatt gestures to the boxes of Titan Fish Fingers in the freezer behind us.

"Napoleon?" I ask as I fiddle with my Dictaphone.

"He's my cat. Fussy little beggar when it comes to dinner-time, but he's been my only companion since Ronald died. He'll only eat this brand of fish fingers, and this shop is the only one that stocks them. Anyway, I was just putting the box in my basket when I remembered that I had a coupon for them. So, I got my purse out of my bag and started to look for the coupon, and that's when the girl came up behind me and snatched my purse from my hand."

"You must have been so scared."

"Not at first. I was angry. What would Napoleon have for his tea if I didn't get him his fish fingers?"

"Did you get a good look at the girl?" I ask.

"I say girl, but she was a teenager. Dark clothes, a hooded

jumper pulled over her head, and pink patterned boots that looked too big for her feet. She was so brazen. Just snatched it from my hand and walked out of the shop as if she'd done nothing wrong."

Mrs Wyatt shakes her head, and I can see some of her anger washing away, the fear she arrived with settling back in. I can't help but think about seventeen-year-old Valdemar and how he had something of value taken from him as easily as this girl had taken Mrs Wyatt's purse.

"Did you report it to the police?"

"Pfft." She scrunches up her face. "And what do you think they would have done? Nothing, that's what. How many crimes are committed in this city that the police have no power to do anything about? How many reports have you covered where a victim has been left helpless because the police are unable to reprimand the criminals?" She folds her arms. "I got the man on the checkout to go and get the manager, and even he said there was no point in calling the police. He told me that theft in this shop has doubled over the last few years, but the police are powerless. They know they can't catch these villains, and even if they did, they have no authority in this city. I don't feel safe anymore, and I've lived here all my life. I should be able to go and buy some fish fingers for my cat without being afraid. This city is going to the dogs. There was a time when someone would have done something about the rising crime. Would have hunted these criminals down and strung them up."

She's right. This city *is* going to the dogs, and I see it now, the influence the Raven Hands had over this city ten years ago, the fear they used to wield over the criminals, the punishments they would dole out so that the law-abiding citizens could live in peace. And I hate that she's right, but even more, I hate the fact that all I can think about is how much I would like to teach these criminals a lesson—one they won't forget.

"Thank you for your time, Mrs Wyatt," I say, switching off my Dictaphone and stuffing it into my bag. "I think I have all I need."

"You have my number if you have any more questions."

"Yes, I do."

We walk slowly towards the exit, Mrs Wyatt hunched up as if she's trying to make herself look smaller, and I wonder how many more people in this city have a story similar to hers.

"I'll keep a lookout for your report, Miss Bransby, and thank you for taking this seriously. I'm sorry to say that some of the other papers wouldn't even come out and talk to me."

The doors to the entrance of The Eldorado Food Emporium open, letting a gust of wind whip at the back of Mrs Wyatt's coat. She smiles weakly, turns, and walks out of the shop just as Jupiter walks in.

Instinctively, I step back, pulling my coat around my body and then stuffing my hands into my pockets.

"Fancy seeing you here."

Jupiter grins, and I take two steps back, hoping to God he's either bumped into me accidentally, which I doubt, or that he's been following me the old-fashioned way and this has nothing to do with his gift. He didn't touch me the last time I saw him, but even so, uncertainty niggles at me.

"What do you want?" Tracking his hands, I keep my distance.

But he picks up on it and glares at me. Holding both hands in the air, he stops moving. "I just want to talk."

"About what?" I ask.

His eyes narrow. "I know who you are."

"Congratulations." I smirk.

"And I know who you work for," he adds.

"So?"

"So, I'm sure you can appreciate my concern over what you're talking to Valdemar about," Jupiter says.

"If he hasn't told you, then it's clearly none of your business," I tell him, sounding braver than I feel.

"See, that's where you're wrong." He takes a step towards me as I try to slip around him, and he reaches out.

"Don't touch me." It comes out louder than it sounded in my head, and I see beneath the glare that he knows I know about his gift.

"It's clear that Valdemar has told you things, things he has no right telling you. I need to know what your intentions are." His voice lowers, dangerously low.

"I don't have any intentions. He asked me to come and see him, so I did." I hold my ground.

"I know he wants to talk to you because of who you are, who your brother was, but I need to know that what he's telling you isn't going to be splashed across the front of the *Amontillado Gazette*."

"Even if I did write about it, do you think anyone would believe me?" I say.

Jupiter eyes me, flexing his fingers, his jaw tensed. "How do I know I can trust you?"

"You don't." Like the flick of a whip, I turn and walk back down the freezer aisle.

Taking my time to steady my breathing, I circle and arrive back at the entrance to see Jupiter has left.

Is that all he's worried about, keeping the secrets of the Raven Hands hidden? Or is there something else? It doesn't sound like he trusts me—or Valdemar, for that matter. What is their relationship like? Does Jupiter want full control of the Raven Hands? He's been the frontman for ten years while Valdemar has been locked up. Is he reluctant to let go of that power now that Valdemar is to be released? Or is he going to fight to retain it by whatever means necessary?

I climb into my black car and pull out the note I've been keeping in my bag, wondering if these are the words of Jupiter Prospero.

I'm alone. Like always.

CHAPTER TWENTY-NINE

Sunday night looms over me with a heaviness that feels stifling.

For three nights, I've endured the dream of being on the stage with the ghostly women touching but not touching me while Valdemar sits and watches, his words stoking things in me that won't be doused.

It's been torment, the lack of physical contact driving me to insanity. I've had to take matters into my own hands to relieve the pent-up pressure, and I've told myself that I don't need dreams of Valdemar Montresor to turn me on, but I'm failing miserably, as every time I try to imagine some other man, my thoughts stray to him.

By seven o'clock, I've showered and changed into loungewear when my mobile rings with a withheld number.

"Hello?"

"Angel." His voice travels down the line.

For a second, I contemplate the viability of his gift extending to reading my mind as I grip the handset.

"Valdemar."

"I apologise for the wait for this phone call, but I only get one a week on Sundays."

"And you've wasted it on me? Wait—how did you get this number?" I ask.

"I have my sources. I don't have long. I just wanted to see if you're okay." The line crackles.

"Why wouldn't I be?"

He pauses. "After last week? The fight that broke out."

"I'm fine. Surely you should already know that having seen me every night."

"Dreams are different. They don't represent you as you are in real life. If you break your arm in reality, you don't necessarily have a broken arm in your dreams," he says.

"Well, I can assure you, I don't have a broken arm. I'm fine. And speaking of dreams, you need to stop."

"Stop what?"

"Don't play games with me," I say.

"I wouldn't dare." There's a mocking tone to his voice that suggests the opposite.

"But you are. You need to stop visiting me." I try to sound firm.

"Not going to happen," he replies.

"Why not?"

"Because until I'm released, it's the only way I get to see you without a stupid table and three guards between us."

His words sink in.

"Until I'm released."

"I can't wait a week until I see you again, so the dreams are the next best thing," he says.

"I don't think I can stand another night of the same dream," I confess.

"Then do something about it."

"How?" This comes out strangled.

"You hold the cards, angel. Only you have the power to change the dream."

Aware of what he's asking, I close my eyes.

"Look, if you really want me to stop, then I will. It'll kill me, but I'll stop if that's what you want," he says, defeat behind his words.

Fuck.

Time ticks away. He can't have much longer on the phone.

"Is it what you want, angel?"

"I don't know what I want," I admit.

A voice carries from the background, faint but undeniable. "Come on, Montresor, time to end the call."

"I think you do, angel."

He has one phone call. This is it until I see him in the flesh next week. Do I stop the dreams, stop his nocturnal visits, or endure the agony for four more nights until I see him on Thursday?

Static cuts down the line, and for a second, I fear he's gone.

"Valdemar?"

No reply.

"Valdemar?"

Nothing.

The thought of four nights of insomnia grips at my insides. Four more nights of not seeing him, or four more nights of the ghostly hands touching me without any sensation.

Which of these can I endure?

"You have my consent," I almost shout.

A buzz sounds in my ear, and I worry I'm too late. Loosening my grip on the phone, I'm about to scream when Valdemar's voice travels through the speaker and into my core.

"Until tonight, angel."

CLOCK-WATCHING IS A NASTY HABIT, ONE I DON'T NORMALLY have the luxury of, but tonight it's been my sole focus. Earlier, I'd taken out my laptop and reviewed what I'd written about Valdemar, now knowing his story can never be told—not without endangering him and the other Raven Hands.

Am I cross about his ploy to lure me in with the promise of a big scoop? No. I would never have agreed to meet with him if he told me it was simply to learn the truth about my brother's death. It would have appeared to me as if he was asking for my forgiveness, trying to assuage the guilt he's lived with for the past ten years. The only way he was ever going to get me to listen was as a journalist.

But I haven't listened as a journalist. I've listened as Ed's sister, his twin, his other half. And although I was shocked by what Valdemar told me, it's also opened my eyes as to why he killed Ed, and it has me wondering if I would have had the strength, the love, to have been the one to pull the trigger.

Slipping under the fresh sheets, I'm hit with the artificial smell of lavender-and-honeysuckle fabric conditioner mingling with the mango body cream I generously slathered on after a long soak in the bath. Changing the bedding had been another way of killing time before I could respectably come to bed—though at nine thirty in the evening, it's still way too early for me to sleep. But I can't ignore the anticipation of seeing Valdemar and of what tonight's dream might hold.

Avoiding an analytical thought about how I feel like a teenager on a first date, I let my head sink into the pillow and wait for sleep and Valdemar to claim me.

The stage is empty, the chairs gone; instead, the hall is brimming with dancers and ablaze with light. Men are partnered with women, women swirl with women, and men embrace men as a symphony of a thousand violins fills the air.

Amongst the glittering ballgowns and sharply cut dress suits, waiters and waitresses weave between the bodies, trays held aloft, their necks extended and arms perfectly aligned, as if they've been choreographed.

Candlelight flickers from elaborate candelabras coupled with an impressive chandelier that hovers above. But even in the blazing glow, I can see the emptiness of the dancers, the haze around their edges, and the softness of their silhouettes. Focussing on a blonde woman, I track her as she twirls to a Viennese waltz, her eyes trained on the man leading her steps. It's as she spins, her blonde curls blurring against the black dress, that I notice the bloodstain on the back of her head.

Looking elsewhere, I clock a man to the right. He's smiling, his suit pressed to perfection, his back as straight as a ruler. The only thing marring this beautiful scene is the red stain on the white of his shirt.

He's not alone in this macabre attire.

Blood envelops some of the dancers, while others suffer a broken limb or greying skin, bloodshot eyes, or thinning hair.

They're dead.

All of them.

This is the dance of the dead.

I'm about to bolt when I spot a flash of black. It's solid, wholesome, not like the shimmering edges of the deceased.

A shoulder, an arm, the dark hair pulled back in a low bun.

It's him.

Valdemar is here, and he's looking for me.

I push my way through the crowd. The dancers continue to churn around me as my flowing silver gown swishes around my legs.

Not taking my eyes off Valdemar, I slide through the throng, wondering how the dead can be so difficult to navigate through.

The tempo builds and the dance along with it, the dancers' rotations increasing to a dizzying speed until I feel like I'm being twirled around with them, thrown between couples like a lost sock in the washing machine.

Fighting the tide, I try to reach Valdemar, glimpses of him getting more and more infrequent as I fear he's heading away from me. I try to call out, but it's as if his name is useless, having no effect at all. Hands reach for me, pale and withered as if the bodies are decaying further with every step they take. My dress catches on something, and I'm forced to take my eyes off Valdemar for the briefest of seconds, but it's long enough for me to lose him amongst the gaggle of rotting bodies.

Sequins swamp me, empty eye sockets glare at me, and tiaras glisten amidst straggling curls as the dead surround me, roiling and curling like a human whirlpool. And just as I'm about to be swallowed by them, they vanish.

Blackness surrounds me. Nothing but blackness until he walks towards me, his white shirt blaring against the black hole we're now enveloped in, his skin glowing compared to the dead who were just here.

Taking my hand, he kisses the back of it.

"I thought you weren't going to find me."

"I will always find you, angel." His eyes smoulder, his touch soft. "Shall we?" When he extends his other arm, the ballroom reappears, empty and inviting.

He holds me like a professional dancer, and the violins return. The room spins as we take flight across the polished floor, Valdemar's swift moves and strong hold ensuring I never miss a step.

It's blissful abandon, sheer frivolity as we cover the entire ballroom until the music slows, and our embrace tightens before he sweeps me up into his arms and carries me over to the abandoned stage, the orchestra having vanished.

Setting me down on the edge, Valdemar stares at me. "Angel." Pushing my hair off my shoulders, his fingers graze my skin and send a pack of wolves howling through my body. "So beautiful. I wanted to tell you that on the first day I met you."

"Then why didn't you?"

He smiles. "Because you wouldn't have believed me." Taking a step closer, he buries his face in the crook of my neck, his arms encircling me like my favourite blanket. "You are more beautiful than the moon and the stars."

Moving my head back to let Valdemar nuzzle my neck, I catch the glimmer above us. The ceiling of the ballroom has melted away and left us with an unobstructed view of the clear night sky. Stars dazzle, blinking in unison, watching us from their perfect vantage point.

I keep my eyes on the stars as Valdemar steps back and runs his hands under my dress and up my legs.

"It was torture, listening to you beg me to touch you, knowing those women were doing my job. It's a good thing they were already dead."

The magnitude of his words means nothing as his hands travel higher.

"You are mine, angel. You've always been mine."

The stars spin as he reaches between my legs and strokes me softly.

"Valdemar."

Clinging to the back of his neck, I push myself against his hand. The last few nights, I've been shaken like a fizzy drink, the pressure having mounted to a dangerous level. Valdemar is about to make me explode, so I tighten my grip and hope I can make this last as long as possible.

"Look at me," he commands.

My eyes rise to his, and I swear I see stars glinting behind the darkness of his pupils. How easy it would be to get lost in his eyes. How easy it would be to become lost in him.

But I don't feel lost.

I feel found.

Circling my tender spot with his thumb, he slides two fingers inside me, and the stars in his eyes dance as I moan.

This is bliss. Pure bliss.

I want to lie back, but I don't want to lose this closeness, the glint in his eyes as he watches me come undone. This is the first time I've been able to see his face when he's made me come, and I can't ignore how intimate it feels to be locked in his gaze, this private moment shared by only us.

"Hold on, angel."

I interlock my fingers, my lips parting as my orgasm mounts, the overwhelming feeling of it about to wash through my body and shake me to my core. He knows I'm near, has done this enough times now to know my body, my little telltale noises, my facial expressions. No one has ever made me feel like this. No one has ever paid me this much attention. No one has ever touched me the way he does.

With a knowing smile, he slips one more finger in, and I'm undone, the stars exploding above me as I press my forehead to his, my body shuddering beneath his touch.

"Valdemar."

He pushes my hair from my face and stares at me intensely as pleasure courses through my body like a dam has burst.

"I didn't think you could be any more beautiful, but the sight of you coming for me is sublime."

Waves crash around me. My body trembles against his. Tears swell at the corners of my eyes.

Cupping my head in his hands, he tips it upwards.

"Angel?" Concern morphs his face as he wipes a tear away with his thumb. "What is it?"

"This isn't real. None of this is real."

It's as if I've been submerged underwater for the last hour as I heave the night air into my lungs. The sheets have been thrown off the bed, and Valdemar's T-shirt has ridden up to my waist, but there's no evidence of him here.

I'm alone. Like always.

It's just a dream.

Always a dream.

And what breaks me more than anything is that it will always remain a dream. How could I let a man like him get close to me in real life? And why would I want to? Because he listens to me? Because he's the only living human with whom I can be myself, who knows what I am and what I can do? Or is it because he makes me feel alive even though I'm surrounded by the dead?

But I shouldn't be feeling these things for him. He's a monster. A murderer. At what point did I forget what he is?

Wiping my face with the back of my hand, I realise that my tears are the only thing that *is* real.

This is fucked up.
All of it is fucked up.

CHAPTER THIRTY

Una stares at me over the top of her mint-laden mojito as Pierre rolls an unlit cigarette between his fingers.

"More so than the rest of us?" she asks.

"Definitely," I reply.

"Is it the dreams still?" Pierre slides the cigarette behind his ear and picks up his pale ale.

"It's not just the dreams." I exhale loudly.

They eye me over the small round table of the new bar in town called Octavia.

Pierre had been the one to choose tonight's venue, an aptly named underground bar on Octavia Alley. Una and I eyed each other as he led us down the stone steps into what felt like a dungeon, and I expected to see half-naked staff with dog collars on. But we arrived in a swanky-looking room with warmly lit tables, plush velvet seating, and a guy perched on a stool softly playing the saxophone.

"At what level can you condone murder?" I ask.

Una stops swirling the ice in her glass as Pierre puts his drink down.

Una is the first to answer. "I don't think you can ever condone murder."

Pierre presses his lips together. "I disagree."

She flashes him a look. "How can you say that?"

"If someone had shot Hitler when he was younger, I'm sure history books would have been a lot nicer reads."

"But that's with hindsight. No one could have known what he was going to do," Una argues. This is the type of debate she loves. Something to get her teeth into, a corner to fight in, a cause to rally for, and she will not back down.

"Okay, say someone had killed him halfway through his murderous rampage. The world would still have been a better place. And he's not alone. There are plenty of barbaric people out there who deserve to die," Pierre says.

Una opens her mouth, about to launch her counter defence, but then she stops and looks at me. "Wait, why are you asking us this?" She arches a heavily pencilled eyebrow, the ruby dangling from her choker wobbling with every word. Her cabaret goth look is one of my favourites.

There's no need for me to answer this question. If I leave them long enough, they'll work it out for themselves. Even though they weren't working for the *Gazette* when it happened, everyone knows about my brother and what went down at Fortunato Casino ten years ago, and they've all heard the rumours about Valdemar's release.

"Wait, is this to do with your brother?" Una asks.

I'm tempted to congratulate her on getting there before Pierre, but it would be in poor taste.

"Is this to do with Valdemar Montresor?" she pushes.

His name doesn't sound right coming from her mouth, and I'm suddenly possessive of it. I fight the urge to say something, to acknowledge him as mine.

Pierre leans in. "This isn't some therapy technique, is it?

Where they suggest you forgive the person who killed your brother to seek closure?"

Una glares at him. "You can't ask her if she's seeing a therapist. That's none of your business."

"I didn't ask," he shoots back.

"You implied," she says.

"Hey, it's fine." I shake my head. "I did see a therapist when it happened—fat lot of good it did me—but I stopped going a few years ago. I think I'm beyond therapy now."

"Then what is it?" Una urges.

After contemplating my next disclosure, I take the leap. "I've been to see him."

"Valdemar Montresor?" Pierre's hand hovers over his glass.

"Yes."

He whistles. "Jeez, you're braver than me, girl."

Una squints. "Why? How?" And I can see the hurt already brewing behind her heavily made-up face that I'm only telling her this now.

"I needed to. I thought it was time." I don't want to tell them that he asked me to—it'll only raise their suspicions, and I already feel like I'm telling them too much, but my mother's empty silences have started to take their toll. It's time to talk to the living.

"Time for what? Wait." Una rests her hand on my arm. "You're not planning on killing him, are you?"

She laughs, not a real laugh but one of confusion, but I don't, and neither does Pierre.

"Shit, Evangeline, you're not, are you?" Her eyes widen.

"No." My eyes flit between them. Their stares are hard, their faces like stone. They don't know what to do with this information, don't know what to say because there's no rule book, no guidance on what to say to a friend who's visited the man who killed their brother. "No—don't be daft. I just needed to understand."

"Okay, this *is* starting to sound like some therapy technique," Pierre says. "It's not some pathway to forgiveness, is it?"

Una flashes me a worried look. "I hope you're not contemplating forgiving him." Her eyes darken. "That would be worse than contemplating killing him." Although Una wasn't working at the *Gazette* when it happened, she knows what I've gone through in the last ten years, five of which she's known me for. She's been the only person who I've confided in about the pills, the depression, the times when I felt like life was just too difficult to navigate, and she's been there for me through all of it. So, I hear her concern when she asks me this, because why would I forgive the man who destroyed my life and took my brother's?

"No." There's little conviction in my delivery. "It's just...."

"Just what?" she says. "He killed your brother in some shitty shoot-out at a casino. That man is fucking insane and should never be let out."

Silence sweeps the table, and Una is the first to pick up on it.

"You know they're letting him out, don't you?" she says.

I nod.

"Shit," Pierre says. "I can't even imagine how you're feeling."

"It's okay," I tell him, even though it isn't. "I've kind of got my head round it now, and it's the reason I've been to see him."

"Captain confirmed it the other week, that he was being let out and that we would obviously have to run a story on it," Una explains, and I don't like that they've all been keeping this from me, but I know it's because they care. They want to protect me, shield me from the bad guy.

"I still don't understand how they can be letting him out so soon," she adds. "It's been how long?"

"Ten years," I answer. "He pleaded guilty."

"They will have taken into account good behaviour as well." Pierre swipes at something invisible in the air.

"But still," Una protests.

"He knows people, doesn't he? I bet he's greased a few palms for an early release," Pierre guesses.

"And people wonder why there's no faith in the justice system." Una puts her hand over mine. "I wish you'd told us. Visiting him must have been really difficult."

"Yeah." I feel bad for not telling her, but judging by her reaction so far, I think I made the right call.

"I take it seeing him hasn't helped you understand?" Pierre presses.

"In some ways it has, but it's left me in even more of a mess," I confess.

"Why?" Una's face is flooded with concern as her hand tightens over mine.

"I can't go into details, but all I can say is that now I understand why he shot my brother, and it's horrifying because I've started to wonder that if it had been *me* holding the gun, what *I* would have done."

Two pairs of widened eyes stare back at me as Una releases my hand.

"No wonder you feel like you're going insane," Pierre says, clearing the uncomfortable silence as Una glares at me like she's seeing a different version of me, one she didn't think existed.

"Are you saying you forgive him?" she demands, her black-and-white version of the world being tested.

"No. I'll never forgive him. He killed my brother; that's unforgivable. What I'm saying is that I understand *why* he killed him."

"That doesn't make it right," Una says. "Murder is murder, no matter the reason for it. He pleaded guilty and never gave any explanation as to why he did what he did. And I get that you might want answers, to be able to understand it, but please don't forget who that man is—a killer."

"Shit, this is heavy stuff." Pierre runs his hand through his messy hair and plucks the cigarette from behind his ear.

"I'm sorry. I didn't mean to drag the mood down," I apologise.

"You don't need to apologise," Una reassures me. "I wish you'd told us sooner. I would have helped you through it. Pierre and I both would."

"Oh. My. God!" he says suddenly, each word dropping from his mouth like the first blobs of heavy rain before a storm.

The room stills, and I'm aware I'm staring at Pierre as the unlit cigarette hangs from his mouth even though he has no intention of lighting it in the bar.

"The dreams you were talking about the other week," he mumbles, the cigarette sticking precariously to his dry lips.

I can see the pieces of the puzzle falling into place in his brain, and I'm dreading the last piece going in.

He plucks the cigarette from his mouth and points it accusingly at me. "Have you been dreaming about Valdemar Montresor?"

My cheeks blaze as a thin layer of sweat coats my back.

"Holy fuck," Pierre says slowly, each syllable emphasising just how messed up this is.

"Why didn't you tell us?" Una repeats, her face paler than the white powder she's dusted it with. And her reaction is exactly why I didn't tell them both. Because, right now, Una is looking at me with such disgust I can feel it on my skin. She's never been able to hide her emotions, never been able to keep back her opinions no matter who's involved.

"Because it's just so fucking weird and odd and wrong and disturbing." Even as I say it, I feel like I'm betraying Valdemar, as when I'm in the dream, nothing is disturbing about it. That feeling only comes after, when I wake up having been consumed by him.

"Well, I'll be damned." Pierre taps the end of the cigarette on the table, a mischievous look clouding his face. "What's he like?" he asks, waggling his eyebrows and smirking. "Hung like a horse?"

Una whacks him on the side of his arm.

"For God's sake, Pierre," she says.

He holds both hands up in defence. "I'm just trying to lighten the mood, and rumour has it he's supposed to be insanely hot."

"Would you stop it already?" Una closes her eyes momentarily before returning her gaze to me. "I apologise for the insincerity of our colleague here. He doesn't know what he's saying."

"It's fine, honestly. I could do with a laugh," I say, relieved that Pierre is trying to douse the tension around the table.

"I'm sure the dreams are just because he's on your mind. People dream about sleeping with other people all the time, even when they're happily married," Una tells me.

"Do they?" Pierre asks.

"You're telling me you've never had an erotic dream about a co-worker or a friend who, in real life, you wouldn't touch with a barge pole?" she asks him.

"Now you mention it, I have." Pierre leans in. "I dream about you, Una, every night, with your skull earrings, black lipstick, and ripped tights." He gnashes his teeth like a dog tearing at a chew toy.

"Not funny." Una glares at him, unable to let the importance of this situation be batted away with jokes. She returns her attention to me. "So, what are you going to do?"

"I don't know. I'm not sure there's anything I *can* do. He's being released, and that's all there is to it."

"Do you feel safe, knowing he'll be walking the streets again?" She places both hands around her glass.

I don't even need to think before I answer. "Yes."

What I don't tell them is that I'll feel safer than I ever have in my life. How would they even begin to understand that when I don't understand it myself?

Tipping my almost empty glass to the side, I stand. "Who's up for a refill?"

Una rises. "I'll come with you."

"It's okay," I tell her. "I got these."

She sits back down, and the pair of them eye me like I'm a priceless vase balanced on a precariously high stand that could topple at any moment.

Heading to the bar, I try not to think about what they'll be saying about me. I wonder what their reaction would have been if I'd told them everything. That Valdemar Montresor can visit me in my dreams, that I'm now addicted to the way he touches me. What would they say if I told them that I sleep with his T-shirt on, that he occupies my thoughts twenty-four hours a day, that I can't sleep without knowing he'll be there, how his words and his touch make me come every single night, and the sadness that swamps me because none of it is real?

I'm unsure as to what level of sanity I've reached by justifying what's been going on these past few weeks, but having said it out loud, I realise how it sounds, how it is.

Una is right. This is fucked up. All of it is fucked up.

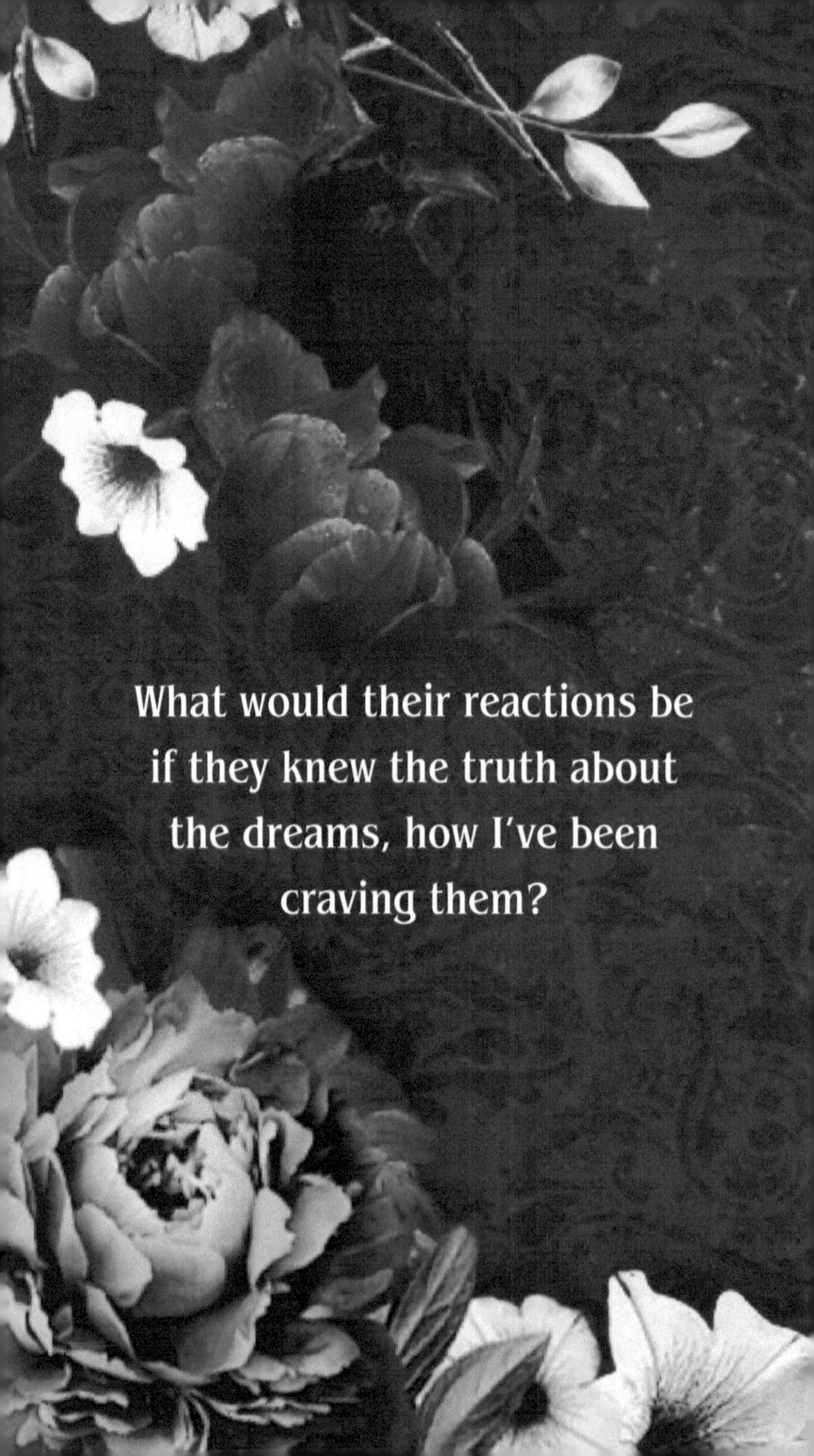

What would their reactions be
if they knew the truth about
the dreams, how I've been
craving them?

CHAPTER THIRTY-ONE

On returning home from the bar, I ransack my bathroom cabinet, pulling out boxes of paracetamol, ibuprofen, congestion tablets, and antidepressants until I find what I'm looking for.

Over the past ten years, I've been prescribed an apothecary's worth of drugs that were supposed to help me feel better. The early days were a blur of chemical-induced survival, my zombielike existence a mist of hazy memories. The drugs all made me feel like I was cocooned from the world, going through the daily motions in a suspended state of reality.

It was a horrible feeling, existing yet not, the side-effects bringing their own catalogue of symptoms, such as sleeplessness yet feeling tired all the time, irritable bowel syndrome, and brain fog. I didn't want to spend the rest of my life blindly fumbling through the haze. So, slowly, I weaned myself off the drugs until I was able to function without them. But until my first meeting with Valdemar, my nights remained troubled, my mind refusing to shut down, the loss clawing at my skull like a hungry beast feeding on my what-ifs.

Holding the box of sedatives, I almost laugh at why I didn't think to try these when I was first attempting to quash the dreams.

I was prescribed them years ago when my sleepless nights were starting to affect my ability to operate and hold down my job. They're strong, and the doctor told me I couldn't use them every night, only for the times when I'd gone days without sleep and my body was struggling.

Flipping the box over, I clock the use-by date—just gone three years.

I'm about to toss them in the bin when Una's face flashes before my eyes, the look of horror on it when I'd told her I'd visited Valdemar Montresor and was beginning to understand why he'd killed my brother. Then I replayed the look when Pierre had mentioned the dreams.

What would their reactions be if they knew the truth about the dreams, how I've been craving them? How safe I felt in his arms during the fight at the prison, how he's the only person I can talk to without holding anything of myself back?

I can still feel the tingling on my skin from when Una had removed her caring hand from the back of mine when I told her I understood why Valdemar had killed my brother.

What is wrong with me? Why have I bonded with Valdemar? Is it because he's given me answers? Because he still has a link to my brother? Was it the way he made me feel the day of the fight? Or is it purely the dreams? Has he manipulated me into feeling things that aren't really there?

I'm starting to lose my fucking mind and my grip on reality.

And it has to stop before I lose myself completely to Valdemar Montresor.

I punch two pills out of the blister pack, pop them into my mouth, and swallow before heading to my bedroom, where I dig out Valdemar's T-shirt from under my pillow.

I should throw it away. Shred it. Burn it. But I can't. Instead, I stuff it into the back of my closet, trying not to inhale his scent embedded in the cotton.

Sending out silent prayers, I climb into bed, hoping to God the sedative works and knocks me out for the night.

The plush carpet is soft beneath my bare feet, my toes sinking into the woven loops, the dark red colour a stark contrast to the paleness of my skin.

Lights bedazzle my periphery like a kaleidoscope flaring at the edges of my vision. Voices of people I can't see rain down around me. With each step, more words reach me.

"Higher."

"Black twenty-nine."

"Place your bets."

There's a drink in my hand, amber in colour, the glass cold against my palm. But when I take a sip, the glass is empty, yet I feel the liquid run down the back of my throat, coating it in a silky syrup.

The woven threads of the carpet become dense, and my grip on the glass tightens as I see him. Ed. Just as he was the very last time I saw him before he left for work—his crisp white shirt peeking out from underneath his sleek waistcoat paired with black pressed trousers.

"Red twenty-one."

"All-in."

"Beginner's luck."

I stumble, going over my ankle as the glass falls from my grip and bounces off the carpet. Ignoring the throbbing pain, I pick up my pace.

Shading his eyes with his hand, he glances around the room as if looking for me. I go to wave, but something heavy has replaced the glass that fell from my hand.

My feet sink into mud as the red carpet disappears beneath a sea of dense dirt. Squelching my toes into the new terrain, I glance up just as he spots me.

There's a pull in my cheeks as the grin expands across my face, and I expect him to mirror my joy, warmth flourishing in his grey skin. Instead, his face drops and his eyes widen, his mouth shaping the word "No."

I'm running towards him now, my strides sluggish through the sludge. Rain batters my skin as the lights disappear along with the invisible people, and a wind whips around my legs.

Unsure as to why he looks so afraid of me, I pull my arms up to wave, but the heavy object in my right hand makes my arm shake.

Feet sinking, I stop, taking in the object I'm holding.

Sleek, cold, and brutal, the gun rests in my palm as if it were made to fit.

Trembling now, whether from the weight of the gun or the weight of its significance, I'm unsure, but my hand isn't steady, isn't trained.

Rope binds Ed across his torso as if by invisible hands, his body bucking against unseen captors. I need to get to him, need to save him, but my feet are fully submerged in the thick clay.

His face is frantic, his mouth forming words that get caught in the wind and the lashing of ropes before they reach me. A wall appears around him, but it isn't finished. Ed stands in the gaping hole as if the wall has devoured him.

The viscous coating in my throat lurches its way up into my mouth as an orangutan-like creature hauls over a crate filled with bricks. Another ape arrives, pushing a wheelbarrow laden with cement.

"Ed!" I call out, but no one appears to hear me. All I can see are the whites of Ed's eyes as he stares at the bricks and mortar.

"No!" Lifting the gun, I point it at no one, my hand too unsteady to aim.

Tearing his eyes from the bricks, Ed stares at me before they close. His mouth doesn't move, but I hear his words in my head.

"Do it."

One of the apes takes up a trowel, digs deep into the cement, and slaps it onto the unfinished brickwork in front of Ed's legs.

"No!" I repeat, waving the gun like it's a flare.

Ed struggles against his bindings, his hair flopping in front of his eyes. The bricks continue to be stacked, the builders fast and efficient and the cement already drying. The wall gains height with every second.

His eyes find mine, and they beg me.

"Do it."

But my finger slips on the trigger, my hand still shaking, the gun so fucking heavy. Tears drench my face along with the relentless rain, blurring my vision and obscuring my target.

I want to pull the trigger, need to pull it now, but my hands betray me. My heart is weak.

Ed's mouth opens wide in a mute scream as the wall engulfs him. He silently screams, and I scream with him.

I scream and scream and scream.

"Wake up, angel. Wake up, now!"

My scream pierces the air, my lungs in overdrive, my body shaking.

I'm in my bed. In my room. Alone.

There's no rain, no bricks, no gun, and no Ed.

And no Valdemar.

I need him...

CHAPTER THIRTY-TWO

 the prison visiting room, I wait for Valdemar to be brought in. This is our last visit before he's released, and I wonder what he'll have to say.

After the experiment with the sedative on Monday night and the horrendous nightmare, I've refrained from using them again. Instead, I've opted to try and stay awake, which, given the copious amounts of caffeine I've been consuming and my insomnia rearing its head like it'd been on holiday these last few weeks, hasn't been as hard as I thought. Working on the hunch that Valdemar must be asleep for him to infiltrate my dreams, I returned home from work on Tuesday and Wednesday and caught a few hours of sleep from five until ten, which seemed to work.

But I'm paying for it today. My body feels sluggish, not conforming to what my addled brain wants it to do. My limbs are heavy, my eyes stinging, and no amount of make-up could hide the dark circles.

Valdemar is brought into the room. I avoid his gaze until

he's sat down in front of me and there's no alternative but to look at him.

Even through my watery vision, I see the mixture of emotions on his face.

"I'm glad you came, angel. I've been out of my mind with worry." His first words belie the anger I can only imagine is simmering beneath his façade.

"Why don't we cut the niceties," I say.

His shoulders rise as he examines every inch of my face.

"Okay, what the fuck did you do?" he asks.

He's angry, yes, but something else hides behind his eyes. Concern?

"On Monday night. How did you...?" His voice trails off as his eyes narrow.

"I had a wake-up call on Monday, a reality check of how fucked up this whole thing is. I feel like I'm losing my mind, and I don't know what's happening here, but it needs to stop. Needed to stop."

"I told you I would stop if that was what you wanted, but instead you.... What *did* you do?"

"I took a couple of sedatives. It was supposed to knock me out enough that I wouldn't dream at all, but instead...." I shake my head, not wanting to return to that god-awful nightmare. "Did you see it?" I hadn't felt him there, not until the end when I'd heard his voice.

"I couldn't get to you. The sedative must have interfered somehow. But I was there. I know the dream well," he says.

"What do you mean, you know it well?"

"I know it well, angel, because it's *my* dream."

Staring at him, it's only now that I see the hurt on his face, his dark beard stark against the sorrow sitting on his brow.

"Yours?" I ask.

"I don't know how. I still don't understand it, but yes, it

was my nightmare—the one I've had every night for the past ten years until you came to see me and I started to visit your dreams. Your dreams have been a welcome break from my own."

"But how?" Pressing my hand against my forehead, I wonder if I weren't so tired, I might be able to understand this.

"I don't know. It isn't your gift, so I don't know how you would be able to cross over like you did, but I can't explain it other than as a fucking fluke, crossed wires, a faulty connection. Who knows? But I do know that I never want you to have to see that again, so promise me that whatever you did, you won't do it again." He leans forwards, alerting the guard behind us, who straightens as he peers at us.

"The sedative was the only thing I did differently, and I haven't taken it since," I tell him.

"I haven't seen you for the past two nights."

"I haven't slept," I say.

"At all?" He narrows his eyes.

"I got a few hours yesterday from five until ten. I figured you had to be asleep to be able to visit my dreams, so I slept while I thought you'd be awake."

There's a hint of a smile. "You guessed correctly. We both must be asleep at the same time. But you can't stay awake forever. It's not safe. How are you even functioning on so little sleep?"

"It's nothing I'm not used to. I've gone ten years without sleeping properly," I say.

"And long term?" he asks.

"You need to stop visiting me."

The silence is thick for a moment before he replies.

"Is that what you want?"

"No. But it's what I need. This isn't right. It isn't healthy." Una's and Pierre's faces spring back into my mind, the look they both gave me the other night when I told them I've been to see Valdemar, that I've been dreaming about him ever since.

"It's better than the nightmares. It's better than not sleeping at all. You've never slept better than you have in the last few weeks," Valdemar argues.

"Yeah, but I started not being able to sleep after you killed my brother. You. You did that. And now you're here trying to help me sleep by seducing me every night. Do you know how fucked up that is?" I snap. The thought of what would have happened to Ed if Valdemar hadn't shot him has not escaped me. I know it was a mercy killing, but I've spent the last ten years knowing this man pulled the trigger, the act of which I was unable to do in Valdemar's dream. Why couldn't I do it? Because I love my brother and would never be able to kill someone I love, yet Valdemar managed to shoot Ed despite their Blood Oath.

And I can't let go of the thought that my brother might have stood a chance of getting away from Fortunato, that he might have been able to escape, to fight back, to kill Fortunato before he bricked him up behind a wall, but because Valdemar shot him, he took that possibility away.

"I know I'm the cause of all of this. I know I am to blame, so you can understand how I want to help, how I want to put things right." He holds his hands up, then places them flat on the table as if showing me he's telling me the truth and has nothing to hide.

"But you can't. You will never be able to put it right. You will never be able to give me what I want."

"And what *do* you want?" he asks.

"I want my brother back. I want to be loved the way my brother loved me—unconditionally, irrationally, the way that only twins can love each other. I want the connection we had. I want a family, someone to rely on, and someone to love just as hard as he loved me."

The air swells as Valdemar runs his hand through his hair.

"My mother died giving birth to me and Ed. Do you know what it's like to grow up knowing you killed your mother?" I let this hang before I continue. "Her death left my dad broken, unable to bond with us, so he threw himself into his work, his friends, his hobbies—anything to avoid spending time with the children who killed his one true love. And when he deemed us old enough to take care of ourselves, he moved abroad for his job." I swallow hard. I've never spoken to anyone about my past before, so these words, although old in my head, feel alien now they're out in the open.

"Ed was all I had, and that was fine, as we had each other. But then you took him, and now I have no one except the ghost of my dead mother who sits in my apartment day after day, smiling at me without having a single word to say. And I can't even take comfort in the fact that I can see ghosts by seeing my dead brother, because he took some stupid fucking Blood Oath that's now bound him to you even in his death. How fucking ironic is that? So, forgive me if I don't relish the thought of falling into your arms every night in your effort to make me sleep better."

Loss closes in on me, the loneliness that my life has been these past few years, and I can't change that. Sleep won't change it. Nothing will.

As if tasting my words, Valdemar sucks the air between his teeth. "There is something we could try."

My neck jars as I straighten up as if on high alert. "What?"

"I could try to bring Ed into a dream."

My eyes widen. The last thing I want is Ed standing there while Valdemar touches me.

As if reading my thoughts, he continues. "Not in the sense

of our normal dreams, angel. That *would* be fucked up. I could try to bring him into a dream so you could talk to him."

"How?" I blink, attempting to understand what he's suggesting.

"I don't know. I haven't done anything like this before, but for you, angel, I will do anything. But you'll have to let me in. No more sedatives or sleeping when I'm awake."

This might be my one chance to talk to my brother. The only chance.

I nod.

"I can't promise anything. The dead don't sleep, so I'll have to talk to him and see how we can make this work."

My insides tighten at the thought of him being able to talk to Ed. I know he said he can't just dial him up, but even so, the idea that he can speak to him at all fills me with jealousy.

The last thing I want to do is get emotional, so I change the subject. "This is our last visit. Monday is your release day, right?"

"Yes. It doesn't feel real even though it's only days away. Ten years is a long time to be locked up. It feels like forever, yet at the same time like the blink of an eye."

"What will you do when you get out?" The note springs to my mind, and I wonder how long he'll last before someone tries to kill him, his enemies vast and plentiful.

My lips part to tell him about the note, but before I can say anything, Valdemar answers my question.

"I haven't thought much past Monday. I know the Raven Hands are throwing me a party. It's in very poor taste and not exactly how I want to spend my first night of freedom, but they've insisted on marking the occasion."

My fists clench at the thought of them throwing him a lavish party, celebrating the fact that he's survived his years behind bars for pulling the trigger and killing my brother. At this thought, my desire to disclose the note shrivels up. And I refuse to get drawn into some old feud. The last thing I need is to be drawn into a gang war.

"I was going to ask if you'd be willing to attend," he says.

"Are you fucking serious? You want me to come and party with you for doing your time for killing my brother? Christ, you *are* insane," I spit.

"I take that as a no." He sits back.

"Absolutely not. Why would I want to be there when they let you out? What would the other Raven Hands think?"

"I don't care what they think," he says.

"I do. How weird would it look when I walk through the door while they're all celebrating your release? And I don't think it would be very safe."

"Safe?" He cocks his head.

"I'm sure they would all think I was there to enact my revenge. Jupiter certainly doesn't trust me." I'm not sure I trust myself.

"It doesn't matter whether Jupiter trusts you. It's whether *I* trust you," Valdemar argues.

"And do you?"

"I wouldn't be inviting you otherwise. And I've enjoyed your company over these last few weeks. It would be nice to speak freely, without such restraints." He pushes at the table that's kept us apart during these visits.

The note is still pricking at my brain. The danger he could be walking into on release day. And not just from his old enemies. Do I trust myself to be alone with this man? The dreams are one thing, but in the cold light of day, will I be able to hold back my anger at him taking my brother from me?

"You've grown too comfortable in here." I throw my eyes

around the room. These walls that have kept him contained for ten years have also kept the real world out.

"Maybe you're right," he says.

"Either that, or you know the hold you have on me."

"And what hold is that?" he asks, his gaze fixed on me.

"You're the only link I have left to my brother."

"And if the dream doesn't work?"

"That remains to be seen," I tell him, not wanting to think about the fact that it might not work and what would happen if that's the case.

"Time, people. Let's wrap things up," the guard calls from the back of the room as another guard begins to collect the inmates.

"Don't sleep before ten tonight," Valdemar tells me. "We have four nights to try this before Monday. Please don't give up hope."

"Okay."

"And I'll send a car for you Monday night at seven, as I'm sure we'll need to discuss things," he adds.

I want to tell him to go fuck himself, but the guard arrives behind Valdemar and ushers him out of his chair.

"I said I'm not coming." I push my hair behind my ears. "Wait. How do you know where I live?"

"Just think about it, please. The offer will be there."

And with that, he's led to the back of the room and out the door with the rest of the inmates.

I'm not sure how I feel about the thought of seeing him outside this room. My feelings on this are as tangled as my conflicted feelings for him. I need him—he's my only link to my brother—and he knows this. But if I do attend his party, there will be a whole new set of eyes on us, no table separating us, and no one calling time.

I can only dream...

CHAPTER THIRTY-THREE

My mother is waiting for me when I return from the prison, her face so calm in contrast to the storm that is my head. She sits at the dining room table like a cat in its favourite spot, waiting to hear how it went and what was said—or at least, I tell myself this is the reason she sits here day after day

And so I tell her. I pour out my heart like it's molten lava from an erupting volcano.

"Valdemar is going to try and bring Ed into a dream. I know it won't be real, but it'll be something. Anything is better than the numbness."

Her hand moves across the table, and I reach for it even though I know I won't feel her.

"Why do I have everyone taken away from me?" Sniffing, I wipe my cheek. "Am I just destined to be on my own for the rest of my life? Because it certainly feels that way."

I can only imagine her words of reassurance as she tells me not to lose hope and that my life won't always be this way.

We remain at the table, and I'm unsure as to whether my mother's eyes are doused in tears or whether it's my own tears that obscure my vision.

At exactly ten o'clock, I climb into bed, a crackling of nerves skimming my skin. I've tried not to get my hopes up. Valdemar said the dead don't sleep, so how he's going to get Ed into the dream, I've no idea. But I pray it'll work, to see Ed again without the bullet hole through his forehead and his bloodstained clothing, to hear his voice again after all this time.

I can only dream, so I do just that.

The hallways are dim, lit only by candles burning in wall-mounted holders and the small flickering flame I hold in my hand. An urgency pushes me down the corridor, my bare feet slapping against the cold wooden boards.

The house is familiar, but not this part of it. This is new, a place I haven't visited before. There's a door to my left that I push open, looking for something.

The room is square, with large plum curtains drawn across what must be an enormous window. Sunlight streams through the small gaps where the two curtains meet, casting the rest of the room in a regal purple hue. Two children sit on the floor, a boy and a girl. I know them both, their silver hair unmistakable.

"It's my turn." The girl bats the boy's hand away from the board, the ludo figures wobbling as she lunges for the die. "I got a six, which means I get another turn."

"Sorry, I forgot," the boy replies, moving back so she can throw the die again. "There's no point in you rolling, though, as I'm going to win the game."

The girl looks at him sharply, her violet dress bringing out the blue of her eyes. "You don't know that. You can't possibly know that. You're just trying to put me off my game." She shakes the die close to her ear and silently whispers a good luck spell before letting it drop onto the board, knocking down the stationary pieces.

"Sabotage will get you nowhere." The boy darts for the fallen pieces as the girl picks up her red figures and places them on the board.

"No, but cheating will."

"Hey, you only had two men out, not all four." The boy moves two of her pieces back to her base as he laughs. "If you're going to cheat, Evangeline, at least be subtle about it."

My heart flares. A memory. One of many.

I close the door and continue down the hall until I reach another door.

Opening it, I expect to see a different room, but instead, I'm met with a graveyard, the rows of headstones blanketed with green moss, fresh grass growing up the sides as if they need tucking in.

Older this time, but only just, the boy and the girl stand hand in hand, a bouquet clutched to the girl's chest, her emerald coat buttoned against the sharp breeze.

"How can you miss someone you've never even met?" the boy asks as the girl shivers.

The girl doesn't look up from the gravestone. "I see her."

"You'll be imagining it. People see what they want to see," the boy says.

"No, it's not my imagination. I see her. Not all the time, just some of the time."

The boy looks at her, his interest piqued. "How do you know it's her?"

"I just know. You would know her, too, if you saw her."

"You're serious, aren't you?" he asks.

"Yes. Why would I joke about something like that?"

"I don't know. Does it frighten you?" he says.

"No. She looks strange, like there's light behind her or she's not *fully formed. I can tell she's a ghost. She doesn't speak, which is annoying. I've tried to get her to talk, but she doesn't." The girl glances at the boy. "You don't believe me, do you? I knew you wouldn't."*

It feels as if the dead are listening when the boy finally answers. "I believe you. Others won't, but I do."

"What does it mean?" she asks.

"It means you're special. You have a gift."

The girl looks at the boy. "Does everyone have a gift?"

"Not everyone. Just some of us."

"Do you have one?" she asks.

"I'm not sure. Maybe."

Another memory. Another snapshot. This is not what I'm looking for, so I close the door on the graveyard and continue down the hall until I stumble, my feet moving faster than my body can keep up with.

The flame on my candle flickers and then goes out, the walls seeming to close in on me as the corridor is plunged into darkness. He must be here somewhere—he has to be—but there are no more doors, just black walls. I push forwards until I hit something hard and solid.

The candle slips through my fingers as two hands grab hold of my arms.

"Angel." Valdemar's face comes into focus.

"I can't find Ed," I tell him, panic setting in my voice. "He's supposed to be here, but I can't find him. It's just memories. All the doors are memories."

"Maybe those memories are what you need to hold on to," he suggests.

"I want to make new ones." Tears sting the back of my eyes.

"So do I," he says.

"You were supposed to bring him." I place my clenched fist on his chest.

He wraps his hand around my balled fist. "I said I would try. I won't give up if it means that much to you."

"It does," I tell him.

He pulls me into an embrace and strokes my hair. "Then I won't give up."

He's the key that will unlock
my brother's silence.

CHAPTER THIRTY-FOUR

FRIDAY NIGHT'S DREAM WAS MUCH THE SAME AS THURSDAY'S. I wandered the house, walking into rooms that were filled with memories. There was one of Ed and me one Christmas when I ate a full selection box before six in the morning and then couldn't open the rest of my presents because I felt so sick. Then a memory of the first time Ed and I went to swimming lessons, and he was so scared of the water that I had to hold his hand as we lowered ourselves in, the instructor scolding us before Valdemar arrived looking sorrowful and promising he would try again.

Saturday night's dream took me back to when Ed first got the job at the casino and how I'd made fun of him in his new uniform even though he knew I secretly admired how smart he looked. But it isn't memories I'm after. I already have these locked away for safekeeping. I want to talk to Ed now, to speak to him, to hear his voice. Is that so unreasonable?

Tonight is Sunday, and it's the last night before Valdemar's release, after which I'll have to decide whether to abandon this foolish quest or go to Valdemar's stupid party and demand he find another way.

Pulling the sheets up around me, I settle into a comfortable position, sending out my silent nightly prayer that tonight will be the night I am reunited with my brother.

The voices reach me first.

"All bets are off."

"What are the odds?"

"Aces high, folks."

My toes squish into the blood-red carpet, my hand clenched around a glass.

A chill works its way down my spine.

I've been here before, but this is not a memory.

This is not my dream.

I try to turn, but it's as if there's a force behind me willing me to keep walking forwards. I know where I'm heading. I know what awaits me.

Staring at the liquid in the glass, I try not to drink it, but unseen hands force it to my lips, the burn of the drink stinging my throat and eyes.

I drop the glass. It bounces off the floor that has now turned to mud, my feet squelching into the claylike soil.

My right hand flexes around the cold metal that has replaced the glass, and Ed is there, right in front of me—the person I've wanted to see for the past three nights, yet now I don't want to see him at all.

My feet urge me on even though my body is screaming for me to turn and run.

Unseen hands grab him.

The wall looms up around him, and the bricks and mortar appear along with the apes.

The burning of my lips accompanies the bile in the back of my throat.

His face contorts, silent words springing from his open mouth as the ropes bind him to his fate.

Raising the gun, I aim, but it's so heavy, just as heavy as last time. My arm shakes as if there's an electrical current running through it. It won't still. My heart beats loudly in my ears as Ed struggles against the ropes, his jaw straining, tears flooding his eyes. And as the wall begins to grow before him, the apes vanish, and it's just me and Ed, my gun held aloft, aimed right at his heart.

The bindings hold him in place as he mouths words that are lost in the silence.

I try to speak, but no words come out. It's as if this place is itself devoid of sound. Placing my left hand over my right, I try to steady the gun, but my arms are weak, my eyes blurry with tears as Ed shouts at me over and over, words that don't reach me until a deafening ringing sound erupts around us.

"Do it."

Shaking my head, I lower the gun. It's him. Ed. His voice. The voice I haven't heard in the past ten years.

"I can't," I tell him.

Pain spears my chest as sadness washes over him, desperation at what is to come and what he knows has to happen.

"Please. I'm begging you. Do it."

The scream pulses in the back of my throat as the wall reaches Ed's chin, his eyes wide, the darkness about to consume him.

I aim the gun at his forehead as my lips part, the scream bubbling to the surface. An arm cocoons me, the gun is pulled from my hand, and my eyes close before the gunshot explodes.

At the deafening bang, everything vanishes as Valdemar steps in front of me, taking my head in his hands and placing his forehead against mine.

"It's okay, angel. I'm here. I'm here."

Vibrations course through my body as I shake beneath his touch, invisible tears waiting to erupt.

"I'm sorry. I'm so fucking sorry, angel."

My eyes flutter open, and I swear I can smell burning.

My chest heaves. Glancing around the room, I make sure

there are no bricks, no cement, and no walls being built up around me—and no Ed.

That wasn't my dream.

Somehow, I ended up in Valdemar's dream again. But how? Last time we thought it was because of the sedative, but I took nothing tonight before I went to sleep. So, what caused me to wander into his dream again?

I switch on the lamp, and my eyes adjust to the amber glow as I wrap my arms around myself, silently wishing they were someone else's.

What is wrong with me? What is happening here? Why do I find myself wanting him when he's the one who's caused me all this pain? What do I need to do to heal? What am I looking for to make this all go away?

That's when I notice my mother sitting on the window seat, her hands laid neatly in her lap, her smile just as permanent as it always is. And she's been at it again, moving things invisibly, leaving me little clues as to what I should do next, because beside her is a dress. My silver dress. The one I wear to all important functions and fancy occasions.

"I'm not going," I tell her, even though I know the words are a lie and she knows it, too, because what choice do I have? If I want to see and speak to Ed again, then Valdemar Montresor is my only chance. He's the key that will unlock my brother's silence.

No guards, no security
cameras, no rules.
All bets are off.

CHAPTER THIRTY-FIVE

The walls of my apartment are shrinking around me as I watch the clock and imagine Una and Dupin waiting outside the prison, Una's lens trained on the entrance, Dupin's Dicta-phone poised, hungry for today's headline.

I can picture it now.

Monster Montresor Released.

Will Una get a good shot of Valdemar leaving the prison? Will his head be covered with a dark hood, or will he hold his head up high, knowing he's done his time and now he gets to live his life as a free man?

Guilt churns in my stomach at not telling Una or Pierre that I'd booked the week off work. Captain knew the signifi-cance of the date and had asked if it was the reason I was asking for the time off. I'd explained that I wasn't sure I could be around the newsroom when all the headlines would be about the guy who killed my brother. He told me he understood, but I'm regretting my decision now, as there's nothing to stop me heading down to the prison to watch Valdemar being released.

Una was the one first on the case regarding my absence from work, sending me a text.

Hey, are you ok?

I'd replied straight away, telling her I was fine and just taking some R & R time. I also told her I wouldn't be meeting up for our Monday night drinks, something I've never missed. I've convinced myself this is simply because I don't want to have to sit there while Una and Pierre try not to talk about the day's headline or be tempted to ask Una how Valdemar looked when he walked out a free man, but in reality, I know it's because of Valdemar's invite to his release party and my mother's insistence that I should attend.

GLANCING OUT MY APARTMENT WINDOW FOR THE HUNDREDTH time in the past ten minutes, I consider the idea that maybe the party has been cancelled or Valdemar never made it out of the prison alive. I've been avoiding the news and social media all day, and my phone has been eerily silent other than a text from Una telling me where to find her and Pierre this evening if I change my mind.

My mother has been perched on the window seat, where she watched with glazed eyes as I got ready earlier. There wasn't a flicker on her face when I strapped the knife between my shoulder blades, the feeling of which I'm still trying to get used to, before slipping my silver dress on. Imagining my mother asking for an explanation, I told her I didn't know why I was taking it with me, just that I knew someone wanted Montresor dead.

Books and movies make it appear easy to strut around with a sharp piece of metal tethered to your back. I'm no warrior, but the cut of my dress means there's no other place for it, and my makeshift knife holder is digging in under my bra.

Am I expecting backlash from the unknown pen person as to why Valdemar Montresor walked out of prison today and wasn't declared dead weeks ago? Or does the note-writer believe I'm playing the long game and have spent the past few weeks worming my way into Valdemar's inner circle?

But I've also considered what I'll do tonight if Valdemar insists there's no other way to contact my brother and that he's giving up on me. Will I need my knife then?

Deep down, I'm not a killer, but I feel a whole lot better taking the knife with me.

Lights crawl across the far wall of my apartment, pulling me from my thoughts.

A sleek black car comes to a stop below my window just as a text lights up my phone.

Your car is here.

The number appears alongside the message, and I quickly save it under VM. He hasn't wasted any time in acquiring a phone.

"This is it," I tell my mother, who simply smiles as I leave the apartment not knowing what the hell is going to happen tonight.

There will be no table between me and Valdemar, no guards, no security cameras, no rules. All bets are off.

Will I see the true Valdemar Montresor this evening—or will I see the true Evangeline Bransby?

He is enough.

CHAPTER THIRTY-SIX

 the driver says as he holds the rear door open for me. He's a small man in a pressed suit, with dark skin and kind eyes. "Abel Phittim. I'm your driver for this evening."

"Nice to meet you, Abel," I reply, wondering if all Raven Hands receive this chauffeur service or whether Valdemar has made an exception for me.

Half expecting Valdemar to be in the back seat, I peer into the car, but I'm met with only sleek leather upholstery that smells of furniture polish and mulled wine.

The driver returns to the front seat, then glances in his rear-view mirror. He looks smaller now, swallowed up by the grandeur of the car, a starched collar encasing his bronzed neck, and I imagine a shock of black hair under his driver's cap.

"Are we good to go?" he asks.

"Yes." The wobble in my voice surprises me, the straps of my makeshift knife holder pinching at my skin as I settle into the seat. "How long is the journey?"

"Traffic is slow, but if I take some shortcuts, we should arrive at the house in around twenty minutes."

"The house?"

"Corvus House." He says this with a note of surprise, like I should have heard of it.

"Corvus House," I repeat.

"Everything okay?" he asks.

"Yes. Thank you."

He nods and then checks his mirror before setting off.

We weave down the side streets of Amontillado, the old stonework blackened with centuries of dirt, hidden door-ways leading to underground bars and clubs, the nightlife spreading under the pavements like roots of the city.

Within minutes, the buildings disperse, and we follow the long road that runs beside the Maelstrom, the prison sitting like a decorative centrepiece.

Lights glow from the many barred windows, giving the false impression of warmth within, the lake shimmering with the reflection. It's hard to believe that only yesterday, Valdemar Montresor was imprisoned behind its walls.

And now he's free.

Though I wonder how free he actually is.

The car takes a sharp left, and I lose sight of the prison. Trees frame the dirt track, and the car bumps its way up the uneven surface.

My mind wanders to gingerbread houses, a girl in a red cloak, and big bad wolves as the trees thicken into a dense forest, the car cutting through them like a scythe. And even though I've never been in these woods, have never driven up this track, the sense of familiarity simmers under my skin.

The darkness before us swallows the car as if we're being devoured until the branches cease and we pull onto a smoother road.

Sitting up, I crane my neck to see through the front window.

Just like the prison, a large building looms in the distance, lit up like it's ablaze.

"Is that the house?" I ask.

"Yes. Have you never been here before?"

"No." But the word feels like a lie.

I have been here. I know this place.

The road leads straight up to the house, the grandeur of the gothic Victorian mansion binding me the closer we get. Abel swings the car around the circular driveway as I drink in the gabled roofs and the impressive tower.

Slowly, he brings the car to a stop right outside the entrance.

Nerves swim in my stomach as he makes his way to the back and opens the door for me.

Now is the chance to turn back, slam the door closed, and tell Abel to take me straight back to my apartment, but the steep steps leading to the large front door are calling me like the stonework is laced with magic.

Heeding its call, I slide out of the car, pulling the hem of my dress down and preparing myself for what's beyond that door.

"It's been a pleasure, Miss Bransby." Abel touches the brim of his hat. "Enjoy your evening." He glances up the steps as if showing me the way.

"Thank you."

Following his gaze, I climb the steps, silently counting them to ease my nerves while taking in the gargoyles perched on the low stone walls and the urnlike planters that have sprawling ivy creeping out of them. Before reaching the door, I inhale deeply as if this might be the last breath I take, the evening air smelling of fresh rain and damp earth.

As I reach the top, the door opens, light from inside spewing out.

"Good evening, and welcome to Corvus House," a man dressed in formal attire says as he holds the door, ushering me inside with his arm.

"Thank you."

"If you head through the foyer and to the door on your left, you'll reach the Great Hall."

I nod, knowing full well where the Great Hall is because I've been here before.

This is the house from my dreams.

This is where I've spent my evenings with Valdemar. This is where he touched me on the balcony, spread me beneath the fountain, and laid me bare on the stage.

The foyer opens up, revealing a large staircase before me, a table in the centre sitting beneath the domed roof—all of it so familiar, it feels like I'm returning to some forgotten childhood home.

Leaving the quiet of the foyer, I turn left and am swept through open double doors and into the bustle of the Great Hall, each step feeling surreal.

Lost in my memories, I see the stage to the right, where a band plays soulful music. My hands flex at the memory of the wood beneath my palms as Valdemar sat me on its edge. Goose bumps flutter over my skin at the thought of the dead hands upon me and how I had wished they were his.

I'm so lost in the dreams that I haven't noticed the whole room has stopped.

Eyes glare at me. Eyes that are very much alive.

Women. Men. Suits. Ballgowns. The chatter has died, the band the only thing to be heard as I walk into the swathe of people.

Anxiety flares under my skin at the heat of their stares. I crane my neck to gaze over their heads.

Where is he?

The men are wearing black suits, and the women are wrapped in black dresses. My silver gown stands out like a red rag being waved at a bull, and I wonder if the simple fact that I didn't get the note about the dress code is the reason for their stares. But I know that isn't the case. They know who I am, and they're wondering, as am I, what the fuck I'm doing here.

Ignoring the looks, I continue my search. He has to be here.

A tray arrives under my nose, brandishing tall glasses of fizzy amber liquid. I shake my head. I need my wits about me. Although, as the tray is withdrawn, I think maybe I was too hasty and that the alcohol might dull the barrage of nerves.

Like a ruffling of feathers, the crowd parts the deeper I wade into the twitter of beaks and plucking of plumage. I'm a cat amongst the pigeons. An imposter to the flock.

The music slows to a halt, as if the musicians have run out of batteries. And it's in the stifling silence that I hear the unmistakable click of a gun.

I stop, the deadly charge reverberating in the air, the twittering ceased and the feathers fallen. The crowd stares over my shoulder, and I deduce that someone behind me has a gun aimed at the back of my head.

Fear paralyses me. I can't run—there's nowhere to go, and they would never let me out.

Is this how Ed felt? Am I about to join my brother in death?

Then we all hear him.

"Put the gun away. Now."

Their heads turn in unison, and I'm flooded with relief as Valdemar emerges from a door in the far corner.

His black suit hugs his lean frame and emphasises his

broad shoulders. His dark hair is sleek and shiny, secured in a neat bun at the back of his head. The command he has of the room is frightening. I would have expected Valdemar to have a gun raised at the person who must have one trained on the back of my head, but as I hear the shuffle behind me, I realise Valdemar doesn't need a weapon to make people listen to him.

He is enough.

His presence.

His words.

His command.

They don't take their eyes from him, some bowing slightly, some staring with open mouths.

He doesn't appear to see any of them as he strides towards me like a lion to its prey, a feral glint in his eye.

He's close now, as close as he was the day of the fight, and I can already feel the warmth from his body.

"Angel." He snakes his hand around my waist and lightly kisses the side of my cheek. Aware of the knife between my shoulder blades, I pull his hand from my body and hold it.

Dark eyes greet me, and I'm done for.

"You came," he says.

"You asked me to."

"Come." Securing his hand around mine, he leads me through the crowd that's still parted for him as if he's royalty. I want to look around, to get a glimpse of the person who held me at gunpoint, but I'm surrounded by stares, held close to Valdemar's side and too relieved at his arrival to be concerned with where he might be taking me and what might await me when we get there.

We head for the door at the corner of the hall, and I think we're going to make it—until Jupiter steps into our path.

"What is she doing here?" He flicks his head to indicate

me as Valdemar pulls me into his back, shielding me with his body.

"She's here because I want her to be here," Valdemar replies with a slight curl of his upper lip, not unlike a dog warning another to back off.

"Do you think that's wise?" Jupiter snorts.

"It's my house, Jupiter. My party. I'll do what the fuck I want."

A woman arrives beside Jupiter. Jacinta.

"At least fucking search her," Jupiter snarls, eyeing me with such hatred that you would think I was the one who killed one of their flock.

"Don't worry, Jupiter, I intend to do just that," Valdemar replies as he pulls me through the door and away from their stares.

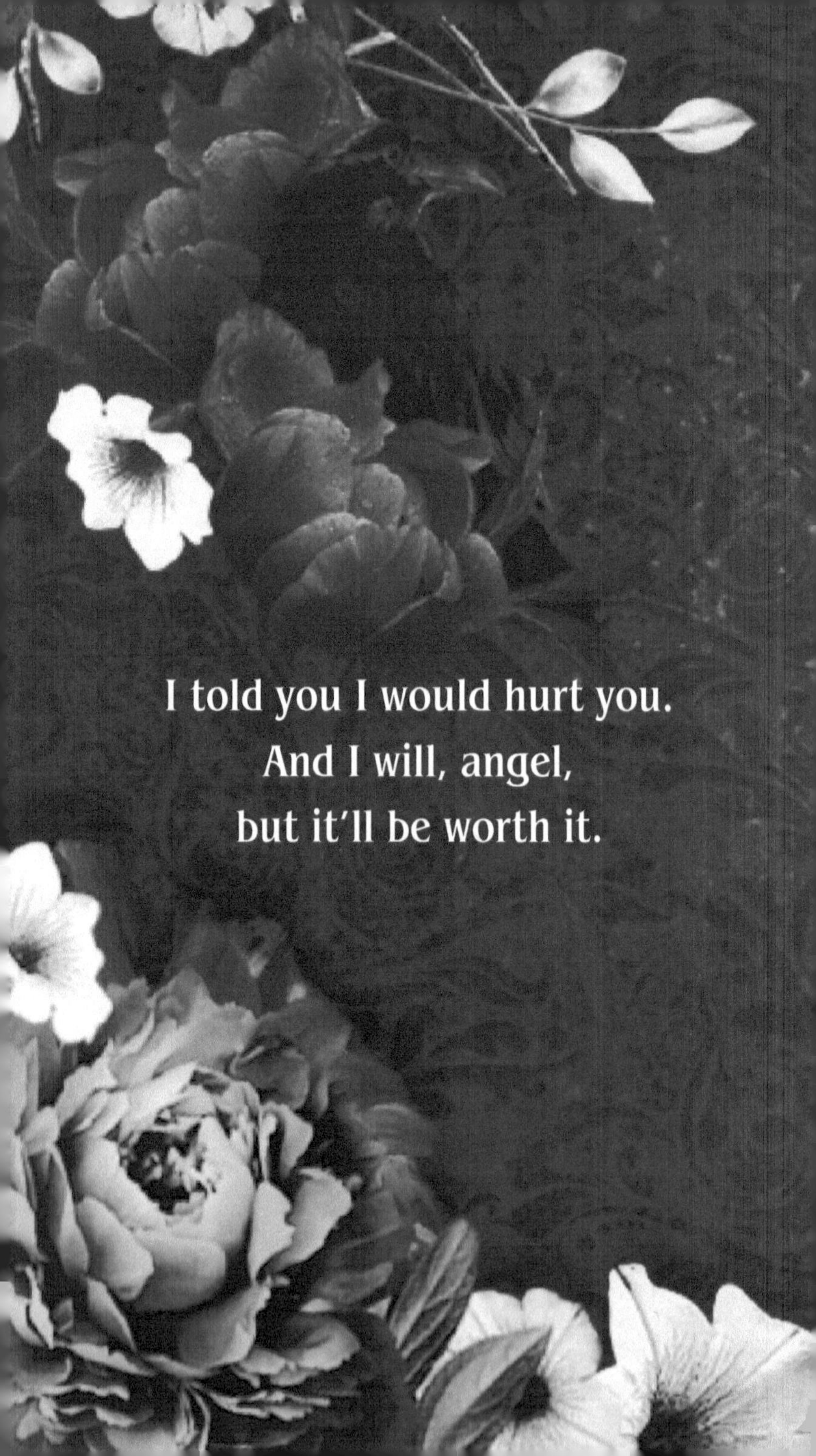

I told you I would hurt you.
And I will, angel,
but it'll be worth it.

CHAPTER THIRTY-SEVEN

THE GLARING EYES ARE REPLACED WITH TOWERING SHELVES housing row upon row of leatherbound books. Logs burn in the open fireplace, two wingback chairs sit opposite each other adjacent to the hearth, and a large desk is pushed under the window overlooking immaculate grounds.

Whether it's the heat from the fire or the heat in the pit of my stomach, my skin burns as a loud click reverberates through the room.

He's locked the door.

"I'm not complaining about your choice of dress; you look beautiful, angel." Valdemar arrives behind me, his breath on the base of my neck as I feel his fingers pulling at the zip. It's like in the dreams, yet this is real. *He* is real. "But if you're going to conceal a weapon, then you need to consider something a little less snug."

Before I have a chance to react, he lowers the zip enough to pull the knife from between my shoulder blades.

Cold steel slithers over my neck as his warm hand holds me flush against his chest, my thighs clenching at the throb between my legs. Why does my body react this way? I thought it was just in the dreams where I had no control, but reality is just as compelling, if not more so.

"I would be disappointed if you hadn't come prepared, angel." Continuing to hold the knife at the base of my neck, he steps in front of me, his hand leaving my waist.

"Are you going to kill me?" I ask.

"No, angel. You're safe here." He holds the knife out.

I take it, eyeing him with uncertainty.

"*You* are the one who is going to kill *me*," he says.

What the fuck? Confusion pushes at me—so much so, I feel as if I might fall over.

Stepping back, he takes off his jacket and throws it over the back of a chair before unbuttoning his shirt. Sweat coats my palm as I grip the handle of the blade. My eyes are glued to his torso. I'm viewing the masterpiece for the second time, the swirling tattoos, the giant raven, and the ripple of his muscles hypnotic as he moves towards me.

Wrapping his hand over mine, he guides the blade to where his heart is.

"Don't hesitate. Just push it straight in, right to the hilt. Don't twist it; quick and clean, that's all I ask," he instructs.

Dread coats my skin.

As much as I've fantasised about Valdemar's demise, this is not what I came here for.

"I'm not going to kill you." I pull my hand from his grasp in case he gets any ideas about pushing himself onto the knife. "I admit, when I first came to see you, I wanted nothing more than to kill you, but not now."

His eyes narrow.

"Then why did you bring a knife?" he enquires.

"I brought it for protection. Someone wants you dead. Somehow, they got into my car and left a note instructing me to kill you."

"I know what it said," he says.

"You know?" I don't understand. How could he know this?

"Yes, because I wrote it, and a Raven Hand delivered it for me," he tells me.

"What?" I search his beautifully dangerous face.

The room is stifling. Heat and confusion bathe me in sweat.

"I took the Blood Oath with Ed. It bound me to him and him to me. Our souls were coiled, our lives interwoven, much like being a twin. He was more than a brother. He was my blood. You of all people should know what it's like to lose someone you're bound to through blood. That's why I gave myself up to the police and pleaded guilty to his murder. I didn't know how to live with myself, with this emptiness that his death created. And I thought I just needed time to recompense, time to grieve, time to heal. But it's only got worse. The emptiness. The feeling that part of me is missing." Pinning me with his stare, he asks me, "After Ed's death, how many times did you try to kill yourself?" He says it so gently, as if to soften the question so it doesn't sound like an accusation but more of a recognition.

It's as if he was with me when I tried to slit my wrists, the razor blade flush against my veins, my pathetic cry when I dropped it just as the skin broke and the blood gushed out. Maybe he sees the drugs, the glass of vodka, how I couldn't get past the second handful of pills before I vomited all over the floor.

"A few," I confess.

"As you know, I'm great at killing other people. But the hardest thing to kill is yourself. And it's nearly impossible in prison. So, I thought of the one person who would want me dead more than anyone else in this world."

A fresh wave of sweat courses down my back. "Me."

"You, angel. You must be the only person in this fucked-up world who deserves my death. You have every right to be the one to put this knife into my chest and end it all. No one else but you. And I can say that I would die a happy man if the last thing I saw was you."

"Stop," I plead.

"Why? Because I'm right?"

"No," I reply.

"Revenge. Justice. Isn't this what you want, angel?" His eyes narrow.

"Is it what *you* want? Has this been your intention all along?" My gut coils, fear, desire, the reality of what he's asking me to do all churning inside me, the knowledge that he's had an ulterior motive, as I knew there would be. I just never thought it would be this.

His eyes look heavy as he regards me. "It was at first. The whole reason I asked you to visit me was so you could learn the truth before putting me out of my misery. But then I met you, and I touched you in your dreams and heard your loneliness and my name on your lips as you came in my arms. I thought there was nothing left worth living for, but then I met you, and now, I want nothing more than to own you."

"This is so fucked up."

"Having your Blood Brother ask you to shoot him because he's going to be bricked up alive is fucked up. But it does make you realise that life is short, so you have to take what you want, and fuck everyone else," Valdemar says.

"I don't know what you want," I admit.

"It's simple. Death or you. Kill me or keep me. Stab me, or I fuck you." He pulls my hand back up to his chest, the knife pressing into his flesh. "The choice is yours."

"Shit. I can't...."

"I know you want this. Your dreams were a testament to that. So wet for me. So pliant. But you won't allow me to give it to you because of who I am. You need to stop thinking about what's right and what's wrong."

The room is hot. Too hot. I can't think straight. I have no logical reasons for this choice because none of this feels logical.

"And what does that say about me? What kind of person wants to fuck the man who killed her brother? What does that make me?"

"It makes you mine." He almost growls this.

"Fuck." I wish I'd taken that drink now.

"Will this make it easier?" He takes the knife from my hand and moves behind me. "I can fuck you at knifepoint. Then when you wake tomorrow, guilt swarming you for what you allowed me to do, you can tell yourself that I made you do it, that you didn't have a choice." His lips brush my ear. "You are safe here, but I can't promise I won't hurt you; those promises are for the weak. We don't go through life not hurting those closest to us."

My pulse reverberates in my ears, drumming at my insides like it's goading me.

"Tell me to stop, and I will. Just say the word." His voice is like a hypnotic fog clouding my brain.

"I don't want you to stop." And I don't. He's right. This is fucked up. I told myself I came here tonight because I needed him to reach my brother, but I know that's not the only reason. I do need him, but I also *want* him. I can't deny how upset I've been when I wake and realise every dream is just that—a dream, none of it real.

But this is real. *He* is real. He doesn't have to be a dream.

The cold of the blade caresses my neck as Valdemar pulls the zip the rest of the way down the back of my dress. "Take it off."

Keeping my head still because of the knife, I slide my arms out of my dress and let it drop to the floor. Valdemar cuts through the straps of the scabbard and pulls it from my body.

Now, wearing only my underwear, I feel the burn from the roaring fire and the heat from Valdemar's skin.

"I haven't touched a woman in ten years, not in the flesh. And even then, my dream was only you. Always you."

The knife comes back up to my throat, and I let out a yelp.

"Go stand by the desk," he instructs.

I do as he says, and he moves with me, the knife never leaving my delicate skin. Placing his other hand in the middle of my back, he pushes me over the desk, moving the knife away so I don't slit my own throat.

My cheek rests against the hardwood, my high heels straining my calves.

"The view of you bent over my desk is worth living for." His words are as sharp as the blade he uses to cut through my underwear before tugging the material from around my legs, leaving me in only my bra. "You have no idea how many times I pictured you like this."

Despite the warmth of the room, a cold draft works its way over my flesh and winds its way between my legs, making me feel even more exposed.

"Fucking beautiful, angel. And you don't need to worry about the guests in the hall, as they won't hear any of your screams; they're for my ears only."

The cold metal slides up the back of my leg, sending a shiver through my core. There's nothing inside my head except him, his touch, and the knife. I want to say something, to tell him how this makes me feel, what he does to me, but I'm lost, words confounding me. Maybe it's the niggle of betrayal that has my tongue. Una, Pierre, Ed. I'm betraying them all, sleeping with the enemy, so I keep my mouth closed.

"I'm on my knees for you, angel," he says.

I hear the shift as Valdemar lowers himself behind me, the blade smoothing over my calf. The air leaves my lungs as he pulls my cheeks apart, and then I'm gone as he flicks his tongue right up my centre.

I claw my nails over the grain of the wood, thankful the desk is holding me up. Valdemar licks me again, his tongue dipping as I shudder against his face.

Unable to keep my mouth closed any longer, words find me in a rush of pleasure. "Oh God."

Holding my hips, the knife clasped in his hand now resting against my thigh, Valdemar fucks me with his tongue, then flicks lightly over my clit with the faintest of pressure, which only makes me want it more.

"You taste just like I imagined—sweet and exotic. God, I could taste you all day, all night, and still not get enough," he says, his husky voice adding to my climbing arousal.

The familiar swirl of an orgasm builds like a cyclone gaining momentum. His tongue is relentless, his pace rhythmic, the sensation intoxicating.

"Fuck." My breathing is laboured, like I can't get enough air though the room is full of it.

Just as I'm about to peak, Valdemar stops and rises behind me, pulling me up by my hair, the knife still gripped in his hand, the blade resting against my head.

I'm about to ask him what the fuck he's playing at, but he beats me to it.

"I want you to watch, angel, while I make you come."

At first, I don't comprehend, my mind still reeling from the fact that I was so close and he just stopped, but then I glance at the window and catch our reflection.

Valdemar is behind me, his shirt open, his chest pressed against my back. I can feel the swell of his cock against my backside, and it thrills me to know how turned on he is by this. His fist is in my hair, clutching the knife, and his other hand trails up my back and releases the clasp on my bra, which slides down my arms. I lift my hands momentarily to let it fall to the floor, my breasts now free, my nipples hard and swollen.

He then snakes his hand down my stomach and lingers over my swollen clit. "Look at how beautiful you are."

Letting go of my hair, he drops the knife down against my throat, and I can't deny how fucking turned on I am by the sight of my naked body against his, his hand dipped between my legs, and his hot breath on the nape of my neck. Plunging his fingers inside me, he cups my clit with the palm of his hand, and my vision blurs.

"What turns you on more, my fingers inside you, the knife against your neck, or the thought of what I'm going to do to you after you've come?"

"All of it." It's not a lie. I wish it were.

Pushing myself against him, I grind my pussy into his hand, the need for him consuming me from within.

He adds another finger, spreading me wider. My heart pounds against my chest as I gulp the air. Then he curls his finger, hitting the sweet spot as he grips my throat, the knife inches from my face.

"Keep watching, angel. I want you to see yourself coming undone."

"Valdemar," I cry out as the edges of my vision distort and the orgasm rips through me like an explosion.

"That's it, angel. Come for me."

Pleasure eats away at me, my legs wobbling under the strain. I lean forwards and place my arms on the desk to hold myself up. Valdemar spins me so I'm sitting on the edge, his hand returning to my clit as the aftershocks course through my body.

"Lie back." He pushes me down, my body slackening as I

let my legs drop. Standing between my open legs, Valdemar removes his hand.

Even though I'm exhausted, I push myself up on my elbows, eager to see what he's about to do next, as I know this is only the beginning.

He drops the knife onto the desk and slides out of his shirt before throwing it to the side, never taking his eyes from me. Using one hand, he unlatches his belt and then his button and zip.

I swallow hard.

"Do you think you can take me?" he asks as he grabs the heel of my shoe and pulls it from my foot, followed by the other. He places my feet on the desk and then pushes my legs apart, letting my knees flop to the side, opening me wider for him.

"I'll try." My answer is hoarse, my throat dry from heavy breathing, but then I salivate as he pushes his hand inside his trousers and his boxer shorts and pulls his cock out.

Fuck. I want to retract my answer. My thighs clench, and my eyes water.

"I told you I would hurt you. And I will, angel, but it'll be worth it."

Thrusting his fingers inside me, he pumps them until they're soaked, then removes his hand and swipes it down the length of his rigid cock. It's beautiful, now glistening with my pleasure.

With his cock in his hand, he traces it across my middle, lingering over my tender clit, rubbing and coating it further. A feverish fire rages between my legs. A hungry need gnaws at me, and I wish I could touch him, but I can't quite reach his arms.

"I'll take it slow at first," he tells me, the hoarseness behind his voice only adding to the inferno between my legs. "But then I'll fuck you hard and fast, angel."

I find myself nodding even though he wasn't asking my permission, merely making a statement of things to come.

Just as he said, he slowly dips the tip of his cock inside me, flirting with my entrance, which only makes me want it more. Moaning through the building desire, I arch my back and push myself forwards.

There's a reflection on his chest from the moonlight pouring in through the window, and it makes his skin shimmer, his body rippling with every movement, the tattooed raven looking like it's in flight. He's something to behold, holding his cock in his hand, my legs spread wide while he guides it seductively inside me.

"Valdemar," I gasp, the necessity growing, the urgency to have him taking over my common sense, my animalistic needs holding the reins.

"You want it all, don't you? You want all of me inside you," he growls.

"Yes." Another truth.

"I would never deny you, angel." Slamming his hands onto the desk on either side of my body, he thrusts himself in deep, taking my breath away.

Quickly, he grabs one of my legs and wraps it around his back. I follow with the other, hooking my ankles to anchor him to me.

"Sit up. Put your arms around my neck." He's pounding into me, thrust after thrust. The heat from his body mingles with my own, his neck damp with sweat as I claw my nails into his skin. "Hold on, angel."

I interlace my fingers, and his pace quickens, the pleasure mounting. He unlocks my legs, spreading them wider, pushing down on the insides of my thighs so he can hit me deeper. I cling on to him, and my eyes threaten to close, my teeth clenching as my orgasm builds.

"Oh God." My mouth is drying out, and the air in the

room suddenly feels scant. My breaths become short, frantic. It's getting harder to keep my hands locked around his neck.

"Lie down," he tells me, one hand going to my throat, the other to my clit, and I'm spinning, my eyes losing focus as a blinding orgasm rages through my body.

"Valdemar." His name is out before I can stop it, his cock swelling as my insides clench it tighter before he comes with such force, I'm left breathless.

For several minutes, we remain still, and all that can be heard is the gasping of our breaths, our bodies returning to their normal, resting state.

Though I'm not sure my body will ever return to its natural state.

Still inside me, Valdemar pulls me up by my arms and wraps them around his neck. Grasping my head, he forces me to look at him before planting tiny kisses on my forehead. "You've no idea what you've just done to me," he says.

I'm still floating on euphoria, drunk on pleasure, my body swaying against his hold, and I have no response for what he's just declared.

Sensing my need for silence, he fishes in his pocket for a tissue, his trousers hanging onto his hips, then slips out of me and wipes himself before cleaning me up and loosely resecuring his belt. He grabs his shirt and wraps it around my body, guiding my arms through the sleeves. He then picks me up and carries me to a door in the far corner of the room.

Once again, I'm clinging to him, my arms around the back of his neck, my head resting against his chest, and a different warmth spreads through me—the same warmth that invaded me the day of the fight.

With great dexterity, he opens the door and carries me down a long corridor, fleeting glances of panelled walls and dado rails skimming past my vision.

I can't help but marvel at his strength when I feel like I'm the one who's run a marathon as he carries me up a flight of stairs and down another corridor. We eventually reach a door that he pushes open with his foot and then kicks closed behind us.

A fresh scent hits me, like a forest after a heavy downpour. He places me on a large four-poster bed covered in dark grey sheets. After the hardness of the desk, I feel like I'm lying on a cloud, my back sinking into the softness of the mattress.

Large windows line the right-hand wall, and the heavy drapes are open, leaving the room drenched in moonlight.

Valdemar perches on the side of the bed, taking in my depleted body. "Do you need to rest?"

"Before we go back to the party?" I ask.

The shrill tone in my reply has done nothing to hide the fact that the party is the last place I want to go. I can't bear the thought of facing those stares again, let alone what they'll look like, knowing what Valdemar and I must've been doing, as my hair is dishevelled, my lipstick non-existent, and I can imagine my eyes look like black holes with my mascara having smudged due to them watering. Either that, or they'll think he's tortured me into confessing my desire to kill him.

"Fuck the party."

"But it's for you," I say.

"No, it isn't." Sensing my confusion, he continues. "It's an excuse for the Raven Hands to invade my home, drink my wine, and get shitfaced."

"Sounds like a party to me."

"A party is when you celebrate something. What exactly are they celebrating?" he says.

"The fact that you're here." It's the only way I can word it. I don't want to mention the prison or what he was there for, as it'll only remind me of how I've ended up here. There's still a bitterness to all of this, despite what he's just done to me, the way he's made me feel.

"After leading my flock into a mission that killed one of them, leaving Adolphe Fortunato completely unscathed and free to run his fucking empire for the past ten years without anyone to challenge him on his depraved morals."

"Didn't the Raven Hands seek revenge after you were put away?" I ask.

"I forbade them from it. It was my fault Ed died. There was no way I was putting any more Raven Hands at the mercy of Fortunato."

"What about now? Do you want revenge? Are you going to go after Fortunato?" My mind races at the thought.

"It's been ten years, angel. Ten years is a long time to plot revenge."

"That doesn't answer my question," I say.

"Sometimes I do want revenge. So much so, I can taste it, see his blood on my knife and the whites of his eyes as I drain him of everything he is. But then at other times, I just want my head to stay quiet, to revel in the nothingness and give myself up to dark abandon. And I don't know which is worse," he explains.

Darkness pools on his face, his eyes misting over.

His gaze returns to me. "The only thing I *do* know is what I want right now."

"And that is?"

"Do you want to know the last physical words Ed said to me before he died?" he asks, even though I would like to think he knows me well enough now to know what my answer will be.

The hairs rise on my arms as if nails have been run down my back, a sickly feeling working its way through my stomach.

"Yes." It's delivered with little conviction, rather guilt at not having been there to hear his last words, jealousy that Valdemar Montresor was the one to hear them, and anger that they were his last words in the first place.

"After the gun went off, I ran to him and grabbed his head so I could look at him. I told him everything was going to be okay and that he just needed to stay with me. Lies. All of it fucking lies."

Sadness overtakes his expression as he continues.

"I had two guns pointing at the back of my head—one held by Fortunato's bodyguard and the other by a very nervous police officer who looked far too old to be in uniform, never mind brandishing a gun. But I never took my eyes off Ed. I told him I was sorry, so fucking sorry, and that I would spend the rest of my life being sorry. I asked him to forgive me. He told me that only an angel could grant such things."

Tears swell behind my eyes, but I refuse to let this man see them.

"Jesus. You think I'm a fucking angel," I say.

"I know you are."

"Well, I'm not, and even if I was, I don't forgive you. I will never forgive you," I tell him.

"I don't expect you to when I can't forgive myself," he admits.

Wrapping his shirt closer around my body, I pull my legs up and hug them. "What happens now?" I ask.

"That's up to you. You can go home, if that's what you want, or you can stay here with me. It's your choice, angel."

Tracing the flock of ravens tattooed up his arm, I know I should be asking for my dress and getting the hell out of here. But the slump in his shoulders and the bleakness of his face won't allow me to. What has he lived with these past ten years? It's been hard enough living with the loss of my brother, but how do you live with that loss knowing it was your fault?

"I don't forgive you, but I won't condemn you. Stay with me." I reach my hand out, and Valdemar looks up, a small light shining behind his eyes that's so far removed from the beast that stalked into the library not thirty minutes ago.

Sliding onto the bed, he takes me in his arms, and I let him.

I'm ruthless, angel, but not
when it comes to you.

CHAPTER THIRTY-EIGHT

Sleep engulfs me. Uninterrupted, dense, and heavy sleep.

I can't recall the last time I slept so well, no dreams, no night visitors. When I wake, it's to foreign sheets, an unfamiliar room, and the warmth of a body next to me.

Valdemar is sitting up, resting his back against the headboard, the sheet covering his legs, his chest bare and brazen. Suddenly aware of my nakedness, I tug the sheet up to cover my breasts as I sit up, moving slightly away from him.

He puts his phone on the bedside table and regards me with curiosity, like he's trying to work out whether I'm going to pounce on him or run a mile. I do neither. Instead, I search my brain for how I've ended up here, naked and beside him in bed, when the reason I visited him last night was for something entirely different.

"What time is it?" I glance around the room for a clock.

"Do you have somewhere to be?" he asks.

"No. I've booked a few days off work, but that doesn't mean I should be here."

"I was right, then," he says, folding his arms.

"About what?"

"The guilt. The shame. You're already berating yourself for ending up in my bed."

"You held a knife to my throat," I remind him.

"So, you've no reason to feel bad; I gave you no choice."

I shake my head. "We both know that's a lie."

"We lie to ourselves all the time. Why should this be any different?"

"This is not what I came here for last night."

"Then why did you come here?" he asks.

"You know why. I've still been unable to talk to my brother. The dreams didn't work." I feel I've lost sight of this these last few weeks.

"No, and I'm sorry about that, but I said I would try, and I did."

"Then you need to try again," I insist.

"I'm not sure that's a good idea."

"Why not?" I ask.

"After the last dream?"

The cold metal of the gun in my hand, Ed pleading with me to shoot him, Valdemar stepping in to take the gun from me, my eyes closing as the explosion shatters the dream.

"You ended up in my dream again, and although I got to you just in time, I don't want you to have to go through that again. *No one* should have to go through that," he says.

"Why does this keep happening? The other dreams weren't like that. They were memories."

"I don't understand it either. No one has ever managed to step over into my dreams," he tells me.

"Then what do you suggest?" I ask.

His face stills, but I feel that beneath the furious darkness, the cogs are working double time.

"I don't know," he says at last.

"Then there's no reason for me to be here." Clutching the

sheet to my chest, I shimmy my way off the bed, leaving a naked Valdemar in my wake.

He's hard, and he gives his cock one long stroke. "You can't expect me not to be turned on by the sight of you."

Squeezing my eyes shut and gulping hard, I find my voice. "Where's my dress and underwear?"

"Where you left them." He's still teasing me, running his hand up and down his shaft, slowly, smoothly as if it's the easiest thing in the world. "In the library."

I take a step towards the door, and Valdemar takes the hint, throwing his legs off the bed and pulling on some boxer shorts he fishes off the floor, the tight material doing nothing to hide his arousal.

"So, are you just going to fuck me and leave?" he says.

"I shouldn't have even done that, let alone still be here." I wave a hand over the room.

He puts his hand on his chest. "I'm hurt."

I scoff. "I doubt that. I'm sure before going to prison you fucked women and walked out on them all the time."

Something drapes itself across the room, a darkness like someone has closed the curtains. I stare at Valdemar, his expression swimming with anger.

"For the record, I don't, and I'm getting annoyed that you think I'm some heartless caveman who has no idea what emotions are."

"You said last night that you haven't had a woman in ten years, so forgive me for thinking that I just happened to be the first one you came across who was stupid enough to fall for your mind games and your pretty face." My anger at him isn't justified. I'm angry with myself for letting him in, for being swayed by him and forgetting what he did and why I came here in the first place—Ed. This has always been about Ed, but I need a punching bag, and Valdemar is the closest thing.

With the sheet wrapped around my body, I go to leave, but Valdemar beats me to it, standing in front of the large oak door.

Glaring at him, I ask, "Are you going to stop me from leaving?"

"No, but I'm going to make you listen to me before you do." He places the flat of his hand against the door and scowls. "I'm not some fucking playboy. I don't fuck women who don't mean something to me. I may look like a complete bastard, but I'm not. And I didn't ask to feel the way I do about you. In fact, it's made things rather complicated. You're the last person I would have dreamt of pursuing, but you don't get to choose who you're attracted to. Fuck, it's not even attraction; it's something else. It's like there's this energy coming from you, and I can't help but gravitate towards it."

I bite my bottom lip to stop its trembling.

I should be arguing with him, but despite my sensible brain trying to bulldoze all my emotions, what he's saying makes perfect sense, and I'm relieved it isn't just me who feels this invisible pull.

"My life has been on hold for ten years, and I thought I wanted it to be over, but last night when you made your choice to not stick that knife into me, I made a promise that I wasn't going to waste the life you were giving back to me." His hand drops from the door. "I will not keep you here, but I would very much like for you to stay."

Something releases inside me, something I've been holding in, and my shoulders drop.

"I didn't mean to make assumptions about your character, but all I have to go on is that you're the head of a notorious vigilante group and have murdered several people, including my brother," I say.

"I'm ruthless, angel, but not when it comes to you."

"You've made your feelings pretty clear, and I won't lie, you make me feel things I haven't ever felt before, but realistically, where do you see this going?"

"What do you mean?" he asks.

"Do you see us dating? How would that even work? I can see it now—bringing you to my work Christmas party. 'Hey, guys, this is my new fella. You know, the guy who killed my brother.' And God forbid, if we were to get married and have kids, how would I even begin to tell them that their dad killed their uncle? And even if there was a remote chance of us ever being together, I can't imagine a day would go by that I didn't look at you and see the man who murdered the other half of me. Even after everything you've told me, that's who you are and who you will be, and I don't see that ever changing."

"And if I hadn't killed your brother?"

The intensity of his stare is too much, his anger gone, replaced with a terrifying sadness. I drop my eyes but am only met with his solid chest and the raven that appears to be circling me.

"Then I would be falling at your feet." My eyes meet his, and my heart cracks. "But you did kill him."

Before I have a chance to change my mind, I open the door and force myself down the corridor, trying to remember the way we came last night.

To my relief, I find the stairs and descend, the sheet tangling around my ankles as if it's trying to stop me from leaving.

In the light of day, the place looks different, with no shadows dancing against the walls, nothing hiding from the moonlight, but I still feel the presence of this house, like something is living in the walls and has been for centuries.

Finding the library, I breathe a sigh of relief and look for my clothes. There's no rescuing the underwear Valdemar cut from me, the memory of which makes me shiver, desire already pooling between my legs. Shaking it off, I slip my bra on and then my dress.

The door opens, and I try to ignore the tension that's arrived with Valdemar.

"Shit," I curse while ducking down to search under the chairs for my shoes. When I stand, he's in front of me, holding both of them.

"Thanks." I tug them onto my feet, then rake my fingers through my hair as I give the room one last glance.

"I have something for you." Valdemar moves over to the bookcase and scans the shelves before selecting a small red book that he hands to me.

It looks old, with no title on the plain front cover. "What is it?" I ask, turning the book over to reveal the title embossed in gold on the spine.

The Raven by Edgar Allan Poe.

"It was Ed's."

I glance up at Valdemar. "I don't recognise it."

"He found it after I met him, when he was about nineteen," he explains. "It was one of the only possessions of his that I kept. He took it everywhere. For some reason, it was important to him."

That was the time when Ed had already closed himself off to the world and I had begun to feel like we were two different people rather than the one I'd always been used to. It breaks me to think he treasured something I didn't even know existed. And also to think that he kept it from me. What else had he been keeping from me?

The spine cracks as I flip open the book, the yellowing pages smelling musty, like they've just been shaved from the oldest tree.

"Do you know the poem?" Valdemar asks, breaking my train of thought.

"Only what I can remember from being at school. I don't understand why…." My words trail off as I land on the title page, the letters resembling an old typewriter font. Underneath the title, there's a handwritten dedication, the copperplate-style lettering fancy and ornate.

To my own darling Lenore, for whom my love shall burn forever more. ER

"My mother's name was Lenore." My eyes shoot up to meet Valdemar's. "This book was given to my mother."

"That would explain why Ed cherished it," he says.

"I don't understand, though. The inscription suggests it was given to her by my father, but the initials don't match." I thrust the book towards him.

"ER," he reads.

"My father's name is William. William Bransby. So, who the hell is ER, and why was he sending my mother a book?"

"You're the journalist. Maybe you need to do some digging," he suggests.

I clutch the book to my chest as Valdemar continues, "Just be careful how far you dig. Some things are better left buried."

His warning should send a chill down my spine, but the sadness on his face indicates pain and suffering rather than fear.

A weariness drapes itself over my shoulders as I head for the door leading to the Great Hall. Unsure of what to say, I opt for silence as Valdemar follows, opening the door for me.

It's strange, stepping into the empty hall, the darkness that shrouds it during the day signifying that this isn't a room to be used in daylight. Gone are the disdainful stares, the wide eyes that tracked my every move. Only Valdemar and I—and the ghosts—the remain.

"I'll get Abel to run you home," he says.

"There's no need. I can get a taxi."

"I insist."

There's no point in arguing with him, and I'd rather leave now than have to wait for a taxi anyway.

"You have my number," he says as we reach the main entrance.

I hadn't appreciated how heavy the doors were last night or the intricate detail of the woodwork.

"Yes." I hesitate, wondering if my next words will make things easier or harder. "I wish things could be different." And I mean it. I wish, more than anything, that my brother's blood wasn't on his hands and that those hands were now holding me.

"So do I." His eyes dim, the darkness mixing with regret.

"Would you tell my brother something?" I ask, trying not to linger in his sorrowful eyes.

"Of course."

"Tell him I miss him." It's a whisper, a fragment of all the things I want to say.

Valdemar bows his head.

I turn and begin my descent, my footsteps heavy, my heart even heavier, and I don't know why I feel this pain now. Is it the knowledge that Valdemar doesn't seem willing to try to help me anymore, or is it the pain of having felt I might belong with someone after such a long time while knowing it can never be?

His question echoes inside my head.

"And if I hadn't killed your brother?"

My reply burns in my chest.

"Then I would be falling at your feet."

I wish things
could be different.

CHAPTER THIRTY-NINE

thoughts are chaotic. Images of my mother clash alongside
her mystery lover, black-feathered birds flapping their wings
against the inside of my skull along with the haunted look on
Valdemar's face as I walked out of his house and left him. My
inner thighs burn with the slightest of movements, my
stomach muscles sore, my throat feeling hoarse—reminders
of what I've just done, who I've just fucked.

"I wish things could be different."

I already know I'll never feel pleasure like it. No other
man will ever compare to him, but what choice have I got
except a life of celibacy? If I were to sleep with another man
now, I know my thoughts would stray to Valdemar. It would
be the memory of his hands upon my skin that would make
me burn, his fingers inside me and his hand around my
throat that would make me come. Not only can I not have
him, but he's ruined me for anyone else.

The slam of my apartment door is loud enough to wake
the dead, and just as I'd hoped, my mother is sitting at the

table, her hands clasped, her back straight, but there's no smile.

"What is this?" I slam the book onto the table, full of anger at my predicament, that I've given in to temptation, that I've slept with the enemy. But he doesn't feel like the enemy. He hasn't for a long time—and maybe that's why I'm so angry.

As expected, she doesn't answer, but she doesn't smile either. She merely looks at the book like I've just slapped a dead rat onto the table.

"Who is ER? Who was he to you?" I ask.

She stares at me, and I wish I could grab her and shake the answers from her.

"Why won't anyone answer me?" I shout at the walls, but they don't answer me either, so I grab my laptop from the middle of the table and fire it up, my fingers itching to surf the keys.

While everything loads, I freshen up in the bathroom, changing out of my dress and into leggings and a hoodie. Mouthwash makes my eyes water, and I rub some micellar water over my tired skin.

Feeling a little more alert, I begin.

My first search is for the poem "The Raven." It must have some significance to my mother. Her name was Lenore, just like in the poem, and she called my brother Edgar, like Edgar Allan Poe. I search for the name Evangeline, wondering if my name is also from Poe, and find out that he composed a poem called "Evangeline" that was part of an essay he wrote and first published in 1884, but I'm lost in the old jargon, so I return to "The Raven." What was her fascination with this poem? What did it signify?

There are chat rooms and forums dedicated to the poem, containing many discussions on its origins, the meaning behind it, and what a master of the macabre Poe was. But after an hour, all I learn is that the poem is about the death of a loved one and how the raven symbolises the never-ending suffering and pain of the narrator remembering his Lenore. The message Poe was sending was to let go, as holding on to the mournful memories will cause eternal suffering—something I can wholly relate to.

Is that the reason Valdemar gave me this book? Is he trying to tell me to let go of my brother and live my life? But it still doesn't answer why my mother had it and who ER was.

In a change of direction, I search for the initials ER, thinking there can't be that many male names beginning with the letter *E*, but I'm wrong. It's a needle in a haystack.

After looking at Edmund, Edward, Egor, and Ethan for what feels like hours, I take a break. The need to shower is compelling, but I don't want to wash the scent of Valdemar off me. The water would pummel away his touch, and I'm not ready to let the memory of him go just yet. That thought only prods at the ache of how messed up my feelings for him are—how I want him but won't allow myself to have him because he can never change what he's done. Instead, I delve into the furthest depths of my closet and pull out the old box that has sat at the back for the past ten years.

I've never looked at the contents of this box. It's always been too painful, but I'm on a mission, and the recollection of Valdemar saying that the book was the only thing he had of Ed's makes me wonder what else I might find if I look.

My father, William, had been the one to eventually clear out Ed's room, and I don't think he kept anything of value except what he gave me in this box.

The room stills as if it's holding its breath over what I'm about to find. And I know she's here, sitting on the window seat, her favourite spot when I'm in my bedroom.

"What am I going to find in here?" I ask her, but she just motions towards the box, urging me to open it.

There's no dust on the surface of the lid, a testament to it having been shoved in the back of my closet for so long, buried beneath old handbags, worn-out shoes, and tatty scarves. The box itself is made of thick cardboard, slightly larger than a shoebox, and decorated with the wallpaper that adorned Ed's bedroom for nearly six years.

Grief fights with my adrenaline, this memory so stark, it almost punctures my chest. I remember him choosing the geometric wallpaper in the DIY store, my father paying someone to come and hang it, and Ed asking if there were any offcuts. My father hated it, saying it made him feel dizzy, but Ed loved it, the triangular design saying something to him that no one else could hear.

Swallowing my tears, I pull the lid off quickly, like a plaster from a wound.

It takes me a few moments before I can bring myself to touch his things.

As expected, his wallet, phone, and keys all stare at me, the familiarity of these inconsequential items almost choking me. Ed was forever losing his keys, so every year I bought him a new keyring that he would add to the bunch in the hope that they would be so large, it would be impossible to lose them.

I gave him so many over the years that he whittled it down to his favourites, and it breaks my heart to see the large red *E* I gave him one Christmas and the stainless steel one that reads "Thank you for being my brother." And then there's the silver one I remember seeing in a souvenir shop. I got it because Ed went through a phase of drawing birds, but the significance of it now has me holding my breath.

The keyring is of two birds facing in opposite directions, their bodies overlapping, their feet touching. I remember being attracted to the swirling patterns on their bodies, the beauty of the design, and the fact that the two birds reminded me of Ed and me, both the same but heading in different directions. It's only now that I realise what I bought him: the two birds are ravens.

I take the keyring off the bunch and place it next to the box.

Next, I pull out a wad of paper, each page small but cut out with precision. I trace the delicate pencil lines with my fingers, knowing that at some point, Ed had touched these. They're drawings, sketches, some detailed, some just an outline, but every single one is a bird. I haven't forgotten how good at drawing he was, but I had forgotten his obsession with drawing birds. At the time, they were just birds, but now I recognise the angle of the beak, the dip of the head, and the sleek black feathers for what they are.

Ravens.

Had Ed seen Valdemar in a vision? Had he known he was to become a Raven Hand?

Ed was very particular about wallets and would only use one he'd purchased himself. He said they had to smell right if he was going to walk around with it in his pocket all day.

Opening it up, I find his debit card, a receipt for a jumper from Landor's, and a ring pull from a can of pop. Shoving my finger behind the small flap at the bottom of the wallet, I pull out three pieces of paper.

Two are photos.

The first is a photo of me and Ed when we were about five. It was taken by our father while we'd been playing in the back garden. There's a smudge of mud on my cheek where I can remember digging for treasure under the large oak tree, Ed watching me with fascination, telling me that I would need to dig really deep before I found anything. The second one is of our mother, smiling softly, eyes warm and happy. She's sitting on a step, a house looming behind her.

The steps look familiar.

I squint at the door behind her and can just make out the intricate detail on the woodwork.

"This was taken at Corvus House," I tell her.

Her hands rest in her lap, and her smile returns.

"What were you doing there? Why were you at the Raven Hands' house?"

Ignoring her silence, I look at the last piece of paper, and my heart skips a beat.

There, in Ed's familiar handwriting, is a name.

Ellison Rue.

It's like he didn't even exist.

CHAPTER FORTY

I FLY BACK TO THE KITCHEN AND PULL OUT MY NOTEBOOKS from the first time I visited Valdemar.

Skimming my hurried writing, I search until I find the name I'm looking for.

Victor Rue.

Valdemar told me that Victor Rue had been the head of the Raven Hands when he joined and that he'd been suffering from some sort of dementia, which had resulted in him asking Valdemar to kill him, and thus Valdemar became the new head of the Raven Hands.

My head swims as I tap "Ellison Rue" into Google.

Nothing. It's like he didn't even exist.

Next, I type in "Victor Rue."

This proves more fruitful. Sifting through all the basic details of being born in Amontillado and what a successful entrepreneur he was when he started his own medical business, I try to find a link, but there's nothing about his family, nothing about his roots.

After several minutes of similar searches, I give in and grab my phone.

Valdemar answers after the first ring, and I leap in without letting him speak.

"You know who ER is."

"That didn't take you long," Valdemar says.

"Why didn't you just tell me?" I snap.

"To be honest, I never looked inside the book, so I had no idea what was written in it, and it took me a while after you left to put the pieces into place."

"What pieces?" I ask.

"Before he died, Ed was looking into his family history. He found the book on a shelf at Corvus House and was set on the trail, just like you are now, although it took him a long time to discover what he found."

"And what did he find?" I push.

"I don't know. He never got the chance to tell me."

"ER is Ellison Rue." The line goes quiet, and I can picture Valdemar scratching his chin, his eyes narrowing as he processes this. "Who the hell is Ellison Rue?" I ask.

"Victor was a very private man, and he never talked about his family, but towards the end of his life, he did mention a brother." He pauses.

My brain whirls. "So, my mother used to have a thing with Victor's brother before she met my dad?"

"Victor told me he'd never got over the death of his brother, who he said died unexpectedly at the age of forty-two—no age for anyone to die. By that point, Victor was remembering things from twenty years ago with such clarity, it was hard to believe his mind was being eaten away. Then he wouldn't remember what he'd done the day before or sometimes even an hour ago."

The phone is heavy in my hand, Valdemar's silence too loud.

"So, my mother and Ellison were together at some point, and then he died?" I guess.

"It's a possibility, but there's something you should know. Something that changes things." Valdemar waits a beat, and I become impatient.

"What?"

"Victor told me that Ellison was a Raven Hand, just like him. It isn't unusual for the gift to run in families, especially when the siblings are twins—and Ellison Rue was Victor's twin brother."

I'm too consumed with
the lie I've been living.

CHAPTER FORTY-ONE

Valdemar's voice fades into the background as I pull the phone from my ear and end the call. I can't think with him on the other end of the phone, and my brain is struggling to fit this all together.

Twins.

Twins are hereditary.

Ellison Rue.

My mother appears in the kitchen. She isn't sitting this time but standing by the table, her hands by her sides.

"Ellison Rue is my father, isn't he?" I ask her.

I imagine tears streaming down my mother's face. My eyes are a blur, so I don't notice the shimmer behind her, but as I blink my own tears away, a man comes into focus, his hand on her shoulder, and I step back.

Slender frame, soft white hair, and ice blue eyes.

He has a striking resemblance to Victor Rue, the man I've just been googling. Same white hair and angled jaw. But what shocks me the most is his resemblance to Ed. The almond eyes, the slight nose. It's like looking at an older Ed, everything mirroring my brother other than the thin lips, which are like my own.

This man is the ghost of Ellison Rue.

My mum lifts her hand to reach for his, and she smiles.

"Why now? Why come to me now?" I ask.

But neither of them can answer me. My back is pressed against the wall, and I slump down to the ground, tears obscuring the vision of my dead mother and father, my world altered so drastically, questions mounting so densely that I'm drowning in them.

THE THUDDING INSIDE MY HEAD STARTLES ME.

It takes me a second to notice I'm still sitting on my kitchen floor, but the sky has grown dark, grey clouds having overthrown the weak winter sun. My dead parents have vanished, and the thudding in my head is coming from my front door.

Unsure as to how long I've been here, I flinch at the sound of the voice coming from the other side.

"Are you in there? I suggest you open the door before I kick it in."

Scrambling to my feet, I bolt to the door and open it before Valdemar resorts to breaking it in and alerting the entire building.

He's out of breath. "Fuck, I thought you'd done something stupid." He grabs my hand like he's checking for a pulse.

It's only then that I notice Wilson, the caretaker of the building, standing behind him.

"I couldn't get into your building," Valdemar explains.

"I'll be off, then. Glad everything's okay." Wilson dips the brim of his baseball cap and wanders off down the hall, keys jangling on his belt.

Valdemar steps into my apartment.

"Why did you hang up the phone? I've been worried sick," he says breathlessly.

"I was thinking," comes my rather lame reply, but my head is still pounding.

"Well, you shouldn't have been thinking alone."

His huge frame pushes past me, and he searches the tiny foyer as if there might be intruders.

He heads to the kitchen, and I follow.

My laptop is still open, the screen black, probably from the battery dying, and my notes on Valdemar are scattered across the table.

"Working on a story?" he asks.

"Trying to find answers."

He nods.

"They were here," I tell him, noting the relief in my voice that I have someone to talk to, someone who knows the strange shit that goes through my head even if he doesn't see it himself, and someone who will talk back to me.

"Who were?"

"My mother and my father."

"Your father?" He holds my gaze as he answers his own question. "Ellison Rue is your father," he guesses.

"Yes."

He glances around the kitchen as if they might be hiding somewhere.

"I take it they've gone?" he says.

"For now."

"What can I do?" He searches my face, still looking for signs that I'm hurt, injured in some way, but there's nothing to see on my face. My turmoil is internal, my insides feeling like they've been wrenched out of me, rearranged, and then stuffed back inside.

"What is there to do? What do you do when you discover

your whole childhood is a fucking lie? Do you know what bothers me the most, apart from the fact that Ed never told me he was looking into our family or what he'd already found out? That I have no idea who William Bransby is and why he's pretended to be our father for all these years."

"Why don't you ask him?" Valdemar picks up my phone from the table and hands it to me. "No time like the present."

My stomach squirms, but he's right. This can't wait. I need answers.

The irony of searching for his name—"Dad"—in my contacts isn't lost on me. He may not have been the greatest dad in the world, but to me, he's always been my father. How do I even begin to unthink something like that?

The call connects and the phone rings as I select speaker, not wanting to hear what he has to say by myself.

"Evangeline." My dad's voice, William's voice, echoes through my kitchen.

"Hey, Dad."

"Are you okay?" he says.

"Not really. Look, I don't want to draw this out. I just have some questions for you, and I would appreciate the truth." I try to sound firm, try to dig out my journalist voice, but this isn't work. This is my life.

"Sounds ominous." He laughs nervously, and I wonder how long he's been contemplating this moment.

I get straight to the point. "You're not my biological father, are you?"

There's a shaky silence before he answers, his voice soft and low. "No, I'm not."

"I know about Ellison Rue, but I need you to tell me exactly what happened to avoid me having a mental breakdown." I push my hair back, feeling like that breakdown has already begun.

There's a rustle down the phone line, and I imagine my

dad swapping the handset to his other ear or adjusting his posture.

"Before I tell you, and I will, I need you to know that I love you. I've always loved you and Ed, and I know I've not been the best of fathers. I tried to do the best I could for you both, but it was hard." He clears his throat. "God, I've been dreading this conversation, but now it's here, I'm actually quite relieved. Are you sure you want to do this over the phone?" he asks.

"I've waited thirty-three years, and if this was a film, this would be the part where you jump in a car to come and reveal the truth and get hit by lightning before you reach me, so no. Tell me now, please."

"Of course. I suppose I better start at the beginning. You got a stiff drink?"

Chewing the side of my lip, I watch as Valdemar opens the cupboards until he finds a bottle of whisky, then takes a cup from the draining board. He pours a slug and hands it to me.

"Yes," I reply, and he begins.

"I met Ellison Rue in my twenties when I was working for the medical firm his brother had set up. Ellison was the one who inducted me, introduced me to my new team, and settled me into the company. He was ten years my senior, and I looked up to him. He was nice, unlike his brother, who was cold as ice. Anyway, the years went by, and Ellison and I became close friends, both in and out of work. He became more than just a boss. And there was a time when I thought we could have been closer, but it wasn't meant to be."

Closer. That word dances in my brain. Little things begin to fall into place. The reason why he never seemed to move on after losing my mother, why he didn't even date anyone. And I always thought it was because no one could ever replace her, that he could never love anyone other than her.

But this? This feels like it should be a huge revelation, like I should be shocked by it, that he was in love with a man, but for some reason, it doesn't feel new; it feels like it's always been there, and I've just never seen it.

"After about nine years of working for him, Ellison met Lenore in a bar where she was working as a waitress. Lenore was beautiful, and not just in a glamorous way. She exuded this aura that affected everyone around her. Even I could appreciate the effect she had on both men and women, so it came as no surprise when Ellison told me he'd fallen in love with her. She had no family, had been left at birth on the steps of the local hospital and had bounced around the welfare system from foster home to foster home until becoming an adult, so it was no wonder she fell for Ellison, this great man, someone who finally wanted her, loved her, and offered her the chance of happiness."

There's a pause, as if my dad is gathering the words he's held on so tightly to and is now finally setting free.

"Then she got pregnant. Lenore was thirty-nine, Ellison forty-two, and I think they thought this might be the last chance they would have to start a family. Victor wasn't happy. He told Ellison he was rushing into things and that having a child would interfere with the running of the business. But Ellison paid no attention to Victor.

"It was a difficult pregnancy due to it being twins and Lenore being classed as an older mother. She was constantly ill, in and out of the hospital with no end of problems right up until the final weeks, when they decided that you and Ed were at risk if they didn't bring on the labour. So, they took Lenore in to induce her, and Ellison went with her. He said he would call me once the babies had been born. I waited for him to call to say that everyone was healthy and that they were the proud parents of twins."

There's a silence down the line, but I wait, hanging on his every word.

"I never got that call. Instead, I got one from a nurse asking me to come to the hospital right away.

"It was the worst car journey I've ever driven. All the possibilities were jumping through my mind as to what had happened. So, when I finally got there, I was overwrought. The nurse ushered me into a small room, and I knew whatever she was going to tell me wasn't going to be good news."

My stomach squirms, as I know where this is heading. I'm finally on familiar ground.

"She did her best to tell me gently that Lenore had died in childbirth due to complications and blood loss. Ellison had to decide whether to save Lenore or his children, a decision no one should ever have to make.

"The nurse told me that Ellison had named you both right after delivery and asked her to call me with the news, as he was too bereft to do it himself. But before she got around to calling me, Ellison collapsed and was rushed into the emergency room.

"Within the hour of you and Ed arriving in the world, Ellison suffered a massive heart attack. I was shocked. He'd been the picture of health, and I always believed he died of a broken heart, but it turns out he had a congenital heart disease that had been brought on by an infection, the symptoms of which he'd ignored, as he'd been so focussed on Lenore and her failing health during the pregnancy."

My hand feels cold as it grips my phone. Two deaths. Ed and I are now responsible for the loss of both our parents, because if my mother hadn't died giving birth to us, my father would still be here. We killed them both. Us. Together.

I feel raw, numb, and I want nothing more than to hang up, to end this call, but I can't. I have to see this through.

"Victor was notified of his brother's death, which he took

hard. But there were decisions to be made with regards to your future. The thought of Victor deciding your fate made me feel ill. He wasn't a family man where children were concerned and would have had you brought up by some agency nanny. I asked if I could take you both home, but it wasn't that simple. As your only next of kin, Victor was given the option to take you in as his own, but he said he didn't want either of you, so you became wards of the state and were put with a foster family until I petitioned the court and was granted custody of you both. There was no battle in fighting Victor for your adoption. His already cold heart had frozen at the loss of his twin, and he blamed Lenore for Ellison's death. You already had your mother's eyes and Ed your father's, and I knew that Victor would also see this, and you'd be a constant reminder of his loss. I feared he would come to hate you both."

The line goes quiet, and I can hear my dad swallowing hard as if he's trying to hold back tears. My own are lodged in the back of my throat, threatening to strangle me.

"Why did you never tell us any of this?" Anger threatens, the numbness gone for an instant. Why have I waited so long to learn this? Would I have ever learned the truth if it hadn't been for Valdemar? Years and years of lies. My life a lie. My past a lie. I'm not sure how much more I can take.

"It was hard enough telling you that your mother had died giving birth to you. I always wondered what growing up with that knowledge did to you both. You were always so insular, so reliant on each other, and the thought of adding your father's death to that was too much.

"So, I told you I was your father. That way you could grow up having one parent, at least. I wanted to give you as much of a chance at life as I could, and I thought that was the best way. What you need to understand is that I loved your father, more than as a friend, a love he simply couldn't return, and that was fine. I never held it against him, and it didn't undermine our friendship. But when you love someone in *that* way, you would do anything for them, and I knew he would have wanted you both to grow up being loved and cherished. And you and Ed were all I had left of him.

"I always intended to tell you later on in life, but there never seemed to be the right time or the right place, and the longer I left it, the harder it became. And then when Ed died, I truly believed that your heart couldn't take any more." His voice breaks, and my chest tightens.

There's a part of me that wants to scream at him, to shout, to let the beast of betrayal out, but I don't have the fight in me. Instead, I reply flatly, "Thank you for telling me the truth, no matter how hard it's been." My voice sounds robotic because I'm numb, angry, reeling, but also deflated by it all. I can't take all this in. It's too much to process. I'm not sure what to do with it and what bearing this has on everything that's going on with Valdemar and my brother. I'm too consumed with the lie I've been living.

"I'm just sorry I never told you sooner and that you had to call and ask. I wish I was there with you. You're not alone, are you?"

My gaze goes to Valdemar. "No, I'm not alone."

I wonder what my dad—William—would say if I told him that the person standing in my kitchen and being my emotional support is the man who shot my brother.

"I'm here if you need me. I will always be here. I know I've not been the best of parents; grief, as you know, does strange things to you, and I wasn't ready to have children. I'd gone from being a single man to losing the only man I ever loved and gaining a family in the blink of an eye. But, at his funeral, I made a promise to Ellison that I would always be here for you, and I feel like I failed Ed. I wasn't there for him like I should have been, and I often wonder if what happened was my fault."

Valdemar swallows hard.

"No. Don't ever think that. His death is not on your hands." I'm shocked at how quick I jump to his defence after what he's just told me, but deep down, I understand why he did what he did. And I'm glad he took us in and didn't leave us in foster care, but I just wish he'd told us all this sooner.

"I think any parent always feels responsible for the death of their child," he says.

"It wasn't your fault. Promise me you'll stop blaming yourself," I tell him.

"I'll try, and that will have to be good enough."

"Okay, Dad." My voice is hoarse, my mouth dry.

"You sure you're okay?"

"Yes," I lie. And as desperate as I was ten minutes ago to speak to him, I want nothing more than to end this call because I need to be alone. I can't process this right now. I need quiet, calm, a darkened room, and time. "I'll call you tomorrow. Goodnight."

"Goodnight, sweetheart. And just so you know, you'll always be mine, my sweet little girl. Even if we don't share the same blood, we share the same love in our hearts, and I love you, my little Evangeline."

"I love you, too, Dad." My voice trembles.

He ends the call, and my arm drops heavily to my side, the phone a dead weight in my grasp.

Valdemar stares at the floor, and I see what he must be going through, the realisation of just how many people were affected when he pulled that trigger.

He chose us.

CHAPTER FORTY-TWO

He lifts his gaze as if ready to argue, and I'm not sure whether it's the look on my face or the lingering resonance of my dad's story, but he holds his tongue.

As I watch him head for the door, I see he's not the criminal I met seven weeks ago. He's a man who has too much to carry, a burden so large, it's pushed him further into the soil, where he's decaying amongst the rotting leaves.

As he reaches the door, he stops. "I know none of this is conventional, that I shouldn't even be here right now, but I am, and I'm not going to hide away from that. I am here, and I will always be here for you. And if you change your mind about anything—"

I cut him off. "Change my mind?"

"Last night, I gave you the choice of ending my life. You made your choice, but I'll understand if that decision changes."

"You're right," I sigh. "None of this is conventional."

"I will stay out of your dreams tonight," he says.

"Thank you." I'm relieved he's at least giving me this.

"But you need to stay out of mine too."

"I don't know how to," I say.

He opens the door, his bulky frame barely fitting in the doorway.

"Call me anytime." And he leaves.

My first thought is that I'm alone, but I know this is a lie. I'm never alone, because even when I can't see my mother, she is always here.

THE HOURS BEFORE BEDTIME ARE A BLUR. I TRY TO NAP, DO some yoga, even read, but nothing can stop the whirling of my brain. The rational side of me is trying to convince myself that there is nothing I can do about the revelation that William is not my father and that I am the daughter of Ellison Rue. William brought me up as his own, his intentions were honourable, and I will never forget that. But the lies hurt. The deception. Living a life that was never real. And that changes everything.

I'm relieved when it's time for bed, but getting ready is a laborious affair. I'm trying to drag it out, knowing I have no idea what will await me in my sleep. Valdemar promised to stay out of my dreams, but I have no way of controlling my own.

I hold the mouthwash in my puffed-out cheeks until it burns my gums. Finally, I spit and watch the dark blue liquid slide down the sink, pondering the thought that today has now been marked with such significance, it will never be forgotten.

William is not my real father.

I let the words play around in my head, wondering if they'll feel different if rearranged, said in a different order.

But instead, they just hang there, losing their impact every time I repeat them.

My biological father was a man I never met, a man my mother fell in love with, a man who couldn't live without her, but it doesn't change the fact that William chose to save us from a very different upbringing and raised two children as his own.

He chose us.

He was the one who taught me how to tie my shoelaces. The one who clapped the loudest when I played Mary in the school nativity. The one who took the abuse when my hormones were raging and I hated the world and everyone in it. He was the one, and that will always make him my dad.

When I slip under the sheets, they feel strange, like I'm not sure what's going to be under them. I wonder if sleep will evade me, the revelations of the day keeping me awake until daylight arrives, but as my eyes flutter, I feel the pull of slumber, the dull heaviness of sleep, and whatever awaits me in the dark.

My toes sink into the mud, the blood-red carpet still visible beneath the murky slime. Ed is in front of me, being held by invisible hands and bound by thick rope.

It's heavy—the gun. Heavy to hold, heavy to look at.

Ed's face contorts, his mouth a gaping hole, the blackness infinite.

"Do it. Do it now."

My hand is steady this time as I raise the gun, aiming it at his chest, but my heart is pounding, and it thunders in my ears like the hooves of an army of horses.

Pulling the trigger always looks so easy on the TV, but the complexity of it now confounds me. My finger slips against the mechanism as if it burns.

Ed is screaming now, shouting at me to shoot him before he disappears behind the infernal wall.

But I can't.

I can't.

I will never be able to pull the trigger.

Never.

I know what awaits him, but it doesn't matter.

Never.

The scream boils in my throat before rumbling out of my mouth with such force that I stumble, the gun wobbling in my hand.

"Angel."

His voice arrives, just like I knew it would, and I know he's going to take the gun from me, relieve me of this burden, give my brother what he wants, and stop the screams.

Strong arms encase me from behind, his hands flat on my stomach as he whispers in my ear. "I'm here, angel."

My eyes close at these words, shutting out the nightmare.

My head rests against his chest, his arms tight around me.

The gun is taken from my hand.

Wait.

Something isn't right.

The gun has gone from my hand.

But how, when both Valdemar's arms remain wrapped around my waist?

I'm about to open my eyes, but then the dream explodes.

Bang!

He hadn't atoned.

CHAPTER FORTY-THREE

I'M CONFUSED BY THE PERSISTENT GUNFIRE UNTIL I REALISE I'M awake, the dream has dispersed, and the banging is not that of a gun but a fist upon my front door.

I drag myself from my bed, pull on a sweatshirt I'd discarded on the floor, and rub the sleep from my eyes as I make my way down the hallway.

The banging gets louder and is now accompanied by a voice.

"Evangeline! Evangeline, are you in there?"

I flip the lock, then swing the door open to find Una with her arm raised, ready to pummel my face in the absence of the door. Pierre hovers behind her, embarrassment mixed with relief on his face.

"Evangeline, thank fuck for that." Una pushes into the apartment, almost knocking me down as she throws her arms around me. "We've been so worried."

"She's been worried. I've been marginally concerned," Pierre says.

"I was worried when you didn't show up for work yesterday. Then Captain said you'd taken some leave, but you haven't answered any of my texts or calls."

Una releases me, and we trail into the kitchen. Their eyes immediately zero in on my dead laptop and the scattered notes and reports on the kitchen table.

"I am allowed to take a holiday," I tell Una.

"Or are you working from home?" Pierre raises an eyebrow.

"This is nothing," I lie.

"It doesn't look like nothing." Pierre tilts his head to try and read one of the loose papers, but I snatch it up.

Una leans against the worktop. "Of course you're allowed to take a holiday. We just thought it a bit suspicious with what happened on Monday, and then when I couldn't reach you all day yesterday, I started to worry."

"I appreciate your concern, guys, but I'm fine. Just thought it would be a good week to take some time off and not be around the headlines for a bit."

"See, I told you." Pierre flashes Una a frustrated look.

The pair regard me with uncertainty before Una speaks. "There was something else."

Pierre rolls his eyes. "It's fine. She is fine. We should just leave."

"What is it?" I ask.

"It's nothing." Pierre stares at me as if trying to convey that this really is nothing, but Una will not be deterred.

"It might be nothing. Or it might be something." She folds her arms.

"Does it require a chair and coffee?" I ask, already pulling out the chairs, then head over to the kettle.

They sit as I busy myself with maid duties.

"I told you we should have just shown up with a Costa and checked in on her," Pierre whispers to Una.

"I am here, you know. I can hear you," I say with my back to them both.

"Pierre doesn't agree with me on the importance of telling you what we know," Una says.

"I just don't think now is the time. It can wait," he argues.

"Sometimes, I question your character as a reporter, Pierre. Remind me again why you became a journalist?" Una says, that infernal tongue of hers unleashing again, but Pierre is used to her by now.

"Very funny," he says, batting her comment away with his hand.

"I'm serious. You don't have your tail in the air when there's a whiff of a story," she pushes.

"This isn't a story. This is our friend and her life," Pierre points out.

With an unintentional thud, I set their coffees on the table and join them.

"Okay, what's the story?" I ask, glad of the distraction from my own affairs.

Pierre eyes Una as if giving her one more chance to back out of telling me whatever it is they've come all this way to say, but she ignores him.

"Yesterday, Dupin and I went to interview some of the witnesses who were at the casino when your brother was shot," Una says carefully, as if her words are landing on the thin layer of a frozen lake.

"Okay." I wonder where she's going with this and why they were talking to old witnesses after Valdemar's release and not before.

"We spoke to Sergeant Psyche, the first officer on the scene," Una replies, clearly testing the ice, watching for a tiny crack. "He's very old now, retired for some years."

She's stalling, which makes me nervous. She'd been so eager to get here, to speak to me, dragging Pierre against his will, but now that the words are forming, she seems to be having doubts.

"We were going for a piece on how the people who witnessed the shooting felt about the release of Valdemar Montresor," Una goes on.

"I get why you were there," I say, now understanding how impactful this story would be. The headline flashes before me: *Cop's Trauma Relived as Monster Montresor Released*. It would have made a great companion piece.

"We started with the obvious stuff. How was he feeling about it all? Did he believe that he'd served his time? Did he think there was something wrong with the justice system? You know the drill." She twirls her hand as she recites the questions as if she's thrown a fishing line out and is reeling it in with the answers hooked on the end. "I know I said he was retired, and when some people retire, they can tend to lose their marbles a bit, their minds not as fresh as they used to be, but I think something like that would stay with you. You would picture it in your head every day for the rest of your life."

The dream is still fresh on the fringes of my mind. It's clear Valdemar hasn't forgotten any of that day.

"I get what you're saying, but can you please just tell me what this is about?" I ask.

Una glances at Pierre, who purses his lips as if to tell her she got herself into this, so now she needs to be the one to get herself out of it.

"It was his answers. They weren't what Dupin and I were expecting," Una says.

"What do you mean?" I fold my arms.

"Dupin was asking him the questions, and I was packing away my camera, as we'd done the photos first, the sun having been in the perfect position through his front window. He kept fidgeting with his hands like he had worry beads in them and glancing over his shoulder.

"When Dupin asked him how he felt about Montresor's release, he started out saying the obvious, that he'd done his time and the public had to have faith in the justice system, but then he went on to say it was a relief." Una's eyes narrow, a quizzical look overtaking her.

"Dupin had also noted the oddness in the answer but ploughed on, maybe thinking the same as I was, that the guy wasn't as sharp as he used to be. But then Dupin asked him if he felt safe with Montresor walking around, and he said he hasn't felt safe for the past ten years, so some things never change. Again, not the most obvious answer, but for the sake of trying to rescue the interview, Dupin pushed on and asked him if he thought ten years was long enough to atone for taking a man's life.

"The silence that followed felt never-ending, and I thought he wasn't going to answer, but eventually, he said that he hadn't atoned in ten years, so he wouldn't expect anyone else to. *He* hadn't atoned. Not Montresor. *Him.*"

Normally, I would be hot on the trail of what Una has told me, my journalist nose to the ground to pick up the scent, but my brain is mush, overloaded by recent revelations. I almost feel like laughing. I'm not sure I can carry anything else right now; my head is full to the brim, and I don't quite feel like myself anymore. It's not unlike how I felt after Ed had died, like the world was carrying on around me and I was just floating, letting the world unravel.

Pierre breaks the silence, disrupting my thoughts. "I told her it was nothing. Just the ramblings of a retired cop who probably has early-onset dementia or something."

"No, it didn't feel like that," Una argues. "Dupin then changed tack and asked him what he could remember about the shooting. He was evasive, told us he couldn't remember the details, and when Dupin pushed him, he shut down, claiming he didn't have long before he needed to get ready for an appointment."

"So, what are you saying?" I ask.

Una looks me dead in the eye as if she's holding a camera and lining up the lens. "I'm saying I think something about that shoot-out isn't ringing true."

"Like what?" But I already have my suspicions. I can still feel the dream, Valdemar's arms wrapped around my waist as the gun was taken from my hand.

"I don't know. All I know is that there's something here, something worth looking at," she says.

Pierre attempts to ease the tension. "I've told her this is a waste of time. It's just an old guy losing his memory. It *was* ten years ago, after all."

"If there was just someone else we could talk to, someone who was there who might be able to shed some light on what actually happened, but there's no one." Una shakes her head.

"There is someone," I say.

"There is?" Una's eyes light up as Pierre rolls his. "Who?"

I just stare at her, no words needed as her face drops.

"You can't be serious."

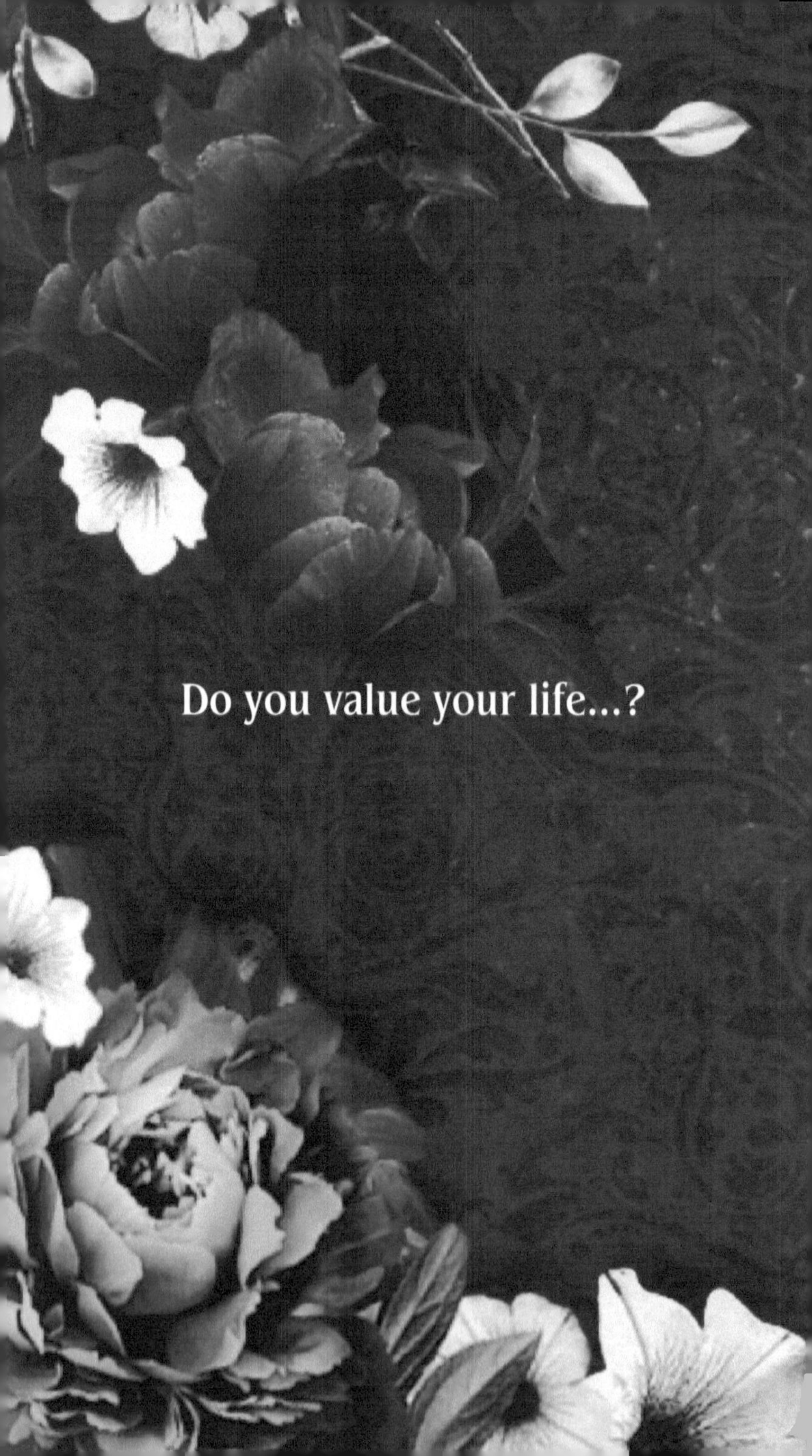

Do you value your life...?

CHAPTER FORTY-FOUR

the weird cop." Pierre throws his hands in the air, staring Una down through his long lashes. "You never said anything about trying to arrange a meet and greet with Valdemar Montresor."

Una holds her hand up to silence him. "It's a great idea, Evangeline, but I don't have those kinds of contacts, and I'm not sure he would be willing to talk to us even if we had a means of asking him."

I'm asking for trouble when I grab my phone from the table and unlock the screen. There's no need to search for his number, as there are already five missed calls from him.

Last night's dream comes back to me.

He'll have wanted to talk to me after that.

His arms were around me, *both* of them, and then there was the noise of the gun going off. It doesn't make any sense.

I dial.

"What are you doing?" Una asks. "Do you have a contact who can reach him? If you do, Dupin will be chomping at the bit for it."

It rings once before he answers.

"I've been trying to call you all morning. Please tell me you're okay," Valdemar says, his words rushing down the line.

"We need to talk." Avoiding Una's gaze, I settle my eyes on the floor, trying to keep my voice neutral and vague.

"Of course. Is everything okay?"

"We just need to talk," I repeat.

"I'll be there in twenty minutes."

It would be so much easier for him to come to us, but there's no way I'm telling Una or Pierre that Valdemar Montresor has been to my apartment.

"No. We'll come to you," I tell him.

"We?"

"I'll explain when we arrive. I take it you're home?"

"Yes. Shall I send Abel?" he offers.

"No. We'll drive," I say.

Ending the call, I drag in a lungful of air and prepare myself for Una's onslaught.

"I'll quickly get dressed, and then we can go," I announce.

Pushing myself out of the chair, I feel two pairs of eyes on me.

"Where the hell are we going, and who did you call?" Una asks, following me across the kitchen.

Unless I want her to come with me while I dress, I'll have to just spit it out.

"I called Valdemar Montresor. We're going to his house."

They glare at me like I've suddenly proclaimed I'm the Virgin Mary and carrying the son of God in my womb.

"You wanted answers," I remind them. Then I step out of the kitchen and into my bedroom.

THE THREE OF US ARE STUFFED INTO PIERRE'S TINY CAR AS WE pull up to the front of Corvus House, Una's mouth not having closed since we set off.

Why the hell do I have Valdemar Montresor's number?

Have I called him before?

How many times did I go visit him in prison?

How the hell do I know where he lives?

Question after question. I was just glad she didn't ask me if I'd fucked him. Her curiosity knows no bounds, but I know she's feeling hurt. I've shut her out, which I shouldn't have done, but there was no way I could have dealt with her disappointment in me that I've been fraternising with the enemy. But *is* he the enemy? I've always thought so. Now, I'm not so sure.

Where I could, I answered vaguely, not committing to anything other than the fact that we've talked.

"Why is the life of crime so fruitful?" Pierre muses as he kills the engine and stares up at the mansion.

Una and I remain silent, her appearing to take in the grandeur of the exterior and me trying not to recall the last time I was at this house.

A black car is parked in front of us, and as we climb out, Abel comes into view, polishing the bonnet.

On seeing me, he tips his cap. "Miss Bransby. Nice to see you again."

"Hey, Abel," I say.

Burn holes are boring into the back of my jacket, and I presume Una's stare is the cause.

"Abel? Nice to see you again?" she hisses, picking up her pace on the steps so she's level with me. "What the fuck is going on here, Evangeline?"

"Trust me, you don't want to know." It's the only thing I can give her.

"Oh, I really do," she says.

"Leave it, will you," Pierre tells Una, shivering as he glances at the gargoyles at the top of the steps. "This place gives me the creeps."

"I'm sure Evangeline will give us a guided tour, seeing as she's been here before. Seriously, what's going on? I don't understand you at all anymore."

"Then stop trying to." I immediately feel awful for snapping at my friend, but she's relentless, and how can I answer her when I don't understand it myself?

There's no one on the door, but a camera mounted above the lintel flashes as we gather underneath its gaze. There's a buzz and a click before the door is opened by Jupiter.

"You again. And you brought backup," he says.

"We're here to see Valdemar," I say with a confidence I didn't have the last time I saw him.

He steps to the side, and I can feel Una itching to ask more questions, but Jupiter leads us into the foyer, where he deposits us.

"I'll tell him you're here." Jupiter disappears up the stairs.

What would Una say if I told her I'd been in Valdemar's bedroom, in his bed, under his sheets, and under his body? Positive her opinion of me would sink further than it already has, I keep this to myself.

Una and Pierre gawk at the open foyer, the grand staircase before them, and the large fresco window in the landing area. They're seeing this for the first time—the opulence, the beauty.

Then their bodies tense as if a dark cloud has blown in overhead and they're bracing themselves for the storm to unleash, whereas my body melts in the presence of the man before me.

Hands in his pockets, Valdemar strides down the staircase, his eyes on me and only me, and I wonder how he's going to play this.

As if answering, he touches the small of my elbow and plants a light kiss on my cheek. "Angel." He delivers it as a whisper, though loud enough for both Pierre and Una to hear.

Fuck.

Una positively hops on her toes, and Pierre just stares.

"Are you going to introduce me to our guests?" Valdemar says.

Our guests, like we're hosting an event as a pair.

"These are my work colleagues." I step out of his embrace, trying to maintain some professionalism. "This is Pierre Zanthe, a reporter for the *Amontillado Gazette*, and Una Ligeia, our photographer."

He nods in their direction.

"And I need no introduction," Valdemar says.

For the first time this morning, Una is speechless.

"We just want to ask you some questions," I tell him.

"Is this going in the paper?" he asks.

"No," I answer quickly, eyeing Una and Pierre, who nod in agreement. "This is something personal."

"Then where would you like to do this? In the library?" He smirks.

"No," I snap, my cheeks heating at the suggestion, the memory of what he did to me in there making me quiver. "Not the library."

"Fine. The drawing room, then." Turning, Valdemar leads us through a door to the left of the stairs.

"Why not the library?" Pierre hisses in my ear. "Is it haunted or something?"

"Yes. It's haunted," I tell him, glad of the lie he's provided.

"Never mind the ghosts," Una joins in. "You have a hell of a lot of explaining to do, *angel.*"

She delivers the endearment as if she's a hissing cat, her words sharp. She's upset. Of course she is. I've lied to her, kept things from her, shut her out when she's been there for me for the last five years. She's bound to be hurting, and just like I do in the same situation, she's lashing out at me.

Even during daylight, the house breeds darkness all its own as we're led down a small hallway, eventually reaching a door that opens into a large drawing room.

Like the rest of the house, its décor is rich and threatening, with dark upholstery, bevelled edges, and polished mahogany. A grand piano sits by the window, the lid propped open, the stool pulled out slightly as if someone has just been playing.

Valdemar motions for us to sit on one of the many chairs and sofas in the room, all of them a deep navy brocade decorated with shimmery red embroidery and strategically placed around a fire that exudes warmth despite it not being lit.

I don't trust myself or Valdemar's hands, so, like teenagers facing the headteacher, Una, Pierre, and I squash onto a sofa, me in the middle. Valdemar takes the sofa opposite us, his huge frame casting a shadow over us.

"How can I help you?" Valdemar asks, his eyes settled on me.

When it appears as though Una and Pierre have lost their tongues, I answer. "We just want some answers to some questions about the night my brother died."

My choice of words is purposeful. I don't want to anger him into shutting down. I would probably have been better off having this conversation with him in private, but then I would still have had to explain things to Una, and I know what happens when I'm alone with Valdemar—no questions would have been answered at all, only new ones raised.

"I'll try, but that depends on the questions," he says.

"What happened that night at the casino?" I delve right in.

Valdemar eyes me with caution. "You know what happened."

"I know what you told me. What I want to know is what *really* happened."

"You don't believe the reports?" He sits forwards, resting his elbows on his knees.

Pierre flinches next to me, and Una hovers on the edge of the sofa.

"You said yourself that there's no truth in any of the witness statements." Before he can react, I add, "And when I think back to our conversations, you've never said the words to me. Never admitted to pulling the trigger."

Valdemar raises an eyebrow.

"Una spoke with Sergeant Psyche," I tell him.

He scratches his chin. "How is he?"

"Old and retired. His memory is a little fuzzy."

"I'm sure it is," Valdemar says.

"You see, that's what strikes us as odd. You'd think something like the murder of a young man would stay with him forever. It's not the kind of thing you forget. Yet he has. He can't remember what happened. Can't recall the details, and some of his answers were, shall we say, a little off," I tell him.

"Off?" Valdemar furrows his brow.

"Yeah, off. So, we would like to know why that is. Why his memory of that day is so hard to retrieve when I'm sure you remember it like it was yesterday."

His jaw clenches. Pierre shifts uneasily.

Then Una speaks, her voice not as strong as it normally is. "We just want to know if there's something you might not have told Evangeline. Something that maybe you forgot." She's clearly scared that I've pushed Valdemar, a convicted murderer, and I'm afraid I have also, but for an entirely different reason.

"Do you value your life, Miss…?" Valdemar stares at Una, taking command of the room in the way only he can.

"Ligeia," she answers.

"Ligeia." He holds her gaze, and I can relate, as I know what it feels like to be held by him.

"Of course I do," Una replies.

"And you, Pierre Zanthe." Valdemar's gaze shifts. "Do you value your life?"

"Yes," Pierre answers with fear in his eyes.

"And you, angel—I know you don't value yours, but I do. So, I'm telling the three of you to drop it."

My blood runs cold.

"What happened on that night is exactly what the police report and the witness statements say, and that's all you need to know. So, unless there's anything else I can be of assistance with, I think this interview is over."

"I didn't think he would help us," Una whispers loudly to me.

"Oh, I am helping you, Una Ligeia. I'm helping you all to stay alive," Valdemar says.

"Thank you for your time," Pierre says abruptly, rising from the sofa, clearly desperate to leave.

"Wait. I'm not done yet." I grab hold of Pierre's arm, my dream coming back to me.

The gun in my hand.

The gun was taken out of my hand.

The shot was fired while Valdemar's arms were wrapped around my waist.

Both of his arms. Both of his hands.

His dream. His memory.

In his dream, I am him. I'm holding the gun. I'm the one who couldn't pull the trigger until someone took the gun from my hand.

His hand.

"You might not be willing to answer our questions, but that doesn't stop us from answering them for you," I say.

"Don't." Valdemar moves to the edge of the seat, his eyes

boring into me, pleading with me not to go there. But I have to do this. I've lived with this for so long, and I came to him for answers, but all he's given me is fiction. It's time to fill in the blanks.

"You were there that night. You held the gun to my brother's head, and you tried to kill him. He begged you to, but you couldn't do it, could you?"

"Angel." He tries to sound stern, but his eyes are watering, the memory too fierce to overcome.

"You didn't pull the trigger. Someone else did. And you took the fall just like everyone else took the bribe. All of you. Who would be worth that? Who has the power to buy so many voices? Who do you fear enough to lock yourself away for ten years for a murder you didn't commit?"

I stare at Valdemar, the man who I thought had ruined my life, the man who I now see lost his own life as much as I lost mine.

"Who pulled the trigger, Valdemar? Because I know it wasn't you."

He can't tell me.

CHAPTER FORTY-FIVE

"Guys, I think we should leave, like, now," Pierre says, pulling his sleeve out of my grip. "I, for one, don't want to know any of this and am going to pretend I was never here, as I have a date at the weekend, and I intend to make said date."

"But what about—" Una begins, but Pierre cuts her off.

"What about ending the week in a body bag? No, thanks. You heard what the guy said." He gestures towards Valdemar, speaking as though he can't hear him. "Does he look like a guy you want to disagree with? He told us to drop it. Now let's do just that and get the hell out of here."

Una glances at Pierre and then at me.

"You coming?" she asks, her shoulders dropping in defeat.

Tearing my gaze from Valdemar, I blink at Una. "You guys go."

She reaches for me. "I'm not leaving you here alone."

"She won't be alone," Valdemar cuts in.

"And that's my worry," Una tells him.

"For God's sake, Una, can we just leave already?" Pierre steps forwards, gesturing to the exit.

"It's fine. I'll be fine," I tell them, staring at Valdemar.

I can feel Una's uncertainty, the internal tussle with herself about whether to leave me here with a convicted criminal. He may not have murdered my brother, but he has murdered others.

"If anything happens to her, I swear to God…," Una hisses at Valdemar, not finishing her proclamation.

"I can assure you, she'll be safe here. I, however, might not be." He smiles at her. "I'll show you both out."

He leads them to the door, and I'm left alone, the stillness of the drawing room wrapping itself around me.

Savouring this moment before Valdemar returns, I contemplate what I've just learned.

Someone shot my brother.

But it wasn't Valdemar.

From his reaction to my guessing game and what I saw in his dream, I know he tried. He held the gun aloft and aimed. But he didn't pull the trigger.

So who did?

Rising, I pace the floor, wishing the fire was lit so I could ponder against the backdrop of its flames like Sherlock Holmes or some other famous detective on the hunt for a killer.

The obvious answer is Adolphe Fortunato. He was the only other man of influence there, a man with enough connections in this city to pull the strings. Ed knew Fortunato planned to kill him, condemning him to a slow and painful death of being bricked up behind a wall while still alive like so many other people who had crossed him. But then why would he shoot him? Did he take the shot when he saw Valdemar falter and then insist that Valdemar take the blame? That could be the case. What other possible solution is there?

"It was Adolphe Fortunato, wasn't it?" I fire the question at Valdemar as soon as he returns.

He closes the door softly, his face grave, his colour drained. "As much as I want to tell you everything, angel, I can't."

"Can't or won't?" I ask.

"Can't."

"Why? Because I might die?" I suggest.

"No, I *can't* tell you."

I stare at him. The way he said the word *can't* is humming on the inside of my ear canal.

"Can't," I repeat, more softly, my eyes narrowing. "Did you make some sort of bargain? An oath?"

"More than that," he says.

Valdemar takes the seat opposite me, a longing now in his expression. He wants me to know. He wants me to guess because he can't tell me.

He *can't* tell me.

"You're bound by something—something you can't break. What happens if you break the oath?"

"Nothing happens. Listen to what I'm saying, angel." He scootches to the edge of the sofa, his knees square, leaning towards me. "I *can't* tell you."

Like with the word games Ed and I used to play as kids, I toss the sentence around before the clarity of it hits me.

"You can't physically say the words, can you?" I ask.

Valdemar closes his eyes.

"Oh my God, what is it? Is it magic or something?"

"Or something. Ancient. Beyond the realms of our understanding."

"But not the realms of Adolphe Fortunato." My eyes roam the drawing room, taking in nothing as this revelation settles. "No wonder he's such a powerful man with so many people in his pocket. Is he some kind of magician?"

"Not him," Valdemar says.

I take note of the simple answers, each one seeming to take such an effort, as if the spell he's under is aware of the topic of conversation and is keeping a tight leash on it.

"Then who?" My forehead knots, but even before the question is out, I can see Adolphe Fortunato and his sidekick. They're never without each other. And they were both there that night, in the very room with my brother and Valdemar when the gun went off.

"Dr Tem-Pest? He's the magic wielder?" I guess.

I'm met with silence, which I take as confirmation. Dr Tem-Pest is the conjuror. He's the one who bewitched Valdemar, Jupiter, and Jacinta.

"So, who killed Ed, Adolphe Fortunato or Dr Tem-Pest?"

Valdemar gulps as if the answer is lodged in the back of his throat.

"You can't even answer questions about it, can you?" I say.

He stares at me as if he's trying to project his thoughts.

"How did you manage to make a statement, to talk to me about it at the prison? I don't understand." I shake my head, all the possibilities loose and jangling about in my brain.

He runs his hands through his hair before he speaks, his words heavy. "I shot your brother. It was me. I held the gun and shot him. It was my bullet. My gun."

Staring at him, I try to see through his words. "You're programmed in some way to tell the same version of events that everyone else was, the magic somehow enchanting you to tell that version and only that version. Am I right?"

He smiles.

"You can only say what Dr Tem-Pest planted in your head somehow?"

Another smile.

"Shit. There has to be a way to cheat this." Rubbing my palms together, I stand and stalk the room as Valdemar watches me. "Okay, let's try this. There was this story I heard once about a famous poet who, one day, went out fishing on his boat, but he died while out on the water. His boat was washed up on the shore a few days later, smashed to pieces, his body arriving with it. The townsfolk had no idea what had happened to him, unsure as to whether a great storm had killed him or the tyrannical sea serpent that the locals feared. Have you heard this story?"

The corner of Valdemar's mouth rises. He knows what I'm doing. A tempest is another word for storm, and he referred to Fortunato as a serpent during one of our early meetings.

"Quite the wordsmith. I haven't heard this particular story, but if I were to advise the townsfolk of anything, it would be not to forget the fair maiden," Valdemar says.

"The fair maiden?" My eyes narrow as if trying to see beneath his words.

"In stories like these, there's always a fair maiden," he repeats.

Pressing my hands to my temples, I squeeze, trying to force my brain to follow what he's saying. A fair maiden. A woman. But who? The only other woman who was there that I know of was Jacinta.

"Jacinta?" It doesn't feel right, and I can tell by Valdemar's face that I'm in the wrong place even when he remains silent, the words unable to form. "No. Not Jacinta. Then who?"

I pace the room again before Valdemar takes my hand and leads me back to the sofa.

"You look tired," he says.

I glance at him, thinking I must look anything but tired. My brain is wired like I've just downed three espressos and chased them with an energy drink.

"Why don't we go to bed?" he suggests.

I glare at him. "What? Are you kidding me? You're thinking about sex while I'm trying to work out who killed my brother?"

"Sleep, angel. You need sleep. And so do I."

"I don't need sleep. I need answers, and you can't give me them." My voice pitches an octave, annoyed at being so close yet still so far from the truth.

"Can't I? You were so close last night, angel. So close." He whispers the last two words.

My eyes widen as the penny drops. "Your dream."

"I'm not certain, but I've been wondering if you've been crossing into my dreams because, subconsciously, I've been letting you, it being the only way I could show you what happened that night." He takes my hand. "Let's go to sleep."

He leads me through the rear door, and we make our way up to his room.

"I'm not in the least bit tired," I tell him.

"I could wear you out if you'd like."

I roll my eyes. "Very funny. Seriously, though, I don't think I'm going to be able to sleep."

"Don't worry, I'll help—and not in the way you think," he says.

As we reach his room, he enters first and closes the heavy curtains, blocking out the low winter sun. The room softens as if convinced it's night-time. He lights a candle in the corner that emits a lulling glow, the flicker of the flame hypnotic against the dim backdrop.

"Come." He beckons me over to his bed.

After kicking my shoes off, I climb on, and he does the same on the other side, so naturally, like we do this every night.

I lie on my side, the soft mattress sighing beneath me as Valdemar pulls me into him.

He strokes my face, pushing my hair from my eyes and smoothing my skin.

"You just need to relax. Shut your brain down. Stop thinking, and sleep will come. You didn't sleep properly last night, and you're so tired. So very tired. You just need to sleep, angel. Sleep." His heady voice settles in the room, the purr of his vowels and the lull of the consonants convincing me that he's right. I am, in fact, so very, very sleepy.

And I'm back in the prison visitors' room, back to when he held me so tightly and I wished, more than anything, that he hadn't killed my brother because there was no other place I felt safer, no other place I'd have rather been than cradled in his arms.

But he didn't kill my brother.

He didn't kill him.

He didn't.

So, who did?

There's a determination in my step this time, like I know where I'm going and what lies ahead, and as much as I don't want to face it, I have to get there.

The red of the carpet is deeper than I remember, almost black as the mud begins to seep from beneath the material and floods between my toes. I let go of the glass, knowing I don't need it, craving to hold the gun in my hand.

I need to see this time.

Need to watch.

Ed is before me, the mighty rope restraining him, but rather than focussing on his tortured face, I look around.

A serpent rises next to Ed, a storm brewing overhead as clouds thicken above us, lightning striking against the bleak backdrop.

"No!" I shout, but it isn't my voice that calls the word.

The serpent moves forwards, its tongue darting from its pursed lips, its eyes regarding the audience.

"Hussssshh," it hisses. "It issss for the bessssst. For what did one exxxxxpect?"

"But I love him."

It's a female voice, but not my own. I search the darkness, but there's no one there apart from the serpent, Ed, and me.

The gun shakes in my hand as Ed pleads with me, silently praying I will end his suffering as the bricks appear at his feet, one on top of another, cement lining them, the wall growing higher as more bricks are placed.

Ed's mouth forms the words.

"Do it. Do it now."

My finger slips against the trigger, my mind pleading with me to put him out of his misery, to end this torture.

The scream swells in my throat, and as it does, the gun is pulled from my hand.

And instead of closing my eyes, I look to my right.

A pale, slender hand takes the gun from me, aims it at Ed, and fires.

The serpent recoils, a hiss emanating from it as if it's the one that's been shot, but it's Ed who slumps to the floor.

Dark hair billows around her tiny frame as she darts over to Ed. She's young, beautiful, and bereft.

"I love you. I will always love you," she tells Ed, cradling his face in her hands, the gun still clutched in her fingers. "And if we cannot be together in life, then let us be together in death." She holds the gun to her temple, but the lightning strikes it from her hand as the serpent coils itself around her and drags her from Ed's body.

Fingers intertwine with mine as Valdemar takes my hand, the pair of us watching the scene unfold.

"I will never allow a daughter of mine to fornicate with a Raven Hand. Never. And sssshe will not bear the weight of hissss death. That burden will be yoursssss." The serpent turns to me. "You

sssshot him. You will pay the pricccccce and forever hold your tongue." At his words, the lightning strikes again, this time hitting my core and surging through my body, the current flowing with lies.

At the hiss of his last word, the serpent coils in on itself, the woman vanishes, and the storm blows over. Only Ed remains, his lifeless body limp on the floor.

And then he moves.

My eyes widen as Ed sits up and stares at the blackness surrounding him until he sees me.

Valdemar releases my hand.

"Go to him," he tells me.

Slipping from his grasp, I make my way over to my brother, my heart beating against my chest. Blood drips from the gunshot wound, and the smell of gunpowder hangs in the air.

Fear coats my skin that Ed will not recognise me, but he reaches out for my hand as I come near.

"Ed?"

"Evan." His voice is just as I remember, soft and mystical, like he has the answers to everything, and the nickname that only he has ever called me because he decided Evangeline was too much of a mouthful sounds so sweet. "I've missed you."

"I've missed you too." Biting my lip, I hold back the tears.

"It's been so long."

"Too long."

His skin is pale, almost translucent, and I feel a sudden fear that he'll fade before my eyes, disappearing once again into the blackness.

"I have so many questions."

"I'm sure you do, so I'll try and tell you all I can. We don't have long," he says softly. "I met her when I started working at the casino. She was on the floor one night, dressed in a light sundress, her fingers drifting over the machines as she looked at everything and nothing.

She wasn't a gambler, and I knew she wasn't staff, but truth be told, I didn't know what she was—I just knew I needed to find out. So, I went over, introduced myself, and asked her if I could help her with anything. She was a mystery, a whisper on the wind, and I was intoxicated from the moment I laid eyes on her and every night after that.

"It was after I fell in love with her, completely and irrevocably in love, that I learned her name. Annabel Lee, daughter of Adolphe Fortunato. And I saw it, the sadness she was living with, the isolation, how he'd shrunk her world so small, she barely fit in it. She was a fair maiden, destined for greatness but locked in a tower by her cruel father. And I vowed I would help her. I would be her knight in shining armour. I would kill her father and rescue her.

"I told Valdemar what I suspected about the spiked drinks and got him on board with taking out Adolphe Fortunato.

"That part of the story is true. The Raven Hands came to the casino, Jacinta pretended to have had a reaction to the drugs in one of the drinks, and I was on hand to ensure the rest of the plan unfolded, but as you know, things didn't quite work out as I'd hoped because Fortunato knew. He'd been spying on Annabel, and he knew all about our relationship and our plan to be together. So, he stepped in, his henchmen seizing me, and told Annabel she would never see me again. I'd told her to stay away, but she was never one for following instructions, another thing I loved about her.

"Then Valdemar arrived and drew his gun, and I knew there was only one way this would end, and I wanted it to be by his bullet rather than behind bricks and cement where I would choke on the thinning air and claw at the darkness. I asked him to shoot me, but he couldn't. The Blood Oath was too strong to allow him to take my life. So, Annabel did, telling me that we would be together in death.

"But that didn't happen. Hasn't happened." Ed stalls as if the pain of all this is too much for him to continue speaking.

I try to help out. *"Dr Tem-Pest knocked the gun from her hand. She's not dead."*

"Yes, he took the gun from her before she could kill herself. After my death, Fortunato had her locked away in a secure unit. Only doctors and nurses were allowed to see her, but one night, I heard her calling my name like she was close but not close enough. It was like she was just over my shoulder. She was looking for me. Through the bond, I asked Valdemar to find out what had happened to her, so he set some Raven Hands off with the task. They told him she'd somehow escaped the hospital and had walked right out into the Maelstrom and kept going until she was fully submerged, her body washing up on the shoreline the next day. My beautiful girl had finally managed to take her life to be with me in death."

"So, she found you?" I ask.

His face drains, his lips dropping. *"No. Because of the Blood Oath, I'm tied to Valdemar, unable to leave his side. She now wanders the unearthly realms heartbroken, calling my name. I hear her, every night, every day, searching for me, but she can't find me, and I can't find her."*

My mother pops into my head, how, even in death, she's always smiling, her face serene like she's at peace with the world, and I realise this is because she's not alone. She's with my father, her one true love. In death, they found each other and are now content in the afterlife, where love knows no bounds.

Ed's face is nothing like my mother's. He's tortured, his shoulders racked with restlessness, his eyes constantly searching. He's lost.

"How can I help you find her?" I ask. *"What do you need me to do?"*

"You know what I need you to do," Ed says, his eyes darkening. *"I told Valdemar to ask you to visit him, told him to write you a letter."*

"Oh my God," I gasp. *"You asked me to kill him?"*

"It's the only way to release me from the Blood Oath. The only way for me to find my love and for me to be at peace. No one else

would do this for me. Only you. I'm begging you. You're my only hope."

His frame shimmers, fading before my eyes.

"There must be another way," I cry.

"You are a Raven Hand, Evan. It's what we do. Now it's time for you to fulfil your role. And there is no other way."

But so much has changed.
I have changed.

CHAPTER FORTY-SIX

THE ROOM SPILLS INTO MY VISION, REPLACING THE DARKNESS where Ed was just standing.

He's gone.

Valdemar is next to me on the bed, his hand resting on mine.

Pulling my hand from his grasp, I sit up, and so does he.

"Ed was there. He spoke to me," I tell him, a little breathless by what I've just witnessed.

"I know," he says.

"You saw it?"

He nods, his eyes watering, his face stoic.

"Then you know what he's asked me to do," I say.

"I've always known, and he's right. It's the only way."

"There must be another way." My words rush out quickly, quicker than I thought they would. Seven weeks ago, I'd have gladly thrust a knife through his chest to get revenge on the man who killed my brother.

But so much has changed.

I have changed.

I'm not who I thought I was. And neither is Valdemar.

Because Valdemar did not kill my brother.

My perspective has shifted. Priorities changed. Life is not about the past or how to contain it. Life is for living—and not living it alone.

Ed wants me to kill Valdemar.

"This was the plan all along. Ed asked you to ask me to kill you. And you did, that night at the party. You asked me to kill you, but then you gave me a choice. Why did you do that?"

"What I said that night was the truth. Before I met you, I would have happily fallen on a blade to end Ed's suffering, but he told me it had to be you who took my life. He knew what was supposed to happen. But that night in the library, I was selfish. I wanted you. I still want you."

"And what is it you want now?" I ask.

Valdemar raises his eyebrow as if this wasn't the question he was expecting. I wonder if anyone has ever asked him what he wants.

"I want you to be happy," he replies.

"Why?"

"Because that's all that matters to me now," he says softly.

I understand this, of course—because I just want Ed to be happy. But that's because I love him.

My eyes shoot to his as something jolts through my chest, the sharp piercing of a foreign object.

Love.

It all boils down to love.

Ellison Rue's love for my mother.

My father's love for Ellison.

My love for Ed.

Ed's love for Annabel Lee.

And now….

It's a vicious circle. Each of us wanting to make the other happy out of sheer, blinding love.

Valdemar reaches for the bedside table, opens the drawer, and pulls out the knife I brought the other night.

"Ed said I was a Raven Hand," I say.

"You are."

His words are like confirmation. Me, a Raven Hand. I'm part of this. I have been all along. My curse of seeing the dead has been my gift, just like Ed's gift, just like Valdemar's and all the other Raven Hands. But I'm a woman.

"I thought women couldn't be Raven Hands," I say.

"You said so yourself how outdated that rule is, brought in during the early days when men ruled the world and women made sure it didn't fall apart. Times change. Things change. The Raven Hands need to change, and I believe you are the one to make that happen. When I met Ed, I thought it was him, that he was destined to make the Raven Hands become something more than just a motley crew of disgruntled men who weren't happy with the way the city was being overrun by lawlessness, but soon after we took the Blood Oath, I realised it wasn't him at all, but you. I felt you through the bond, could feel you through Ed, and I knew then that you were destined for great things."

My pulse floods my ears, the deafening pummel of blood rushing through my veins reminding me I'm alive, that this is real and not another dream I've stepped into. But this is how it feels, dreamlike, ethereal, as if Valdemar has been brought to me on the wings of a raven.

"What are you saying?" My words are slow, laden with uncertainty. I've always thought my ability to see the dead has been a curse, something to be afraid of even though it's never scared me. But now…. Is this really what this is about, what it's all been about? The fact that I am and always have been a Raven Hand?

"I'm saying there are hundreds of women throughout history who have been blessed, cursed—call it what you want

—with gifts and should have had the sanctuary of the Raven Hands to help support them in making a difference, using their gifts to make the world a better place. But they've been denied this chance. Your mother was one of them."

"My mother?"

"She had a gift, I'm sure. That's why she ended up with your father, here at Corvus House. But she would never have been allowed into the fold, and that needs to change. And you, my angel, have the power to make that change."

I'm about to challenge him. How can little old me make such a change? How can I bring about such a monumental turning of history, something women may have tried and failed to do before me? What makes me so special?

Then it dawns on me. It's not what I have or what makes me special—it's about the choice I have before me and whether I act upon it.

"You told me that if another Raven Hand kills the head of the Ravens, then they become the new leader."

Valdemar runs his finger over the blade, his lips curling at the corner.

"So, if I kill you, I inherit your title, and I become the new leader of the Raven Hands," I guess.

"The first ever female Raven Hand and their new leader."

Pressure pushes down on my shoulders. I could make a difference, give a voice to all the women who have lived with gifts yet gone neglected all these years, give them a chance of help and support in dealing with whatever gift they've been born with. The Raven Hands could be something different. They could be a whole lot more than the vigilante group they've become. They could take back the city that once belonged to them. And I could make that happen. I have the power to change things for the better.

All I have to do is kill the man before me. The man whom I've grown to care about, the man who makes me feel safe, the man who has shown me my true self. The man who, right now, has my heart thoroughly in his grasp.

Valdemar places the knife in my hand, stroking my fingers as he rests it in my palm.

"This is no different from what I had to do to claim my title. To end someone's life at their request. I know you can do it. I believe in you," he tells me.

Ed appears at the side of the bed, reminding me that he's affected by this just as much as Valdemar. It's his eternity, his forever destination I have control of, not just the fate of the Raven Hands.

Fuck.

When did I become so important? When did the fate of others fall into my hands, hands that now wield a blade I must use?

There has to be another way.

What if Valdemar is right, and this is my destiny? This might be what I was born to do. And if so, I should know deep down what the right thing to do is. If I am to be the new leader of the Raven Hands, I must have some historical blood somewhere down the line that will show me the way, that will lead me to the right decision.

Closing my eyes, I inhale this new-found power. I let it run through my body, fill my lungs, and spread inside me.

This is me.

This is who I am.

For once, I am in charge.

And I must decide.

I don't hear their words,
but I don't need to.

CHAPTER FORTY-SEVEN

My life has been marred by death. Before I'd even taken my first lungful of air, I had murdered my mother, my father quickly following. Why do I always end up killing the ones I love? Why does it always have to end in death?

There must be another way.

I don't want to save my brother from eternal unrest by killing the man I've fallen in love with, the man I've given myself to, the man who has made me feel alive.

Valdemar's question comes back to me.

"And if I hadn't killed your brother?"

And my response hits me full force in the chest.

"Then I would be falling at your feet."

He didn't kill my brother. He couldn't pull the trigger back then any more than I could pull it in the dream.

And it comes to me, the answer I've been searching for to the question Valdemar asked me. What will make me happy? What is the only outcome that would deliver my happiness?

Snapping my eyes open, I find Valdemar and Ed staring at me, waiting, watching as I clutch the knife in my right hand, bracing myself.

"Open your shirt," I tell Valdemar.

He doesn't hide the gulp or the sadness in his eyes as he reaches for the buttons, his fingers releasing the material to reveal the smoothness of his chest.

I straddle him, his eyes never leaving mine as I run my hand along his skin, smoothing down the canvas I'm about to deface. Will it be the raven's head, a wing, or a tail the knife punctures?

"Quickly. Don't hesitate," Valdemar says, but as I place the knife on his skin, he grabs hold of my hand, his eyes widening before they soften. "Before you do this, I want you to know that I wish things could have been different. I wish I could have been someone else to you. I wish I could have been what you are to me."

I lean closer. "And what is that?"

His lips brush mine, his other hand gripping my thigh. "Everything."

As I drag the blade slowly across his chest, it punctures his skin, blood leaking from the open wound. I sit back slightly, admiring the colour and the richness of his blood as it runs down his body.

Keeping his attention trained on me, I ask him, "And what makes you think I don't feel the same about you?"

As Valdemar absorbs my question, its hidden meaning filtering through his brain, I slash my palm quickly with the blade, the sting making me feel alive.

His eyes go from my face to my palm, realisation not dawning on him quick enough to act before I place my hand against the open wound on his chest.

His eyes meet mine, wild, frenzied.

"What are you doing?" He tries to pull away, but the force of my hand pushes him back as I speak.

"I, Evangeline Bransby, swear the Blood Oath to you, Valdemar Montresor."

"No!" he cries.

The words come to me as if I've always known them and they've just been waiting for this moment. "I bind myself to you and you to me, body, mind, and soul, in life and in death, forever joined, releasing you from any previous Blood Oath you may have sworn."

I only just manage to finish before Valdemar launches himself up and pushes me back onto the bed, pinning my arms on either side of my head.

"What the fuck have you done?" he screams, his face contorted in rage.

"Exactly what I wanted to do," I tell him as he takes my hand that still grips the knife and holds it firmly, angling it towards the open wound on his chest.

Valdemar secures his grip, readying himself to fall on the blade. Struggling, I push myself up and try to pull the blade from him, but he's too strong.

Something drips into my body, a tingling sensation like warm water trickling through my veins and seeping into my extremities.

"Do you know how much harder this will be now? You will never be able to kill me once the Oath takes hold. It has to be now," he pleads.

But I already feel it, the heat upon my skin, the surge of his emotions enveloping me. He feels it too. So much so that he can't quite bring himself to thrust the blade into his chest.

Gritting his teeth, he tries to lean forwards onto the knife.

"Wait!" I yell, and he stops, like he's physically unable to ignore my command. "Look." I nod over his shoulder. He follows my gaze.

Ed is next to the bed, his image shimmering in tiny squares, as if the signal is bad. He's looking around, patting his body.

"I can see him," Valdemar says.

For a second, I'm confused, but then I remember Valdemar telling me that as he pointed the gun at my brother in the casino, he saw what Ed saw and received the vision as if Ed had handed his gift to him for the briefest of moments. Is that what's happened here? Is Valdemar receiving my gift and seeing the world through my eyes?

We watch as a woman materialises through the closed door. Her long black hair hangs damp around her shoulders, her white dress clings to her body, and water drips onto the floor as she makes her way over to the bed.

Ed sees her.

It's the strangest thing, like watching a silent film as they find each other, their embrace like a carefully choreographed dance that is beautiful and mesmerising. Annabel's clothes are drying, her hair is curling, and a pink tinge appears on her cheeks. Ed's bullet hole melts away, the blood disappears from his clothes, and his sad face finally looks serene, just like my mother's.

My heart erupts as they hold one another, gazing into each other's eyes, a sense of peace descending upon the room. I'm not sure how long they remain in each other's arms, but eventually they break apart and turn to face us, Ed standing behind Annabel, one arm wrapped around her waist, his other hand resting on her shoulder, just like my mother and father did yesterday in my kitchen.

I don't hear their words, but I don't need to.

Thank you.

I swipe at a stray tear as they smile before vanishing into thin air.

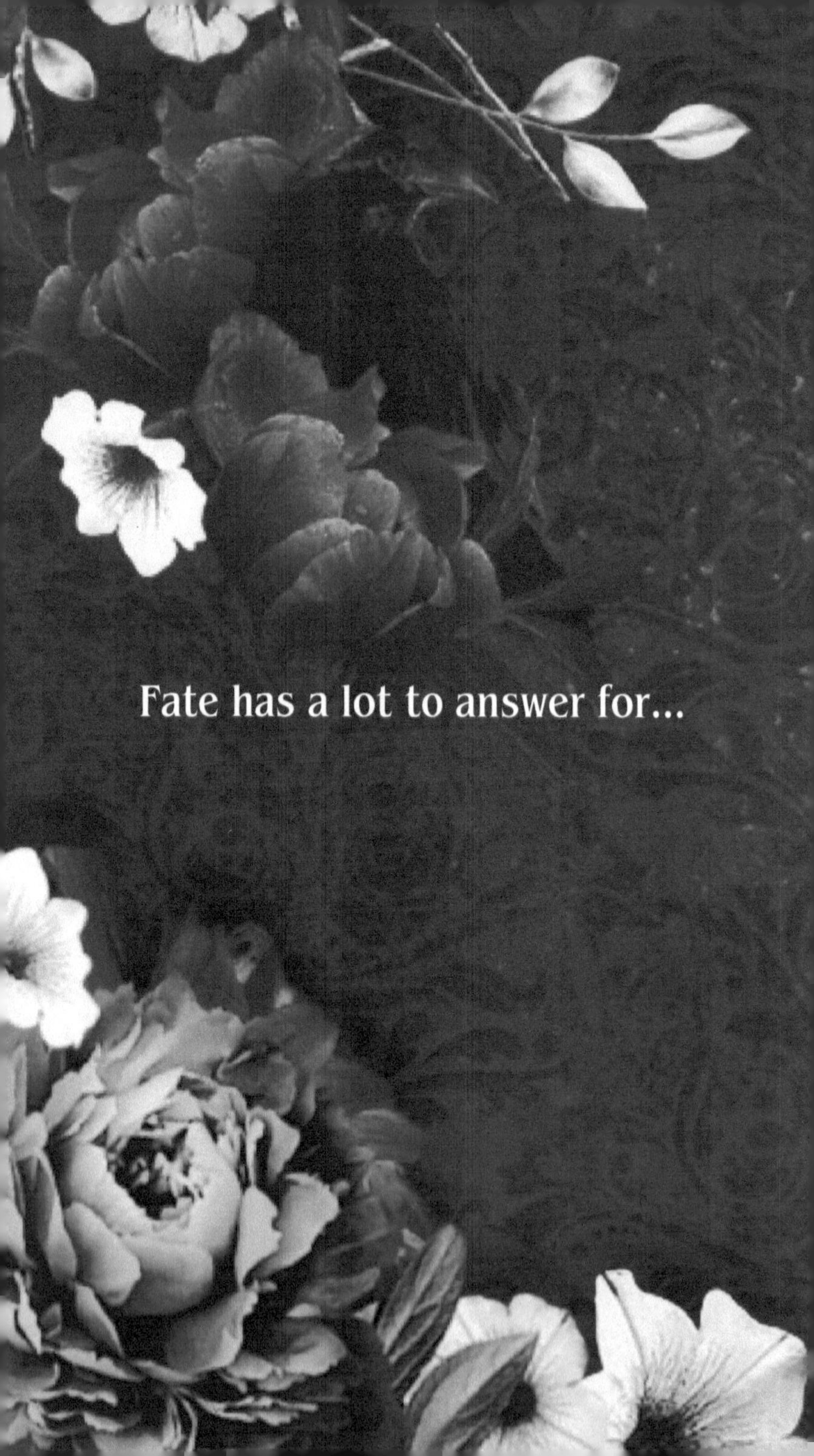

Fate has a lot to answer for...

CHAPTER FORTY-EIGHT

"It worked." The words slip out as Ed and Annabel dissolve, the room suddenly feeling less crowded.

"What do you mean, it worked?" Valdemar snaps. "You say it like you had no idea what you were doing."

"I didn't. Not really," I confess.

"Fuck." Valdemar drops my hand and the knife along with it and leans back on his heels, squeezing the bridge of his nose between his thumb and finger.

"It worked," I repeat with a little more force. "It released Ed, and now he's found Annabel. You're both free."

Dropping his arm, he glares at me, and a strange feeling washes through me. Anger, distress—but these emotions aren't mine. I'm relieved and overjoyed that my brother has found his true love and is now happy in the afterlife. The other emotions I feel are his—Valdemar's. It has to be the bond already working its magic, filling me with… him.

"He is free, angel. Ed is free. But *you* are not."

Gulping hard, I blink, trying to see past the temper that's erupted on his face and now tingles beneath my skin.

"You've bound us, angel. Do you even know what that means?"

"Yes. Yes, I know what it means. I'm not a fucking child. But what was the alternative? If I'd done nothing, then Ed would still be tethered to you in eternal unhappiness, and if I'd chosen yours and Ed's idea, then I would be sat here now, holding on to your dead fucking body."

"Instead, you're bound to my body for the rest of this life and the next," he says.

Fear washes over me, pain, anguish—a hurricane of emotions, some my own and some Valdemar's. He's everywhere. He's under my skin, behind my eyes, running through my veins, my heart pumping him around my body as if my life depends on him.

I stare into the wide eyes of the man who's consumed me day and night for the past seven weeks. The man who I thought had killed my brother. The only man who knew what it was like to be inside my brother's head.

"I am a twin. I already know what it's like to be tethered to someone. Ed and I were made in the same womb with the same blood. His pain was my pain, his joy was my joy, his life was my life until it wasn't anymore, and I had to survive on my own, something that doesn't come naturally to a twin. So, if you're asking me if I know how it feels to be bonded to someone, then I already know."

Tearing his eyes from mine, he thrusts his hand through his hair. "You've sworn the Blood Oath to me."

"Yes," I confirm.

"For life," he adds.

"I'm aware."

"You and I will be…."

"One."

"Is this what you wanted?" he asks.

The room swims.

Over the past few weeks, Valdemar has become a part of me whether I wanted it or not. In that time, things have changed, my perception of the past altered, and my feelings for him evolved into something unfamiliar.

"I didn't want you to die. I didn't want to lose you. I didn't want to spend the rest of my life being alone like I have for the past ten years," I tell him.

A sigh wooshes from his mouth.

"You're cross with me." I read his thoughts so easily. Too easily. "This isn't what you wanted, is it? I didn't have time to ask you."

His eyes narrow, and he grabs my hands.

"You didn't need to ask me, angel. I've always been yours."

My heart swells.

"Have you heard of the red string theory?" Valdemar asks.

I shake my head, unable to answer him, words getting lost amongst the blossoming in my chest.

"In Eastern philosophy, there's a belief that when you're born, there's an invisible red thread connecting you to all the people you're destined to meet and will be connected to throughout your life. That's the only way I can explain how I feel—it's like I'm tethered to you by an invisible force," he tells me.

"When I met Ed, there was the pull, an unfathomable fascination with him, which is why we swore the Blood Oath. And I thought it was him. But the feeling never went away, this feeling that I was looking for someone and hadn't found them yet.

"He never told any of us he had a sister, let alone a twin, but not long after we completed the Blood Oath, I could feel you through him, this presence, like a humming in my bones, a song in my head.

"I asked him about it, asked if he had a sibling, and he told me about you. I wanted to meet you, but Ed was reluctant to bring you into this world until, he said, the time was right. I wanted to push further, wanted to know everything about you, but I respected his wishes until he died and asked me to contact you. And the day you walked into the prison and I saw you for the first time, I knew it wasn't Ed whom I was meant to be bonded with. It was you. It's always been you." He takes a breath, pondering something before he continues.

"I've often wondered if Ed knew your fate all along. After you'd visited me in the prison and I knew it was you who I was supposed to be bonded with and not Ed, I asked him if he'd always known, if he'd had a vision of things to come. But his reply was that sometimes you just have to let fate play out because there is no other way. As you know, he knew he could never change the future, never influence it enough to stop things from happening. Ed knew this. And that's why I believe I've had to wait these last ten years to meet you. Because that's the way it was always supposed to happen."

My body trembles. Fate has a lot to answer for, and I'm awash with anger. Why did we have to walk this road to get here? Why did my mother have to die? Why did my father have to die? Why did my brother have to die? Why have Valdemar and I had to grieve for the last ten years to get here? Why has he had to spend the last ten years paying for a crime he didn't commit?

But fighting my anger at fate's cruel hand, there's hope, an awakening at this new turn of events, of the love I feel for this man and the place we're at now, and what lies before us.

The future.

I smile at Valdemar, knowing this is where I'm supposed to be, that at last, we're together, but he doesn't share my smile.

"Why are you so sad?" I place my hand on the open wound on his chest, our blood already starting to clot, as his sadness washes over me.

"You were supposed to take over the Raven Hands, to revolutionise them," he says.

This thought takes hold. Like the big scoop I've been waiting for all these years, I know this is the moment my life is set to change. It feels right, warranted, as if Ed is here now, telling me that this was my destiny all along. Fate may have sent us down the rocky road, the one that makes you bleed, makes you cry, and brings nothing but pain. But it's worth it to reach the end, to the place where you're supposed to be, where you've been destined to be.

"And we still will. Together," I tell him.

He puts his hand over mine, securing it to his heart.

"I hope you're ready for this." His lips don't move, yet I hear his voice.

"What the fuck?" I pull back, searching his face for signs of trickery.

"The telepathy is part of the Blood Oath."

"How are you doing that?" I ask.

"You can do it too. Just relax and think of what you want to say to me, and I'll hear you."

I inhale deeply, clearing my mind before thinking of something to say to him.

"Boo!"

He raises an eyebrow.

"Oh my God, can you turn it off?" I ask.

He smirks. "In time, you'll learn to block me. *But for now, hear me."*

"Was this what it was like with Ed?"

"When you swear the Blood Oath to a friend, it feels like a loyalty bond, a comradery that you're united for a common purpose. This feels different," he explains.

"Why?"

"Why? I think it's because of the way I feel about you. It

changes the bond to something deeper, something primal that I'm going to have a hard time getting used to."

"How so?" There's so much to learn, so much to take in. My heart races in my chest.

"Like if someone even looks at you in the wrong way, I'm going to want to rip their fucking throat out."

"Better keep me locked away, then."

"That's not a bad idea." His gaze intensifies.

I thump him on the side of his arm.

His lips quirk before his face settles back into a hard stare. "Are you sure this is what you want?" he repeats, this time speaking aloud as if to clarify it.

"You shouldn't need to ask me that. You should be able to feel how I feel, know that this is what I want. *You* are what I want. I told you in my dreams, and I told you in the real world. I want you," I tell him.

"I feel it, but I'm not sure I'm going to be able to keep my thoughts from you. It was bad enough before we took the Oath, but now.... Now you're my all, my everything, and it frightens me, as I'll do anything for you, anything and every-thing, no matter the consequences. It's you. You are mine. I am yours. Like a sunrise without the sun, like thunder without the lightning, without you, there is no me. And it scares me, angel, because you're the light and I'm the dark. You're the saviour, and I'm condemned."

Stroking his face, I kneel on the bed and press my lips to his forehead.

"Stand," I tell him.

He pulls back and regards me with uncertainty, but he does as I say, sliding from the bed and standing next to it.

"You asked me what I would do if you hadn't killed my brother," I remind him as I rise from the bed too. "There is no good without evil, no angels without a devil. And I would rather dance with the devil than float on a cloud playing a harp no one can hear." I trail my hand down his chest before I fall at his feet.

Valdemar drops to his knees and takes my chin in his hand. "Never kneel before me unless I tell you to," he says.

He kisses me, softly at first, as if his lips are testing the waters before his hands search my body, pushing my shirt up and grasping at my bra.

Helping him, I pull my shirt over my head, and then my bra joins it on the floor. Valdemar shrugs his shirt off, his skin brushing against mine. This feels different from the night in the library, and I'm not sure if it's because of the Blood Oath, but it's closer, deeper, like a ritual we've performed over centuries, practised, and perfected, our bodies in tune with each other.When he pulls me into him, I wrap my arms around his neck and thrust my tongue into his mouth, the taste of him making me hum.

"I've dreamt of this moment," he tells me, taking a break from my mouth, his lips travelling down my neck.

"So have I."

"I don't mean in the dreams; I mean in my waking hours. I have dreamt of you fitting perfectly in my arms, happy to be here," he says.

"It's where I belong. I know that now." I knew it that day in the prison, the first time he touched me, as my body sang for him and my heart pounded.

"I've always known it."

I tug down my trousers and underwear, and Valdemar helps to pull them over my feet.

Taking his face in my hands, I press my chest against his, a buzz erupting at the contact. Our bodies bind together, arms entwined until I can't tell where I begin and he ends.

"Then you better fuck me like you own me," I demand.

I swear he growls, fucking *growls* in my ear before leading me back to the bed, pushing me down, and clasping my wrists in one hand above my head.

"I *do* own you, angel, and you own me." His mouth travels down my neck and onto my breasts, momentarily pausing on my nipple, pulling at the swollen bud and nipping with his teeth.

By the time his mouth reaches my waist, the need has grown between my legs, a feral wanting flirting at the edges of my sanity. If he doesn't do something about this, I'll have to take matters into my own hands, but I shouldn't doubt him. There's no need. He knows exactly what he's doing.

Just as I'm about to grab his head and push it between my legs, he looks up at me and smirks. "You're about to learn the first advantage of the Blood Oath."

The roguish grin is back before he dips his head and flicks his tongue over my hardened clit, the buzz of it arching my back and making me gasp.

"You see, angel, I can talk to you with my mouth full, so you can hear all the dirty things that are going through my brain as my tongue fucks you inside and out. How does that sound?"

Through the shiver of pleasure, I manage to reply, "Like fucking heaven."

His tongue dips inside me, leaving my clit bereft and pulsing with need.

"I could spend an eternity tasting you, and I would remain hungry for more."

His tongue slides back to my clit, flicking it, circling it, lapping up my arousal.

Fisting his hair, I moan through the waves of euphoria. Flattening his hands on the insides of my thighs, he pushes my legs further apart, spreading me wide as his tongue goes back inside me deeper, and he fucks me with his mouth.

"Valdemar." My voice scrapes the back of my throat as I try to contain the building orgasm.

"Not yet, angel. I've only just started."

His voice in my head only drives me into more of a frenzy, his tongue everywhere.

"You want me to fill you everywhere, to own every part of you, and I will. You are mine. All of you, and I'll take every bit of you just as you have taken every bit of me."

With one long lick, his tongue travels up my centre, landing on my swollen clit as my orgasm breaks through my body like a crack in the ground during an earthquake.

"Fuck!" I cry as I pull at his hair, thrusting in his face as the throes of ecstasy rack my body. Valdemar grips my hips, pushing his tongue ruthlessly inside me as I come.

I'm shaking, the aftershock of such a powerful orgasm still flaring over my skin as he pulls away and wipes his mouth with the back of his hand.

I press my thighs together to try and steady the pulsing between my legs.

"Are you okay, angel?"

"Yes," I pant through ragged breaths.

Without taking his eyes off me, he unfastens his belt and pulls his trousers down.

"You're so fucking wet, angel," he tells me. "You're ready to take me. Now spread your legs and get ready to come again."

I hook my hands under my legs and pull them apart.

"Look at you—you're fucking glowing."

I salivate as he pulls his cock from his boxers and fists his length while sliding three fingers inside me.

"Fuck." I bite my lip as he thrusts his fingers until they're soaked.

He removes them, then slides his cock in, slowly at first, spreading me with just the tip before plunging his full length deep into me.

The room blurs. He doesn't take his eyes off mine as he

pulls his cock out and switches back to his fingers. He pumps them fast and hard before replacing them with his cock, his movements now slow and deep.

It's fucking torture—delectable, addictive, and fucking moreish torture.

"I want your cock," I tell him as he swaps again and fucks me with his fingers.

"I know you do, and you'll get it. All of it. You just need to be a good girl."

His fingers linger before his cock goes back in, and I raise myself onto my elbows to get a better view of him. "Please, just fuck me."

He rubs at my clit, and I let myself fall back onto the bed, the pleasure too much for me to be able to hold myself up. His movements are deliberate, drawing out each thrust, each dip of his cock so that I'm snowballing into a frenzy, clawing at the bedsheets and trying to thrust my hips against him. I feel like a cat in heat, a feral rage consuming me.

"I want it hard. I want it fast. I want you to pin me to the fucking bed with your cock," I demand, holding him with a stone-cold stare.

He just grins at me. "Be careful what you wish for," he tells me, his fingers brushing against my clit so gently, it makes me shudder.

His cock is inside me but barely moving, his rigid length pushing against my inner walls, spreading me, filling me. He kneels forward slightly, stops halfway inside me, and looks down between my legs before spitting onto my clit and then rubbing it in with his fingers.

Black spots dance before my eyes. Rolls of pleasure crash over my entire body as my orgasm swells.

"Hold on, angel," he says as he grabs my hips and lifts them off the bed before thrusting into me with such force, I swear I feel it against my back teeth.

And I get my wish.

Hard and fast.

My eyes water.

"Oh my God!" I barely get the words out as I'm pinned to the bed, my body consumed by him and his cock, his relentless fucking filling me, claiming me, and breaking me until I come undone, my body limp, my resolve gone, my world altered forever.

I'll never get tired of this.

CHAPTER FORTY-NINE

I RAKE MY FINGERS THROUGH THE SOFT CURLS OF MY HAIR, cursing myself for not putting on my new silver dress before I'd done my hair and makeup.

Light bounces off the full-length mirror, making me look like a model standing under a spotlight, promoting a new range of white underwear. I look the picture of calm, yet inside, my nerves are in overdrive.

It's been a week since my brother was reunited with Annabel Lee and I was bonded to Valdemar. And in that week, we haven't left each other's side, taking the time to get used to our new-found bond. It didn't take me long to work out how to block his thoughts, a much-needed skill when I returned to work, but it's been a comfort knowing he's there even when he isn't with me.

We've talked about the future of the Raven Hands, where we see the group going, and what we would like to change, the first and foremost being the recognition and induction of all the women with gifts. We've arranged a formal dinner this evening at Corvus House for me and Valdemar to disclose our Blood Oath and the fact that we'll be running the Raven Hands together as a team.

All week I've been telling him my worries about how everyone will react. What will they think about letting women become Raven Hands? Will there be anarchy, an uprising, a rebellion? Valdemar hasn't belittled me by telling me not to worry about such things or that everything will be fine, because he knows as well as I do that things might not be fine, and that might be something we have to work through, but we'll work through it together. There's bound to be resistance from a group of men who've been together for years, some of whom cling to tradition, but there'll also be those who welcome it, who've been waiting for change and will embrace it with open arms. Those are the people who will support us.

I can't let myself think about their reaction to the fact that I've taken the Blood Oath with the man who they believe killed my brother. The discussion about sharing this little titbit with the rest of the Raven Hands was short-lived. Although Valdemar is unable to tell the truth about what happened that night, I am not. But he's stressed how dangerous it would be to let that information roam free. He said it was bad enough that I know, but at least he knows he can keep me safe. He will not endanger any other Ravens or put them in harm's way. Adolphe Fortunato has kept his distance for the past ten years knowing that Valdemar, Jupiter, and Jacinta have been unable to reveal the truth about what really happened the night Ed died, and Valdemar doesn't want to give Fortunato any reason to aim his sights at the Raven Hands.

After putting on my heels, I reach for my dress hanging on the side of the mirror when his voice arrives.

"Where are you, angel?"

"I'm still getting ready in the dressing room."

Although I don't officially live here, I've spent more time at Corvus House than I care to admit. I feel a pull to this place, and it's not just to do with Valdemar; it's more than that. It's knowing my mother was here, that she fell in love here and made beautiful memories in this mansion. There's so much history and emotion binding me to Corvus House that I find it hard to leave when it's time to go back to my apartment. I'm not sure who I'm kidding when I tell Valdemar it's too soon for us to be living together. He insists that the leader of the Raven Hands has always resided in Corvus House, and so my rightful place is here with him. And given that I want to be here more than I've wanted to be anywhere, I know he'll get his wish soon enough.

My mother still visits me—and my father, Ellison Rue. They'll appear in my apartment or occasionally at Corvus House, always together and always looking blissfully happy. But the visits aren't as frequent as before I swore the Blood Oath to Valdemar. It's almost as if my mother knows I'm happy, that I've found my way in the world of the living and have no need to be hiding amongst the dead.

"Where are you?" I ask him.

"I'm in the Great Hall." There's a silent beat, and I sense the change in his voice before I even hear it. *"Tell me what you can see."*

My smile spreads as I stare at my reflection.

"I'm standing in front of the mirror."

"And?"

"And my hair and make-up are done." I glance at my freshly curled hair and smoky eyeliner.

"And?" he presses.

"My underwear is on."

I hear him tut down the bond. *"Shame."*

"I was just about to put my dress on," I tell him.

"I'd rather you took your underwear off." Even in my head, his voice is commanding, roguish, and unrelenting.

"But I've just put it on," I argue.

"Don't complain. It'll be worth it. Now do as I say."

I take the bra off first, my nipples already hard at the thought of where this is going. Then I pull my knickers down and kick them to the side.

"Are you naked, angel?"

"Yes."

"I'm so fucking annoyed that I can't see you right now."

I smirk, the thought of him squirming making me even more aroused.

"You'll just have to use your imagination."

"Oh, I am, angel. I'm imagining you right now, standing in front of that mirror, looking at your naked skin, running your hands over your breasts."

"I'm not touching my breasts." The thought alone embarrasses me.

"Don't ruin my fun."

Licking my lips, I imagine him in the Great Hall, directing the staff, setting up the stage, all the while picturing me naked.

"There's a chair in the corner of the room," he tells me.

I turn and see it, a low-backed chair covered in floral material that doesn't go with the décor in the rest of the house.

"Put the chair in front of the mirror."

Excitement brews. This isn't the first time he's used our little Blood Oath bond to play games with me, and as much as I pretend I don't like it, I fucking lap it up.

"Okay, the chair is in front of the mirror," I reply.

"Sit."

There's another beat of silence before he continues. *"Are you sitting in the chair?"*

"*Yes,*" I confirm.

"*Good girl. Now spread your legs and place them over the arms of the chair.*"

Gulping down his words, I hook my legs over the arms of the chair, leaving myself exposed.

"*Now, look in the mirror and tell me what you see.*"

I'm sure I'm not the only woman who's never looked at themselves at this angle before. Sure, I analyse my face, or I might check how my clothes fit me, but I've never studied my naked body for any length of time.

I'm met with a view that Valdemar has seen on numerous occasions and knows intimately, so he'll know if I lie or don't play along with his game.

"*Angel?*"

"*Yes.*"

"*Tell me what you see.*" His voice curls around the question.

"*This is embarrassing.*" Heat flames across my cheeks.

"*Why?*"

"*Because it is.*"

"*It's not embarrassing. It's fucking sexy as hell, and if our roles were reversed, I would have no qualms about describing how my rock-hard cock was pulsing in my hand as I thought about you sitting there naked and splayed out for me in that chair. I would happily tell you how I stroked my balls before sliding my hand up my shaft—*"

"*Okay. I get it. Jesus.*"

"*Am I making you wet?*" he asks.

"*You know you are.*"

"*No, I don't. You need to tell me.*"

Biting my lip, I begin.

"*I'm on the chair, naked, legs spread, waiting for you.*" I swallow, trying to ignore the awkwardness of my inner voice and how I wish I sounded sexier. "*My nipples are hard, and I'm playing with them and wishing it was your mouth.*"

Desire sparks, and my eyelids flutter as I settle into the role.

"All of me is on display, just for you. My fingers are in my mouth now. I'm sucking hard and imagining they're your cock. I'm sliding my hand down my stomach to my clit. It's swollen and tender, and as I touch it, I think of your mouth and what your tongue would feel like if it was there.

"I move my fingers over my clit, and I'm sinking them inside me. I'm so wet. I can see how wet I am in the mirror, and my fingers slip in so easily. Three fingers now, and I'm thrusting them, wishing it was your hand, your fingers, your cock because that's all I want, all I need. Fuck, my hand is soaked. This feels so fucking good, and I want more, need more as I think about your cock and how hard it must be and how you must be trying to concentrate on whatever you're doing, but all you can think about is my fingers doing your job."

I'm glued to the mirror, the image of me getting myself off far hotter than I ever thought it would be. My orgasm is rumbling low in my core, and I'm lost, Valdemar's silence almost making me forget he can hear me.

And just as I feel myself peaking, the door busts open, and I hear his voice fill the room.

"Stop. Now."

His face is primal, a warrior claiming his prize as he stalks into the room, his dress shirt already unbuttoned as he loosens his belt.

As he reaches me, he takes in my dishevelled state.

"Fuck." He grabs my hand and slowly sucks at my fingers, closing his eyes and savouring the taste.

Some masochistic part of me wants to tell him that his little game has backfired, but I value my life, so instead, I flutter my eyes and hope to God he's here to put right what he started.

"Put your hands behind the chair, and don't fucking move

them." His gaze is predatory as I loop my arms behind the chair.

"Have I disappointed you?"

He grabs my throat and tips my head back.

"You could never disappoint me, angel. Never. I'm here to take over." He kneels and then pushes on my inner thighs as his head dips, his tongue claiming me.

"Oh God." There's little work for him to do as his fingers curl inside me, his tongue caressing my clit.

"Fucking hell, Valdemar. Fuck." I come, my body exploding to the crescendo of his name.

Breathing hard, I wilt, but before I have time to return to earth, he's unzipped his trousers.

"Get on the floor on all fours," he commands.

Almost sliding off the chair, I do as I'm told.

His cock eases into me as he goes to grab my hair.

"Not my hair," I tell him. "It took me ages to curl."

"Fine. But this is for teasing me." He wraps his hand around my throat and pulls my head back.

"You started it," I tell him.

"And I'm going to fucking finish it."

He lets go of my throat, then grabs my waist and pounds into me, bringing tears to my eyes. He's rough, he's carnal, and I can't get enough of him. I push back, grinding myself against him as his hand snakes between my legs and rubs my clit.

Pulling me up so my back is flush with his chest, he whispers in my ear. "Look in the mirror."

There's no embarrassment now, only raw sexual desire as I watch him take me from behind, one hand massaging me, his other squeezing my breast. It's the most beautiful thing I've ever seen.

Just as I peak, he comes, hard and fast. I shudder against him, my climax tearing through me like a power surge. His hold is tight as my body descends from the high and sags from exhaustion.

"I'll never get tired of this," he tells me.

"Noted. But we have a dinner to attend in less than an hour."

"Plenty of time." Valdemar pulls out and tells me to stay put.

I can still feel the tremors of my orgasm, and it makes me want us to lock ourselves away in his bedroom and cancel the dinner.

When he returns, he's armed with a warm washcloth, which he uses to clean me.

Sitting up, I try to fan out my curls.

"I bet my hair is a mess now," I say.

He offers me his hand. I take it, and he pulls me up.

"It's perfect, just like the rest of you."

"Make yourself useful and pass me my dress," I say, holding out my hand.

He takes the dress off the hanger, then helps me into the silver gown, zipping me up and smoothing down the long skirt.

We stare at our reflections in the mirror, Valdemar behind me, his hands on my shoulders.

"You look like the angel you are."

"You're biased."

"Always." He lifts my hair away from my face and plants a soft kiss on my neck, then my cheek. "Now, let's go and show them who's boss."

Today marks a new age...

CHAPTER FIFTY

The Great Hall mirrors its name with the chandeliers lit, the rich oak floor polished to a slippery shine, and the guests milling about in their finest suits and gowns, their hands laden with crystal glasses, probably wondering why Valdemar has commissioned another party so close after his release day.

As agreed, I hang back in the library as the party gets underway. If their reaction to me last week was anything to go by, my attendance would only spark a hot debate, and the floral tattoo adorned with several ravens now decorating the back of my left hand and arm would certainly set tongues wagging before Valdemar has had the chance to explain. The visit to the tattoo parlour had been painful, and not just for me. Valdemar was positively bristling at the male tattooist putting his hands on me. When it was done and we walked out of the parlour, Valdemar declared that if I wanted any more, then he would do them himself.

"You're not trained," I'd laughed while adjusting the cling film that was wrapped around my arm.

"I'll learn," Valdemar had replied.

Jupiter joins me in the library, holding two glasses of whisky. He's the only other person, along with Jacinta, who's bound by Dr Tem-Pest's magic in not being able to reveal the truth about the night my brother was shot. In their silent world, they know what happened yet have been unable to tell anyone for the past ten years.

And they're both the only Raven Hands to know about our Blood Oath. We'd sat Jupiter down in this very room, the fire roaring, the walls listening. I'd wanted Jacinta to be present as well, but Valdemar had suggested that we tell Jupiter first, seeing as he's next in the chain of command, and he thought Jupiter would want to tell Jacinta himself, so I agreed to speak to Jupiter alone.

He was shocked, colour draining from his cheeks, and my anxiety peaked; if we didn't have Jupiter's blessing, we could have mutiny on our hands. But then he nodded, his face settling.

"A woman in the flock." He scratched his chin.

"Not just the flock, Jupiter," Valdemar pointed out. "At the helm."

"Jacinta will be pleased." He glanced at Valdemar. "I assume I can tell her?"

"Of course," Valdemar replied.

Jupiter leaned back in his chair, which creaked as if it was absorbing the news. "She's wanted to be a Raven Hand for as long as I've known her. She's even designed her own tattoo." Jupiter laughed at this, and then his face grew more serious. "Her gift is one we've been using for many years, and I'm sure she isn't the only woman who will be excited by this turn of events."

Valdemar had told me that Jacinta has a photographic memory, something that often comes in handy.

"How do you think the rest of the Raven Hands will take the news?" I asked, unable to bite my tongue any longer.

"It doesn't matter how they take it," Valdemar snapped.

"If Jupiter's reaction to me is anything to go by, then they'll be sceptical."

"Hey, that was when you were visiting him at the prison," Jupiter cut in. "I knew you were a journalist, and I had no idea what you were going to print about him, about us, about what we can do. I thought you were going to expose us all."

"And I told you to trust me," Valdemar reminded him.

"Yeah, well, this gig hasn't exactly been easy." Jupiter ran his hand down his throat. "They don't listen to me like they do to you. There's been unrest. Talk of breaking off from the flock. It's been a nightmare."

"I know it's been difficult, Jupiter, and you should never have been put in this position, but I'm here now, and I'm not alone," Valdemar says.

Jupiter stared at Valdemar and then at me, as if sizing me up to see if I fit the role.

"I can get on board with this," he said at last.

My shoulders relaxed.

"Good." Valdemar squeezed my hand as if he'd never questioned Jupiter's loyalty.

Jupiter clears his throat, pulling me back into the present, and I can't help but hope everyone else has his unwavering allegiance.

"How does the crowd look?" I ask Jupiter as he downs his drink and winces before placing the empty glass on the table.

"Puzzled," he answers. "There's a buzz. Has been ever since the night he got out of prison and left his party with you."

"Great." I slump down on the arm of the chair, then stand back up and resume pacing.

"It could be worse." He shrugs. "They don't have pitchforks."

"Not funny." I throw him daggers but can't help the smile that erupts.

"I think everyone is here. It's time to move," he says.

I abandon my glass, and we exit through the rear door, turning left and following the corridor back to the front of the house and into the foyer.

The double doors to the Great Hall are now closed, all the Raven Hands contained inside the hall.

Nausea whips at my insides.

Valdemar's voice travels down the bond. *"There's no need to be nervous."*

"Easy for you to say."

"Nothing is ever easy, angel."

Jupiter stalks to the huge double doors to open one of them a crack, and I hear the chatter die and applause erupt.

"I take it he's on the stage?" I edge over to Jupiter so I can hear what's going on.

"Thank you, thank you," Valdemar says.

The rapturous welcome simmers down, and I picture Valdemar standing on the stage in his pressed suit, addressing his followers, smiling to put them at ease.

"I don't deserve such a welcome, and certainly not after absconding from my party last week. For that, I must apologise. But as I'm sure you can understand, it was a strange day. It's been a long time since I was here, in my home. And I know there've been some doubts and questions about what's going to happen now I've returned, so tonight, I'm here to answer those questions."

Through the crack in the door, I see a snapshot of the faces trained up to the stage, mostly male, but there's a scattering of women, the loyal followers like Jacinta who've been bestowed a gift but have never been accepted into the fold due to the archaic rules. They've remained due to fear of being an outcast in the regular world, where people don't understand the power they wield—a world I know only too well.

"Ten years is a long time to be caged. And it gave me a lot of time to think. A lot of time to wonder about the future and what it looks like. And I'd like to start by thanking Jupiter for keeping me so well-informed and Jacinta for keeping Jupiter sane while I've been away."

I duck behind the door as Jupiter opens it, then makes his way through the crowd and onto the stage.

I close the door but leave a small enough gap so I can hear Valdemar say, "Come on up, Jacinta."

From my vantage point, I can't see Jacinta go onto the stage, but I hear the applause ripple through the crowd.

"You guys have done such a great job, and I'm so grateful for everything you've done," Valdemar tells them.

"But he's back now, so move aside!" someone shouts from the crowd, and silence descends, everyone assessing Valdemar's reaction.

"You're right. I'm back. And it's time to make a few changes."

Silence continues to brood as my stomach somersaults.

"Thirteen years ago, Ed Bransby and I swore the Blood Oath, and, as you all know, the Blood Oath holds even in death. But I'm here tonight to tell you that I've been released from that Blood Oath," Valdemar tells the crowd.

Murmurs flitter through the hall, gasps of disbelief and confusion erupting as some of the Raven Hands look to one another for reassurance that they're hearing this right.

"And I have the greatest honour of informing you that I've sworn a new Blood Oath to our very newest member of the Raven Hands."

Heads swivel as people search the room, looking for tell-tale signs of who the lucky Raven Hand could be.

I hear Jupiter's name bandied about, see glances cast his way. He would be the obvious choice.

I feel sick. What if they throw things at me? What if they boo?

"It's without further ado that I would like to introduce you to not only my new Blood Oath Raven Hand but the person who will co-lead the Raven Hands from here on in."

"*It's time,*" Valdemar says down the bond.

If his previous announcement hadn't piqued their interest, then this one now has the room held in rapturous anticipation.

I step back from the doors as they're opened by two footmen on the other side.

It's exactly like last week, stunned faces pinning me with icy glares as Valdemar jumps down from the stage and heads towards me.

Willing my feet to move, I step forwards.

Our eyes lock, and I'm so grateful that all I can see is him as we walk towards each other, the Raven Hands parting before us.

He takes my head in his hands and kisses me gently.

"It's time," he repeats aloud. Taking my hand, he leads me to the stage, his fingers squeezing mine.

"*I know you're nervous, but don't be. Just remember what I did to you the last time you were on this stage, my angel.*"

My skin heats at his words as I recall reenacting the dream we'd had. We've reenacted all the dreams, my favourite being the fountain in the middle of the maze.

Once I'm standing on the stage, blank faces stare at me, eyebrows furrowed and mouths slightly open. I don't need to hear them to know what they're thinking. *What is she doing up there? Is that a raven tattoo on her arm? What the hell is Valdemar playing at? Is this some kind of joke?*

"I would like to introduce you all to Evangeline Bransby, who is not only the first woman to become a Raven Hand but also the first to swear the Blood Oath."

"You were found guilty of killing her brother," a man with thick ginger hair shouts. "How can you trust her?"

Valdemar glares into the crowd, and I feel his anger running down his arm and fingertips and flowing into my hand. "I trust her with my life, and so should you."

But it isn't enough. These people need to know what happened, but to reveal the full truth of that night could get them killed, so a snapshot will have to suffice.

"Valdemar didn't kill my brother," I begin, Valdemar flinching beside me. "He took the fall to keep everyone else safe. He can't tell you who did kill Ed, as it would put your lives at risk. But if there's anyone in this room who believes he would kill one of his own, then you aren't in the right place."

Silence, thick and dangerous, swamps the hall, and I'm worried it will swallow me until I hear the slow clap from the front.

Jacinta. Jacinta is clapping.

She knows the truth. She knows Valdemar didn't shoot my brother.

"It's about time someone spoke up about what happened," another woman calls from the back, and as she joins in, so do the other women, followed by some men. Not all of them, but enough that the room is filled with noise.

And it's then that I see them. My mother and father are at the back of the hall, my father with his hands on my mother's shoulders, and Ed is there with Annabel wrapped in his arms. They nod to me, my brother and my mother. My family—all of them here to watch except William, my dad, who's since visited me and Valdemar. It was an awkward visit, Valdemar's presence a difficult one to swallow, until we told William an edited version of what really happened to Ed that didn't disclose the Raven Hands' gifts. Luckily, he was more focussed on me and relieved that I'd accepted the news about my birth father without too much scorn.

"Thank you," I say to the four ghostly figures.

The crowd stills.

I address them next. "Thank you for your enthusiastic welcome. I can't begin to tell you how nervous I've been. And I know this change might fill some of you with doubts and fears, but isn't that what great change is all about? What discovery hasn't been met with danger and uncertainty?

"The Raven Hands have been dwelling in the darkness of tradition for too long. There are loyal women amongst us who've been bestowed with gifts, yet they have gone unrecognised and haven't been allowed to be called a Raven Hand just because of their gender. Today marks a new age, and I'm honoured to be the one to bring the Raven Hands out of the darkness and into the light."

A riot of applause follows, and I find myself smiling and clapping along with them.

"But what does this mean for the future of the Raven Hands?"

The clapping dies down as all eyes fall on a tall man in the centre, his hair thick and unruly, a raven tattoo peeking above the collar of his shirt. And I wonder if this is the man who had a gun to my head the first time I walked into the Great Hall. I never have learned who that was or if he remains a Raven Hand after threatening my life.

Valdemar turns to me.

I clear my throat. "It means more recruits. More bodies. More people with more diverse gifts to fight the cause," I tell them.

"And what is the cause?" the man shouts.

"The same as what it's always been," Valdemar answers. "To rid the streets of Amontillado of the filth and rubbish. To make this city a safer place to live, and for people like us to not have to hide or be made to feel like lepers."

"Does that include Adolphe Fortunato?" the tall man asks, and I feel Valdemar's hackles rise. "We've followed your orders for the past ten years and not taken retribution against him or his corrupt organisation. We all know that what went on that night is not what it seems. You would never have killed your Blood Brother," he continues, the people nearest him taking a step back as if to distance themselves from his words. "But ten years is a long time, and in your absence, Fortunato has held this city in a firmer grip. So, what do you intend to do about Adolphe Fortunato?"

Valdemar doesn't answer. He can't. I know his thoughts. He lost Ed because of Adolphe Fortunato and, along with Jupiter and Jacinta, is now under the spell of Dr Tem-Pest. He doesn't want to risk losing any more Ravens at either of their hands. This is a fight he isn't willing to have.

But I am.

"Let me assure you, Adolphe Fortunato will be dealt with," I say.

Valdemar stiffens. I can hear him screaming his protest in my head, but I ignore him.

"He will pay for what he's done. Mark my words. He will pay," I tell them.

A fraught silence hangs before the applause erupts. This is what they've been waiting for. This is what the unrest has been about. They want revenge. They want blood. And the first thing I've done as their leader is to promise them it.

I smile as I feel Valdemar's anger flap under my skin.

"What the fuck have you done?" he hisses down the bond.

I turn to him.

"I'm giving them what they want. What I want. And it's long overdue."

"But—"
"Trust me. I've got this."

It will start a war.

CHAPTER FIFTY-ONE

The rest of the evening is a blur of Valdemar fighting questions, receiving slaps on the back of congratulations, and never-ending drinks. I'm dragged away by various women who've associated with the Raven Hands either through being involved with a Raven Hand or knowing they have a gift themselves but have been unable to become full-fledged Ravens.

But it's when Jacinta pulls me to one side that I truly realise what tonight means.

"Hey, I want to thank you for what you've done, the way you saved Val. And I also need to apologise for how hostile I was at the prison." Her eyes are large and watery, her nails rounder and smoother.

"There's no need to apologise. You didn't know who I was, and you were just being protective."

"And I want to thank you for finally making this official." She rolls up her sleeve to reveal a large raven tattooed on her left hand. "I can't tell you how many years I've waited for this. How many meetings I've sat through, knowing I wasn't really part of them, that I would never be considered one of the flock. Val was great and would always include me, but it was never the same. I've never truly felt like I was a Raven Hand. Not like the men. And it's been hard, knowing you've finally found your calling, knowing there are people out there like you who can do extraordinary things but still not feeling like you belong because you're the wrong gender. Tonight, I think I speak for all the women when I say that we finally feel like we belong. Tonight, we have become Ravens."

I smile, an unfamiliar sense of pride swelling in my chest. Who the hell am I? What has happened to the old Evangeline, the one who relied on prescription medication and talking to the dead to get her through the day? But it feels right. So right. Like fate.

"Thank you. This means a lot, and I'm so glad that people are happy about this. I've been so nervous about this whole thing, worried that people wouldn't accept this change. I feel more confident knowing I've done some good already," I say.

Jacinta goes on to tell me some of the less than savoury endeavours the Raven Hands have got themselves into over the years, all in aid of making Amontillado a better place to live. And this conversation has the added benefit of keeping me and Valdemar apart, which means I can continue to dodge his raging temper at my impromptu outburst during the speech.

"*What were you thinking promising them Adolphe Fortunato's head on a stick?*" he'd shot down the bond as we'd been separated soon after we'd left the stage.

"*I promised no such thing.*"

But truth be told, I don't fully know what I promised. I simply acted on gut instinct and a dormant hope that Adolphe Fortunato would get his comeuppance. It was his fault my brother lost his life, his fault his daughter killed herself, and his fault Valdemar, Jacinta, and Jupiter are compelled to keep quiet about what really happened that night. And these are only the incidents we know about. What about all the other victims? How many bricks has Adolphe Fortunato used to hide his crimes and build his empire?

And isn't this what being a Raven Hand is all about? Making the city a safer place to live? Standing up against tyranny?

It's when I go to the toilet that Valdemar appears, pushing his way into the bathroom behind me and locking the door.

"Fucking hell, angel." He pushes his hand through his long hair. "You sure know how to rouse a crowd. They're gunning for blood out there. And only Adolphe Fortunato's will do."

"I'm more surprised at how well they've taken the news," I say.

"They would love anyone who told them they were going to deliver Fortunato to them in a box."

I fold my arms, and he picks up on his error.

"I'm sorry, I didn't mean it to come out like that. Of course I'm glad they've accepted you, but one of the reasons they have is that you've promised them something they've wanted for a long time. And I promised I'd uphold the safety of the Raven Hands, even if that meant not seeking revenge. Peace for our people. No more dead Raven Hands. Isn't that what's more important?"

"I'm not disagreeing with you, and I know what you did was right, but that doesn't mean we can sit back and let him continue to monopolise this city. So many people are scared of him, and he holds so much power—even more so since you've been locked away. Do you know he wants to buy the *Gazette*? Do you know what that would mean for the future of this city along with me and Una and Pierre?" I say.

"But it will start a war. A war I'm not sure we can win. You do anything to harm, threaten, or even slightly annoy Adolphe Fortunato, and he'll be on us faster than you can say

Raven Hand. He'll shoot us down and pluck out our feathers. Is that what you want?" Valdemar argues.

"No, of course not. But I can't sit back and do nothing."

"Then what do you suggest? Running into his casino with guns blazing?" He wafts his hand in the air.

I raise an eyebrow. "There's more than one way to skin a cat."

"What's that supposed to mean?" he asks.

"Exactly what I just said."

"Jesus." Valdemar whistles.

"Look. We have the advantage. We have the element of surprise. We have what Adolphe Fortunato doesn't even think we have. We have the ultimate weapon."

His eyes bore into me, and when it's clear he still has no idea what I'm talking about, I tell him. Then and only then does his scowl turn into a smile.

What I see next is not
what I expect.

CHAPTER FIFTY-TWO

"To the best fucking headline we've had in years!" Una raises her glass, her hands clad in silver rings, nails painted a deep plum to match the new purple streaks in her hair. The glare of the stark lighting illuminates the champagne, making the bubbles look like tiny diamonds floating in a yellow ocean.

Pierre and I join our glasses to Una's.

"To the ultimate headline," Pierre says.

"To the best news," I chime in, clinking my glass heavily against theirs before we all take a glug of champagne.

Pierre winces, bringing the glass down. "God, I hate champagne." He shivers as if the bubbles are attacking him from the inside.

"It's not my drink of choice either," Una agrees.

"Then why the hell are we drinking it?" I ask. I'm not a huge champagne connoisseur—I can take it or leave it—but we've just split the cost of an eighty-quid bottle.

"This is too big not to celebrate, and you can only celebrate with champagne," Una informs us.

"She's right. I want to remember today, and you always remember champagne." Pierre holds his glass by the stem and swirls the golden liquid.

"I don't think any of us are going to forget today in a hurry." Una raises her eyebrows before putting her glass down on the table. "When Captain found out that fire engines and police cars were surrounding the Fortunato mansion, I thought he was going to explode. He couldn't get Dupin and me out of the building fast enough." She lowers her gaze, and I wonder if she's picking up on how similar today has felt to the night my brother died.

Twisting one of her silver rings, she asks, "But what the hell actually happened?"

"I know as much as you guys," I reply, dodging the question as Pierre swipes at his phone, keeping tabs on the social media posts about today's events. "Una, you were there. You must have some idea about what went down."

"I took photos of Fortunato's derelict mansion, the walls crumbled in on themselves as if the whole place had been made of cards and a strong gust of wind had come along."

"We had confirmation that Adolphe Fortunato and Dr Tem-Pest were inside," Pierre adds. "And Una took a great photo of two bodies zipped up in thick black body bags being carried out on stretchers, so it's safe to say they're both dead. But no one knows why or how."

"People are guessing. A landslide. A freak earthquake. Structural damage to the house. Everyone has a different idea as to what brought that house down around them." Una stares at me, the heat from her glare making my hands sweat. "Except you, Evangeline. You haven't said a word."

"So?" I say.

"So? Don't give me so. You know." Una stares at me, as if trying to pull an answer from me with her eyes.

"How could I possibly know?"

"This is us," she whispers. "Pierre and me. No one else. We know you better than anyone—well, except *him*, maybe, but you can't bullshit us. The Raven Hands were behind this, weren't they?"

It's painful, not being able to confide in my closest friends, especially after keeping so much from them for so long, but to do so would expose not just my gift but all the Raven Hands'. And I can't do that. I won't do that to my people.

After Una had been the first one to smell a rat concerning Valdemar's culpability surrounding Ed's death, there was no chance of me fobbing her off once I'd discovered the truth. But I'd been unable to enlighten her and Pierre as to what actually happened the night my brother died, as I didn't want to compromise their safety, which Una accepted begrudgingly and Pierre accepted gladly. However, I did tell them Valdemar was innocent and that I was in love with him, something that's taken them both a while to get used to, along with the raven tattoo now adorning my hand and arm.

As the weeks have gone on, they've come to accept that Valdemar is not the monster the world portrayed him to be, even if Pierre still won't look him in the eye for fear of turning to stone.

And regarding today's events, I don't know exactly what happened. I can guess like the rest of the citizens who've been left scratching their heads. The only people who truly know what happened in Adolphe Fortunato's house are Fortunato himself and Dr Tem-Pest—and maybe my brother and Annabel Lee.

Maybe.

I set something in motion, the wheels of justice rolling, in the hope that Fortunato and Dr Tem-Pest would be dealt with.

When I'd told Valdemar my plan, he'd laughed, wondering how the hell the ghosts of my brother and Annabel help could get rid of Fortunato.

"I'm going to ask them to haunt him," I explained.

"This isn't a scary story, angel. You can't really think that a couple of ghosts will affect Adolphe Fortunato."

"You don't think the ghost of his dead daughter will affect him? I'm not talking about just seeing her in a dark room or her scratching at the windows on a rainy night. I'm talking about *haunting* him, *terrorising* him, sending him over the edge into the darkest place he's ever been until he feels there's no return."

"This is Adolphe Fortunato we're talking about. He bricks people up behind walls—alive. His whole fucking house is probably held up by the bodies of his unfortunate victims," Valdemar pointed out.

"Then my brother and Annabel just need to find a way to make those walls fall."

I had to wait a few weeks until I saw my brother again. It was the first time I'd seen him since he was released from Valdemar and reunited with Annabel. He looked blissful, an aura of calm and contentment surrounding him in a halo of pearlescent light. They both looked beautiful, shimmering in my kitchen as I got ready for work one morning.

I felt bad asking them. They probably wanted nothing more than to move on and forget what had happened to them when they were alive. But I knew my brother. He had started this war, and it wasn't over. It was far from over.

I'm still unable to hear the dead, but they can hear me, so I asked them to wreak their vengeance on Adolphe Fortunato by driving him to the brink of insanity. Ed smirked and nodded before the pair vanished.

Back in the present, Pierre and Una are waiting for me to make my big reveal.

"I'm sorry, guys. I know as much as you do," I say at last.

"God," Una says. "What's the point in having a Raven Hand for a friend if you won't spill the beans."

"There's nothing to spill. I don't know what happened in that house." Putting my glass down, I rise from my seat, Una's eyes following me. "Just going to the toilet."

We'd chosen a small bar on the fringe of the city centre, knowing it would be quiet and we might get some privacy to discuss the day's events. The bathrooms are up a small flight of stairs, which I climb, my limbs feeling heavy, like I'm scaling a sand dune. I head to the cubicle in the far corner and relieve myself quickly, glad of the peace.

I wash my hands at the row of porcelain sinks, the square units chic and modern, the chrome taps polished to a mirror sheen. Glancing at my reflection, I gasp as I see Ed standing behind me with Annabel next to him.

My breath catches in my throat. "Jeez, you scared me," I whisper.

Holding on to the side of the sink, I stare back at the pair, trying to read the situation. It's a strange place for him to visit me, but I don't have time to wonder what he's doing here before Ed reaches out his hand and places it on my shoulder, and a ringing fills my ears.

I'm about to ask him what's going on when the mirror clouds, and Ed, Annabel, and I disappear.

What I see next is not what I expect.

Der-dun. Der-dun. Der-dun.

CHAPTER FIFTY-THREE

Adolphe Fortunato sits upright in a shiny leather chair, bushy eyebrows resting above beady eyes, his skeletal fingers entwined, elbows resting on the dark mahogany desk. Although I've never seen the interior of Fortunato's extensive mansion, for some reason, I just know this is his home, his study, his man cave where many a meeting has gone down alongside other, darker dealings.

He's talking to a man sitting on the other side of the desk, who I know from his dark skin tone, large amber eyes, and stony expression to be Dr Tem-Pest.

Fortunato looks unamused, bored, even, by his companion; his thin lips are tightly closed, his gaze fixed on his hands until his eyes sharpen, and he glances to his left.

It feels like something has entered the room, crept in uninvited, and spread itself thinly down the walls and over the surfaces.

As if someone has turned the volume down, Dr Tem-Pest's voice quiets as the ringing grows louder before becoming more distinct—a beat, a rhythm, a vibration that thuds through my body.

Der-dun. Der-dun. Der-dun.

Removing his finger from his ear, Fortunato's eyes skim the room. He hears it too.

Der-dun. Der-dun. Der-dun.

Seemingly unaware of what has caught Fortunato's interest, Dr Tem-Pest keeps talking, his voice now a low hum in the background.

"The purchase of the *Gazette* could be good timing, don't you think?" Dr Tem-Pest asks.

Fortunato holds up a pale hand. "Shut up," he snaps, his eyes still roaming until he levers his wiry body out of his seat and starts to pace, scanning the large bookcase behind his desk. "Do you hear that?"

"Hear what?" Dr Tem-Pest says slowly.

Der-dun. Der-dun. Der-dun.

"That noise. It's a low, dull, quick sound."

"No. Are you having any building work done?"

"No." Fortunato continues to inspect the shelves before returning to his desk, picking up the phone, and dialling a short number. "Mary, what is that god-awful noise?"

I don't hear her reply.

"What do you mean, you can't hear it? It's so loud. It's a thumping noise, sounds like it's bouncing off the walls. You sure you haven't got any workmen in today or any on the grounds?"

Der-dun. Der-dun. Der-dun.

He slams the receiver down and scratches his chin.

"You don't hear it?" Fortunato asks.

"Nope."

He eyes Dr Tem-Pest warily, like the man is playing a trick on him.

Der-dun. Der-dun. Der-dun.

The daytime scene blends into night, and I now see Fortunato with his jacket off, his white shirt straining against his angular back as he pulls books from the shelves, gently lifting them away and placing them back with care, the dull noise resounding around us both.

Der-dun. Der-dun. Der-dun.

He picks up his pace, a damp patch appearing between his shoulder blades as he pulls books carelessly from the shelves, letting them drop to the floor as he mutters under his breath.

"Where the hell is that noise coming from, and why won't it stop?"

Der-dun. Der-dun. Der-dun.

The scene cuts away and is seamlessly replaced with Fortunato now standing in his basement, pulling out bottles of wine that line the walls of a purpose-built unit. The grey hair at the nape of his neck rides up against his collar, his face frantic, his top button undone, no smart tie to hold him together.

Der-dun. Der-dun. Der-dun.

"Adolphe?" A female voice travels down into the basement. "Adolphe, are you still down there?"

"Yes, yes. I'm here," Fortunato answers, but there's a shake in his voice, a quiver that isn't unlike the strings being played by a nervous violinist.

"You only went down to choose a bottle of wine. You've been ages. What are you doing?"

"Just getting the right wine." He presses his hand to his forehead, dabbing away some of the sweat that has accumulated.

Der-dun. Der-dun. Der-dun.

"Well, the food will be ruined if you don't choose quickly. Just grab a bottle and come back up."

Taking a deep breath, he grabs a bottle from the shelf, but not before running his eyes up and down the walls.

Der-dun. Der-dun. Der-dun.

There's a flicker across the surface of the mirror as the

scene vanishes and is replaced with Fortunato sitting in a chair in what appears to be a formal sitting room covered with garish wallpaper and adorned with ornate vases with oversized dried flowers. He's with Dr Tem-Pest, who looks crisp and clean in a navy suit, his dark skin making the blue look even more striking. Despite the expense of Fortunato's suit, he looks like he's drowning in it, the material swallowing him as he slumps in the chair.

"You look like shit," Dr Tem-Pest tells him.

"I didn't sleep."

"I can give you something for that."

Der-dun. Der-dun. Der-dun.

"No. No drugs." Fortunato looks at Dr Tem-Pest, the stubble grainy across his chin, his eyes bloodshot, his hair wild. "Something is happening. Something...."

"What?"

"That noise," he hisses through gritted teeth. "And then last night, I couldn't sleep, so I went out and sat on the balcony, and I saw her." His mouth is open, gaping at Dr Tem-Pest.

Der-dun. Der-dun. Der-dun.

"Saw who?"

"Annabel. She was walking out of the lake."

"You saw Annabel walking out of the lake?"

"Yes."

Der-dun. Der-dun. Der-dun.

"Sleep deprivation does strange things to the brain." Dr Tem-Pest's voice is deep and grounding, the kind of voice he's practised over the years in order to lull his patients into trusting him.

"It wasn't a hallucination if that's what you're suggesting. I saw her. She walked out of the lake and up to the house. I watched her take each step until she was right under the balcony. Then she stopped and looked up. And it was horrible. Her face was white, her eyes black, her hair dripping and stuck to her skin. She opened her mouth as if to speak, but instead of words, a flood of black water rushed from her, and I screamed and ran. I fucking ran from my dead daughter. I hid like a baby. Because I was afraid, scared out of my mind. So, I remained in my bed, trembling and weeping. Then I must have drifted off, because when I woke, there was water on my bedroom floor. Pools of it surrounding my bed. How do you explain that?"

Der-dun. Der-dun. Der-dun.

Dr Tem-Pest scratches his chin before answering. "You could have washed your hands in the night and not dried them properly."

Der-dun. Der-dun. Der-dun.

"No," Fortunato jumps in. "The water was dirty, and I could see the footsteps."

"Well, whatever is going on here, I'm sure there's some explanation, but in the meantime, you need to let me help. If you don't want to rely on my usual methods, I can give you regular drugs."

"Goddammit, I said no drugs."

Der-dun. Der-dun. Der-dun.

"Okay." Dr Tem-Pest holds his hands up, palms flat. "But we need to do something. We have a meeting at the casino this afternoon, and you can't go looking like that."

"You want to do something?" Fortunato glares at him, the whites of his eyes blazing. "You can find out where that fucking noise is coming from."

Der-dun. Der-dun. Der-dun.

The light changes, and now I see Fortunato sitting at a large rectangular table, heading up a meeting. A woman in a red dress is talking. Fortunato seems to be staring at his notepad. He looks better than he did previously, encased in a starched shirt and grey business jacket, but his face remains gaunt, his eyes absent, as if they're looking but seeing nothing.

Der-dun. Der-dun. Der-dun.

At the sound, his wild eyes search the people who are all paying attention to the woman, who's talking about the potential for improvements for the casino to make an upwards trajectory and other business jargon that gets lost as soon as she utters it. And then Fortunato freezes, his eyes like that of a startled deer, his mouth open, a silent scream working its way out.

Der-dun. Der-dun. Der-dun.

Because there, sitting at the end of the table, is Ed, the bullet wound dripping blood down his forehead, his eyes locked on Fortunato as the blood runs down his face and pools on the stack of papers in front of him, staining the stark white a brilliant crimson.

"What the fuck?" Fortunato gasps as the room stills.

The woman's voice trails off as the entire table looks over at him.

Der-dun. Der-dun. Der-dun.

"Sir, are you all right?" the woman asks, but Fortunato glares at Ed.

"Get out," he mutters.

"Sorry, what did you say?"

"I said get out. All of you. Get out. Get out. Get out!"

Der-dun. Der-dun. Der-dun.

The scene cuts again, and we're back in the basement as Fortunato swings a sledgehammer at the wall, bottles of wine smashing on impact, the wooden shelving splintering at the force of the blow.

"Stop. Just fucking stop!" he hollers.

Der-dun. Der-dun. Der-dun.

He swings again, his scream echoing amidst the shattering of more glass and the sloshing of wine upon the concrete floor.

"What in the blazes?" Dr Tem-Pest comes down the steps and stops before entering the room, assessing the devastation, the feral look of Fortunato, and the angle at which he wields the sledgehammer.

"I know what the noise is," Fortunato tells Dr Tem-Pest, saliva foaming at the corners of his mouth, his face cracked with anguish, and his white shirt streaked with dirt. "I know where it's coming from."

"What the hell? We've been over this. There is no noise. Only you can hear it. No one else. You're sick. You need help. I will help you, Fortunato, if you'd just let me."

Der-dun. Der-dun. Der-dun.

"Don't come any closer." Fortunato swings the sledgehammer towards Dr Tem-Pest, who freezes and holds his hands up in surrender.

"Look, whatever you think you're doing, it's not the way to deal with this," he says in his best bedside manner, softening his consonants and elongating his vowels.

Fortunato pauses, the good doctor's words issuing their magic.

"Put the sledgehammer down. Then we can go and talk about this and see if there's another way to deal with whatever is going on here."

Fortunato's shoulders slump, his back loosening as the sledgehammer drops to the floor. "Yes," he breathes, his chest slowing after the exertion. "You're right. This isn't the way."

"Good. I'm glad you're coming to your senses."

Der-dun. Der-dun. Der-dun.

The basement flickers, and the backdrop remains, but the time is different. Fortunato is here on his own, the smashed shelves having been cleared away, the broken glass swept up, and the cracked brickwork patched.

Der-dun. Der-dun. Der-dun.

Fortunato is bent over by the wall, fiddling with something and murmuring to himself.

"The doctor was right. The sledgehammer was never going to work. But this will."

He's hunched over, so I can't see what he's doing.

Der-dun. Der-dun. Der-dun.

"It's taken me so long to work out what the noise is and where it's coming from, but now that I know, I can make it stop. And this is the only way to stop it for good."

"Fortunato."

The voice travels down the stairs. The doctor's voice.

"Fortunato. What are you doing?"

Fortunato doesn't look up at the sound of footsteps descending the stairs. "What you suggested. I'm putting a stop to it, once and for all."

The doctor enters the basement and stares at Fortunato. "We talked about you going away for a while. I don't remember talking about the basement."

"No, but I know what the noise is. I know what's driving me insane."

"What is it?"

Der-dun. Der-dun. Der-dun.

"It's them. All of them. Behind the walls. Every single person who I've put there over the years. It's because they were alive when I put them there. And they still are." Fortunato glares at the doctor, his eyes frenzied. "It's the beating of their hideous hearts."

He stands, and as he does, Dr Tem-Pest's eyes go down to the device on the floor.

But it's too late.

Fortunato has pressed the button.

Boom!

We become Ravens.

CHAPTER FIFTY-FOUR

My blue eyes.

My thin lips.

My silver hair.

My face stares back at me as I grip the side of the sink, half expecting the ceiling to collapse or the floor to crack at the sound of the explosion.

But it was just an image.

Looking behind myself through the mirror, I see that Ed and Annabel remain, their faces stoic, their eyes boring into the glass. Ed is no longer touching me, his hand now by his side.

"You came to show me what happened, what you did," I say.

They don't respond. They don't need to.

"Thank you," I tell them.

Ed nods before looking at Annabel, and then they disappear.

Heading back to the bar, I wonder how long I've been gone, whether I'm going to have some explaining to do, and what bullshit story I can cook up to satisfy Una's insatiable curiosity. But as I reach the bottom of the stairs, I feel him.

Valdemar.

Feet tap-dance in my stomach.

Una is laughing, Pierre looks scared to death, and Valdemar sits at the table looking like he's been added in by the artist as an afterthought.

As I reach the table, he stands.

"Angel."

"No talking through the bond. I can't keep it up in front of Una and Pierre."

"Hey, what are you doing here?" I say aloud as he pulls me into his chest and plants a kiss on my lips.

We sit, Valdemar gazing at me as if it's been days since we last saw each other rather than the nine hours I've been at work since we parted this morning.

"I'm here for you," he says.

"But it's Monday night. I told you I was meeting up with Una and Pierre."

"I know, and I hate to spoil the evening, but in light of today's events, there's now a meeting," Valdemar explains.

"A meeting?"

As soon as the news broke, I rang Valdemar, and we exchanged our shock at what was being reported. I told him I had to go, as the newsroom was buzzing, and he promised me he would try and find out more details about what had happened at Fortunato's house.

"You should go." Una puts her hand on my arm, right on top of my raven tattoo.

I raise an eyebrow.

"Yeah, you should go," Pierre echoes. "You've spent all day with us. Go be with your people."

My people.

"I promise never to steal her on a Monday night again," Valdemar reassures them.

"It's fine. I think Pierre and I can manage the remaining champagne by ourselves." Una smiles.

"I'll see you guys tomorrow," I say, giving them a small wave.

Una salutes, and Pierre nods, still avoiding looking at Valdemar.

Valdemar stands, places his hand on the small of my back, and steers me out of the bar.

The car is close, and Valdemar opens the passenger door for me before climbing in the driver's side.

We don't speak until he's pulled out onto the road.

"Are you okay, angel?"

"Yes. Why wouldn't I be?"

"We've been trying to find out what happened," he says, changing gears. "But the police are all over it. It's made it hard to get any answers."

"I know what happened," I tell him.

Valdemar whips his head round, eyeing me carefully before returning his eyes to the road. "You do?"

"Yes."

"Through the paper?" he asks.

"No."

"Then how?" He glances at me quickly, not able to take his eyes from the oncoming traffic.

It takes me the rest of the journey to tell him about Ed and Annabel's visit and how Ed showed me what they'd done through the mirror. By the time I'm finished, he's pulling the car into the drive at Corvus House.

"Fuck." Turning the engine off, Valdemar sits back. "It's fucking insane."

"I know."

"But it's done. And nothing will lead to us?"

"No."

He sits up and leans over, closing the gap between us. "I still can't believe it. That he's dead. It feels like a dream. And all thanks to you."

"I didn't do this," I say quickly.

"No, but it was your idea. You set it in motion. If it weren't for you, Fortunato would still be sitting behind his desk, counting his money and dealing his drugs, the bodies stacking up."

"Men like Fortunato always get their comeuppance."

"Not always, but on this occasion, you were clever enough to uproot him." He pushes my hair from my face. "You are a truly exceptional person, Evangeline." Hearing him say my name, which he very rarely uses, unfurls something inside me.

I bow my head, the compliment heating my cheeks.

"Don't you dare look away from me," he says, tipping my chin. "You listen to me. You have saved your brother and Annabel from eternal unrest, you have released this city from the clutches of a tyrant, you have brought the Raven Hands into the twenty-first century, and you have saved me. How is that not the work of an exceptional person?"

"It's nothing you wouldn't have done."

"But I didn't do it, angel. I buried my head in the sand and hid away in prison for ten years rather than fight this war. You did it. You. So, hold your fucking head up high."

"I just feel like it's too little too late. All those people he killed. All the lives he's ruined. All the things he's done. It's too late for them. Too late for Ed. Too late for Annabel."

He shakes his head. "You can't keep looking behind you. What's done is done. Think of the people you've saved—the ones who were on his list, the ones who would have crossed his path in the future. You saved them all."

"I guess."

"Ever the humble warrior." He smirks.

"I'm no warrior."

"I beg to differ. Just because you don't wield a gun doesn't mean you're not a fighter. You are intelligent, brave, and resilient, and I'm honoured to have a front-row seat in your life."

"Are you getting soppy on me, Montresor?"

My effort at deflecting his compliment seriously backfires when he grips my chin and says, "No, angel, I'm getting fucking hard for you."

He presses his lips to mine, and I'm enveloped by the taste of him.

"I wish we had time to extend that kiss, but unfortunately, we'll have to postpone, as everyone is waiting for you."

I furrow my brow. "Everyone?"

"You didn't expect this to go down lightly, did you? You were the one who rallied them eight weeks ago with your promises."

"I guess. I just…."

"What?" he pushes.

"I don't know." I shrug.

He smiles. "Take it as a win, angel. We don't often get them, so enjoy it." He goes to open the door, but I stop him, pulling at his arm.

"There's just one thing before we go inside."

Valdemar eyes me carefully.

"I want you to tell me what happened the night my brother was shot," I say.

There's a beat before he speaks. "You know what happened." He regards me. "You saw it for yourself."

"I know," I say. "But Fortunato and Dr Tem-Pest are dead, so I want you to tell me."

It takes a second before he realises what I'm getting at.

Then Valdemar takes a breath and tells me everything, word for word.

When he finishes, I place my hand on his. He looks like a different man, like a weight has been lifted, like the shackles have finally been removed.

"How does it feel?" I ask him.

"Strange. Like the words don't belong to me. I've been telling the lie for so long that I almost believed it was true."

"I'm sure Jacinta and Jupiter will feel the same," I point out. "I just wish we could tell the world." I smooth over the back of his hand. We both know that can't happen. It would reveal too much about the Raven Hands, who we are, what we can do.

"The world doesn't need to know," Valdemar says at last.

"But the Raven Hands do." I smile.

"Then we shall tell them."

"*You* will tell them, in your own words."

He kisses me lightly before we exit the car, ready to face our people.

When we enter Corvus House, I can already feel the energy of the Raven Hands. They're assembled in the Great Hall, all of them looking different from the evening of the party. Some are in uniforms, having just come straight from work, others in jeans and sweats, and some in hijabs and shalwar kameez.

As I enter the hall, they applaud.

I marvel at how far I've come from having a gun aimed at me.

My face heats as Valdemar leads me to the stage.

We stand on it together, Valdemar raising my arm, and I can't help but smile at them.

"Ding dong, the witch is dead!" a Raven Hand calls, and the crowd laughs.

"Speech!" someone else shouts.

"No, I...." But I don't get far, as Valdemar lets go of my hand and ushers me forwards.

And as I stand in front of my people, something awakens inside me, like it did the last time I stood on this stage and faced this crowd.

The applause and cries die down as my mouth opens. Words tumble out, and I've no idea where they're coming from, but I can tell that they're listening, all of them, hanging on my every word.

"Today is only the beginning. It marks the start of a new age, a new generation of Raven Hands who will do whatever it takes to stand up for what is right, what is just, and what is fair. We no longer hide in the shadows of a tyrant but walk in the daylight of freedom, hand in hand, side by side."

As I say my last word, Valdemar joins me.

He looks at me, and I look at him, and we smile as he takes my hand in his and raises it in the air.

"The Raven Hands!" he calls, and the crowd chants it back.

My people.

Our people.

And in that moment, something Valdemar said to me at one of our first meetings in the prison comes back to me.

Raven Hands aren't chosen.

We become Ravens.

ACKNOWLEDGMENTS

This has been one of the most enjoyable books I've written to date, but also one of the most difficult. Researching the works of Edgar Allan Poe was a dream, and then having the crazy idea to use all his character and place names within the story was very hard work, but worth it.

I would like to begin by thanking my editor, McKinley Hellenes Krantz, who waded through my appalling grammar and punctuation like a woman possessed and made this whole thing make sense. Despite the hard work, she makes it such fun, and I can't thank her enough for making the laborious editing process such a joy.

I'd also like to thank my acquisitions editor, Kristin Scearce, whose shared love of Poe is probably the only reason this book got a big fat yes from Hot Tree Publishing. To have found a Poe fan within my publishing house feels a little too much like fate.

To my beta reader, Andrea Robinson, I thank you for your encouraging comments and swooning over Valdemar just as much as I do. And to Mandy Pederick, who is like a book detective, trying to solve all the clues I've left. I love reading your guesses as the plot unfolds, and I'm so grateful to you.

It goes without saying that a huge thank you must go out to Becky Johnson at Hot Tree, who is always on the receiving end of my stressed emails and answers them at all hours in such a calming way. I would be a mess without your guidance.

And Claire from BookSmith Design deserves a medal for coming up with the awesome cover after having to interpret my many—some ill-fated—design ideas. As expected, she nailed it in the end.

A huge thank you goes out to Lori, Donna, and the rest of the PR team for their wonderful PR package and for dealing with all those little niggles that seem to crop up at the eleventh hour.

To all my ARC readers, book bloggers, and reviewers—I am indebted to you. Thank you for taking a chance on my books and posting all your wonderful thoughts and getting on board with the book tours.

I must thank my mum, who, all those years ago, bought me an audiotape—yes, I am THAT old—of Edgar Allan Poe's short stories. I would fall asleep at night listening to the hauntingly dramatic voice of Christopher Lee reciting "The Tell-Tale Heart," because fairy stories just weren't my thing.

And I can't forget the man himself, Mr Edgar Allan Poe, whose inspiration is what holds this whole novel together.

My writing world would look pretty bleak without my rock, Author Kerry Williams, who holds my hand (virtually) every step of the way. I would be lost without you, my lovely. Creepy hearts together forever.

All my love goes out to my husband, who has to endure me being locked away in my office for hours on end but also has to read my work when he hates reading.

A shout-out to my kids, who I embarrass on a daily basis because it's not cool to have an author as a parent, especially considering the stuff I write. And not forgetting my dog, who never lets me write alone.

And lastly to my readers, who are the reason I do what I do, because if you're anything like me, you live for a good book.

ABOUT THE AUTHOR

Maria Dean is an author from Yorkshire in England, where she lives with her husband, two boys, and her faithful Boston terrier. Her short stories have appeared in various publications and range from fantasy, sci-fi, and the supernatural, but for the long-haul, her heart remains rooted in romance.

WWW.AUTHORMARIADEAN.COM

instagram.com/author.maria.dean
tiktok.com/@authormariadean
bookbub.com/authors/maria-dean

ABOUT THE PUBLISHER

Hot Tree Publishing loves love. Publishing adult romantic fiction, HTPubs are all about diverse reads featuring heroes and heroines to swoon over. Since opening in 2015, HTPubs have published more than 300 titles across the wide and diverse range of romantic genres. If you're chasing a happily ever after in your favourite subgenre, HTPubs have you covered.

Interested in discovering more amazing reads brought to you by Hot Tree Publishing? Head over to the website for information:

WWW.HOTTREEPUBLISHING.COM

facebook.com/hottreepublishing

instagram.com/hottreepublishing

tiktok.com/@hottreepublishing